Sam's Creed

SARAH McCARTY

Sam's Creed

Spice

Spice

SAM'S CREED

ISBN-13: 978-0-373-60523-1
ISBN-10:   0-373-60523-4

Spice and Colophon are trademarks used under license and registered in Australia, New Zealand, Philippines, United States Patent and Trademark Office and in other countries.

www.Spice-Books.com

Printed in U.S.A.

To Joanie, Sam's Woman of Enticement. May you always have that twinkle in your eye and your alpha by your side.

1

1858, Texas

Sam was getting tired of death.

He pulled Breeze up. The horse tossed his head and sidestepped a protest. Taking a draw on his cigarette, Sam surveyed the scene below the rise. Whether or not he was getting tired of death didn't seem to matter. It haunted him from one day to the next. He blew out a long stream of smoke. Today it lay spread across the hollow before him in a perfect example of how miserable people could be to one another.

The burnt-out shells of two wagons lay tipped on their sides in a loosely stacked V. Charred black, they were just more skeletons on a landscape used to absorbing the death of hope.

From where he sat, Sam could see two bodies bloating in the June heat. Their colorful serapes blazed red and yellow in the bright sunshine. The serapes and state of the bodies probably meant the attack had come at dawn. June nights could still be cool.

At least the wind blew from his back, sparing him the stench of the decomposing bodies, but he didn't need the wind to remind him what he was missing. The memory of that particular odor lingered in his memory, etched there in a moment that had defined his whole life.

Breeze tossed his head. He wasn't a fan of death either.

Sam kept the reins taut. Wagons like these usually meant women. Maybe children. He wasn't in the mood to bury women and children. Especially on the first nice day he'd seen in a week of downpours. The air was hot and clear without the humidity that had plagued everything unmercifully the last few days. Above him the sky stretched endlessly in a crisp blue. It was a day that lent itself to thinking of picnics by the lake and flirting with a pretty girl. The kind of day that made a man realize all he'd given up.

It wasn't a day for funerals.

He urged Breeze forward. The horse tossed his head again and backed up a step instead. Beside him, Kell whined and lagged back. Sam couldn't blame the horse or the dog. Between the stench and the flies there wasn't much to draw a body forward, but if he didn't investigate the area, his conscience would gnaw him raw. If there had been women, their kin would want to know their fate. And he would need to bury them. He didn't leave women and children to the care of carrion eaters.

"Stay, Kell."

Kell whined again but didn't insist like he would if they were talking a big body of water or a pot of stew. Kell had a real liking for both and couldn't be trusted to hold a command when faced with either.

Breeze's hooves sounded a steady clop as he reluctantly headed down the slope. Sam unfastened the strap locking his shotgun in its sheath, the little hairs on the back of his neck twitching.

The closer Sam got to the wagons, the worse the stench of smoke, death and hope-gone-wrong became. A flare of pink material protruding from under one of the wagons caught his eye. There *had* been women. He set his teeth and flicked his smoke to the side. Hell.

A couple more bodies became visible as he guided Breeze to the right of the carnage. All male, at least. That made four total. Three men and a boy who looked too young to pick up a razor. A kid trying to be a man meeting his end way too early. Sam shook his head as he dismounted, dropping the reins to the ground. Damn.

He patted the sorrel's neck. "Wait here, Breeze."

Behind him Kell yipped. Sam motioned him to stay and surveyed the hard-packed dirt for tracks. Nothing worth studying had made an imprint. He turned his attention to the rest of the campsite.

Open trunks listed against the interior of one of the wagons. The contents were strewn about in an array of color. A white glove fluttered on a stand of grass as he passed. He stepped over the charred remnants of a red skirt crumpled in the dirt in an obscene splash of gaiety.

The attackers had to have been white. Indians wouldn't have wasted such a valuable prize. Their women might not wear the dresses, but they would make use of the beautiful material. Indians didn't waste much.

He knelt and fingered the trim on the skirt hem, wondering against his will what had happened to the owner, what she'd suffered, might still be suffering. Hell, he wished his thoughts didn't always go there. A slight rasp interrupted the silence. Kell growled and stalked forward. Sam dropped his hand to the butt of his revolver. The warm wood fit comfortably into his grip.

"Come on out. Now."

The stillness was absolute in the wake of his order. The noise didn't have to have been made by a human. Death always drew carrion, but every hair on the back of his neck said someone was hiding in the wreckage. He stood slowly, pulling his revolver. Had someone survived the massacre? Had the robbers left one of their own behind? Ambush was a tried and true tactic of doubling up the income produced by a raid. Leave the scene looking like it'd been picked over, hide in the surrounding countryside and then swoop down on anyone who came along to investigate.

There weren't many places for someone to hide. The

most obvious would be the bed of the other wagon that was half tipped over. A body could hide up between the seat and the floorboards and prepare for whatever it wanted to do.

Cocking his revolver, Sam kicked the top edge of the wagon hard, toppling it over with a loud crack of wood and a jangle of metal. Kell snarled and dove in, his attack silent of barks, betraying his wolf blood more than his masked face and size.

The scream that rent the air was female. It ended when the wagon hit the ground with a suddenness that put a sick feeling in his gut. Sam grabbed Kell by the scruff and hauled him back.

"Stay, damn it!"

The dog growled and whipped his head around.

"Snap at me and you'll be doing without your share of tonight's stew."

Kell stood his ground, hackles up, ready to leap at the smallest provocation, but at least he stayed. He was learning. When he got back to Hell's Eight Sam would have to have Tucker take a hand in his training. No one could sweet-talk an animal like Tucker.

Keeping his gun ready, Sam circled the bed of the wagon. The first sign of life was a foot. Black-booted and tiny, it protruded out from under the toppled conveyance. Clearly feminine. He touched it with the point of his boot. It wiggled. The woman wasn't dead. And if that was a curse echoing around inside the wooden interior, a far cry from unconscious.

Another muffled sound and then a thump inside the wagon. Another thud. Another curse. The wagon was too heavy for the woman to lift.

"Ma'am?"

The foot jerked and then froze. A very cautious *"¿Sí?"* seeped through the floorboards. Angling his gun away, he bent down and hooked his fingers under the edge of the rough wood, ignoring the immediate protest of old injuries. "Don't be afraid. I'm Sam MacGregor, Texas Ranger. I'm going to lift the edge of the wagon, *señora*. When I do, I need you to back on out, nice and easy. You understand?"

"*Sí.* I understand."

Her English was softly accented with the melody of her native Spanish, muffled yet still strangely compelling. "Good." He braced his knee and got his body in alignment. "You got your fingers shy of the edges?"

"What?"

He'd have to ease up on the color in his language if he wanted her to understand. "Are your fingers away from the edges?"

There was the sound of hands being quickly shuffled across the ground. "Yes."

"Fine. Then here we go."

Kell came snuffling around.

"Get on back now."

"What?"

"Not you, I'm talking to the dog."

"He is friendly?"

He waved Kell back. Kell lifted his lip. "When the mood takes him."

"I will wait while you restrain him."

He cocked his eyebrow at the foot he could see. That sounded distinctly like an order. "He's not fond of restraint."

"Did you ask him?"

"He's made his preferences known." He tensed his muscles. "Are you ready?"

There was a pause and then, "You will control your dog first."

"Is that a question?"

A longer pause, then, "I can make it one if you would prefer."

The honesty caught on his sense of humor. "That won't be necessary, I can pretend."

That might just have been a snort. Or she could have sneezed. He kind of thought it was a snort. With an un-familiar smile tugging the edge of his mouth, he hefted the wagon up. He got it up twelve inches and braced himself. "Back on out."

She didn't move immediately.

"I can't hold this all day."

"Your dog, he is restrained?"

He glanced over. Kell had found the glove. The fingers were in his mouth. The rest flipped up over his head like a lopsided bonnet. "He's sitting here as pretty as all get-out."

"You are sure?"

"Yup. Now back on out of there before my arm wears out."

A second foot joined the first. There was the inevitable wiggling and riding up of the black skirt. He didn't want to notice, but the calves that were exposed above the ankle tops of her shoes were trim and lightly muscled, the skin the color of milk spiced with a touch of cinnamon. She kept wiggling and the skirt kept riding. The backs of her knees looked soft, young.

He wiped the sweat from his temple on his shoulder. What in hell was wrong with him? Getting ideas about a woman from nothing more than her lower legs. The woman probably had ten kids waiting for her at home and more than likely was grieving. Her next wiggle had the skirt rising to dangerous territory.

He grabbed the material and yanked it down. The woman squealed and grabbed at her thigh. "What do you do?"

The hand, as small and as delicate as her feet didn't look that old either. "I'm keeping you decent."

She felt around as if to be sure that's what he was doing and then she said, *"Gracias."*

"You're welcome, now if you wouldn't mind hurrying?"

"I am sorry."

She scooted back, those trim legs a forerunner to surprisingly full hips that sashayed from one side to the other in an unconscious invitation that made his palm itch to cup the plump cheeks. Damn, there were times when his good side was sorely tempted. This was one of them.

She backed the rest of the way out. A long, thick, black braid stood out in stark relief against the white of her shirt. He was actually eager to see her face. The novelty of feeling eager was enough to give him pause. He couldn't remember the last time he felt any emotion, least of all a positive one.

She turned. Only his survival instincts kept him from getting plugged as she swung the revolver in her hand around. The weapon discharged. She screamed and dropped the gun.

"Shit!" After surviving all the outlaws that had drawn down on him, he'd almost met his maker by accident.

Grabbing the pistol, he tossed it to the side. Since when did he make mistakes like that?

The woman lunged for the gun. "Give that back!"

Like hell. Snagging the back of her shirt he let the wagon fall. Wood and metal rattled as it crashed back to the ground. He stood, hauling her with him. "So you can shoot me?"

Quick as light she found her balance and sprang to her feet. She tossed her head. The braid slid back over her shoulder. Her hands hit her hips. Her chin came up. "If necessary."

She reminded him of a pissed-off kitten with her triangular face, pointed chin and big brown eyes blazing bravado. A beautiful, sexy kitten.

"You'd better get some height on you before you go spouting threats."

She took a swing at him. He hefted her up. She missed. "Let me go before I kill you."

She was an amusing little thing. "Doesn't seem to me like you're in any position to be making threats."

She stopped struggling and met his gaze squarely. "I do not have to kill you now. I can wait until you sleep."

He just bet she could, which just piqued his interest more. There weren't many men that could stare him down and not many woman even worked up the courage to try, but this woman was ready to fight. "Seeing as I came here to rescue you, I'm not quite sure why you plan on killing me."

She reached behind her head and tugged at his arm. "You tried to kill me first."

He didn't let go, but the spot where her pinkie met his skin warmed beneath her touch. "How?"

"You knocked the wagon on top of me."

She said that as if that proved her point. "I knocked the wagon on top of whatever was lying in wait."

She blinked, drawing his attention to her eyes. She had very thick, long lashes that highlighted the intriguing flecks of near-black in her brown irises.

"I was in the wagon."

"I got that."

"You flattened me!"

From what he could see of her front, there wasn't much to flatten, but her hips more than made up for the lack up top. Full beautiful curves just like he liked on a woman. "You don't appear any worse for wear."

She gasped and her eyes narrowed. Before she could launch into the tirade clearly on her tongue, he asked, "You got any more weapons on you?"

"Yes. Many."

She couldn't lie worth a damn but she did make him smile. "That's what I thought." He let her go. She tugged down her shirt. Kell snarled.

She spun on him. *"Silencio!"*

It was an order given in a tone that expected obedience. Obedience wasn't Kell's strong suit. He just lifted his lip higher, revealing sharp teeth. The woman's chin went up, revealing a stubborn streak as big as the dog's. To his surprise, Kell backed down.

"How'd you do that?"

She dismissed Kell with a wave of her hand. "A woman cannot take seriously a dog wearing girl's clothing." She smoothed her hair back. "What do you do here, Mr. Ranger?"

A kitten with the attitude of a duchess. "I'm looking for someone." With a wave of his hand he indicated the carnage around them. "A better question would be how are you alive when everybody you were traveling with ended up dead?"

He felt like a heel the second the words left his mouth. The woman must be scared out of her wits. She was stuck in the middle of nowhere, surrounded by dead bodies, facing down a stranger twice her size and all she had to wield as defense was a peck of attitude. And he was trying to undermine that.

"I had yet to join them."

It was his turn to blink.

"That's not your stuff tossed about?"

She shook her head. "They were going to sell it."

"But you were joining up with them?"

"Yes."

"Why didn't you join them in town?"

"My joining was a secret."

"A secret? As in you were running off with one of these yahoos?"

She looked hopeful. "Would you believe that?"

He didn't even have to think about it as he reholstered his revolver. "No."

She sighed. "I did not think so."

The silence stretched. "Sweetheart, you wouldn't be thinking up a lie to spin me would you?"

"Isabella."

"What?"

"My name, it is Isabella."

It was a very pretty name and when her lips shaped around the syllables, it made a man think of other things that sexy little mouth could ease around. His cock, which had been twitching ever since she'd backed out from under the wagon, filled in a low pleasurable ache. She ran her tongue over the full curves in a nervous betrayal. She was more worried than she was letting on.

"Nice to meet you, Isabella. Now, what's the real truth?"

"I *was* supposed to meet up with them."

He looked around. They were a good four miles out of town. He crossed the few feet to where the pistol lay and picked it up. "Why am I still not finding that any more believable the second time around?"

"Perhaps you are a man of suspicion?"

He was that. A check of the chamber revealed two bullets. He glanced over. "You weren't planning on putting up much of a fight."

"I grabbed the *pistola* when I heard you come."

He looked up the slight rise. It was possible she'd heard him coming. "Next time grab some bullets, too."

Isabella eyed the gun in his hand with an ill-disguised hunger. "I will remember."

He just bet she would. "You're planning on there being a next time?"

"I need to get to San Antonio. There is much trouble between here and there."

She had that right. Pretty much certain death for a woman alone. Tucking the gun into the back of his waistband, he moved onto the bodies. "You got family there?"

"No."

The first man had nothing of value. He let him roll back to the dirt. "What's the draw then?"

"I have heard it is pretty."

"Are you expecting me to believe you hooked up with these four because you thought San Antonio was pretty?"

She shrugged. "It is the truth."

Maybe part of it. "A gently reared woman would have to be pretty desperate to join a bunch like this."

"What makes you think I am gently reared?"

Sam shook his head. As if he didn't know when quality and innocence was looking at him. "Come clean. You weren't planning on traveling alone with these men."

"I was."

"Why?"

"I had no choice."

At least that made sense though the why needed exploring. "You do now."

She blinked. "I am not traveling with you."

He jerked his thumb over his shoulder. "You were eager enough to go with them."

"They were not dangerous."

Interesting she felt he was. "I think about a mile out you'd have changed your mind on that."

About a mile out the men would have had the clothes stripped from her body and that sexy mouth too full to scream.

"You do not know that."

"True." He checked the next body. "They might not have waited to leave the campsite before raping you."

Those full lips pressed into a flat line. "I do not believe that."

"Then you're a poor judge of character."

There wasn't anything left on any of the bodies worth

scavenging except for a broad-brimmed hat. He grabbed it. The woman might need it. Skin that creamy wouldn't hold up well under the sun.

"The padre made them promise to give me safe passage."

He shook his head, rolling the third man onto his back, glancing up at her smothered gag as congealed blood slid off. "And that's all it took for you to leap trustingly into their arms?"

She pressed her hands to her lips a second before answering, "A man would not break a promise to a padre. It would mean his soul."

Sam straightened. "I'd be willing to bet these men lost their souls long ago."

"You will not say such things." The fingers of her right hand clenched in the fabric of her skirt. "They lost their lives because of me."

"You weren't even here."

She shook her head. "It is still because of me." Her gaze met his. There was no mistaking the anguish in the depths. "If you force me to go with you, you will lose yours, too."

He'd heard that before. "What makes you think I'm so easy to kill?"

"Easy or hard, when *he* finds you, you will still be dead."

"He?"

Her lips clamped closed.

"You might as well tell me."

"You do not need to know."

He liked the way she spoke, the syllables coming together in a melodic flow, the accents falling in the wrong places in such a way that made a song out of normally harsh words.

"Since we'll be traveling together, I'd like to know who's going to be on my tail."

"I will not allow it."

"You don't have a say."

"Yes. I do."

Because she thought he couldn't figure it out. There was only one man in this territory powerful enough to be labeled *he*. When Sam combined that with the fact that San Antonio was the first large town outside Tejala's territory, it wasn't hard to figure out who had her running scared.

He reached for her arm. She stepped back. "I cannot let you be hurt."

Damn, what happened to thinking he was dangerous?

"Anybody ever tell you you have strange notions?"

From the way she immediately drew her pride around her like a shield, he'd say yes.

"That does not make the ideas wrong."

No, but it did make them hard to hold on to. "Do you have any belongings?"

She pointed under the wagon bed.

He flexed his shoulder. Shit. "Figures."

"If I am holding you back, you may just leave."

"When I leave you're coming with me."

"Not unless it is to San Antonio you go."

Kell growled again. She turned on the dog, pointing her finger. "You, you will behave."

Kell, being Kell, ignored the command.

Sam folded his arms across his chest and leaned back against the wagon wheel. "You figure out how to make him do that, I'll take you straight to San Antonio."

She shielded her eyes against the sun and frowned at him. "He is your dog."

"Not exactly."

"He's not your dog?"

Sam shrugged. "We're working it out."

"I do not understand."

"He showed up a few days ago on the trail. We've shared a few meals but nothing's permanent."

"It seems permanent to me."

"Appearances can be deceiving."

She nodded. She took another step, not toward Kell, but apparently he thought she was taking liberties. He lunged. Sam jumped forward. He was too late. With a rapid spate of something in Spanish, Isabella cracked the dog across the nose. He yelped and dropped back. Hands on hips, she glared at the dog. "No more out of you."

Sam shook his head. If that didn't beat all. "I think he likes you."

Isabella bent down and worked her arm under the wagon. "Why do you say this?"

"Because the last man who tried that got his throat ripped out."

She didn't even blink, just scrounged deeper. "Then it is good we have reached an understanding."

Sam supposed it was. The view she was unwittingly giving him of her rear was also good. So much so she had to repeat herself when she needed his help. Bracing her palm on the bed, she said, "You must lift the wagon again. I cannot get my bag out."

Her bag. The wagon. Shit. He couldn't afford to be this distracted. "Got it."

In a matter of seconds she had the small satchel out. She'd packed light. Too light to plan on having more than one change of clothes. Too light to have any resource once she arrived at her destination. "Who'd you say you were running from?"

"I did not say I was running."

He reached down and helped her to her feet. The top of her head came to the center of his chest. She just seemed bigger. "But you are. And a little thing like you needs all the help she can get."

"I am not little."

"Petite then." He tugged her toward Breeze, who was patiently waiting. Kell fell into step beside them.

"I am not this petite either."

"You're taking two steps to my one," he pointed out.

"You are a giant."

He took her satchel and hooked it over the saddle horn, hiding a grin. Her height, or lack thereof, was obviously a sore spot, "How about tiny? Can you live with tiny?"

"No."

Her nails dug into his wrists just atop his gloves, the gloves he resented because they kept him from feeling the softness of her skin.

"Wait. We have to bury them."

"Duchess, whoever did this is probably still around. That being the case, we don't have time to dig holes."

Her lips flattened. "You must."

"I don't have to do anything."

"I owe them."

"I thought the padre arranged the deal."

"But I was to provide money."

For all her high manners she didn't look like she had two coins to rub together. "Did you have any?"

"No."

She said it as if those four men would have traveled anywhere with something as sweet as her without taking their payment out of her hide. "They would have been ticked when they found out."

"Yes."

"You'd have probably ended up on your back working the cost off."

She didn't look shocked. "It was a possibility."

A woman would have to be seven kinds of desperate to take off with those odds staring down at her. She headed toward the front of the wagon where there was a gap between the ground and the sides. He grabbed her arm, pulling her up short.

"What the hell kind of trouble are you in?"

She looked at him with big brown eyes that were the color of warm chocolate. Eyes that forgave him ahead of time for the desertion she expected. "Tejala wants me as his intended."

"Interesting phrasing. I take it you are not in agreement?"

"No."

From what Sam knew of Tejala, Isabella's objections would mean nothing. "So what are you going to do after you reach San Antonio?"

"That is not your concern."

She was right. It wasn't. She likely wasn't even a Texas citizen. He could walk away and no one would hold him accountable. Tension arced between them, extending from his shoulder down his arm to his grip. Beneath his hand, her muscles jerked, sending the tension right back. She was a strange mix of courage and desperation. Innocence and sass. A smart man would leave her and her problems to her people to sort out. She licked her lips again, the gesture leaving the bottom one invitingly wet and pink. Vulnerable.

He swung up on Breeze. "Maybe not, but I've decided to make it mine."

And maybe her right along with it.

2

The woman was as infuriating as all get-out. Sass, spit and fire with an autocratic manner that was bred into her bones, she didn't shake an idea once she had hold of it. And the only idea she had her teeth sunk into right now was that San Antonio was her safe haven. She was determined to get there, by herself if Sam wouldn't take her. On the hard-used nag they'd come upon about a half mile from the massacre. As if he'd let that happen. The woman would be raped or dead within minutes of striking out. But she didn't see it that way.

"There are laws against capturing a woman against her will," Isabella pointed out in that logical tone in which she'd been presenting all her arguments for the last few hours.

Sam glanced over his shoulder to where she rode just behind. "You don't say."

"Yes." She kicked her horse, an animal who wore its

hard life in the scars on his hide, to force it to catch up. "I believe it is a hang by the neck offense."

"Damn. Guess I'm in trouble then." He motioned to the horse with his cigarette when she kicked it again. "You're hurting him for no reason. He's got bad knees. It pains him just to walk."

His opinion of her went up a notch when she immediately stopped kicking and started petting and crooning to the animal. It took a nosedive when she stopped the animal and dismounted. It was more of a slide and tumble than a dismount, but since she landed on her feet, he'd call it that.

"What are you doing now?"

She pushed the too-big hat back from where it flopped over her face. "Walking."

Kell growled. She cut him a glare. He didn't stop growling but he did sit with a look at Sam that clearly said he expected him to handle the crazy woman so they could be on their way.

"If I thought the horse couldn't carry you, I would have shot him when you brought him forward."

She gasped. "You would not shoot Sweet Pea!"

If that didn't add insult to injury. "You named the poor thing Sweet Pea?"

She bristled and patted the black's shoulder. "It is a good name. He is very sweet."

"Well, being sweet isn't something a man wants shouted to all and sundry, so you might want to not call him that in front of the other horses."

For a split second she looked concerned and he wanted to smile, but then she caught on with a shake of her head.

"You make fun, because I do not want to hurt him."

He made fun because she was sexy as all get-out when those deep brown eyes gathered sparks and anger drew that full mouth further into a pout that naturally had a man wanting to lean in and kiss it soft again. "Just a little."

How a woman so short standing so far beneath him could manage to look down her nose at him was a mystery, but she managed it. "This makes you not so nice as a person."

"I never said I was nice."

"No," she sighed. "You did not."

He dismounted and came around to her side. Her whole body went taut.

"What do you do?"

"I'm going to help you back up." He quirked an eyebrow at her. "Unless you think you can get up by yourself?"

The horse might be broken down, but he stood sixteen hands easily, too big for her to just hop up.

If looks could kill he'd be dead but she was gracious in her defeat. "Thank you."

He ground his smoke out in the dirt.

She frowned at the gesture. "You smoke too much."

"I'll keep that in mind."

"It would be good that you do."

Turning, she raised her arms and waited. He probably should tell her she just needed to present her foot. He admired the line of her back, the dramatic flare to her build, but since he'd already admitted he wasn't nice, there wasn't actually a *need*.

Her waist easily accepted the span of his hands. Damn, the woman was built for a man's pleasure. With a heft he had her up. For a second her hips were mouth level. His mouth watered. The complete unawareness in her "thank you" as she grabbed hold of the saddle horn and fumbled for the stirrup was like a splash of cold water. He was lusting after an innocent. After checking her stirrups and unwrapping the reins from around her palms while she stared at him, oblivious to the havoc she wrought, he headed back to Breeze. Kell chuffed as he passed.

"You want to deal with her?" he asked under his breath. The dog walked away. "That's what I thought.

"Town is just over the next rise," he said as he got back in the saddle. He reached for his makings.

Isabella frowned. He pulled the pouch out. She sighed and shook her head. He smiled and pulled out a paper. "There might be a hotel. You'll be able to take a bath."

Her mouth set tighter and her chin went higher. She clearly wasn't in a mood to be placated.

"Everything's bound to look better when you've got yourself set to rights."

"Even being dead or captured by others?"

She did have a dramatic turn. "The word you're looking for is kidnapped." He tapped tobacco into the paper. "But being all cleaned up would save time for the undertaker."

She clearly didn't appreciate his sense of humor.

"I would prefer he have to work."

Even with promise of an honest-to-goodness bath, a luxury every woman had to crave after time on the trail, Isabella was being stubborn. Sam wasn't entirely sure what to do about that. A woman not getting excited about a bath was downright unnatural.

Not that he'd spent a lot of time with women outside the bedroom. There just hadn't been the opportunity. Nor, he admitted in a moment of honesty, the inclination. At least on his part. He wasn't a man who liked ties though plenty of women had attempted to tie themselves to him. He rolled his smoke and put his makings back in his pocket.

They topped the rise. The town, such as it was, came into view. Ten ramshackle buildings formed an uneven cross in the middle of nowhere. It was doubtful a town so small had a hotel. He hoped to hell Kell had town manners.

"You might be right about that bath."

"I am right on many things."

He smiled, struck the sulphur and lit his smoke. She did stick to her guns. The ride to the edge of town was completed in tense silence. As they cleared the first building a sign on the third one down caught his eye: *Hotel*.

"Looks like you might get that bath after all."

Isabella's response was a harsh gasp. He'd heard that sound too many times before to mistake it for anything but fear. Looking over his shoulder, he had a clear view of her. Not her expression as the hat had slipped over her face, but he was able to determine the direction she was looking. Her attention was focused down the street to where five horses were tied outside the saloon. One of them was a paint with distinctive markings.

As if his glance was a cue, five men came stumbling through the doorway of the saloon, spilling onto the dirt street in a drunken roar of laughter. Breeze whinnied. Kell snarled and dropped his head, ears flat to his skull in warning. Out of the corner of his eye, Sam saw Sweet Pea's head jerk as Isabella yanked him to a halt.

The men looked their way then dismissed them as yet another couple of saddle bums blowing into town on the good weather. As long as no one looked too closely, they'd be fine, but Sam wasn't going to hinge Isabella's safety on a hope that flimsy.

Backing Breeze up until he could reach over and grab Sweet Pea's reins, he tugged them out of Isabella's hands. It wasn't hard. She was still staring at the men, her face a chalky white. Keeping his voice low and soothing, he ordered, "Duchess, I want you to throw your leg over to this side and slide on down."

The shake of her head was barely discernible. He was

tired, hungry and even if she didn't want that bath, he sure did. And the sooner he settled this, the sooner he could set about enjoying the pleasures of town. "Do as I say."

The order had no more effect on her than the last. Leaning over, he handled the matter by grabbing her forearm and giving a tug. Instinct had her grabbing for the saddle horn with a high-pitched, undeniably feminine squeal as she listed to the side. Fortunately, Sweet Pea stood solid. Unfortunately, the men heard, stopped and looked back. They exchanged words. Pointed. Retraced their steps.

Sam untied his shotgun from its sheath, double-checking to make sure it was loaded before sliding it back in. He pulled his revolver from its holster and rested his arm across the saddle as if he had nothing better to do on a hot, sunny afternoon but sit in the middle of the street. "Isabella, go on into the hotel."

For once she didn't argue with him, scooting behind the horse and up onto the wooden walk. The glances the men shot Bella as she stood at the door provided a good clue to the topic of their conversation.

"Get inside, Bella."

"It is locked."

Shit.

"Knock."

The bandits were an ugly-looking bunch, none too clean, but colorful in their assortment of clothing. Their spurs clinked softly as they swaggered forward.

That swagger worried him. It meant they felt pretty comfortable doing whatever they planned on doing.

He nodded to the leader when they got to about twenty feet away, "Howdy, boys." In case they mistook his greeting for an invitation, Sam centered his revolver on the leader's chest. "That's far enough."

The man ran his hand over his full moustache, his fingers lingering on the straggling ends of the right side. "The woman you have with you looks familiar."

"Who rides with me isn't any of your business."

Two of the bandits fanned out in a loose flanking maneuver. Sam glanced around the streets. The smattering of locals that had been walking about had disappeared inside buildings faster than he could wave his hand. Down the street a door slammed shut.

"Isabella, I thought I told you to get inside."

"You did."

"Then why are you still standing out on the street?"

"Because the people of this place seem to want me outside."

A lanky man with a black hat, dirty chaps and shiny guns headed toward Isabella. Sam adjusted the point of his revolver. "Mister, you take one more step, and it will be your last."

"You're awfully unfriendly for somebody who just came to town," the leader said with deceptive civility.

Sam gave him back an equally civil smile. "Consider it a character flaw."

He glanced over at Isabella standing on the walkway.

She was too exposed. "Duchess, I want you to go around to the alley over there."

She waved toward the man at the edge of the walk between her and her goal. "How?"

"Just walk on by."

Her tongue flicked over her lips. Not a single man missed the provocative sight. Damn, that woman had a mouth made for loving. "But—"

"If he moves I'll put a bullet in his brain. You can trust me on that."

Two breaths and then she turned those eyes on him. "You promise you will shoot him?"

"I promise."

"You will not miss."

"Not likely."

"Likely is not a guarantee."

"Get moving."

"Fine, but if you miss I will be unhappy."

Even from here he could see her hands shaking at the thought of passing by the bastard.

"Then for sure I won't miss."

With a short nod she headed toward the alley. Sam waited until Isabella disappeared around the corner of the building, and then he straightened, settling easily in the saddle, letting the coldness that preceded battle cloak him. "Now that she's gone, we can talk."

"There is nothing to talk about."

"Fine, then I'll just lay it out for you. It's been a bitch of a day. I'm hungry, tired and been stuck on the wrong end of that woman's tongue for the last four hours." From the alley came the faint echo of a gasp. He smiled. He thought that would get her going.

"If the woman is such trouble, my friends and I would be happy to take her off your hands."

He just bet they would. Leather creaked as he shifted his weight in the saddle. "And who would you be?"

"Juan Zapatos."

"Well, Juan, I only mentioned that because pretty much all I want is a couple shots of whiskey and a soft bed."

The man near the walkway moved. Sam met his gaze and gave a small shake of his head. He settled back.

"There's no reason you can't have what you want," Juan said.

"As long as I give you what you want?"

Juan nodded. *"Sí."*

"That's not going to happen."

"The woman is Tejala's."

"Then Tejala is going to be disappointed."

"I don't think so."

"What's mine stays mine." He nodded toward the alley where Bella hid. "And the woman's mine."

Another gasp.

"And who are you to think you can take what is Tejala's?"

Centering the revolver on Juan, Sam answered. "Sam MacGregor. Texas Ranger."

There was a murmur from the man near the walk. A

whisper of unease spread through the group. A little of the starch left Juan's stance. But not all of it. After all, Sam's reputation notwithstanding, they had him six to one.

Juan spat. "Your badge means nothing here."

Sam shrugged. "A badge means nothing anywhere. It's the man behind the badge you've got to be afraid of." He smiled. "And quite frankly, y'all are wearing on my last nerve. So if you don't mind, I'd like to get this over with."

"And what is 'this'?"

"*This* is me either peaceably passing through or plugging a hole in some of you." He turned the revolver on the bandit closest to the alley. The shotgun he lined up with Juan's midsection. He didn't need accuracy with a shotgun. "Which way I go is entirely up to you."

Metal slid across leather in an audible hiss as Juan's men drew their guns. Behind him, the unexpected scuff of a boot on sand. Sam dove to the ground, turning and pulling the trigger as he fell, swearing as he saw his target jerking the gun to the left just in time. The bullet whizzed past Isabella's head. She screamed and crouched down, covering her head with her arms.

"Son of a bitch!" She must have circled around the building.

He rolled under the horses' hooves toward the center of the street, taking the line of fire away from her. At least he knew why Kell hadn't given a warning.

"Get your ass back in the alley," he hollered. "Kell, guard."

He hoped the dog knew to guard.

Bullets hit the ground around Sam in rapid succession. Kell hesitated.

"I will help," Isabella yelled. Sam didn't know how much help she expected to be with her hands over her face.

He scanned the street, noting positions. "You can help by getting your butt to safety." He glanced at the bristling dog. "And take Kell with you."

Juan laughed from behind a post. "You cannot even get your woman to obey, and you expect us to fear you?"

"Nah, I just expect you to die."

Rolling to his back, dropping the shotgun beside him, he palmed the hammer on his Colt, unleashing a spray of bullets. Three bandits dropped, two didn't. Shit.

Return fire was immediate. He didn't have any cover. A bullet struck him in the thigh with a hard punch and a sickening splat. Isabella screamed. He only had a few seconds to act before the pain came calling. Jumping to his feet, Sam ran for Bella, catching her around the waist as he got even, half carrying, half throwing her into the alley. Kell was right behind. Bullets peppered the building in the spot they'd been a split second before. He pressed his back against the wall. Splinters of wood flew, stinging his cheek as he shoved Isabella to the ground.

"When I say to stay put," Sam growled. "Stay put."

Pointing the shotgun around the corner, he fired blindly, relying on the scatter to do damage. A high-pitched yell told him he had hit something. The swearing afterward meant probably not fatally.

"Son of a bitch."

There was a tug at his belt. He turned, another curse on his lips. He did not need an hysterical woman on his hands. Isabella grabbed his hand and slapped something into his palm. His fingers closed around familiar shapes. Bullets. He met her gaze. There was steel beneath that softness.

"Thanks."

Bullets whined past the alley opening. He cocked the other barrel of the shotgun, waiting for a pause before pointing the barrel around the corner again and pulling the trigger. As soon as it discharged, he tossed it to Isabella along with the pouch of ammunition.

"Do you know how to load that?" he gritted out.

She didn't waste time on words, just set to work with an efficiency that answered his questions. He shoved bullets into the chambers of his revolvers, keeping an eye on the movement beyond the alley as best he could. "It's going to get messy here in a minute."

Her glance fell to the blood on his thigh.

"It already is."

He was bleeding like a stuck pig. Yanking his bandanna from around his neck, he held it out. "Do me a favor and tie that off."

She did. He bared his teeth against the pain. "Thanks."

She yanked the knot tight before handing him back the shotgun. "Do not miss."

She was a bossy little thing. "I'll do my best."

"It would be best if you succeeded."

Very bossy.

Things were too quiet out there. Sam inched along the wall, being careful his gun belt didn't scrape. A rhythmic jingle of spurs approached. He shook his head at the foolhardiness of trying to sneak while wearing spurs. He leaned back and waited. The thin barrel of a rifle extended past the corner. Sam didn't move, holding his palm out flat behind him to warn Isabella not to make a sound. Two heartbeats passed. The gun barrel jerked. Sam dropped to his knee. Fire burned up his thigh. The man leapt around the corner. Sam fired. The bullet hit the outlaw in the heart, stopping him midleap. He dropped, a stunned expression on his face.

Cocking the hammer again, Sam wiped the sweat from his brow with his shoulder and waited. There was no sound.

He spared a quick glance at Bella. Her face was white and her eyes were big with terror, but she was kneeling beside Kell, holding his jaws shut. Sam added quick-thinking to bossy.

Holding his finger to his lip, he indicated she should continue to be silent. She nodded back. Sam inched closer to the corner of the building, blood dripping down his leg in a warm flow. As soon as he took care of the last bandit, he'd have to see just how bad it was. At least the bullet had missed the bone.

"Your friends are dead," he called out.

No answer.

"I'm willing to let you live, for a price." Something crashed to the ground. From the splintering aftermath it sounded like a crate. "You promise to take a message to Tejala, and I won't plug your sorry ass."

Still no response.

"I'm going to count to three. If I get to three I'm going to take that for a no."

Another crash. He stepped around the corner. A barrel tumbled off the stack against the livery. Beside it listed a broken crate. A quick scan revealed no guns poking out of windows, no new additions to the battle cluttered the streets. Apparently the citizens of the town were no more married to Juan and his companions than he was.

"One."

He got to the edge of the barrels, his leg aching like a son of a bitch. Ahead of him he could see the bandit scramble backwards across the ground, one arm held awkwardly at his side. Sam advanced, guns cocked, eyes watchful as the man tripped and fell back to his elbows. A hoarse shout punctuated his fall onto his injured arm. He pushed with his feet but there was nowhere for him to go. Behind him was the building and in front of him was Sam. The wall would be easier to get through.

"Two."

The bandit finally realized he was trapped. He threw up his hand. "*¿Qué quieres?*"

Sam didn't answer. He let the man stew in his own sweat while he bore down on him. A trickle of blood rolled down his cheek and more blood seeped down his leg.

He kicked the gun away from the bandit's useless arm. "What does Tejala want with this woman?"

"I don't know."

"That wasn't what I asked you." Sam fired a bullet into his other shoulder.

He had to wait until the man's shouts dropped to a panicked gurgle before he could repeat his question.

"To marry her! She is supposed to be his bride!"

So that part of her story was true.

"If she's supposed to be his bride why isn't she married to him?"

"Because I have refused the marriage contract."

Sam should have known Isabella wouldn't stay put. She stood beside him, staring down at the man, no expression on her face. "I don't remember inviting you to this parley."

Kell worked his way between them, his yellow eyes locked on the bandit. Bella folded her arms across her chest. "I do not remember asking you to capture me."

He cocked the other hammer of the gun. "And yet we're both here."

"And here is where?"

It was the bandit that answered with a sneer. "Here is where you will die."

Sam was tempted to end it right there. Instead, he placed his foot on the bandit's injured shoulder and pressed. "Care to share what makes *here* so damn dangerous?"

It took very little for the bandit to spill what he knew. Pretty much one hard push and he was telling all. "Tejala owns this town. Owns this territory. No one will help you for fear of his retribution."

"I never asked for help."

The bandit leaned to the side and spat out a mouthful of blood. "You will need it." He jerked his chin toward the dead. "You killed his cousin. He will not rest until he kills you."

"Which one's his cousin?"

Sam looked at Isabella. She shrugged. The bandit was more accommodating. "The one with the moustache."

"The stupid son of a bitch who came between me and my dinner?"

The man spat again. "In a few days, we will see who is so stupid."

"If you kill him, no one will know who did this," Isabella interjected helpfully.

Kell growled as if he approved the plan.

"True." Sam removed his foot from the bandit's shoulder as he pretended to consider the notion. "Of course, the thirty or so townsfolk peeking at us from behind the window curtains might be a problem."

"How many bullets are in your gun?"

Damn if she didn't have a sense of humor. Swallowing back a chuckle, he shook his head. "Not that many."

The bandit grimaced, showing rotted teeth stained red with blood. "There is no hope for you, ranger."

Suppressing an urge to kick those ugly teeth down his throat, Sam kept his voice even. "I wouldn't go that far. As long as I have the woman, I have a bargaining chip."

Isabella gasped. A sly glint came into the bandit's gaze. "Tejala would pay much for her." He hitched his weight up higher against the wall. "I could bring you to him. We could share the profits."

"I don't share."

"You will need me to find him."

Sam caught Isabella's hand, keeping her from getting any further out from his side. "Or I could just plant my feet somewhere and give a shout as to what I've got."

He ignored Isabella's "Bastard."

"What do you think of that?"

The bandit spat again. He wiped his chin on his shoulder. "I think that you are a dead man."

Sam straightened. "I think you're right. Which means I've got nothing to lose."

Curtains were fluttering like crazy down the street. The town's residents were getting nervous. Nervous people made him anxious. Isabella tugged on his hand. He looked down.

"If you let me go," she said, in a voice that shook, "No one will chase you."

"Now where would the fun be in that?"

"You don't want me."

She had to be shitting him. The woman was a curvy little keg of dynamite that had a man thinking about making her explode with his first look. "Darling, there isn't a man alive that wouldn't want you."

He didn't like the assessing look in her eyes as she cocked her head to the side and placed her hands on her hips. "You also?"

"Sure. I'm as red-blooded as the next man."

"Good." The too-big hat fell over her face. She pushed it back with an impatient hand. "Then I will hire you."

"I'm a ranger. I'm not for hire."

She didn't bat an eye. "Then you can hire me."

"For what?"

"You're a ranger in Tejala territory who's going to have *bandidos* on his trail in a very short time. You're going to need a guide if you plan on surviving."

He pushed his hat back with the back of his hand. "I suppose you're offering your services?"

"Yes."

"You got any references?"

She waved at the nearly unconscious bandit at their feet. "I have been evading men such as he for the last six months. That must mean something."

What it meant was she'd been running scared longer than any woman should have to. "Well, I might be impressed if you could prove it was true."

That chin came up. The hat came down. She rounded on the bandit. "You will tell him it is true."

The man shook his head. Isabella kicked his calf, then his thigh. Sam figured the family jewels were next. The man grabbed her boot. "I'm not telling him shit."

Kell lunged in and snapped at his arm. Isabella stomped on his fingers as he jerked it back. "Tell him!"

Sam chuckled as he pulled out a sulphur. They sure were a bloodthirsty pair.

The bandit lurched to the side, cradling his arm. Isabella drew her foot back. Kell stalked forward. It was probably time to step in.

"Hold up."

Bella whipped around. "Make him speak."

He quirked an eyebrow at her. "You don't think you've tortured him enough?"

"He must tell."

He put his hand on her shoulder, soothing the panic rippling through her in visible tremors. "Yeah, he must."

But not the way she thought.

Grabbing the injured man by his shirt, Sam yanked him to his feet. "You're going to carry a message to Tejala for me."

"What makes you so sure?"

Stupidity ran deep in this bunch. "Because otherwise," he said, jerking his thumb over his shoulder, "I'll let those two have at you. Make a choice."

The bandit grunted. "What is this message?"

"You tell Tejala that if he comes after Bella, he's coming after Hell's Eight."

The man shook his head. "He will not care. He is crazy that way."

"Funny," Sam said. "So am I."

3

He was crazy. Isabella watched as Sam rested his rifle against the cave wall and propped three sticks shoved through several cleaned fish beside it. A dark stain spread downward and outward from the bandanna tied around his thigh. Blood from where he'd been shot, defending her. She did not know much about bullet wounds, but it looked like a lot of blood. Enough blood that they should have stopped back when she'd told him to instead of continuing on to this cave. Kell slid up beside Sam, sniffed his wound and then whined. The wag of his tail knocked one of the sticks. Sam caught it before it could tumble to the dirt floor. "Easy on dinner, mutt."

Kell stepped back. Isabella wanted to move back, too, when Sam turned toward her. Except she couldn't. The wall was to her back and her pride was in her face. After all her bold talk, it would be very humiliating to cower now that they were alone.

She motioned to the wound on Sam's thigh. "You must take better care of yourself."

Shadows hid his eyes, but she could tell from the angle of his head that he was looking at her. "Worried about losing your guide to San Antonio?"

"*Sí*. You are very important to me right now."

He favored his leg as he brought the fish over. "Good for a man to know where he stands."

From where she sat, it seemed he wouldn't be standing much more. The firelight highlighted the paleness of his face and the lines carved deeper at the corners of his eyes. He was hurting and tired. Because of her. She motioned to the boulder across the fire and against the wall. "You will sit and let me tend to your wound."

"I will?"

"Yes." Standing, she brushed the dirt from her skirt. "Unless it is your wish for your wound to fester and for you to die."

His gaze burned a path from her head to her toes. "I can't say that I'm anxious to meet my maker just yet."

The intensity of his gaze made her uncomfortable, but oddly enough, not scared.

She pointed to the boulder. "Sit."

"Is that an order?"

It had been, but maybe ordering a man like Sam around was not such a good idea. She crossed to the saddlebags and rummaged around. "You should think of it as a reasonable request."

He followed her with that miss-nothing gaze of his. The hairs on the back of her neck rose in response to the look—so strong that it felt like a touch. Her fingers closed over a silver flask.

"When you were thinking of this reasonable request, did you stop to think I'd have to remove my pants to accommodate it?"

She had, but thinking ahead did nothing to stop the blush from rising to her cheeks. She had never seen a man naked. It wasn't done for a young woman of her station, but Sam did not need to know that. "I will do my best to preserve your modesty."

While gaining as much of an eyeful as she could. She was very curious about the male body.

Sam didn't answer immediately. His boot sole scuffed over the sandy cave floor. A glance wasn't any more revealing as to his mood. The press of his lips could be anger as easily as it could be amusement. He was a very hard man to read.

"Well, I appreciate that."

Uncorking the flask, she took a sniff. The odor of strong drink made her eyes burn.

Sam grunted as he sat down. "That you can pass on over."

She tapped the cork back into the bottle. "You will drink it if I do."

His holster scraped rock. "That's sort of the point."

He was always so on guard. "I will need it to clean your wound."

"Like hell."

Frowning over her shoulder at him, she pulled out a flat packet tied with rawhide. "There is no need for such language."

"You ever had rotgut poured over an open bullet hole?"

"I am not so foolish as to throw myself in front of a bullet."

It angered her that he had. Even more that he wasn't taking the wound seriously. People died from infection.

"Duchess, I was saving your life. That makes me a hero, not a fool."

She opened the packet and found a needle and catgut inside along with plenty of strips of material for bandages. She didn't want to think how dangerous Sam's life must be that he carried such things with him. Nor did she like how little catgut there was compared to bandages. He must be injured often. She snapped the packet closed and brushed the hair from her eyes with the back of her hand. "You were needlessly reckless."

"That's my job."

He said that as if it was the truth, but she did not think so. Grabbing up the items, she headed back toward him. He watched her the whole ten steps. There was something in his eyes that had not been there before.

She dropped to her knees by his injured leg, wincing as her muscles protested. She was not used to riding so much. "I think you are too enthusiastic in your doing of this job."

The soft leather of his glove skimmed her temple, tangled in her hair before curving behind her ear, taking the annoying strand of hair with it. "Pardon me, duchess, but what you know about about my job wouldn't fit on the head of a pin."

She carefully placed her hands on his thigh, feeling very bold. Women of her station did not get this close to strange men. It was nothing like touching her leg. There was no softness beneath her fingertips. Just rock-hard muscle. Which only led her to wonder how else men were different. "I do not think I need to know a ranger's job to know what I see."

"And what do you see?"

Muscle bunched under the press of her fingertips. She glanced up, catching his gaze. The answer just popped out. "Trouble."

For one heartbeat Sam didn't react, and then he laughed, a deep soft sound that slipped over her nerves like warm honey. She slid her hands higher toward the blood-soaked bandage.

"On that you've got the right end of the stick."

"So maybe I have the right end of other sticks, too."

"I wouldn't lay money on it."

She noticed he didn't deny it outright. Sam Mac-Gregor was an honest man, if maybe a little evasive. The makeshift bandage was stiff with dried blood. It took her a few minutes to work the knot free.

When she parted the edges, she had full view of the hole in his pants and a glimpse of the raw wound beneath. Her stomach heaved. She swallowed it back. She no longer had the luxury of weakness.

"I think I will decide for myself where to put my money."

And right now everything she had was riding on Sam. Placing the dirty bandanna on the floor, she indicated his pants. "As I have laid my money on you, I would appreciate your help."

The humor clung to his expression as he pushed his hat back. "You want me to shuck my pants?"

Her blush rose and her mouth went dry. "This would be helpful."

Again the brush of his fingers over her temple. And then his fingers were under her chin, lifting her face up. Her senses tuned to the four points of pressure, the softness of the leather glove, the scent of his skin, the cool blue of his eyes.

"You ever ask me that with something more light-hearted in mind, I'll have them off before you can blink."

It took her a second to process the meaning through the intensity of awareness arcing between them. He was telling her no. She blinked the cobwebs from her mind. That was unacceptable. "They need to come off now."

So she could get to that ugly-looking wound, among other things.

The fire popped. The aroma of roasted fish drifted

closer. Isabella wrinkled her nose. Sam grinned. His thumb touched her lips.

"Hand me the flask and the kit."

He couldn't mean what she thought he meant. "Why?"

"Because I'm tired, and hungry, and I'm not wearing long johns."

Now, that was an interesting fact. "You cannot treat yourself."

His smile broadened. His thumb pressed harder. Her breath caught as her lips parted. The scent of leather and smoke—the scent of Sam—invaded her mouth on a lazy drift, strong enough that she could savor the illusion of his taste. "I can do a lot of things that would stretch your imagination."

"We are no longer talking about stitching your wound, are we?"

"We should be."

His fingers pressed upward in a silent command. The stiffness in her legs made standing more difficult than it should be. The hunger in his eyes made staying put even more difficult. Even Tejala had not looked at her with such want.

"For future reference, Bella, getting on your knees in front of a man is not a good idea."

"Why?"

His grip shifted to her upper arm as he helped her up the last few inches. "That you will have to ask your husband."

It was not her imagination that his fingers lingered on her upper arm. Nor that where his fingers lingered, tiny fires seemed to start under her skin. "I am not married."

"Then you'll have to wait for the why until you are."

"This would require patience." She stepped back, the heat from his gaze strangely finding a home under her skin. "I do not have much patience."

"So I'm beginning to understand." He reached into the top of his boot. "Turn around."

"Why?"

Pulling out a wicked-looking knife, he slid it into the hole in his pants. Material ripped under the lethal blade. "Because today's been bad enough without you puking up your guts on the floor."

He saw too much. "I can control my stomach."

He stuck the knife blade in the fire. A quick glance showed the furrow carved in the hard muscle of his thigh. Blood seeped out in a sluggish flow. Her gorge rose and for a split second she thought she would actually throw up.

With a sigh, he stood. She felt like a monster when he winced. As a result, she offered no resistance when he took her shoulders in his hands. "Do us both a favor and show me how tough you are tomorrow."

With that, he turned her around. The weight of his hands was not unwelcome. Her reaction to him was very confusing.

The minutes stretched. No sound came from him. Isabella would have felt better if he had moaned or groaned. The silence left her with nothing but her own imagination to fill the emptiness.

"You should let me help."

He grunted. Something fell to the ground with a small thunk. "Nothing much to do. It's just a crease."

"Then why do you need the knife?"

"The bullet was stuck a bit under the skin."

The small thunk. "It is out?"

"Yup."

She turned around. He was tying a fresh bandage over the wound. "You did not sew it."

"No need."

"It will scar."

The thought of that bothered her.

"One more isn't going to kill me."

"It is unnecessary."

"A needle and thread is what's unnecessary. Especially with dinner waiting."

Isabella couldn't forget the size of the furrow now hidden by the white bandage. The scar would be large. Unnecessarily so, forever marring the beauty of his thigh. The danger of infection was very real. "Your leg is more important."

He grabbed up the flask. "Tell that to my stomach."

Anger, unreasonable and hot, snapped through her. He hadn't sewn the wound, and now he would waste the only thing they did have to treat it? She snatched the container from his hand. "You are not so big and bad that an infection will not visit."

"Hand that back, Bella, before I paddle your butt for messing with a man's liquor."

The warning in his tone just fed the resentment pouring through her. He had no right to talk to her so, threaten her like a child. Risk himself so needlessly.

She dumped the liquor over the bandage. Too late, she realized what she'd done. She dropped the flask. *"¡O, madre de Dios!"*

Sam's face flushed red and his mouth settled into a grimace of agony. She'd never heard such words as what came from his mouth as he grabbed at the soaked bandage. Nor the ones that followed once the alcohol found his wound. He would kill her.

Sam stood. Isabella ran. He caught her before she made it five steps.

"God damn, you get back here."

She went with his tug, spinning around, fists up as she'd seen her guard Zacharias do when he was going to throw a punch.

Sam just stood holding her, breathing as if he'd run miles, eyes narrowed, mouth set in a flat line…and stared.

And then, catching her fists in his hand, he laughed. A real laugh that scalded her pride. A laugh that made her not care how handsome he was. A laugh that had her struggling wildly as he drew her arms wide and dropped a kiss on the end of her nose. And then her mouth. Their first kiss, and he had not asked!

She struggled harder. He paid no mind, just kept his

lips on hers, letting her struggles dictate the pressure in soft slides and quick jerks. Her thighs brushed against his, her chest against his abdomen. Her struggles slowed as anger changed to something softer, something as fragile as the next skim of his mouth over hers. Her arms were pulled wider, bringing her body flush against his much bigger one. His lips parted just a hint. There was the moistness of his breath and then the shocking glide of his tongue, gentle and tantalizing, along the seam of her lips. Lightning flared in a brilliant arc along her nerve endings, jerking her up onto her toes before tossing her back.

Sam let her go. She did not immediately back away, anger and something else keeping her feet planted in place. Though he stood a foot away, Isabella could still feel the pressure of his lips, the heat of his breath, the temptation he presented. Why did he fascinate her so?

She clenched her fists. "You had no right to do that."

"You're right. I'm sorry."

He didn't sound sorry, but she was. "I am sorry I poured the spirits on your wound. Though it needed to be done, I should not have done it like that."

He cocked his head to the side and a grin ghosted his lips. "You just can't help it, can you?"

"What?"

"Sounding so high-and-mighty."

"I think my poor English gives the impression of arrogance."

Sam's smile broadened. "Yeah, that's likely it."

She had the distinct feeling he was laughing at her. He had no right to laugh. He was as wrong as she was. Putting her hands on her hips, she challenged him. "Kisses should not be stolen."

"I agree."

"They should be given freely."

He turned and headed back to the fire, obviously favoring his injured leg. "No one's arguing with you, Bella."

He didn't need to be so agreeable when she wanted to fight. She followed more slowly, her conscience nagging her. The alcohol must still burn. The truth popped out as it always did when she felt guilty. "Maybe I am arguing with myself."

Sam sat back on the rock and pulled one of the sticks off the fire. A piece of the fillet fell off. In a move almost too fast for her to see, he caught it, tossing it in his hand to cool it. Shadows jumped on the wall in wild accompaniment. Her heart jumped with the same silly excitement as he cocked an eyebrow at her. "Now, why would you do that?"

She owed him for the manner in which she'd cleaned his wound. "Because I think it is wrong to enjoy stolen kisses."

His expression closed up. "Very likely."

She'd chosen honesty as a penance, but she had no idea it would be so hard to see it through. It would be easier to let him continue to think what he obviously was—that she was talking about him—but that wouldn't be fair. Her cheeks burning hotter than the heat coming off the fire, she whispered, "But I enjoyed yours."

He dropped the fish into the fire. It was the only sign her words had thrown him.

"Why?"

There was a limit to how far she would atone, and he had reached it.

"I do not know why." She glared at him. "You are a very provoking man. By rights I should shoot you."

He fished dinner out of the fire. "The man who saved your life?"

She sat down on the rock a couple feet away. "That would make me ungrateful."

He handed her the other fillet. The one not covered in ash. The consideration made her feel even more guilty.

"But?"

He was an astute man to hear the *but* in her voice. "You are aggravating."

"Because I won't stitch a crease?"

That and other things, but since the other things were nameless worries in her mind, she settled for a simple "Yes."

He took a bite of his fish. She tore off a piece of hers. It was a little big, but she was in a cave, in the wilderness eating off a stick. Surely manners could be flexible?

He waited until she had the too-big piece in her mouth before saying, "If you think that's aggravating, I sure don't want to see what you're going to make of the fact we'll be sharing a bedroll."

4

Sharing a bedroll with Sam had not been the exciting thing the forbidden should be. Here it was the next day and she was as much an untouched virgin as she had been lying down the night before. Darn it. She had not wanted him to rape her, but she would have liked to have a little tale about the night she'd slept with the infamous Sam MacGregor. Something more than that he'd rolled up a horse blanket into a bundle, set it between them like a bolster, rolled on his back and ordered her in a gruff voice to go to sleep. That was not what she expected from a man with his reputation.

Which just went to show how inflated legend could make a man's reputation. Even in her little town of Montoya they had heard of Hell's Eight and Wild Card MacGregor—a man so cold he could supposedly seduce or kill with a smile. She completely understood the former, and had witnessed the latter, which left only the question of why he had not seduced her. Was she so unappealing to him? The question nagged at her just as thoroughly as the leather of the saddle nagged at the insides of her thighs through her worn, fine lawn bloomers. This land could be very hard on the finer things.

She braced her hands on the pommel of the saddle and pushed up. The brief relief to her rear was welcome. Ahead of her, Sam rode easily, sitting in the saddle as if he was an extension of the horse. None of the weariness dragging at her showed in his posture. The setting sun behind them reflected off the silver conchos rimming his black hat. She glanced over her shoulder. The sunset was gorgeous. Even more gorgeous was the silhouette of another town backlit by the pink-and-orange glow. She bet there was a hotel in that town, and a soft mattress. She scanned the rickety outline of the buildings. Well, maybe not soft, but less hard than the saddle.

"No sense hankering about what's not going to be," Sam called back.

How had he known what she was thinking? She lowered her rear gingerly to the saddle. "I was just admiring the sunset."

"I thought you were pining on the luxuries of town."

It annoyed her that he did not even bother to look at her as he talked, just presumed to know what she was thinking. Even if he was right. "I do not see what would have pained to stop for one night. You defeated Tejala's men."

"Hurt for one night."

"¿*Qué?*"

"The phrase is 'What would it hurt.'"

"Hurt, pain." She dismissed his correction with a wave of her hand as she gently urged Sweet Pea to catch up. She might have succeeded, except the packhorse they'd taken after the battle yesterday put up a protest. Sweet Pea jerked back. A nip from Kell's teeth soon changed the packhorse's mind. Sweet Pea picked up his pace until his nose drew even with Breeze's flank. "None of it is good."

"You've got a point."

"So why could we not stay in town?"

"I'm a cautious man."

"Not that I have heard."

He shifted in the saddle, enough so she got a glimpse of his profile. It was as uncompromisingly handsome as the rest of his face, and just as compelling. Especially with the hint of a grin denting the corner of his mouth.

"And you believe everything you've heard?"

After watching him defeat the bandits of the last town and boldly step in front of a barrage of bullets to save her life? "Yes."

The dent grew into a crease. He slowed his horse until she pulled alongside, and turned to face her. "I'll keep that in mind."

She pushed the hat brim off her face. He had a gorgeous smile—even white teeth and finely shaped lips.

There probably was not a woman he had ever asked to his bed who had turned him down. She wondered if they had noticed how rarely his smile reached his eyes. "Where exactly do we go?"

He ran those eyes over her in a slow perusal, making her vividly aware of the fact that she was still braced on the pommel and also of her promise not to slow him down. "Getting a bit saddle sore?"

"Not at all."

It was probably the biggest lie of her life. She would have much to confess to her priest when she returned home.

Sam tipped his hat back the smallest bit. The sun reflected off his face, turning the deeper flecks in his eyes to shards of blue fire. For all that he sat relaxed in the saddle, he radiated an energy that crackled. Or maybe it was just her awareness of him that gave the impression of sizzle. She'd never met a man who made her so conscious of the weight of her breasts, the softness between her thighs, the very unique differences of male and female.

"Good to know. I was hoping to get another three hours in."

Three hours? Her thighs would be raw meat by then.

"It'll be dark in the next half hour."

He pointed to the left. "The moon ought to give us enough light to travel by."

She hadn't noticed the half-moon rising. She tried again. "What about dinner?"

He reached behind him, flipped open the saddlebag and pulled out a cloth-wrapped parcel. "Here."

She had to let go of the pommel to take it. Try as she might to hide it, she knew he saw her wince as her thighs took her weight. *"Gracias."*

She unwrapped the cloth. Inside were two biscuits and four strips of jerky. Not a whole lot of food. Her stomach growled. She had not eaten since this morning, and not that much then. Fish was not her favorite. Sam reached over and took Sweet Pea's reins. With a flick of his wrist he tossed them over the horse's head.

"I'll lead Sweet Pea here while you eat."

Sweet Pea jerked away from the flip of the reins. The food tottered in her hand. Dinner almost fell in the dirt. "Be careful!"

"I'm always careful."

She took a piece of jerky before wrapping up the rest of the food. "This I do not believe."

"Why not?"

She cocked her head to the side. How much to tell? "I think you do not care much if you live or die, so you do crazy things."

He blinked and his smile slipped. "That's what you think?"

"Sí."

"You think too much."

It was either think too much or moan over the condition of her thighs. "For this you should be grateful."

"What makes you say that?"

"If I did not think, I would have nothing to take my mind off the town we are passing. Thinking of the town would make me think of hotels and soft mattresses. Thinking of the mattress left behind would make me realize how unhappy I am. Being unhappy makes me sad. Being sad…"

He held up his hand. "Go ahead. Think."

"Thank you." She smiled and took a bite of the jerky. There was kindness in him.

He waited for her to start chewing before he asked, "Are you settled? Can we head on now?"

Good manners dictated she not talk until she was finished eating. If she followed good manners, they would still be standing here tomorrow night. The jerky was very tough. The only option was a nod.

"Let's move, then."

She couldn't stop her groan as the horse took the first step. Sam glanced over his shoulder. "When you were evading the Tejala gang the last six months, you didn't spend a lot of time on horseback, did you?"

"No." She took another bite of the jerky. It was salty, and flavored with a spice she didn't recognize, but to an empty stomach it was very good.

"Where did you hide?"

"In a cave."

"What drove you out of hiding?"

"Men found the cave." Vile men with rape on their minds.

"Tejala's."

"No. Others."

"That must have been a bitch."

"It was not my best day."

With a cluck of his tongue, Sam urged Sweet Pea to pick up the pace. The horse immediately complied. Isabella had noticed that always happened. Animals liked Sam. Truth was, so did she. Sometimes for reasons she could define and others for reasons she did not understand but which were more compelling than the ones she did. She took another bite of jerky. He was a very interesting man.

"Where do we go?"

He pointed toward the setting sun.

"Another town?"

"No."

She chewed some more and tried again. "A place that at least has a tub?"

She held the jerky in her mouth while she waited for the answer.

"No, but there's a pond."

She swallowed the jerky. "That will do."

Another tug on the reins had Sweet Pea catching up. "You're looking forward to a bath?"

"Are you not?"

The side of his mouth she could see tipped up in a familiar smile. "Are you hinting I'm getting a bit ripe?"

"I would not suggest such a thing to a man."

"You just plan on suffering in silence?"

SARAH McCARTY

She opened the napkin and broke off a piece of biscuit. "I am rarely silent, especially when I suffer."

If she thought his smile was handsome before, it was nothing compared to how handsome it was when emotion filled it.

It took her a moment to remember to breathe.

He tugged his hat down, covering his eyes, leaving only his mouth to focus on. It was a very expressive mouth, given to nuance rather than exaggeration. And right now he was amused. "I'll keep that in mind."

With a cluck of his tongue he went ahead, leaving her with a strange tingle in her stomach and a heat that infused her skin with a radiant sensitivity. What was it about this man? Why did he have such an effect on her? There were many handsome men on the Montoya ranch. Many men who walked with grace, fought with power, faced death with courage. Men who had a dangerous edge, but none of them had what Sam had. None of them had his bold masculine appeal that sank beneath her skin like liquid lightning. He could have any woman he wanted, be anywhere he wanted to be. But he was here. With her. That had to mean something. And if it didn't, there had to be a way for her to make it into something. Something good.

The first time she'd seen him coming up the rise, she'd been praying, asking God to send her a solution to her problem. Folding the rest of the biscuit into the napkin to keep it from crumbling, she wondered—did that make Sam the answer to her prayer?

She bit off more jerky, chewing contemplatively. It was a strange idea, but it had also been a strange prayer. Besides, what was the point of praying if one was not going to believe that occasionally a prayer would be answered?

Even if the timing of Sam's arrival was coincidence and not divine intervention—she was aware she might be convincing herself because she wanted it to be so—Sam was still a solution to her problem that she could easily live with. She did not kid herself that Sam was a forever man, but he was a man who could probably provide the happiness it was rumored a woman could experience in bed. He would not worry about her modesty, about offending her. About right or wrong. He would merely take what he wanted, give her what she needed. No more, no less. Exactly what she had prayed for. This could work.

Tejala wanted her as a virgin sacrifice to his power. Proof to the people of his town that he was invincible. That they owed him for their existence, and his benevolence could be counted on only as long as they submitted to his will. That's why he hadn't taken her by force. He'd left her lying in the dirt, vowing that before he would marry her she would crawl to him begging for the honor to be his wife—the honor she'd rejected. First he would take her pride, then he would take her home and lastly he would take her life. If she let him.

She did not feel like letting him.

Studying Sam, taking in his naturally aggressive posture, his broad shoulders that narrowed to his lean hips, the revolver that rode his hip, she saw a man designed to give Tejala headaches. Tejala would never accept being second to this man, just as she would never accept Tejala as her first man. She might not be able to win their war, but on the subject of whom she gave her virginity to, that battle she could win.

Sam was a warrior like Tejala, but with a difference. Tejala made her skin crawl, but Sam made her want to crawl under his skin. Where she'd be safe. Maybe that was the difference. She took another bite of dry biscuit. Her father had always told her that when she met a man who made her feel safe, who made her heart race, one others held in respect, then she would be looking at the man God had made for her. She grimaced. As a child she had believed him. As an adult she knew things were more complicated.

Her father had been a romantic. A good man, but impractical in some ways. Still, there was merit in his words about looking for a lover. Much more than in the advice her mother had handed out.

Her mother was the opposite of her father—practical to the core. Isabella had always thought her mother had very little respect for her father. Their marriage had been arranged. A good marriage producing a contract that joined property boundaries. She did not think her mother had ever forgiven her father for being caught up in the excitement and romance of making his fortune, for leaving Spain and coming to the territory.

Her mother would have been content being the wife of a third son of a respectable family. She was not content being the wife of the only aristocrat in the new land.

That dissatisfaction drove her to want more for Isabella. In her mother's eyes, Isabella needed to return to Spain to find a husband. Short of that, she needed to marry Tejala and secure the family's future in the land to which her father had chosen to bring them. Her mother was a great believer in exploiting the rules of the society in which she found herself. So was Isabella. Just not in the same way.

Her parents' different views had torn their family apart, forced Isabella to flee, killed her father. She closed her eyes against that memory, everything going black around her, leaving only the sound of her father calling her name, Tejala's laugh, a spray of blood hitting paper, an awful gurgle and then nothing. No more pain, no more dreams. Nothing except flight and the knowledge that each day might be the day Tejala found the way to force her to crawl. As if she would ever crawl to that son of a dog.

"If you don't ease up that grip, your dinner is gonna be crumbs."

Isabella looked down. She was holding the napkin so tightly the contents squeezed out between her fingers. "I am sorry."

She pulled the corner of the napkin back. One of the biscuits had survived pretty much intact. The jerky was invulnerable to the assault. She urged Sweet Pea closer to Breeze, gritting her teeth against the agony in her thighs. Holding out the food, she offered the intact biscuit. "This one did not suffer too much."

Those too-observant eyes of his touched on her face. She had not looked in a mirror lately, but she knew from how her face felt when she washed in the streams that she'd lost the plumpness in her cheeks. Her father would be horrified. She was unconcerned with that, but she wished she would lose a bit of the plumpness in her chest. The binding that kept her more-than-ample breasts from bouncing painfully was hot. And it made her break out in an irritation rash if she had to exert herself. As she had had to the past two days. Just thinking about the rash made her think of the itch, which immediately became in dire need of scratching. Of course, with Sam watching her so closely, she could not scratch a thing. She held out the biscuit. "You must hunger."

His blue eyes went dark. His nostrils flared and his gaze traveled her figure. "I can wait."

Her breath caught. He was not talking food, but because she could not think how to answer, she kept on with the pretense. "It is not possible I can eat all this."

Sweet Pea stepped in a hole, jerking her thighs along the rough edge of the saddle. The pain was too much. Dropping the packet of food, she grabbed the pommel, a groan grating past her lips. Kell made short work of her dinner. A blur of gray, a snap of teeth and it was gone.

Strong hands cupped her waist. She squealed as Sweet Pea sidestepped, and suddenly she was falling. But only for a second. Then she was lifted and her rear connected with Sam's hard thighs. His arm came around her stomach, securing her in place. Her hat fell back off her head, getting caught between his shoulder and her back. The string dug in like a noose around her neck. She grabbed for it, kicking with her feet, wrenching at the tie.

Sam's hands replaced hers, working between the string and her neck. "Easy, now."

She could not breathe. Harsh noises clogged her throat, struggling to get free. He was choking her. She clawed at his hands.

"Isabella!"

The call for attention slipped under her panic, giving her something to hold on to. She opened her eyes. Sam's face was inches away. Sam. Not Tejala. His hand was on her shoulder. He was talking to her.

"The string's gone. You can breathe, Isabella. Just open your mouth and suck in some of this nice cool evening air."

He made it sound so simple. Just breathe in and out. No big deal for most people. But she had a horror of being choked. It came at the strangest times. And usually in front of people she would prefer didn't know. Like now. With Sam.

His thumb brushed her jaw. "Now, Isabella."

She held his gaze and tried. The obstruction in her

throat cleared. She took one breath, and then two. The night air was sweet. Then again, any air was sweet after choking almost to death. She touched her neck, tucked her fingers under the lax string of the hat and yanked it over her head.

"Yeah, I think we can do without that for a bit." Sam took the hat and hooked it over the saddle horn. His fingertips replaced hers at her throat. Just the tips, tracing the spot where the sensation of a noose lingered. As if he knew. She went breathless again. He moved his hand to her shoulder, just under the collar of her shirt. For no reason she could discern, she apologized. "I'm sorry. I do not like my throat touched."

His eyes lingered where his fingers had been.

"So I noticed. Any particular reason?"

She shrugged her shoulder, rubbing against his chest. It was a scandalous thing to feel his chest on her arm, his thighs under hers. "I just dislike it."

The callus on his fingertips tickled her skin. She was almost grateful when his hand left her shoulder and moved to the fabric of her shirt. The rough callus caught on the fabric, dragging just a little as his fingers traced down her arm, over the bend of her elbow before arriving at her hand. For some silly reason she expected him to hold it. He didn't, but his fingers did move from her hand to her skirt, opening and closing as they gathered up the material. His gaze was so intent, his eyes so beautiful, the tingles that stretched from her neck to her hand so fascinating, she didn't realize what he was doing at first. But when cool air hit her knees, reality came crashing back.

"What do you do?"

"Well, I could be planning on tossing up your skirts."

"We are on a horse."

"I'm not getting your point."

People could do that on horses? "You cannot be serious."

It was hard to tell with her vision blocked by the setting sun as it was, but she was pretty sure the creases at the corners of his eyes deepened, which meant he was amused.

"Duchess, someone has sadly neglected your education."

"Women are not educated in such things."

"Uh-huh." His response was low and deep, sensual nuance thickening his accent. She loved his accent. It was so different from her natural language, and different from the English spoken by the few white people she'd seen. His word choice was fuller, his grammar better. "Mine would be."

She gasped, and not because it was such a forbidden thing to say, but because it found such a home inside her. She could imagine this man doing wild things with his woman. She could imagine his woman enjoying it. She could imagine being his woman.

Just the imagining sent the tingles in her arms leaping to her thighs, sensitizing the skin that seemed to swell into the curve of his palm. Between her legs her private parts swelled, too, and her heartbeat picked up the pace. This was desire, she realized. The evil thing that kept her on her knees in church. The downfall of mankind. This was the reason Tejala chased her. To feel this with her. To be the only one to feel this with her. It would not happen.

She closed her eyes as Sam's hand continued to pull up her skirt, drawing courage from her purpose, but not brazenness. She could not just smile and make nice while Sam exposed her legs. There was enough of her upbringing still healthy to make that impossible.

"What's going on in your head, Isabella?"

"Is it really possible to have relations on a horse?"

His hand stopped moving. Against her side, his chest expanded on an indrawn breath and then stopped. She had actually shocked him. She had the feeling not many people did that.

He let the breath out on a slow, even expulsion. "Feeling adventurous?"

Adventure implied risk. "Are having relations on a horse more difficult than relations elsewhere?"

His eyes narrowed and his head canted to the side. "I'd feel a whole lot better about answering that question if you didn't keep referring to things as 'relations.'"

"My grasp of your language is not that good. I do not know another word."

"I've picked up a bit of Spanish here and there—why don't you run the words you do know by me?"

And admit she did not know any words at all? She did not think so. "I do know one word in English, but I do not think it is one a lady uses in front of a gentleman."

His eyebrows rose. "You don't say?"

"Do not look so eager. It is not a word I will say."

He grinned. A real one. "Chicken."

Yes, she was. In many ways.

She caught her lip between her teeth. This was a big step she was taking, probably one she shouldn't be taking without a lot of thought—one that would have her forever banished from her family, ruined in society's eyes, fallen in God's. But Tejala's men were close, and tomorrow might be too late. She was not foolish enough to think she could win in this game with the outlaw forever. Someday she would be outmaneuvered and her innocence would be taken from her. And she would still be banished from her family, ruined in society's eyes, still be fallen in God's eyes. So either way there were consequences, but one way she made the choice. The other, the choice was made for her.

She licked her lips again. Sam's eyes dropped to her mouth. There was a tension in his muscles that hadn't been there before. A hardness under her buttock that hadn't been there before. In contrast, everything in her body softened.

This man who'd risked his life for her interested her. She did not fool herself that Sam was a gentle man. There was a razor edge to his personality, a coldness to his expression that spoke of purpose, but there were also those flashes of humor, and moments of softness. But what she noticed most about him was the lack of cruelty. He was kind to his horse, kind to his dog. Kind to her. Taking him as a lover might not be her worst choice.

She closed her eyes, daring and apprehension rippling through her at the same time, riding the same thought. A lover. She shivered. She was considering taking a lover. And not just any lover, but the infamous Sam MacGregor.

It seemed so much more brazen when she thought in specifics. But the alternative was losing her virginity to rape and becoming the trophy of a man she hated. That was by far more horrifying. She didn't want the only things she knew of relations between a man and a woman to be taught to her at Tejala's hands. She didn't want to hand him one single victory, especially the prize of her virgin's blood. Taking a lover accomplished many goals. Taking a lover was practical. Her mother had raised her to be very practical.

She opened her eyes. Sam was still watching her mouth. In an experiment, she ran her tongue over her lips again. His gaze followed every movement. Taking a lover was also going to be very fun.

"Do you find me pretty, Sam?"

"Anyone would find you pretty."

He was still watching her mouth. The dying scream of her mother's lectures on the dangers of being promiscuous echoed in her mind as she placed her hand over his on her thigh. "That was not what I asked. Do you find me pretty?"

"You're beautiful."

It was so hard to be brazen with the sun shining in her eyes, exposing her to every nuance of Sam's expression. So hard to be confident with Sam watching her as if she were a prisoner intent on escape, his hand on her knee a vivid distraction. Her diaphragm constricted. She took a careful breath and asked, "Beautiful enough to have relations with?"

"Why?"

She was prepared for a simple yes, had her next line rehearsed. She was not ready for "why." Men did not ask why. They just leapt on the opportunity. Asking why was an insult.

"What do you mean, *why?*"

5

Bella forgot herself and pushed at Sam's shoulder. It was like hitting a wall in every way except for the inclination her fingers had to linger against the surface, to explore the solid ledge of muscle and bone, to move the shirt aside and know the warmth of his skin intimately. She yanked her hand back. "A man does not ask this of a woman!"

"Seems to me to be a sensible question when a respectable woman propositions a disreputable man."

He was not disreputable. She knew disreputable. He was not it. The heat of his flesh dallied on her palm, teasing the nerve endings into wanting. She closed her fingers around the need. "It is a very rude question. And the fact that I am sitting as I am is the proof that I am not respectable."

"I notice you don't argue my being disreputable."

The sun was too bright. She could not see his face, but she had a suspicion he was laughing at her. "You had best not be smiling."

She shaded her eyes. He was.

"You're real fond of giving orders, aren't you?"

He was very handsome when he smiled that way, one corner of his mouth a touch higher than the other, his blue eyes darkened with the emotion he usually kept contained. His hand squeezed her knee, reminding her how intimately placed his fingers were. She should have been shocked. Instead, she was taken with a strange breathlessness. "I have not thought about it."

That was a lie. She tended to be too focused on what she wanted and grew impatient with politeness. Sometimes it was just easier to direct the person. "And you have not answered my question."

His smile deepened at her pushing. "No. I haven't."

His control annoyed her. And excited her. A strange combination. "The question is simple and only requires a yes or no answer."

Not a muscle on his face moved, but she had the impression he was delving deep into her mind, seeing beneath her skin to motives she didn't want him to notice. Fear. Desperation. Desire. Finally he spoke.

"I think we've already established that I'm the contrary type."

It was her turn to frown. Contrary was not good for what she had in mind. "This is not a recommendation for a lover."

Sam's smile softened as his hand slid higher, edging beneath the thin lawn of her pantaloons, finding excruciatingly sensitive flesh. Deep inside, her very womb spasmed in an ache so sharp she gasped. Sam's eyes narrowed.

"Now, that's where you're wrong." His fingers slid in the barest of touches, skimming up the inside of her thigh, raising goose bumps and anticipation for... more? Her breath caught and held. How far would he go?

"If I were of a mind to accept your offer, my being contrary could be a real benefit to you."

She bit her lip as his fingers crossed the line between smooth flesh to chafed.

"And this would be one of them."

Even the whisper-light touch of his hand burned. She cried out. The arm around her waist tightened. Sam's mouth brushed her ear. "Anyone less contrary, duchess, would have you straddling his lap and his cock nice and snug in your body by now."

Shock held her still. No one had ever talked to her as he did, touched her as he did. Always she had been sheltered, protected, pampered. Never had she heard the word *cock,* but she knew from his wording what it referred to. And she was reasonably sure it was not a polite word for that body part. If there was such a thing.

She wondered if this was the way men spoke to the woman they desired or if it was a sign of disrespect. She did not hear a sneer in Sam's tone, but there was a richness to his drawl that had not been there before. His hand opened over the raw skin, sheltering it from the sting of the air, covering almost half her thigh with just the placement, reinforcing in her mind the difference in their sizes.

"But being contrary," he continued, "I don't like my pleasure to be a solitary thing."

She had no idea what he meant by that. "This means you do not find me pretty enough for relations?"

He removed his hand. Her skin whimpered a protest at the loss of his touch, while her nerves retained the imprint of his hand long after the stinging stopped. It was a strange sensation, but not unpleasant.

Sam reached behind him. She was jostled around as he searched for something in the saddlebag. He brought out a tin. "It means I don't find you in any condition to have relations."

Small and gray with no markings, the tin was more suspicious than impressive. "What is that?"

He uncorked the lid. "Something to make you feel better."

He tugged her skirt up until it bunched just below her hips. She was very aware of his gaze on her legs, of the breeze on her calves. Never in her life had she exposed even the hollow of her throat. And now this man had her out in the open displaying herself. She should be outraged. And maybe it was outrage bubbling along the nerve endings just under her skin, frothing like water at the peak of a rapid, but it felt an awful lot like excitement. He dipped his fingers into the sweet-smelling salve.

"Part your thighs."

She gasped and jerked. She couldn't help it. The man was shocking.

As he tilted his head, the last rays of the setting sun bounced off the conchos banding his hat, blinding her.

"For somebody in a hurry to have relations on horseback, you're awfully jumpy."

What was she supposed to say to that? She blinked against the brightness. "I am sorry."

If Bella squinted, she could probably see his expression. She had no intention of squinting, for the simple reason that she had a feeling he was going to be a lot more shocking, and she needed some distance to handle it.

"No need to be sorry. I just need you to part your thighs so I can rub this cream on them."

Maybe she should have squinted after all. At least with a little tension in her face she might have avoided her jaw dropping and in all likelihood looking like a landed fish struggling for breath.

"How can you say things like that?"

She felt his shrug all along her side. "I believe in plain speaking."

Before she could suck in a fresh breath she discovered he also believed in plain touching. On the inside of her thighs. Where no one had ever touched her.

The dip of his head blocked the sun, and she could once again see his face, the tightness over his cheekbones, the darkness of his eyes. He wanted her. This, at least, was good.

The salve was cool on her skin as he applied it with methodical thoroughness. A soothing balm to the irritated nerve endings. It was too bad this magic could not be smoothed over her fractured composure. She told herself she had no need to be embarrassed—Sam was just treating her wounds. And even if he took liberties, she'd invited them. It didn't help. She was embarrassed and unsure.

When his hand reached the softest part of her inner thigh, she couldn't help herself. She grabbed his wrist, halting his progress. "I can do the rest."

Instead of leaning back, he leaned in. His lips brushed her ear, sending hot tingles down her spine that leapt straight to her thighs, coaxing them to part. He hummed his approval at the slight movement. The ache between her legs spread right along with her thighs.

"You sure?"

Again she couldn't see his expression, but she just knew he was looking at her with that half amused, half provoking smile on his mouth. And she wanted to slap him for having so much control when she had none.

But she couldn't. Women that propositioned a man while on horseback really had nowhere to go with their expectations of respect.

"I am sure." She held out her hand for the tin. For interminable seconds her hand lay between them, her request dangling with it, waiting on his decision. She suspected that he deliberately made her wait. Did he think she would give in? He had a lot to learn about her. She could sit there on his lap until hell froze over or morning came without surrendering. She was very good at stubborn.

Sam placed the tin in her hand. The other hand stayed on her thigh, the fingertips rubbing in tiny movements down low. She scooped up the salve and applied it to her other thigh, her knuckles occasionally brushing his. It seemed so intimate. So daring. And still he didn't remove his hand from her thigh. The longer it sat there, the longer she got to think about it. The more she thought about it, the more aware of it she became. The more aware she became, the more her skin seemed to heat to the imprint of his fingers....

She cleared her throat. "We are wasting time."

"Duchess, I never consider it a waste of time when I've got my hand between a woman's legs."

"You are outrageous."

He took back the jar. "I'm not the one proposing relations on horseback with a stranger."

"It is not like that."

"Can't see where I got it wrong."

Feeling vulnerable, she rubbed the remnants of the cream between her fingers and tugged her skirt down with the other hand. She made it one inch before he was tucking it back up again. Higher than before. She shot him a glare and held tight, barely preventing full exposure. One corner of his mouth quirked up in a grin. If he had not been intent on exposing her privates, she would have found it very endearing. The man had charm when he wanted to use it.

"You forgot to do this side."

She hadn't forgotten a thing. "Your hand was in the way."

"Then it's only fair that I help."

His hand engulfed hers, directing her salve-covered fingertip back to her flesh, guiding her as he eased the cream onto her other thigh, first down then up, higher each time on the up, coming closer and closer to her woman's flesh. He wasn't touching her, but it felt as if he was. So much so that she felt she needed only to let him go just a little bit farther and something important would be revealed. He brought her hand back down, and then up in a slow seduction that was sinfully decadent. Lushly erotic. And totally out of her control.

Isabella yanked her skirt out of his grip and her hand from under his.

Sam chuckled, but didn't fight with her. It was a deeply inviting, highly sensual sound. It made her want to laugh, too, for no other reason than to join in. She frowned and concentrated on applying the salve. It was easy to get down by her knees, but higher up required her to lean back. Back was about a six-foot drop to the ground. She settled for rubbing more in where it was.

"Here." Sam's arm came behind her back. "Lean on me."

"It is fine." If he dropped her she would break her neck.

"I won't drop you."

"Do you read minds as well as everything else?"

"You're not that hard to read. Lean back."

She did tentatively. His arm was solid as a wall.

"I won't let you fall."

She glanced up at him. He was no longer smiling, and his expression was strangely soft.

"Why should I trust you?"

"I am a Texas Ranger. My job is to protect."

"This does not reassure me."

"How about I take care of what's mine?"

"I am not yours."

"You will be if I take you up on your proposition."

"You have not accepted."

"I'm working up to it."

That was not the only thing he was working up to. His hand guided hers higher, past the softest part of her thigh to the valley between, coming to rest against the center of her ache.

"You missed a spot."

His fingers pressed hers against the hard point beneath the cotton. Fire shot through her body. She cried out. He held her through the shock, supporting her through the delicious trauma. Distantly she heard Kell whine.

"Easy, Bella. Don't fight."

He made her sound weak. "You will know when I fight," she gasped.

His lips pressed her temple, and his finger slid between hers, finding the slit in her drawers and dipping beneath. "I bet."

His finger was hot, intrusive, but oddly exciting as it

tucked between her folds, forcing her own finger to slide against that erotic point as his found the hollow below.

She didn't know whether to curl up in embarrassment or to drop backward in a full-out sprawl.

"There, that feels good, doesn't it?"

Caught as she was between mortification and joy, she could only nod. He rocked his hand on hers, pleasuring her even as she pleasured herself.

"Don't pull away. Just let yourself get used to the idea."

Of what? Going up in flames at the direction of a man who was practically a stranger?

"It is a sin to touch oneself."

"Why?"

She frowned. "I do not know."

His hat brim brushed her head as he drawled in her ear, "Now, that *is* a sin. And one that should be rectified."

She shivered as the dark promise of something wicked coming slid down her spine. She'd always been attracted to wicked. Always longed for the forbidden, and now, as if the devil had heard her thoughts, here was a man who seemed to understand the part of her she'd spent so many years on her knees burying in prayer. And she didn't know what to do with him. She said so, bracing herself for ridicule. If anything, his expression grew softer, more sympathetic.

"Just follow my lead."

The problem was he was not leading her anywhere. His hand just covered hers as it rested on her mound. She kept waiting for him to move, to attack, but he did not. He merely squeezed his knees and the horse began to walk, adding a light rocking shift of pressure to the contact.

"What do you want me to do?"

"You're doing fine."

She was not doing anything but feeling him, the strength in his arms, the power in his touch, the threat of his shaft pressing into her buttocks. She became vividly aware of all the places his body touched hers, the fragility of her hand blocking his from the ultimate intimacy. An intimacy she'd invited. Even reminding herself of that fact didn't stop the tension within winding tighter, and while she felt distinctly threatened, her body continued to soften and flower outward as if in invitation. Her next breath came on a shaky realization. A woman didn't have any control in a situation like this.

"Breathe, Bella."

The amused reminder came in another deep drawl that slid like dark molasses over her nerves, soothing some, stimulating others. She loved his voice, the deep timbre rich with nuance that conveyed so much, but right now revealed nothing. She could not imagine what he thought of her. A woman who so boldly invited him to be her lover. His finger probed her tightness. She jumped, bumping his chin with her head. Instead of swearing, he pressed his lips against her temple.

"A bit nervous, are you?"

What harm was there in honesty when the truth was so evident? "A little."

Sam's hand left hers. It felt wrong to leave hers there

without the guidance of his. He stopped her before she could take it away.

"No. Don't."

She froze. "Why?"

It just came out. Wishing it back didn't do any more good than wishing Tejala didn't want her. Sam responded with brutal honesty.

"Because I like the thought of your hand there ready to pleasure yourself if I tell you to."

She couldn't imagine doing that. Didn't even know how to do that. "Touching oneself is a sin."

"So you said, but for someone I doubt even has a kissing-cousin relationship with the concept, you seem to have an awfully long list of things on your list that are sinful."

"We are schooled in such things."

Beneath her hip his shaft jerked.

"In sin?"

"*Dios,* no." Too late she saw the teasing in his eyes. She shook her head at herself. "You are not serious."

His smile was beautiful, making her forget for the moment the intimacy of their position and her discomfort with it.

"Not fully, no."

Not fully implied he was partially serious. She shifted on his lap. His shaft jerked again, brushing her more intimately than his hand. She paused, absorbing the uniqueness of the sensation. It wasn't unpleasant. That had to be a good thing in light of what she was planning.

"But you were a bit serious?"

"Just wondering what's going on in that head of yours. Good women don't just go throwing away their innocence."

Ah, his conscience needed soothing.

"Maybe in my eyes it would not be a throwing away."

"Uh-huh." His lips grazed her again. She shivered from head to toe and the ache in her womb swelled.

"So." He smiled against her temple before repeating the caress. "I take it you'd consider it too much of a sin to touch yourself like this for me?"

"This" was a slow draw of his finger upward from the well of her vagina to the hard point above, before wandering back down again.

Did she? Her face felt as if it were burning, the muscles so tight she couldn't form the words. His finger pressed against her opening, gentle in its demand. She clutched at his shirt and nodded, as for the first time, her muscles parted to take a man. She cried out as the tip of his finger entered in a tiny consummation. Digging her nails into his shoulder, she arched, inviting more.

He froze. "Damn."

The curse buffeted her temple. Heat transferred from his skin to hers, summoning an answering heat deep within her core. A heat that melted all that it touched. A foreign wetness invaded her flesh. He tested it with a light press. His finger slid deeper, easier.

"Maybe I should take over, then," he rasped. "Just to spare you the burden of penance."

Embarrassment twined further with desire, giving birth to doubt. "You are *católico*?"

For some reason it would feel better sinning with a member of her faith.

"No, but I'm familiar with the breed."

The moisture spread as his fingers glided higher before slipping back down. Horror blended with an agony of embarrassment. Her time of the month had just finished. It could not be that. How did one ask if such a thing were normal? She stalled, searching for the way.

"You are a heathen?"

"Pretty much."

A shiver went through her, and his smile grew. "You like the thought of that?"

How did he know the wildness in him attracted her? He couldn't know. He was just guessing. She licked her lips again and clenched her fingers against the probe of his balm-covered ones. "Of course not. It is wrong to enjoy the misfortune of others."

His fingertips worked between her legs in smooth glides, always ending at that shallow well, always ending in that erotic stretching as he forced her to take that first bit. Always her body welcomed the intrusion. Always her mind struggled with the reality.

Was she as swollen as she felt? Could he feel the unnatural wetness? O Dios, *please do not let him mind.*

"But maybe I'm happy being a heathen." His drawl deepened until it was almost a growl. "Maybe you're happy I'm a heathen, not bound by restraint and 'must nots.'"

He removed her hand completely, placing it on her thigh while she was paralyzed with a dread that felt a lot like anticipation.

"Maybe," he continued, "you like the thought that I'll do what I like with you without one thought to proper."

Maybe he was right.

The thrust of his finger was a shock, driving deep between her thighs when he'd trained her to expect a tease and withdrawal. The burning ache whipped along her nerve endings, flaying them with the rapture caught in the bit of pain. It was too much, but she didn't fight, just accepted the burn and the pleasure. Accepted it because she'd asked for it. Accepted it because it felt right.

"Ah, duchess," he growled in her ear before catching the lobe between his teeth, "I do think you like my heathen self."

She did, and the proof was in the moan that accompanied the withdrawal of his finger.

"Now, that was a sweet sound."

She thought it was a humiliating one. She wanted to be as in control as he was. Nothing made it clearer that that wasn't going to happen than the slow reinsertion of his finger. Searing heat shot from her groin outward, jerking her muscles taut. She would have fallen off the horse if his arm hadn't wrapped around her waist, trapping her arms at her sides, holding her for the pleasure he insisted she experience.

"Like that, sweetheart?" he asked as if he expected her to be able to answer. "Do you like it like that or do you prefer—" an equally slow retreat followed immediately by a shallow thrust "—that?"

The thrust was harder to take, but it delivered such sweet joy.

"Both," she managed to gasp. "I prefer both."

He chuckled. "Greedy, too."

The urge to turn her mouth to his was almost irresistible. "You asked."

"So I did. Hold on, now."

She already clung to him as if the bottom was about to fall out of the world. His teeth nipped her ear. His fingertips grazed her hungry flesh. She thought the rough callus might hurt, but right now it merely provided an intriguing drag. A tingling ache followed in the wake of the caress. Instinct drove her hips up the fraction it took to renew the contact. It wasn't the same, though. It wasn't enough to get the goodness back.

Sam's chuckle could have been mocking. She recognized his experience the same way he had to recognize her inexperience. But it wasn't mocking. Neither was his tone as he circled the hard nub at the top. "So nice and wet for me. I like that."

When Isabella opened her eyes and checked his expression, she found merely an openness that comforted. Sam was enjoying touching her. Enjoying the effect of his touch on her. It gave her the courage to ask, "The wetness is normal?"

"When you're having a good time, yes."

He made another pass with his finger. The tingles flared to fire. She caught his hand, stilling the caress. There was something she had to know. "It does not repulse you?"

The arm supporting her back shifted, sliding up her back until his big hand cupped her shoulder. Her torso naturally shifted into the hollow created by the curve of his arm. She might be innocent, but she recognized desire when it stared at her, and Sam desired her.

"If you weren't such an innocent, I'd show you just how much I'm not repulsed."

She didn't know if she could survive it. Sam clearly came from a different world than she. She'd always been pampered and sheltered from the coarser side of life, tucked away from reality, whereas Sam clearly kept his boots firmly planted in daily life. He was as earthy as he was dangerous, and, *madre de Dios,* he appealed to her.

Sam changed the angle, forcing her to lean back. Off balance, she felt her thighs splay farther, his hand cupping her more fully.

It was as if another person possessed her. A wanton woman who burned for the stroke of his fingers, who lived to see the satisfaction in his face when she pleased him. A woman who yearned to burn at his command.

She just didn't know how to burn, but looking up into Sam's face with his sensual mouth set above that square jaw and strong neck, she bet he knew how to set the fire. She licked her lips. If she was brave enough to hand him the sulphur.

His hand cupped her cheek. He held her now cradled against him, anchored at her most vulnerable points—her face and her groin. Again, she should feel threatened, and yet again she just felt...cherished. His thumb tilted her chin up.

"Tell me something."

"What?"

"Are you giving yourself to me because you think it'll guarantee you protection?"

She had to think about it.

"Would this matter if it were true? You would still have a willing woman in your bed."

His thumb stroked her lips, pausing in the dent in the middle. "You hinting I've been hitting a dry spell?"

She couldn't even find the coordination to swallow. She wrinkled her nose. "Probably not."

"So what would be the draw?"

"I am a virgin." Everyone knew men lusted after virgins.

"That means you lack experience."

Shaking her head, she twisted her hand until she could grab his wrist. "Even I know that is not a negative to a man."

"It is if you've reached a point where you're not wanting to do all the work."

"You are telling me you are lazy?"

"Laziness is a highly underappreciated quality."

The man had not stopped moving since she had met him. He must be teasing her. She could tease, too. "But just think about it—you could train me to what you liked."

He canted his head to the side, his gaze still on the point where his thumb touched her lip. "That would take a long time."

"I could be a woman who learns fast."

He pulled her lip down, seemingly fascinated with her mouth. "You have the look of a woman who'd be a lot of work."

"I might be worth your while."

"Keeping you around could get me killed."

She caught his finger between her teeth. "Letting me go without teaching me will definitely get you killed."

"By who?"

Nipping his thumb, she answered, "By me."

Some of the seriousness slipped from his expression. "Is that a fact?"

She nodded, looking as mean as she could. "A rock-solid one."

The smile she suspected was lurking just out of sight teased the corners of his eyes. "You think a little bit of a thing like you could make me shake in my shoes?"

She scooted down into his embrace, clutching like

a talisman the inner conviction that said she fascinated him the way he fascinated her. "I think if you taught me right, I could make you quake."

"Hell."

He was imagining. So was she, but she did not think her images were as clear as the ones putting the heat in his eyes.

"So that is a yes?"

"Not yet."

She liked the fact that he did not prevaricate. "But you will think about it?"

"I doubt I'll be thinking of anything else."

Neither would she. Her whole body was a restless ache for the satisfaction he withheld. She ran her fingernail down the placket of his shirt. "Maybe you would like me to convince you to a yes?"

His nostrils flared. Oh yes, he would like that.

"What I'd like is for you to think over the invitation while I consider it."

Watching him watch her, seeing the goodness in him that he hid behind a cold exterior, she realized why he was hesitating. He worried she had not thought this through. He was wrong.

She knew what she was doing. Her mother had warned her that there would come a time when she would not be able to run anymore. She had finally reached it with this man, in this wild place. And it felt right. "You think I'm running away."

"Yes."

"I am not."

"Then what are you doing?"

She curled her fingers over the hand that cupped her cheek, holding on. "For once, I am taking what *I* want."

"And you want me?"

She had never been more sure of anything in her life. "Very much."

His eyes narrowed. "For how long?"

She would not ask him for more than he could give, and he was not a man who gave a woman promises. "As long as it lasts."

His big hand settled on her thigh, weighing heavily. The utter stillness with which he touched her implied more significance than a caress. She sorted through the notion, trying to understand what it meant, but came up with no answers. Just more questions. Finally he gave her thigh a squeeze and pulled her skirt down over her legs, causing her to look at him again. Did he want her or not?

"Hold on."

As the horse broke into a canter, only one thought perked through the conflicting messages he sent her. *To what?*

6

Isabella held on as long as she could, but by the time they reached the small hollow in the side of the cliff where Sam decided it was safe to spend the night, she could barely hold her head up.

"You awake?" Sam asked as soon as Breeze came to a halt.

"*Sí.*"

"Your legs feeling strong enough to hold you?"

"Of course."

His hand wrapped around her upper arm. "Then slide off, and we'll get settled for the night."

Nothing had ever sounded so good. Grabbing Sam's wrist with both hands, she turned her body and slid off Breeze. It was not her most graceful moment. She kicked the horse's shoulder and then his knee on her way down. Beyond a snort, he made no complaint. Even when her knee hit his stomach, he didn't move. By the time her feet touched the ground she was extremely grateful for his training. Every muscle from her ankles to her shoulder blades screamed a protest. She collapsed against Breeze's side. If it hadn't been for Sam's hold, she would have fallen to the ground.

"Whoa, there."

She glanced up, wanting to cry with the sheer frustration of being so weak at a time when she wanted to be so strong. "Maybe I am not feeling so strong as I thought."

"It looks that way. Grab on to the saddle for a second."

She did, wrapping her fingers in the rawhide straps that dangled off assorted leather decorations. Sam swung down behind her. Immediately he wrapped his arm around her waist. Letting go, she let him drag her against him. His shoulder knocked her hat. It fell over her face.

She pushed it back and off. "I hate this hat."

Before it could slide off her head, he tipped it right back. "Unless you're fond of mosquitoes in your hair, you might want to leave it on." With his free hand he untied the bedroll from the back of the saddle. Propping her against the wall, he made short work of rolling out the blankets. Locking her knees, she leaned against the warm rock, too sore and too tired to care anymore how weak she looked to him.

He motioned to the bedroll. "Here, sit."

It was a long way to the ground. "I think I will stand, thank you."

"You'll be fine once you sit down."

How would he know? She didn't even turn her head, just stayed propped against the wall. "That is easy for you to say, but much harder for me to do."

"Are you saying you need help?"

"I am saying I need a whole new body."

He chuckled, more a vibration of his chest than actual sound.

"Don't go ordering it until I get done appreciating this one."

She glared at him. "You have a very inappropriate sense of humor."

"Seems to work just fine for me."

"This explains why you are alone."

"I am not alone. I'm Hell's Eight, remember?"

He held out his hand. She placed her palm in his.

"You are alone in every way that matters."

He shook his head. "You think too much."

"You said I could."

He braced his arm. "So I did."

His palms were laced with ridges of callus. Beneath the edge of his shirtsleeve she could see the thick edge of a scar. He was a hardworking man who breathed violence the way she breathed air. He should be violent. And he could be violent. He just never was with her and, as opposed to many of the men she met, her stomach never twisted in warning that he ever would.

"So maybe you should control your humor."

"Why?"

"I already said. So you would not be alone."

"That's a woman's way of looking at things."

She snorted. "I am a woman."

"That, duchess, is evident." The way he said *duchess* made her heart flutter. He said it with a touch of affection supported with a base of possession. "Bend your knees now and I'll get you settled."

She clutched his wrist. "If I do this, does it mean I do not have to move again for the rest of the night?"

"That it does."

"Then I will sit."

"Glad to hear it."

He didn't rush her, just waited. Watching her. Eventually it was the guilt of making him stand there that unlocked her knees. The descent wasn't pretty, and it was accomplished only amidst many groans and one small squeak, but eventually she was sitting on the bedroll. Sam untied the saddlebags and placed them beside her. "There's another piece of jerky in that pack if you want it."

"I am not hungry, thank you." Truth was she was starving, but she didn't have the energy to chew a piece of jerky. She barely had the strength to sit and watch Sam get the horses settled. As he loosened the girth on Sweet Pea's saddle, she closed her eyes and leaned back against the wall. Solid rock had never felt so good.

She let out her breath in a long sigh. "I will have to name the packhorse."

"Why?"

"It is not good that a soul go nameless."

"I thought the church preached animals didn't have souls."

She cracked her eyelid. His back was to her. It was a very nice back, and as she followed the natural line of his build it ended in very tight buttocks. Buttocks she would soon have the right to touch. She licked her dry lips. "Do not tell the padre."

"What will you give me to keep quiet?"

She cracked her other lid. He was looking at her over his shoulder, that invisible smile hovering around him as he raised his brows at her.

"Does everything with you have a price?"

"Yes."

"Then I promise I will not snore tonight."

It was a pretty safe promise, as she was sure she did not snore.

"I guess that's a fair exchange, seeing as I'm dog tired and might be forced to take action if you started sawing logs."

Despite her tiredness, she couldn't help her smile at the colorful expression. Sam had so many it would be hard to remember them all, but she wanted to. More than that, she wanted to use them. Her mother would be horrified at her lack of decorum. Her father equally so. It was the one thing they agreed on—that she should behave impeccably at all times. Sam was the first person on whom she had had the opportunity to try out her sense of humor. That he seemed to appreciate it just made her like him more. "Good."

She drifted off to the sound of packs hitting the ground and Sam's croon to the horses. There was magic in his voice when he pitched it like that. Low and deep—not quite speech, not quite song, but a wordless melody that lulled and soothed. She let that magic work through her. It was hard to be afraid of a man who crooned like that, but it was easy to speculate about him. To wonder what made him laugh, what brought the passion to his eyes, the hunger to his soul. To wonder if, with her inexperience, she would be woman enough to please him. To wonder what had brought him to her in the hour when she needed him most.

Dios, *I need a hero.*

The prayer she'd whispered in despair as she'd watched the men who had been going to take her out of town slaughtered by Tejala's banditos came back to her. Opening her eyes, she watched as Sam rubbed down Breeze. There was no doubt he was hero material. But hers? She glanced at the vastness of the night sky, dotted with stars, a black canvas stretching into infinity. It was possible. She did believe in fate. She glanced back at Sam and sighed. But not likely. Men like him had bigger things in their destiny than to save one hunted woman, but maybe she would believe so for now. It would make everything easier.

Heat from the day seeped from the rock into her muscles, soothing her aches. It felt so good not to have to worry for a minute. To have nothing to do but enjoy the peace of the night and the sounds within it. To give her cares to one more able to handle them. To let time and awareness drift away…

Isabella came to swinging. Sam ducked her fist, unable to see her eyes as his shadow covered her face. Her kick caught him in his shin. Stepping to the side, he evaded the next.

"Easy, duchess. It's just me."

She stilled, her breath coming in hard pants. "Sam?"

Firelight cast unsteady light across her features, but it was enough to see the residual fear in her eyes. He pushed the hair off her face. A woman like her should wake up expecting kisses, not blows.

"Yeah. Sam."

She blinked and yawned. He worked his arms under her knees and shoulders. "Are we done?"

"Appears to me you're about done in." He straightened, taking her with him. "Put your arms around my neck."

She did, slowly, as if she was lifting boulders instead of her own limbs. With a slight toss he angled her into his torso. Her head fit perfectly into the hollow of his shoulder. He carried her over to the fire where he had a makeshift bedroll covered in his oilcloth slicker. He nudged Kell off with his foot, ignoring his grump. Isabella glanced around as he knelt. "I'm sorry, I should have helped set up the campsite."

"Next time you can do it all."

She nodded. *"Gracias."*

"Don't be thanking me too soon. Setting up a camp-site can be hard work."

"I am not afraid of hard work."

No, she probably wasn't. He set her as gently as possible on the bedroll. Sam was beginning to think not much scared her once she got the bit between her teeth, but he doubted Isabella had seen much hard work in her life. Her hands had blisters with only a light layer of callus beneath, and her curvaceous little body was very soft. The kind of soft that came from pampering.

He balanced the end of her braid on his finger, imagining her in a fancy house, imagining how her day might go if she wasn't running from Tejala. Maids to do the work. Servants to bring her food. A man to protect her from the harsher realities. He liked the thought of her being pampered. He wanted to pamper her. He wanted to protect her. He wanted…her. Which didn't make any sense. He wasn't a settling man.

There was a smudge of dirt on Bella's cheek. He wiped it with his thumb, noting the differences in their skin. His was dark and rough, marred by scars. Hers was pale and smooth, as perfect as sweet caramel. The smudge didn't come off. If they were back on Hell's Eight, he'd follow Caine's example and indulge himself by drawing her a bath. He'd never bathed a woman before, but there was something intrinsically pleasing in the thought of caring for Bella on that intimate a level. Hell, the woman was just damn pleasing, period. "I'm going to lay you down now."

Not even cracking her eyes, she asked, "Do you need to?"

He bet she was as sore as all get-out. "Yes."

She sighed, one of those long-suffering ones he'd already heard from her a time or two. It seemed her favorite mode of expression when she wanted to avoid an argument but still make her opinion known. "All right."

She immediately went stiff as a board, obviously braced for the worst.

"If you tighten up, it's going to hurt more."

She shook her head. "Not possible."

"Try to relax anyway."

After a deep breath she nodded for him to proceed. Sam smiled at the unconscious arrogance coming from someone so defenseless, and angled her back. She groaned as her muscles stretched and protested and then slowly relaxed into the knowledge they didn't have to support her anymore. He watched the process, inordinately interested in every nuance of her expression, noting how her mouth firmed when she prepared herself, how her dark lashes fluttered against her cheek just before the pleasure took her and she relaxed.

He curled his fingers into a fist to keep from reaching out and tracing the curve of her lashes against her cheek, their deep black merely accentuating the dusky color of her skin with its undertones of peach. Her lips carried the same peach tint beneath the pink. Her nipples were probably that color, too.

The knowledge punched him in the gut, driving straight to his cock, pounding hard within the swollen shaft. Damn, she was a sexy little thing. Tracing his fingers along her jawline, he studied her face, looking for the reason she appealed to him so much. She was beautiful. A triangular face with angles that gave an impression of haughty aristocracy softened with full lips that betrayed her vulnerability—plump, pouting, the upper fuller than the bottom, and drawn up just short of a kiss. It was easy to see why Tejala was chasing her all over the territory. The woman screamed wild nights and sultry mornings. If she came from a good family, Tejala could have his cake and eat it, too. Respect in town and a hellcat in his bed. Sam brushed the hair off her other cheek. Except she didn't want Tejala. She wanted him.

Sam still didn't know how he felt about that. Rubbing his thumb in small circles at her temple, he contemplated the sheer anomaly of indecision. It was not, he decided, an emotion he liked. He did like, however, the way Isabella naturally turned her cheek into his touch, confirming another of his suspicions. She was a very sensual woman, ripe for the plucking.

You could train me to what you like.

Talk about waving a red flag in front of a bull. He shook his head, staring down at her. There were lots of things he wanted. Those lush lips wrapped around his cock, her hair wrapped around his privates, the taste of her on his tongue, her moans in his ears. A lot of things he wanted to do to her, but he couldn't shake the feeling that the price was going to be higher than he wanted to pay. He nudged her cheek with his finger.

"Are you awake?"

"Yes."

Barely, if the weakness of that "yes" was anything to go by.

"I'm going to unbutton your shirt. Don't start screaming."

Her thick black lashes rose off the shelf of her high cheekbones. A touch of pink accentuated the peachy tan of her skin. Through her lashes he could just make out the deep brown of her eyes. "Are you going to drop a spider in the opening?"

"Hell, no." Why in hell would she think he was going to do that?

Her lashes fluttered back down. "Then you do not have to worry about my screaming."

"Ah." The first button gave easily. "You're afraid of spiders?"

"They're disgusting. All those ugly legs and fat hairy bodies…"

The involuntary shudder that took her knocked the second button out of his fingers. "I'll keep that in mind."

She stiffened. It wasn't hard to tell where her mind was going. "As a thing to avoid," he clarified.

She relaxed infinitesimally. "Thank you."

The third button gave. He glanced over at the small kettle sitting over the fire. The water should be warm by now.

The fourth button gave without a protest. He could just make out the edges of her collarbone. His breath was coming hard, like a horse blown after a run, and he hadn't even gotten a decent look at anything interesting. There was just something about her that teased his interest, caught on his lust, drowned his better judgment.

The fifth button revealed something wrong. A wide band of cotton. He explored it with his fingertip. It ran horizontally across her chest. "Are you injured?"

"Oh, *madre*." She clutched at the lapel and her lids popped open. "I forgot."

He let her hold the lapel up high while he worked the buttons below. "Forgot what?"

She tried to sit up, hit the wall of muscle pain and flopped back down with a groan. "It is my bindings."

"Bindings?"

"Could we not do relations without undressing? It is not pretty beneath."

That gave him pause. He cocked an eyebrow at her. "You think I'm planning on making love to you?"

"Why else would you be undressing me?"

Why else indeed. "To see what's beneath this bandage."

"It is not a bandage."

The death grip she had on the top of the shirt didn't

hinder at all his spread of the bottom. The wrapping went all the way down to her surprisingly narrow waist. He pulled his knife from his boot. "What is it, then?"

"It is binding to contain my...chest."

The binding was substantial. It only stood to reason that what it contained would be, too. Sam's mouth went dry as he put the edge of the knife beneath the wrap. Her stomach sucked in, creating a gap between the material and her abdomen. His imagination galloped ahead while his cock throbbed and his pulse raced like a green boy's. Isabella grabbed his wrist.

"Do not."

"Why not?"

She was blushing so hard he could see it in the near dark. "I do not have any other bindings."

"You won't need them with me."

He would never let another man touch her.

Her eyes met his, as soft and velvety smooth as melted chocolate, dark with embarrassment. "It hurts—"

The knife sliced through the bindings.

"To not have support," she finished in an agonized whisper as the bindings fell to the side.

"Hell!"

He just bet it did. *Bountiful.* That was the first word he came up with to describe her breasts. Bountiful, plentiful and gorgeous. The full curves belled inward from the compression of the shirt, all but the nipples revealed. He opened his hand over her midriff, the palm itching with the need to touch. More than a handful. Maybe even two handfuls. Damn, she couldn't have been created more perfectly to his taste. "Perfect."

"Are you looking at me?" she squeaked.

He glanced up. She'd retreated into the only defense she had left. She'd closed her eyes.

"Yup, and getting an eyeful." He slid his hand up toward the treasure she'd hidden from him. Her lips moved, but no sound came out. Her hands slid down the lapel. He stopped her with a shake of his head.

"No."

"I am not comfortable."

He could see that. The binding had left her breasts reddened and swollen. They'd look like that after he loved them, too, but they wouldn't have an angry rash surrounding them from the bindings, and they'd be swollen from pleasure, not abuse.

"You won't bind your breasts again." He rubbed his fingers along the ridges left by the bindings. She gasped and arched away. He followed her down, supporting her as he promised. Firelight played across the pale flesh. Anger snapped through him when he saw the shadow of a bruise. "It's a wonder you haven't damaged yourself permanently."

Her hand closed almost convulsively around his wrist. "I need support."

He hefted a heavy globe, grazing his thumb along the underside. He just bet she did. "I'll take care of you."

"You cannot walk around all day holding my breasts!"

He laughed at her expression. She clearly hadn't

realized how that was going to sound when she spit it out, but now he had a feeling that if she could have dug a hole, she'd be in it in a second.

"The thought has merit." He said that just to get her going. It worked. She sat up so fast the bottom of her head barely missed his chin. One look at his face and she figured out his game.

"You said that just to shock me!"

Her breasts bobbed with indignation, the aftershocks reverberating along their heavy curves. He looped his arm around her chest, supporting her breasts on his forearm as he pulled her back against his shoulder. From here, he had a bird's-eye view of her impressive cleavage. Deep and dark, it would take his cock perfectly. All he'd have to do was unbutton his pants, straddle her torso and he could be in heaven. Shit. She made him want. It was a struggle to find his voice. "Yes, I did."

She yanked the shirt as closed as she could over his arm. The garment wasn't cut to contain such largesse. The best of her efforts still left him with a fine view.

"Why?"

That was an easy question. He gave her the easy answer. "I like you better spitting fire than I do apologizing for your existence."

"I was not apologizing for my existence, but I am not used to undressing in front of a man."

"Technically, I was undressing you."

She just stared at him. As if maybe she was losing her mind, or maybe she thought he was losing his.

He dropped a kiss to the top of her head before leaning over to open the saddlebag. He fished around inside until he found the tin of salve. Leaning back, he said, "There is a difference, you know."

Her tongue eased over her lips in a slow glide of pink on pink. "I do?"

He couldn't take his eyes off the natural sensuality of the gesture. "You're going to be hell on fire in bed, aren't you?"

"Honestly?"

"Yes."

"I would like to think I could be."

He opened the jar of salve and scooped some onto his fingers. "Move your hands away from your chest."

She did cautiously, obviously having no idea how inflaming the slow tease of gradual exposure could be. He smoothed the salve over the patches of prickly heat on the side of her right breast.

"So why the 'could be'? Not that I'm complaining, but most young women aren't concerned with the bedroom much, let alone how wild they're going to be once they get there."

His forearm brushed her nipple. And every time, she gasped, his cock jerked, until he was pretty much one big throb, and it was all he could do to keep up the pretense that the only thing that was going on was him treating her injuries.

"Eventually, Tejala will catch up with me." She twisted her fingers together. "That will not be pleasant."

He stopped rubbing ointment into her breast and cradled it instead. She needed comfort. He wasn't good at giving comfort.

Her voice dropped to a whisper. "I do not think I will ever want to be touched again after that, so I think I would like to know the full pleasure of being a woman before it is taken from me."

Shit. "There's such a thing as telling too much."

Her lashes rose, revealing what he didn't want to see. Hurt. He'd hurt her. "I am sorry." Buttoning her shirt, she inched away. "I talk too much."

She talked more than any woman he'd ever met. But strangely, it didn't bother him. Because she also made him smile more than any woman he'd ever met. He sighed. "You might as well know from the get-go, I'm not good at this."

She sat stiff and unyielding, buttoning those damn buttons, not looking at him. "What is *this*?"

He tipped her chin up, cupping it so she couldn't look away. "Soft words. They're never there when I want them."

"Did you want them to be?"

"Yes."

"Then we will trade. I will teach you soft words and you will teach me to love."

Sam wedged the lid back on the salve. He took longer than needed doing it. Bella didn't struggle or fight, just rested against him. Accepting his decree the way she wouldn't accept Tejala as her fate. If he was smart, he'd turn tail and run.

"Making things between the sheets perfect for a woman is a tall order."

"I understand." With a wave of her hand she granted him absolution. When he didn't want it.

He captured her hand midwave. It felt natural to bring her fingers to his lips. To make her promises. "He won't touch you, Bella."

There was a long pause. Her gaze searched his for answers to questions she wouldn't voice. He didn't think she was even aware how tightly she clung to him. "I pray daily for that miracle."

"Then you can stop praying."

Another pause. She took a deep breath. He found he was inhaling right along with her. A flush rose to her cheeks, emphasizing her youth. He couldn't follow her there. He didn't think he'd ever been as young as she was, ever had such innocence. But he had easily been as desperate. Tucking her hand against her chest, he took over fastening the buttons of her shirt. "You don't have to bargain with your body, duchess. My protection won't cost you a thing."

"That is good." To his surprise, she opened her shirt back up, not all the way and not without a new flush spreading over her creamy skin, but enough to tease him with the silky inner curves and the shadowed hollow between. "Because what I want between us should not have a price."

"Everything comes with a price."

"Then maybe this price I want to pay."

"Maybe I don't."

She nodded. "Ah, so it is not for me you fear."

No one had ever looked at him with such softness and understanding. He didn't like it.

"The hell it's not. A whore's future isn't pretty."

She blinked, and the softness left her expression as if it had never existed. Her spine snapped straight. "You will apologize for that, Sam MacGregor."

"Why the hell should I apologize for the truth?"

She pushed off his lap, gasping from the pain, and turned around. She was kneeling so her face was level with his. This close there was no mistaking she was ticked. She poked her finger into his chest. "Because it was mean and I did not deserve it."

"Why should I care?"

She sighed and shook her head. "Because my feelings are damaged and because you like me."

This was her with her feelings damaged? He opened his mouth. She cut him off.

"In case your eyes have not seen, this is a time for soft words. Nice words. Words of apology."

"I wasn't calling you a whore, but—"

Holding up her hand, she glared at him. "Know that if you ask me another question that I must answer with 'because,' I will cry."

Son of a bitch. "Are you blackmailing me?"

She shook her head and touched his shoulder fleetingly before sitting back on her heels. "I am just tired and sore and I have not much resistance left."

That might be a tear in her eye.

"So you're going to cry?"

"Men do not like tears." Her lips trembled, then firmed. "I understand this, but I do not think mine will stay away much longer if you continue to damage my feelings."

"Hurt my feelings."

"Damage. Hurt. What difference does it make?"

Not a bit, and she was right. He hated to see any woman cry, especially Bella. And she understood that and warned him, because to her that was fair play. He didn't think he'd ever met another woman like her. He wasn't sure he wanted to. She left him too off balance. He sighed. "What do you want from me, Bella?"

"I'm afraid to ask now."

She wasn't afraid of anything. "Ask."

It was practically a growl.

Instead of flinching in fear, her eyes heated with hunger.

She caught his hand and brought it to her breast, straightening his fingers one by one until they straddled the hollow and flattened against the succulent flesh on either side. "Will you give me pleasure, Sam? Will you teach me to be a woman?"

In the end it was an easy decision to make. He cupped his fingers behind her neck, drawing her forward into the press of his palm, feeling her heart leap, hearing her breath catch. Oh, yeah, he'd teach her. "Better than that, I'll teach you to be my woman."

7

"Lean back."

Leaning back meant making muscles work. Leaning back meant committing herself to the path she'd taken. Leaning back meant trusting Sam.

Bella reached out. "Could you help me?"

"Absolutely."

He handled her as competently as he had handled his horse. One hand behind her shoulder, the other holding hers. He made it easy. All she had to do was give him her weight, and he took care of the rest.

"Are you going to make it all this easy?"

He cupped her cheek in his hand. It was a gesture of comfort. A declaration of intent. "Yes."

She turned her head until she could press a soft kiss into the center of his rough palm. "Thank you."

He smiled, a real smile that reached his eyes. "I think that's usually the man's line and comes much later."

She could not help but smile back. "We are doing many things differently—why should this be any different?"

"Why indeed." He gave the shirt a tug. "You want to lighten your grip a bit?"

The shirt. He wanted her to let go of the shirt. She tried, but her fingers wouldn't obey the dictates of her brain.

"Problems?"

"My fingers will not listen."

"Second thoughts?"

"I think it is too many years of being told I should keep it closed."

"Then this must be your lucky day."

"How?"

"I spent a lot of years learning how to convince women to get buttons open."

Bella tried not to think about that. Not only because she didn't want to know about other women, but because, despite her brave talk, she wasn't sure she had what it took to satisfy a man like this. And she did not think she would find relations satisfying if Sam was not fulfilled.

But maybe Sam didn't know that. Her mother had talked to her in vague terms that had touched on the mechanics, but her talk had not touched on the emotions involved.

"Sam?"

"Yeah?"

"I want to find this fun, too."

He paused and looked at her, surprised. "That was always the plan."

"Ah, I did not know. *Mi madre* only told me that my responsibility was to please you, but not that it's possible for me to be pleased." She licked her lips, the next words lodged in her throat as a flush burned her from toe to head. She had to swallow twice before they would come out, and even then they came out in a high-pitched airy rush. "I would like to have some pleasure."

She could not believe she'd said all that without burning up from embarrassment.

"That's another thing I like."

"What?"

"A woman not afraid to ask for what she wants."

Bella let go of the shirt. "Then maybe I was an answer to your prayers, too."

He met her gaze squarely. "I don't pray."

Dropping a bandanna around the handle of the kettle, he lifted it off the fire and set it beside the packet of soap.

What did he want her to say to that? "Then I will pray for you until you remember how."

"Don't waste your time."

No matter where she put her hands, they felt awkward. She tried her stomach, then her thighs and finally settled for resting them on the slicker beside her. "It is my time. I will waste it however I want to."

"Suit yourself."

He dipped the bandanna in the pot, wrung it out and

then placed it against her neck. The warm water felt heavenly against her skin.

"Oh, yes."

Sam chuckled. "You're easy to please."

"My easy is good for your lazy side, yes?"

"Oh, definitely." He wiped at her skin with surprisingly gentle strokes for such a big man, but then she'd seen the way he'd handled the horse and she realized she shouldn't be surprised. There were many layers to Sam MacGregor. The more interesting ones were the ones he didn't show the world.

The bandanna moved across her collarbone, taking the dirt and tension with it. When Sam removed the cloth, the night air felt cooler. She felt cooler. Her nipples tingled and puckered. "No one has ever bathed me before."

Water sloshed in the kettle as Sam rewet the cloth. "A lot of people have been missing out."

She closed her eyes and smiled. "Men, you mean."

The fragrance of pine-scented soap got stronger. "Yeah. Men."

She didn't care about other men. Just Sam. When the cloth returned, gliding across the tops of her breasts, she arched her back, just a little. The shirt fell to either side in a whispery caress. Sam's indrawn hiss of breath was an equally elusive caress.

"I am glad then that the only man to give me this pleasure is you." She sighed, keeping her voice soft so as not to disturb the emotion burgeoning between them.

Another glide of the cloth, this time lower. "This is just for now, Bella."

Internally she smiled at the hard tone. He was so leery of strong feelings. "So, you would have me not enjoy it?"

"Not hardly."

With a lethargic wave of her hand, she motioned him on. "Then hush and continue."

The cloth paused in the valley of her breasts. "Anyone ever told you it's not your place to be giving orders?"

She shook her head. "No."

The bandanna left her skin. The spot where it had rested chilled. "Then let me be the first."

There was that hard note in his voice again. It shivered through her more powerfully than a kiss. There was something about that tone that resonated with something wild in her. Something primitive, feminine and hungry. She opened her eyes. Sam was staring down at her with the same implacable resolve deepening his drawl. A second shiver joined the first. His gaze sharpened and his nostrils flared. Did he sense that part of her that struggled for freedom?

"If you're going to be my lover, you'll have to learn to temper that side of you."

If? What had she done to bring the "if" back? "Why?"

The little smile that curved his lips tweaked her as hard as a dare. "Keep giving me orders and find out."

"That was unfair! You know I will not be able to resist."

He rewet the bandanna as calmly as if he had not just

thrown down a challenge. "Got to admit, the thought had occurred to me."

Excitement thrummed through her blood, kicking up her heartbeat. She licked her lips and asked, "What happens if I fail?"

The cloth swirled over the surface of her breast, circling upward, encompassing her nipple. His fingers closed over the hard tip through the damp cloth and squeezed lightly, drawing it away from her body in a sensual tug, drawing out the tension, the heat. Intensifying the pleasure. "When you push me too far, I'll take you in hand."

The spasm that rocked her womb was akin to pain. The aftershocks were a prelude to a savage need she did not understand, but Sam did. She could see it in his eyes. He understood what she needed. Her "How?" was a soft whisper of sound. *Por Dios,* she wanted to hear how.

The soft pinch he delivered to her nipple tore a cry from her lips and jerked her up. Pain lanced through her from her abused muscles, drowning the pleasure from his teasing. Immediately he was there, cradling her head in his hand, easing her back. Concern mellowed out the harshness of desire. "Easy, Bella. You've got to be easy."

"I cannot when you do that."

His eyebrow quirked. "This?"

He squeezed her nipple again, a little harder, a little longer, and this time the sensation did not come as a surprise. This time she could enjoy it, savor it.

"Yes." She wanted to arch into the feeling, into his hand. His palm on her shoulder prevented it.

"Stay still, and we'll see if you can take a little more."

"We? Where is this 'we'?"

He laughed and leaned in, his mouth meeting hers in a deep kiss, his words flowing into her mouth like a lure. "Little innocent. Don't you know nothing gets a man hotter than when his woman burns at his touch?"

Bella slipped her fingers between the lapels of Sam's shirt, feeling very daring as crisp hairs tickled her fingertips. "Not even my hands on your skin?"

Sam shuddered and smiled, his mouth moving over her cheek, nuzzling into the corner of her mouth, waking up nerves she did not even know were there. Nerves that clamored only for him.

"That's good, but it's nothing without the other."

She slid her fingers farther inside. "And you like the way I come alive for you?"

"Very much."

Popping the button beneath her fingers, working her hand deeper, she asked, "And when it is my turn, will you come burn for me?"

His grip clenched convulsively on her nipple. Pain and pleasure combined in an erotic bite. She gasped and grabbed at his shirt, holding on as the thrill wove through her.

"Damn!" Sam smoothed his thumb over the taut peak. "I'm sorry. I lost…"

Shaking his head, he sat back.

She finished the thought for him. "Control."

"I didn't lose control."

But he had with her. She smoothed the crease from between his eyes with her index finger. "I will forgive you if you do it again. It was very…exciting."

The lines beside his mouth deepened, the tension in his fingers spreading through his body. His eyes narrowed. "You're going to be hell to keep in line, aren't you?"

"Would it make me bad if I say to the point that it is probably not even worth the effort of trying?"

A real laugh accompanied the chuck he gave her chin. "If I didn't succeed, what kind of man would that make me?"

Isabella did not want to know. She liked Sam just as he was with all his bossiness, his sense of honor, and she definitely liked his sense of humor. "The man I want as my lover?"

The cloth fell to the side, and then it was the heat of his hand on her damp flesh, plumping it as his head bent. Though she knew it was coming, his mouth on her breast was a shock, burning hot, the lash of his tongue across the sensitive tip a surprise. Lightning whipped across her skin, picking up sparks as it went, igniting fires across the landscape of her torso, sending a shower of sparks careening down her spine, throwing her into a wild storm that swept her up and tossed her about with nothing familiar to grab on to. The scrape of his teeth was more than she could stand. But it was not enough. She needed more. Wrapping her fingers in his hair, she dragged his mouth to her. "Harder."

Oh, please do it harder.

With something that sounded like a growl he complied, drawing hard on her nipple, nipping with his teeth, soothing with his tongue until she was arching up, pulling down, panting with pleasure.

"Sam!"

Another rumble followed by a small nip. Ah! It felt so good. He was so good. She rubbed her breasts against his beard-roughened cheeks, trying to keep the magic even as he pulled away. "Your mouth is wonderful."

He swore and dropped his forehead to her breastbone.

"What?"

"You are hell on a man's good intentions."

"I like these intentions."

His chuckle blew across her belly. "And I'll get back to them, but first I have other plans for this sweet little body."

"Will I enjoy it as much as this?"

"Right now, I think you'll enjoy it more."

She pressed his hand to her breast, sighing when he obligingly stroked the tender skin. "This will be hard to better."

With a last hard kiss, he knelt beside her and tested the water in the kettle. "Trust me."

She missed his warmth and weight immediately. No wonder mothers preached that their daughters have nothing to do with men. If all women felt with men the way she felt with Sam, there would be no virgins.

Trust me.

He picked up the bandanna and dipped it in the kettle again. She did trust him, but she did not understand. He would prefer to wash her? "This is what you wish?"

He nodded, his expression strangely intent. "Yes."

He rubbed the wet cloth on the soap. Pine scented the air. Starting at her neck, he wiped away the dirt and heat of the day. She studied his face as he repeated the action on the other side before moving down to her shoulders. Every move was carefully planned; every stroke overlapped the first. And with every pass the tension in him eased and the satisfaction in his eyes grew. Bathing her fed a need in him. She didn't know what it was, but if doing this gave him a measure of peace, then she would not complain.

Bella sighed as the warmth from the cloth sank through her skin. Not that she had anything to complain about. Sam was very good at this. He never let the cloth get too dry, never let the water get too hot. And while relations with him were exciting, this was as good in a different sort of way. This made her feel special. Pampered.

"Feel good?" he asked as he lifted her arm.

"Muy bueno." It was almost a purr.

The quirk of his lips indicated his approval. "Good."

The water was hotter now, the heat almost stinging her skin before soaking beneath to the sore muscles of her arms. It felt so good. She moaned, flexing her fingers as he brought the cloth back up her inner arm. "You may do that all night."

"I did intend on getting some sleep."

"Then I will just appreciate your care until you sleep."

His lips twitched. "You do that."

"But I do not think your reputation will survive."

He dipped the bandanna in the water, this time wiping the soap from her skin. He seemed fascinated by the process. "What reputation was that?"

She couldn't believe she was saying this. "That you can please a woman from dusk to dawn without stopping in between."

Unbelievably he smiled and moved the cloth down, sliding it over her breast in gentle motions.

"Is that a fact?"

Her breast tingled and drew taut. "Yes."

Firelight played across his features as he cut her a glance from under his hat brim. "Then maybe you want to reconsider your proposition."

He was giving her an out. Another one. Some cold-blooded seducer he was turning out to be. "No. We made a deal. I am holding you to it."

His head tilted slightly as he put the cloth aside and eased his hands under her. "To the letter?"

"Yes."

"That's my girl. Roll over."

"I am comfortable." And she really didn't want to go through movement.

"You'll feel better afterward." He started the rolling for her. *Madre,* he was strong. Tucking her arms under her, she went with his urging until she flopped onto her stomach, moaning as the protest rippled through her muscles.

"Easy."

"I was easy until you had to have your way."

"It'd serve you well to remember I always get my way."

Another warning? "I am used to getting my way, too."

Cool air wafted over her back as he lifted her shirt. It was quickly followed by the warmth of the cloth making gentle sweeps over her back. She rested her cheek in her hands. Her eyes drifted closed on the surge of bliss.

"I like that little noise."

She did not realize she'd been humming in her throat. She did not know what to say. She settled for "Thank you."

The cloth swished in the kettle. Droplets fell like rain as he wrung it out, and then once again he was moving it over her back in those long sweeps that encouraged the tension to leave and relaxation to set in.

"Admit it," he whispered in her ear. "Turning over was a good idea."

She did not want to say no and lie, but she also did not want to say yes and prove him right, so she settled for another hum in her throat, hoping that would satisfy him. It didn't.

The swat Sam gave her right buttock stung, hot and sweet, the foreign pleasure flowing into the space between her legs, pulsing for two heartbeats before flowering in anticipation.

"Answer my question."

It was an order, spoken in that tone that found the wanton chord in her. The one that delighted in his dominance, lived to challenge it.

She did not answer immediately, in part because it was her nature to fight authority and partly because of the lingering heat. If he spanked her again, would it grow or had it been the surprise that made it such an erotic little experience?

The oilcloth rustled as Sam changed his position. Her muscles drew taut; anticipation ran rampant. She forgot to breathe, every muscle quivering.... Would he? *Dios,* would he?

The spank did come, a little lower, a little harder, the sharp bite throwing her off balance. She rocked forward. His hand pressed in the middle of her back. "Hold still."

Burying her face in her arms, she groaned. Another spank, another surge of hot pleasure contained by the weight of his hand covering her buttock. "Answer my question, duchess."

"Yes."

"Yes what?"

"Turning over was a good idea." If she had wanted him to know how depraved she was. Which she had not really wanted him to know. Her mother had said her wild side would bring her nothing but harm. Maybe she was right. A grown woman enjoying a man spanking her could not lead to good.

This time when Sam's hand settled over her buttocks it was not a spank but a caress.

"What's put that tight note in your voice?"

She didn't look up. "I am not used to a man... handling me."

He continued his gentle washing of her back, removing the grit and grime. "Is it that you're not used to a man handling you or you're not used to how you feel when a man does?"

"Both."

"At least you are honest."

He tugged her shirt down.

"I always try to be honest."

He patted her butt. "Unless a lie will serve you better?"

"No." He rolled her back over. It did not hurt so much this time. She stared up at him as the shadows played across his face—the smile on his lips and the speculation in his eyes.

"So why are you upset that you enjoyed that little spank?"

He would notice that. "Why does it upset you to like me?"

He went still, just for a second, but it was enough to prove to her that she was right. He did feel something for her. He just didn't like it.

"What makes you think I like you?"

"What makes you think I liked your spank?"

His head canted to the side. His shadow shifted with the move, surrounding her in darkness. "Instinct."

"It is also instinct that tells me you like me."

"You're not old enough to have instincts."

She propped herself up on her elbow, shoving a stray tendril of hair out of her eyes. "How old do you think I am?"

His gaze fell to the open front of her shirt. "Too damn young for me."

So this was his problem. "Is that why you bathe me and spank me, because you think of me as your child?" She did not know how she would get around that if that was the case.

The vehemence with which he said "Hell, no" was a relief. But now he had her curious. "Then why do you?"

"I wanted to."

That was not the whole truth. "And what Sam wants to do, Sam does?"

"Pretty much."

From the left, Kell growled. The change in Sam was immediate. Gone was the lover and in his place was the killer. Placing his finger over her mouth and his hand on her shoulder, he pushed her back down.

"Don't move."

She gave a short nod to let him know she understood.

He ran his knuckles across her cheek and touched

the corner of her mouth as something soft moved through his eyes, but then it was gone and so was he.

It was the hardest thing she had ever done to lie there, knowing something, someone, was out beyond the firelight, waiting to attack. Sam had no such problem. With a nonchalance she envied, he moved the kettle off the fire. With a scream that made her jump, a man leapt out of the shadows straight for Sam's back. Except Sam was not there anymore. So fast she was left blinking, he rolled back in the direction of the attacker, his body catching the other man under the knees, flipping him down beside her. The stranger landed with a thud two feet away. He reached out.

Isabella twisted to the side, her body screaming, her mind screaming, her teeth biting into her lip so she would not actually scream and distract Sam. Scrambling to her knees, she tried to crawl away. Pain slashed through her scalp as she was yanked back. Clawing at the hand that held her braid, she twisted and fought. The man grunted again and then she was free. She scrambled away, watching as two shadows rolled across the fire. Sparks flew and smoke puffed. Kell came up beside her, a dark snarling menace. Kneeling up, she shoved at his side. "Get in there and help!"

The dog snapped at her hand and then turned back to the fight, head low, his snarl in a constant rumbling accompaniment. She wished she could snarl. All she had were backed-up screams waiting to be released.

The shadows rolled again into the darkness, away from the light. One shadow rose above the other in a faint silhouette against the deeper black of the night that stretched beyond the firelight. She recognized it immediately. Sam. She sagged in relief. It was Sam.

For one second he was silhouetted against the glow from the scattered flames, arms extended downward to the head of their assailant. Then with a quick jerk and twist, and the snap of bone against bone, the fight was over. Sam straightened.

Isabella grabbed her stomach as he came over. He'd just killed a man. With his bare hands. Kell whined and thumped his tail in greeting. Sam bent and patted his head. "Good dog."

Though she could not see Sam's eyes, Bella knew he was watching her. Watching her shake like a coward. She tipped her chin up. "He did not help at all."

A rustle beyond the firelight made her jump again. Sam didn't even turn his head. "He did just like I told him to do. So did you."

"Why wouldn't you want him to help you?"

Why wouldn't he want her to help him?

"He'd be in my way."

She rubbed her hands up and down her arms, looking past Sam to the body lying on the ground. She kept expecting him to get up.

"He's dead. He's not getting up."

She glanced at him, shocked. "How did you—"

Squatting in front of her, he cupped her cheek briefly

in his hand, a gesture of comfort, approval. Of caring. "You have a very expressive face."

He'd just snapped a man's neck. How could he be so tender now? "Oh."

"Are you hurt?"

"No. Just a little scared."

"You don't need to be."

She motioned to the body. "Was he one of Tejala's?"

"Nah. Just someone wanting company for the night."

She blinked as his meaning sank in. "He wanted me."

"I think we settled he can't have you."

Her knees buckled. He caught her against him. "I am sorry. I did not realize there would be any other threats."

For so long Tejala had been the one consuming threat; she had lost sight that there could be others. She had been blind, selfish. "When I asked you to let me stay, I did not expect…" She glanced at the body again. "I thought there would only be Tejala. You would take me to San Antonio. There would be no complications."

"You trying to back out of our deal?"

She couldn't get past the image of the man jumping Sam, wanting to kill him because of her. She twisted her fingers into the front of his shirt, trying to go beyond the realization. But she couldn't. "I did not think there would be others.…"

Sam shrugged, the heavy muscles under her cheek flexing with the movement. "There will always be others like him."

As if that were nothing. "They would not bother you if it were not for me."

Sam turned her face back to his. "Don't even think it."

"What?"

"Setting out on your own."

Her mind had not gotten that far, but it was the logical solution.

"I will not have anyone else killed because of me."

She wouldn't have him killed because of her.

"I'm not that easy to kill."

She closed her eyes as the memories howled. "I thought the same about my father, yet Tejala killed him."

"While you watched?"

She shook her head. She could feel the rope around her neck again, feel the incredible pain, the terror. "I had my eyes closed."

"Because he was strangling you."

She jumped. "How do you know?"

His lips brushed the top of her head. "You're touching your throat."

"It is a bad habit."

"It's a hell of a bad memory."

As if that justified anything. "And I do not want your death to be my next one."

He held her for a minute, not saying anything, just holding her. "Bella?"

"*Sí.*"

"I'm not letting you go."

It took all her willpower to untangle her fingers from his shirt and push to her feet. "Then you must take me to San Antonio directly."

"I can't."

She blinked. "Why?"

"I'm looking for someone."

"Who?"

"A woman."

Her stomach dropped into her toes. Of course a man like him would have a woman. She took another step back. He let her, watching her. Too closely. Too intently.

"Are you hurt?"

"No."

"Good. Go sit on the bedroll while I clean this up."

The bedroll was four feet behind her. Closer to the darkness. "Maybe he had friends."

"He didn't."

"How do you know?"

"His kind never does." Sam snapped his fingers and pointed. "Kell, guard her."

She went to the bedroll, knees weak, heart pounding. Kell paced by her side and stood in front of her as she sat. The only plus she could find was he blocked her view of what Sam was doing. Stiffening muscles made lying down awkward. She did not care. Pulling the blanket over her, she stared at Kell's leg, counting the spots from his shoulder to his knee. Eight, he had eight. And counting them was not doing anything to take her mind off the knowledge that Sam had a woman.

Was she beautiful? she wondered. Isabella shook her head at her foolishness. Of course she was beautiful. She probably had pale white skin, beautiful blue eyes and long blond hair. She probably was everything proper, everything right. She heard the sound of something being dragged. Isabella pulled the blanket over her head. Sam probably loved her very much.

All too soon the blanket was pulled back. Sam slid in beside her. As if it were the most natural thing in the world, he tucked his hand under her shoulder and pulled her into his embrace.

"What's wrong?"

The words just popped out. "Do you love her?"

"Who?"

"This woman you search for."

"No."

That was it. No other explanation, but it eased the knot in her stomach. Sam would not be so casual about a woman he loved.

"Anything else you want to know?"

"No."

He shifted, jostling her as he found a more comfortable position. Pulling his hat down over his face, he ordered, "Then go to sleep."

She closed her eyes. Sleep didn't come. The ground was hard, her shoulder began to hurt and her mind kept racing, speculating about the unknown woman, about Sam, about how he made love to a woman.

"Can't sleep?"

She jumped. "I thought you were asleep."

"You're too restless to allow nodding off."

"My shoulder hurts."

"I can fix that."

Cooler air washed over her again as the blanket was lifted and she was lifted, too, until she was draped across Sam as thoroughly as any blanket. "Better?"

In some ways yes, in others no. Lying on top of Sam was like lying on top of pure temptation. Her mouth dried to a husk, and every point where her torso touched his tingled and burned. She could feel his heartbeat against her breasts, rode the rise of his breath. And against her stomach, his cock pressed. The ache she had been trying to suppress inside broke free, spiraling outward. She dropped her head to his chest. "Yes."

His big hand came up and cradled her skull, keeping her against him. She expected him to say something. He did not, but the expectation would not go away, just built right along with the desire between them. His breaths grew shorter, choppier, his grip tighter. He felt the attraction, too. Finally he asked, "So how old are you?"

She smiled against his shirt. Ah, he was working his way around that obstacle.

"Old enough."

8

"That was not an answer to my question."

Mischief was in Bella's eyes as she looked up at him. "It was as clear as any answer you give me."

The mischief drew Sam harder than the call of battle, soothed him better than aggressive sex. Working his fingers into her hair, sliding them down until he reached the base of her braid, Sam said, "Ah, but you're not me."

He felt her smile, the hard peaks of her breast, the softness of her stomach, the inviting V of her thighs. He remembered the way she'd instinctively reacted to that little spank. His cock throbbed. He needed her to be old enough.

Weariness and desire meshed together. On top of him, Isabella shifted with the same combination. Inexperienced, she had less ability to disguise the havoc going on inside. He changed his grip from her back to her buttocks. The muscles tightened in a provocative clench. She groaned as her muscles protested, but when the pain finished its arc, her rear lifted, pressing up into his palm. She was a hot little thing.

"Sam?"

"What?"

"I can't sleep like this."

"Now, that is a shame."

"Yes, it is. And you need to do something about it."

"Are you giving me orders?"

In the faint light from the dying embers of the fire, he could see the nervous lick of her lips, before she nodded. "Yes."

He tugged her up until her face was over his and her forearms were braced on his shoulders. The thick rope of her braid fell between them, linking them. "That's a dangerous thing."

"So is leaving me like this."

He liked that she was open with him. "And how exactly is this?"

"Achy and feeling like I have missed something."

"Are you by chance seducing me?"

"Am I succeeding?"

He slid her onto her side, rolling over her as her nails clung to his shoulder in protest at being dislodged. Nudging her hips with his, he let her feel the readiness of his cock. "You're pretty close."

"What do I need to do to succeed?"

"Convince me you know what you're doing."

Her fingers touched his cheek with the delicacy of a butterfly. "For this night I just wished to feel like the woman that I want to be. I wish for you to plant the sensation of how a good man can make a woman feel so deeply inside me that, no matter what happens in the future, I will never forget this time."

It was so very Bella. A practical solution for a woman who lived with the knowledge that she was hunted, that she would eventually be found, and when she was, she would be raped and possibly killed.

"You want a lot."

Her hands linked behind his neck. "Not so much for you, I think. You are the infamous Sam MacGregor."

The woman was nothing if not single-minded. And incredibly appealing with that witchy smile that dared him to take her in hand.

"You're asking for more than you know."

"But you will give it to me."

It wasn't a question. "Maybe."

Her fingertip pressed deliberately in the middle of his chin. "I think there is no maybe. I think I will be most irresistible to you."

Hell, she was probably right. He smoothed the hair back off her temple, exposing the soft blue tracery of veins beneath her silky skin and the too-fast beat of her pulse. Fear or excitement? With Bella it was hard to tell. Touching his thumb to the pulse he asked, "Anyone ever tell you you talk too much?"

"No."

It was so obviously a lie said deliberately to amuse him that he laughed as he lowered his head to hers, hearing that catch in her breath she couldn't disguise, smiling because she was as aware of him as he was of her. And also because he had the advantage. He knew how to use her desire against her. "Good."

"Why—"

It was incredibly easy to silence the rest of the question. All he had to do was drop his head that quarter of an inch that brought his mouth to hers. All he had to do was catch her gasp in his mouth, take it as his, and she was his. Body and soul, even if her mind didn't agree. She could fight him all she wanted, but she was right on one point. Attraction this strong didn't happen every day.

Grabbing her hands, he pinned them above her head, moving fully over her, settling his thigh over hers, his chest to hers, hating the barrier of clothing between them. Hating the barrier of her innocence. Hating himself because he was going to take it from her. Because he couldn't help himself.

Isabella arched up and whimpered. Beneath his palms her wrists worked. Too much. He was putting too much weight on her hands. Sam eased back on his kiss, lust surging as she lifted her head, prolonging the contact.

He brushed his mouth over the side of her neck. "I'm not going anywhere, duchess."

She whimpered and turned her head, her mouth blindly seeking for his. Anchoring both her hands in his, taking most of his weight on his forearm, he did, delving into the sweetness of her passion, the openness of her desire. She might be innocent, but she burned hotter, brighter than any woman he'd ever kissed. And he needed more.

So did she, if her response was anything to judge by. She drove her hips up into his, the angle of the rhythm reflecting her inexperience, but the eagerness... Damn, the eagerness.

Taking care not to rub against her chafed thighs, he directed her movement. "Like this."

It only took a slight tilt in her hips to deliver the pressure to where she needed it.

Her *"Dios"* exploded past his ear.

"Feel good?"

She nodded, those fine white teeth sinking into her lip.

"How good?"

"I cannot describe it."

"Try."

"How does it feel to you?" she shot back, exasperation pitching her question high.

He didn't have to think about it. "Like sweetest fire beckoning."

"Yes," she gasped, her head arching back as he pressed into her softness. "It burns."

"I like that." He unbuttoned the fly of his pants. "You burning for me."

He worked his cock free. It fell thick and heavy to the thin wool of her skirt. The scratchy material teased the sensitive length. His hips bucked involuntarily. Her skirt rode up as he notched the blunt head between her legs, adjusting it with his hand until she gasped and arched again.

"Damn, when I get you naked, we're going to have fun."

"I want fun now."

She had no patience. He wished he could find it as a fault but he was as eager as she was.

He rolled to the side pulling her against him.

Her arms wrapped around his neck. "I do not have time to wait for you to fight with your conscience, Sam."

Because she thought Tejala or another would find her and take her choice away. Sam didn't bother to tell her again that would never happen. That he wouldn't let it happen. She wouldn't believe him. "I know."

Her lashes fluttered against his neck. "So you will hurry?"

He stroked her hair, catching her braid in his fist,

sliding his hand down to the bottom and working the tie free while his heart twisted in his chest. The tie came undone. He unraveled the braid one loop at a time, letting the thick silky strands of her hair glide across his fingers.

"Relations…" he used the word to spare her sensibilities "…are not supposed to be rushed."

Wrinkling her nose at him, she said, "You can stop calling it that now."

"I think it's cute."

"You think it is funny."

She was a quick little thing. He smiled, easing her back down, gathering up her skirt. "That, too."

With a flick of his wrist, he tossed her skirt up over her hips. She squeaked, but held still. The sight that greeted his gaze as her skirt cleared her thighs made him frown. Very gently he pressed on her left knee. She instinctively moved her leg away from the intimate touch. The delicate flesh on the inside of her thighs was raw and raised with blood spots. "Hell."

If her thighs were raw her pussy had to be bruised. He cupped his palm over the warm pad, holding it to her. He should have foreseen her inexperience. Seen her difficulty riding earlier. "I'm sorry."

She frowned. "For what?"

"For not seeing you were having so much trouble."

"I was hiding it from you."

There was no way she could have hidden it from him if he hadn't been doing his best to keep from staring at her like a green boy. "Uh-huh. Well, if you ever hide your hurting from me again, I'll paddle your sexy little rear."

Isabella smiled that bad-angel smile. "Do you promise this?"

He tucked his finger between the slit in her pantaloons, working between the silken folds of her pussy, testing, exploring. "Absolutely."

Her legs spread farther. "Good." In a slow languid movement, she put her hands back over her head.

"So accommodating."

Her hips lifted to the rhythm he set. "I want to please you."

The confession went straight to his cock.

"That's not a hard thing to do."

She shifted under his touch, gasping when she created a deeper pressure. "I think it's a very hard thing to do, so much so that I think I'm going to have to 'study up' on it."

She was throwing his own words back at him as she taunted the lust forward with a complete disregard for the consequences, seeking the pleasure with reckless enthusiasm that summoned an equal enthusiasm in him. Sliding down between her thighs, knowing he should put the salve on her injuries again, knowing it was going to wait, he asked, "You do, huh? Well, maybe you should see what you're getting into first."

She groaned as he lifted her legs over his shoulders. He gritted his teeth. He was a goddamn animal. She couldn't move without pain and he was all over her, breathing in the scent of aroused woman like it was ambrosia, anticipating how good the juices coating her folds were going to taste on his tongue, coaxing her into accepting the pain so he could have the pleasure.

Animal or not, he wasn't stopping. Couldn't stop. Two more inches and he had the first taste of her on his tongue. Tangy sweet, like a summer storm, rolling through his system. Perfect. She made that little squeaking noise again. He recognized that sound. Sweet, generous surrender.

A second later there was a soft thud as her head fell back.

"You are sure this is right to do between men and women?"

"Very sure."

"But it is not proper?"

"Not a bit."

"Then proceed!"

He did just that, laughter rippling through him as he lapped at the spill of her pleasure, listening to her soft cries, her gasps, the occasional moan of dismay which directed him back to where she needed his touch most. Satisfaction infused passion as he let her pleasure wash over him, fill him deeply with her uninhibited joy.

He dipped his finger into the well again, coating himself with the promise of pleasure. His cock throbbed. He breathed deeply, inhaling her scent. Womanly spice and musk. A very potent combination. One he wasn't going to be able to resist much longer. He'd never been long on honor or self-sacrifice.

"Just relax and enjoy."

He nudged his finger aside with his tongue, penetrating her the only way that was safe, the only way he would allow himself. He didn't rape women and taking one knocked out of her good judgment by fear was the equivalent of it in his book. But he wasn't above stealing a taste. He was risking getting his ass shot off. He deserved at least a taste. A deep, lingering, thorough taste of what he'd be giving up.

"Spread your legs further," he growled. She did, immediately, naturally, parting her thighs until he could feel the muscles tremble, all the while watching him with an expectancy that spoke of a deeper need. One that he was more than ready to feed.

"Come for me, Bella."

"I can't."

"You can." He pushed her thighs a little wider, keeping the tension stretched tight as he lapped delicately at her clit, easing her back into the storm before picking up the pace and pressure, driving her into the passion, holding her legs apart when she would have closed them, keeping her still for the lash of his tongue, the softness of his kiss, the graze of his teeth, keeping her put as the climax rocked her. His name broke from her lips, a breathless mix of fear and joy.

"It's all right, Bella. Let it happen. Come for me."

Her fingers fisted in his hair as she jackknifed up into the press of his mouth, holding him to her as the next spasm took her. He backed off the pressure as the contractions lightened, laving her gently, easing her through her shock to the satisfaction on the other side. Her hands opened on his skull as her breath shuddered out on a long sigh.

Bracing himself on his elbows, Sam looked up only to find Bella watching him in a combination of wonder and fascination.

"All right?"

She nodded, leaning forward, touching her forehead to his. Her hair fell about them in a silken curtain, creating the illusion of just them, just now.

"You were right. I do not think that was at all proper."

"But it was fun?"

"Oh yes." She nodded, sending her hair swishing about his shoulders and back. "Very fun."

He eased his shoulders out from under her thighs, steadying her with a hand on her arm when she swayed. "Good, because we're not done."

"I think I am."

"You have no idea how much pleasure I can give you." He released her arm, watching to make sure she had her balance. Her fingertips riffled through the hair at the nape of his neck, soothing and stimulating at the same time.

"There is more?"

"A lot more. Lean back."

Isabella didn't hesitate. She didn't imagine anyone hesitated when Sam used that deep sexy tone of voice. She caught herself on her hands. The pull in her shoulder muscles blended with the shiver of arousal as she arched her back, thrusting her breasts up, shaking her hair out of her eyes. "Like this?"

"Oh, yeah." Each deep syllable stroked her desire in a rough caress. "Exactly like that."

Sam came up on his knees, palming her breasts, catching her nipple between his thumbs and the edge of his hands, grazing the sensitive tips with a touch so light she had to strain to feel it. Then he did it again, a little harder, the echoing pulse lodging deep in her core, setting off tiny explosions of delight that detonated outward.

A quick glance from beneath her lashes showed his amusement gone, the sharp planes of his face once again etched in harsh lines as his entire focus centered on her chest. His hair skimmed the tops of her breasts in a thick cascade as he bent, joining the stroke of his hands down the sides of her breasts. His beard roughed her delicate skin before his teeth tested her resiliency. Goose bumps sprang up in the wake of the caress, flaring outward on a shiver as he blew across the damp flesh.

Years of pent-up longing welled. She licked her lips, forcing back the response she wasn't sure she should reveal. She thought she had a prayer until he started nibbling. Oh, why hadn't she been born flat-chested? With curves like hers, a man had a lot of room to play. Too much for her to withstand. Especially when it was Sam. He'd learned how sensitive her breasts were and just how she liked to be touched. She gritted her teeth and clenched her thighs against his hips, reaching for the strength to endure as her pussy pulsed and flowered with every brush of his teeth, every lap of his tongue.

By the time Sam reached her aureole, she was panting, her control in shreds. She should pull away, but she could not. Not yet. Not when he was nipping a circle around the puckered flesh, shooting sparks of wicked delight outward in a brilliant shower. He sucked her aching nipple into the blistering heat of his mouth, gathering those sparks in a concentrated bundle beneath the fragile tip, torturing her with the slow drag of his tongue across the heated embers. Her nails scraped against the oilcloth, the sound blending into a hiss of the dying fire as she squirmed under the lash of his tongue, the rough surface fanning the flames of need to flash point.

Dios mío, she could not stand this. She grabbed his head with one hand, wrapping her fingers in the cool strands of his thick hair, falling back into the palm of his hand, letting him support her as the fire raged, burning unbearably, the rasp of his tongue both a balm and a curse as it first soothed then tortured. Broken gasps of "please" poured from her soul, filling the space between them.

"Tell me what you want."

The order, shaped around her nipple, was just more fuel to the flames. Isabella tugged, but he did not come closer, did not give her what she needed. She looked down. Sam's head blocked most of her view, but she could see the fingers of his free hand gripping her breast, his skin so much darker than hers, his big hand encompassing only half the mound, leaving the rest plumped for his pleasure. She took a hard breath as he kissed her nipple, a gentle, totally frustrating caress. She needed more, damn it, and he had to know it.

She dug her nails into his scalp. His response to the silent demand was a pulse of laughter and a murmur of "tease." The satisfaction in that one word made her want to scream. Sam was deliberately driving her crazy. And he would not stop until she gave him what he wanted. The surrender he asked for.

"Your mouth," she gasped. "I want your mouth."

He lapped at her delicately, tantalizing her unbearably with what could be. "Where?"

"On my breasts." Oh God, her breasts.

Another of those delicate laps. "How?"

She yanked at his hair, for once hating his strength as his muscles easily vanquished hers, leaving her with no other option but to concede. With one last pull borne of total frustration, she collapsed against him, desperate sobs stealing her breath as her full breasts crushed against his mouth, for one second delivering the sensation she craved before he pulled back, once again taking control.

"Hard." She shuddered as he nipped her breast gently, the small ensuing specter of feeling just another tease. She closed her eyes and rubbed her forehead against his skull, defeat conflicting with need. "Oh please, do it hard."

As if her plea pierced his armor where her demands could not, his big body shuddered against her. His head tilted back, the stretching of her nipple a prelude to bliss as it pulled taut. She couldn't help her moan any more than she could help her response to the sting. She wanted him. Her nipple stretched between them thinner and thinner, an insubstantial binding that could not continue, but had to. It simply had to.

But it didn't, it never did. With a soft pop of despair, her nipple slipped free. Bella didn't move, didn't do anything, just let Sam's hair slide against her skin in a silken rasp until his forehead rested on hers, waiting for what he'd do next. He didn't do anything, just held them both there, connected yet not as desire palpitated between them in a tangible link. She opened her eyes. He was looking at her, his eyes burning with blue fire. His expression remained harsh, demanding, but there was something fascinatingly tender in the smile that creased the corners of his lips. She stared at it, wanting to understand. His left hand spread under her spine, each fingertip balancing her weight, pressing up.

His eyebrow arched up. "Enough?"

She felt completely exposed as she whispered, "I need more."

So much more than just this physical moment.

The tenderness in his smile spread over into his touch. "All you have to do is tell me what you need, duchess, and I'll give it to you. You have to know that."

Not this. He might not give her this. "You should not make such rash promises."

"Why not? I'm feeling very generous right now."

"Because I could take advantage," she managed to gasp as he found the slick nub of her clitoris with the tip of his finger. *Madre!* He was a warlock with the darkest of magic in his hands.

He was definitely taking advantage, Sam decided, watching Bella's face as the pleasure speared deep, feeling an echoing stab of pleasure that had nothing to do with desire snaking down his spine. Watching Bella burn could become his favorite form of recreation. There was nothing more erotic. Nothing more enjoyable. Nothing more enticing. Sweet silky cream slicked his hand as he rubbed delicately, and she arched into his hand. When she shuddered and collapsed, he followed her down, notching his cock along her pussy until the head tucked into the hot crease of her ass. She gasped and froze, but then her hips lifted, encouraging him deeper as her breath came in seductive little whimpers. "What is it you want from me, Sam?"

He nipped the tendon running up the side of her neck, a chuckle spreading as she whimpered again and subtly arched her neck, giving him better access. He obliged, running his lips over the feminine line until he reached her hairline behind her ear. Goose bumps sprang in the wake of his caress. He opened his mouth, touching a pale freckle with his tongue before sliding down along the betraying roughness, stopping when he reached the sensitive curl of her ear, letting the moist heat of his breath bring more of that roughness to her ultrasmooth skin before whispering in her ear, "Whatever you can afford to give me."

It was two heartbeats before she summoned the breath to answer.

"Then I must have rules."

Everything in him said she'd take him and take him on his terms. "No."

She flattened her palm against his chest. A butterfly challenging a hawk. It made him smile almost more than the properness of her. "I insist."

He tugged her hips up, pressed his cock deeper into the hot cradle of her ass, his irritation soothed by the completeness of her response. She was his at a touch. "Doesn't appear to me you're in a position to insist on anything."

Her fingers curled in a silent plea. "Still, you will listen."

She was too damn fond of giving orders. Brushing the hair away from her cheek, needing to see her expression, he grimaced as her buttocks squeezed him in tense rhythmic pulses that shredded his control. "You're a bossy little thing."

"I know my worth."

"But you seriously overrate mine."

"Maybe."

He stroked her little clitoris harder, kissing her cheek

as she cried out and her body stiffened. She was so close to coming. And in a minute, he'd let her. "Maybe?"

"It depends on how often you intend to satisfy me."

"As often as you can take, duchess."

A shiver shook her from head to toe. "I have but one rule. You cannot ask from me what you will not give."

He traced the whorls of her ear with his tongue and savored her instant response.

"A fair exchange, yes?"

"*Sí.*"

"What if I can't give what you need?"

She turned her head. Her eyes were velvet soft in the dim light. "Then you do not ask it of me."

She was putting the responsibility for keeping it fair on him. Damn, she was clever. Rubbing his lips against the pulse throbbing in her temple, he asked, "Starting tonight?"

"If you are sure."

He wasn't sure of anything except she knocked him six ways to Sunday for reasons he couldn't define, and that he couldn't walk away from her. Not yet.

"Are you sure you want to give me your innocence?" He caught her clit between his thumb and forefinger and rolled it gently.

Her breaths came in staccato pants as he increased the speed and pressure. "Yes."

"Good." He kissed her cheek, the corner of her eyes

and the tips of her deep brown lashes before squeezing the flange of sensitive flesh and milking it with a firm pull. "Then, come for me."

She did, with a riveting cry of his name, her head snapping forward into his shoulder and then back as she shuddered under the lash of fulfillment. The flush on her cheeks deepened. Her face twisted with the stark expression of pleasure so intense as to be pain before gradually fading to the sultry expression of a woman satisfied.

"Sweet. So sweet, duchess." As sweet as he'd imagined. Sam cupped her still-convulsing pussy, cradling it protectively even as he ripped her pantaloons off and lined up his cock with the pulsing entrance to her body. She bucked and cried out. He groaned and pressed. Tight. Damn, she was tight. The realization snapped him back. Shit. He couldn't do this. Not and live with himself. Flipping her over, his own drive to climax riding him hard, Sam laid himself along her back, lubricating his cock in her cream before tucking it back into the seductive seam of her ass. A pulse of his hips and she was pushing back, arching her spine into his chest, her head tipping back, presenting her mouth for his kiss, her body to his desire.

"Ah, damn."

Silky cream pooled in his palm and flowed over his fingers, bathing them in the rich scent of her arousal, tempting him toward his own release. He pushed his cock along the crack of her ass. It slid smoothly between the soft mounds. He centered his attention on the burning surge of lust, the satisfaction in her face and the residual pulses of her orgasm, riding her pleasure to his own, fucking that slick crease the way he wanted to fuck her pussy. Hard, fast and deep, imagining the spasmodic grip of her buttocks was the hard clench of her inner muscles, groaning as his cock caught on the edge of her anus, her gasp and jerk at the ensuing tug putting him over the top.

With a harsh groan his seed erupted from his balls, tearing through his cock to spill in a hot silky jet onto her back. He pushed back on his arms, watching as the next spurt landed higher than the first, blending into the creamy expanse of her skin, marking her as his over and over again until she had all he could give.

His heart thundering in his chest, his breath sawing in and out of his lungs, Sam shifted his weight to the side, retaining his hold on her pussy while covering his seed with his hand and massaging the silky fluid into her skin, like an invisible tattoo.

His. She was his.

The blanket rustled and tugged as she turned her face to his, pushing the hair out of her face, letting him see her full expression. The soft pout of her lips, the fan of red across her cheeks and the wariness in her eyes.

"You did not take me."

He smiled and kissed the corner of her mouth. With a nudge of his fingers he urged her onto her back. She followed his lead easily, only losing her balance in the last instant. He tumbled with her, keeping her head from hitting the ground with the cushion of his palms. "Don't read too much into that."

Even with the doubt he was throwing at her, she didn't flinch, just studied his expression with those soft eyes, touched his throat with those soft hands and whispered. "Someday you will tell me why you hide from me."

"Maybe."

"Until then I will wait."

She would wait. He wanted to shake her. He wanted to hug her. He wanted to run.

He tapped his thumbs to her full lips in a parody of a kiss, guilt eating at him, desire driving him. "You should have a young man with stars in his eyes courting you. Someone to dream with."

She narrowed her eyes. "Do I get to pick a woman for you?"

"No."

"Then you are stuck with my choice."

Him.

Hell. She was muleheaded. And damn if he wasn't glad of it. Feathering his fingers over her cheeks, he pulled her mouth to his. Her lips didn't part immediately. He kissed the right corner and then the left, smiling at her stubbornness. She had a ways to go before she could hope to outmaneuver him. He shifted his left hand so his thumb cushioned her clitoris. One rub, two and her lips parted in a shuddering moan. He took full advantage of the moment, tickling the inside edges with his tongue until she squirmed before going deeper, searching for and finding the response he knew was his. Finding it, taking her gasp and moan as his own before withdrawing just far enough to drawl, "I hope the hell you know what you're doing."

Her arms came around his neck. "I always do."

9

Bella did know what she was doing, but Sam was messing up her plans with his misplaced sense of honor that insisted he protect her from herself. No matter how much she had tried to tempt him the last two days during which they'd "rested up," he remained resolute. She could have used a kidnapper with less moral fortitude.

She glanced across the small clearing where Sam sat sewing on his "long johns." She had offered to handle the task for him, but he had turned her down the way he turned down every other offer she made. It was almost as if he was afraid if she took over any of the chores, she'd start seeing him as something other than temporary.

She sighed and shifted to a more comfortable position against the fallen tree that was serving as her backrest. Being a notorious virgin was not as exciting as it sounded. The notorious part she did not mind so much, but the virgin…that was the part she resented. For the fifth time since yesterday morning she brought up the subject.

"What you are doing makes no sense."

"So you told me before." Sam pulled the thread through the worn red material.

That did not bode well for today's discussion.

"You should take me like you want to. Everyone assumes you already have."

"It doesn't matter to me what others think."

"It should matter to you what *I* think."

"I always take into consideration what you think."

She kicked a rock in front of her. "If this happened, I would still not be a virgin."

He bit down on the thread, looking at her from under his lashes. "You think it's inevitable that Tejala will get you."

"He will."

"And because you believe that," he went on as if she hadn't interrupted, "you're throwing away your future on me."

"They are going to blame me anyway. In the eyes of those that determine my future, I am already soiled."

"Your husband, when you find him, will know the truth."

She wished there was another rock close enough to kick. She wished she was close enough to kick him. "What he knows won't be important. All that will matter in his eyes is what others say."

"You're smart enough to pick a better husband."

"Women do not pick husbands in my culture."

"But they pick their lovers?"

He did not have to mock. She pulled the too-large hat down over her eyes in the gesture she'd seen him do when he wanted to convey disdain. "If they are lucky enough to have the opportunity. Yes."

"And you consider me your opportunity?"

"Yes. And if you did not have such stubbornness, I would not be the subject of gossip with no reward."

"What makes you think you're the subject of gossip?"

"Tejala has announced all over the territory that he wants me back. People will always wonder why I ran, where I am, and what he will do to me when he gets me back. I think I am the subject of much gossip."

"Well, at least you're giving folk something to do."

He shook out the long johns and came over. "These should protect your legs better."

She took the garment from his hand. The material was clean and soft from frequent washing. He'd sewn a drawstring at the waist. She stood up and held the pants to her waist. They were almost the perfect length. Just a touch too long. She glanced up. A long way up. She forgot how tall Sam was. "You have a good eye."

"I spent the last two days studying up on the subject."

She supposed he had. For all he tried to keep distance between them, he spent an awful lot of time making sure she was comfortable. It could be he was that way with everyone, but she didn't think so. A man did not insist on sewing clothes for someone that he was eager to be rid of.

He handed her another bundle of material. "This might come in handy too."

She looked at the band with the two pieces of material attached. He waved toward her chest.

"It should keep the ladies from hurting."

The ladies. Her lips twitched. "Thank you for making these for me."

"Don't go reading anything into it. If those legs of yours get worse, it'll slow us down."

She sighed. He always made a point to say something mean when he thought she was looking on him too favorably.

"We are leaving today?"

"If you're feeling up to it."

It was questions like that that ruined his cold killer image. She thought they were ready to go yesterday, but he'd taken one look at her thighs and declared they needed one more day. "I am not sure."

He glanced at her suspiciously. "You were ready enough to go yesterday."

She shrugged and ran her hands down her thighs, being careful to delineate the width of her hips as she did. He very much liked her hips. "I was, but after last night's loving I am feeling a little—" she shrugged "—raw."

She wasn't actually. Sam had been very considerate as he had pleasured her. He was very sensitive to the fact that she suffered anything and he saw himself as some sort of debaucher of innocence. Even when she kept throwing herself and her innocence at his head.

"Damn it. I knew I should have shaved."

She leaned back against the rock wall, and started pulling her skirt up. One inch at a time. "Perhaps you should check and see how much damage was done."

He was halfway bending down and she had her skirt almost up to her hips, when he paused. Darn it. She thought she had him.

As quick as lightning he spun her around to face the rock. The warm stone pressed against her breasts. Hard to her soft. He pinned her arms behind her back. His cock pressed into her buttocks. More hard. Her pussy moistened. More soft.

His lips grazed her cheek. Both hard and soft at once. "Playing with fire, duchess?"

She pressed back into his groin. "I am doing my best."

The swat on her rear caught her by surprise. "You're going to get burned."

"Why?"

"Because that's what happens to little innocents trying to run before they can walk."

"What makes you so sure I am not ready?"

"What makes you so sure I'm the one?"

She bit the hand trying to push her away from him. His gloves kept her teeth from doing any damage. "Instinct."

She twisted her head and found his wrist. No leather blunted her teeth. He didn't flinch or pull away, which just annoyed her more. She was so tired of no one paying attention to her. She bit harder. He caught her chin, freeing her teeth, turning her face to his.

She couldn't look away from his eyes. So cold. So hot. So bone-meltingly sexy. "I bite back."

The low drawl sent a shiver down her spine. Heat suffused her body. Her breasts swelled and ached. She reached for the buttons on the shirt, imagining how his teeth would feel there. "Is this where I must scream with virginal fear?"

His eyes searched hers. "Yes."

"I am sorry. There are no screams in me."

"Why?"

"I want your mouth. Any way you want to give it to me."

He shook his head, his hat brim shadowing his expression. He turned her around. She placed her arms above her head the way he'd taught her, the way he liked, offering him with one gesture whatever he wanted from her.

The weight of his torso pressed against her chest. Her nipples ached with a sharp pain as they were pressed back into the fullness of her breasts.

"I told you I won't take you."

"And I told you I would change your mind."

"It's not going to happen."

"Sam?"

"What?"

"If you would just make love to me I would stop hurting."

"I told you, I don't make love."

"It is the only word I know. You won't teach me the others."

"Uh-huh."

His lips moved to the corner of her mouth. She tipped her head back giving him better access. "Teach me the words and I will use them."

"You'd be irresistible if you used the words."

His honesty in the face of his resistance was confusing. "So do not resist me."

"I have to."

"Why?"

"Because there's still part of me wanting to be able to look in the mirror when I shave."

She cupped his cheek in her hand. "I like your beard."

"It's too rough for your skin."

She rasped her nail down his jawline. He only said that because he thought *he* was too rough for her. "Your beard excites me." She hated the blush heating her cheeks. The blush that made her look naive when she was trying for worldly.

A sound that closely resembled a growl rumbled from his throat. "How the hell did you stay a virgin this long?"

That answer was easy. "I was not given temptation."

His eyes were almost black. "Bella?"

"What?"

His head came down, blocking the morning sun. Just before his lips met hers, he growled, "Shut up."

The man had the control of a saint and if she ever got back to her hometown, Isabella was going to have the priest look into nominating him for sainthood.

Right now, she just needed a way to get around it. Sighing loudly, Isabella shifted in the saddle. Sam didn't turn, just rode ahead, the smoke from his cigarette drifting back to tease her with the scent of the tobacco he used. A sweet, spicy scent she associated only with him.

The tingle began between her thighs. Not wholly unwelcome. He was a fine-looking man with a good heart. And a penchant for testing himself. Something she intended to take full advantage of. No man was made of steel and eventually he would either underestimate her or lose his control.

"Where are we going?"

"The next town over."

"Is that not dangerous?"

"For whom?"

He was in a snit. "For me. Someone will tell Tejala that I am here."

"By the time the news gets back to him, we'll be long gone."

"But he will track us." She did not want to be tracked. She hated the feeling of having someone on her trail, always looking over her shoulder. Never knowing how close they were, never knowing when they were going to strike, just living with the terror that it was coming.

"I have no doubt he'll try."

She tightened her grip on the reins. "He will succeed. You do not know him."

Leather creaked as he looked over his shoulder. "I've

never met the man personally, but I've met a hundred just like him."

She shook her head. There had never been another like Tejala. He was intelligent, cunning and obsessive about some things. One of them being her. "I cannot go into town."

"I'm sure not leaving you out here, a sitting duck for anybody that comes along."

"Someone will tell. Tejala will come and he will kill them if they do not tell them what he needs to know—what he thinks they should know. Just like he killed the men at the wagon train." Just like he had killed others before. Like he had killed her father.

Sam slowed his horse, waiting for her to catch up. "We don't have any choice."

"Why?"

"I'm looking for someone. I got a lead she might be in this town."

She. The pronoun hit her like a punch in the gut. Of course, the woman he searched for. She was probably beautiful. Experienced. A woman he did not feel he had to protect.

"I suppose she is very experienced?"

"That's what I'm told."

"Experience is not everything."

"I'm sure she'd agree with you. So maybe you could send a prayer up to your God that I find her here."

"What does she have that I do not that makes you so determined to get her?"

"A sister that wants her home."

He was watching her carefully. Bella knew better than to reveal that her mother wanted her home too. If only to give her to Tejala. As long as Sam thought her family did not want her, she had a chance of escaping Tejala.

"Did she run away?"

"She was stolen." So not a lover, but a job. She felt better.

In the distance she could make out rooftops. They were almost to town. "How old is she?"

"Twenty."

An adult woman stolen would only have one destination. "Have you been searching for long?"

"About three months." She wished he would look at her.

"Are you in love with her?" she asked again.

That did get him to look at her. "No, but I'm very close to her sister."

She couldn't hold back. "How close?"

"Desi's married to my best friend."

There was a warmth in his voice when he said Desi's name that made her uncomfortable. He would not be the first man to be in love with his best friend's wife. If he was, it would explain a lot.

"How long has she been missing?"

"Over a year."

A year was a long time. The things that could happen to a woman in a year could be life-altering. "And no one has seen her?"

Sam tipped his hat down the way he did when he was angry. "No."

His horse pulled ahead of hers. Obviously, he did not want her to see his expression when he thought of this woman. She kicked her heels against Sweet Pea's side and reined him over until she could touch Sam's thigh. His muscles jumped under her fingers in a silent rejection.

She didn't take her hand away. It hurt her to see him in pain. "You think she is going to be in the next town?"

"I've got word there's a blond whore working in the cantina." It was a calm statement of facts, but it still made her wince.

Eyeing the tension in his shoulders, she sighed. "You do not think she is there willingly."

"I never knew a woman who was."

That made her blink. Most men she had met liked to think women worked in the saloon because they wanted to, not because there was no other choice. "Have you thought that maybe she does not want to be found?"

"The subject has been brought up."

"What will you do if that's the case?"

"Bring her back to her sister anyway."

"That may be more than you can do."

There was no way Bella could go back to her life, if many men had used her. Sam's hand caught hers before she could take it from his thigh.

His fingers wrapped around hers. "If you were in her position, what would you do?"

"I would find a place of forgiveness and I would stay there."

"Forgiveness for what?"

She shrugged. The "what" was pretty obvious. "For breaking the rules."

"Even if you broke them to avoid being raped?"

She jerked her hand free. "Yes."

Assumption counted sometimes more than reality. To avoid Tejala she had broken her family's rules, the church's rules, and society's rules. There was a price to be paid. "And if I'm going to be condemned regardless—" she met his gaze squarely "—then I wish to experience the pleasure."

The corner of his mouth quirked in a smile. "You never stray far from that subject, do you?"

"It is dear to my heart."

"I told you you're safe."

And she'd told him that she wouldn't let him sacrifice himself for her. "Thank you."

She glanced toward the town, the rooftops getting larger with every clop of the horses' hooves. She licked her lips, thinking of the woman he sought. "She may not want to come back with you. She may be more comfortable in her position now than the one being rescued would put her in."

He glanced sharply at her. "What makes you think so?"

"It is another subject on which I have thought."

He pulled his horse up short and then leaned over and caught Sweet Pea's reins.

"When—" she began.

"If."

She ignored the correction. "*When* Tejala catches me, my world will change. About this I do not fool myself."

"What the hell does that mean?"

"When he does what he feels he must, I will no longer be seen by myself or those around me the way I am now. I will be dirty, soiled. It will change everything."

Sam swore, low and vicious. His hand cupped her chin, jerking her face up, nearly unseating her. "Explain."

"I will not live with his touch on my skin."

"Fuck."

She blinked. Even in her sheltered upbringing she knew the filth of that word. "You will not use such language around me."

"Then you'd better not be spouting such nonsense around me."

Sam might think it was nonsense but he was not the one who would have to live through the rape, live with the sense of violation, bear the lingering imprint of the man's touch. She had experienced enough of Tejala's touch to know it was not something she could endure. Breeze tossed his head and pranced away, breaking Sam's hold. She held his gaze as the distance grew between them. "I will not give him that victory."

"The hell you won't."

Breeze spun around in response to his master's command, easily countering her pull on her mount's reins. In a blink, she was yanked off her horse's back to land painfully across Sam's lap. His arm was a steel band around her waist, the fingers on her chin a vise, but his eyes, it was his eyes that put the fear of God into her. They blazed anger down at her from the shadows of his hat, the thunderous blue-gray of a violent storm. And that fury was focused on her.

She shivered, but it didn't change her resolve.

"I will not."

"You goddamned well will."

"You cannot make me."

"The hell I can't."

She threw the truth out. "You won't always be around."

Sam looked into Isabella's small face, large brown eyes, soft creamy caramel-colored, finely grained skin and wanted to shake her. He'd never leave her while Tejala was a threat. The thought of another man touching her burned his gut. The thought of Tejala raping her was obscene. The thought of her taking her own life over it was even more obscene. "I'll always be there when you need me."

"No, you will not. You will be far away arresting criminals, making love with other women, living your life and I will be wherever you leave me, living mine."

The woman wielded the truth with the sharp edge of a razor. "But you will be living."

"I've seen the women Tejala uses. I will not want to live when he is done with me."

Sam didn't let her duck away. "But you will live. For me."

She shook her head. "So I can see the disgust in your eyes too? I do not think so."

"There won't be any disgust in my eyes."

"But maybe there will be pity? This I will not live to see either."

"Damn it, Isabella. If you ever need me, I'll come."

The anger left her expression and she palmed his cheek, her hand a soft counterpoint against his morning beard. "I know."

He didn't like the acceptance in her voice. It said more than anything else that she didn't believe him. Shit. He had to tell her the truth.

"After I return you to your home, I'm going after Tejala."

She stiffened. "I do not want this from you."

"I don't recall asking your permission."

"He is very dangerous."

She was afraid for him. "So am I."

"He is also crazy."

"Then it will be up to me to put the bastard out of his misery." He stroked his thumb over her lips.

He loved her mouth, always rosy, always full, always tempting, and when it touched his skin, it always burned like fire. He couldn't stand the thought of that fire being extinguished.

"But you, Bella, you're not crazy. You're smart, courageous and a hell of a lot more than anything that could ever be forced on you."

"You do not underst—"

He didn't let her finish. "I'm not saying rape wouldn't be a hard thing to get past, but you'd try and I'd be waiting on the other side."

"You might be married by then."

"I won't be." She was the only one who'd ever tempted him. "And even if I were, I'd still come."

"Why?"

"Because that's what friends do for each other."

The flicker of pain in her eyes hit him straight on his conscience. He should never have touched her. As young as she was, she couldn't separate passion from love.

"I cannot make you this promise, Sam."

She would. Before he left her, she would. "You're so much more than any man's touch, duchess."

"Only to you, but you cannot see that, can you?"

"There's a bigger world than you know just waiting for you, Bella."

"I do not care about that."

"Only because you don't know what you're missing."

She sighed and wiggled up, her elbows gouging into his ribs as the oversized hat slipped off the back of her head, flopping against his arm.

"So you keep telling me."

10

The town was far from bustling. Buildings stood in disrepair. Few pedestrians walked the streets. About the only life came from the adobe structure midway down the street, in front of which two hitching posts were driven into the ground. Tied to those two posts were five horses. Above the arched doorway was a wooden sign with the word *cantina* painted in red across the rough surface. That would be the place to start asking questions. But first he had to find some way to keep Isabella busy and out of trouble. From beside him came a harsh sound. He glanced over. The hat had fallen over Isabella's face again which probably meant that sound was a curse she thought too unladylike to say out loud. He smiled. She had some strange notions. Apparently propositioning him right and left was fine, but swearing would ruin her forever.

Bella looked up. The sun kissed her face with bright light. Not a single line blurred the smooth surface. And while there was a world of worry in her eyes, life had yet to touch her face. In contrast he could feel every line life had carved into his. He might be thirty-one, but some days he felt sixty. Today was one of them. Not only because of Bella, but because of what he might find at the cantina. Desi wanted her sister back very badly. So much so she couldn't conceive of what might be left of the woman she remembered. But he knew. And he didn't think he could be the one to hurt both of them by forcing a reunion if Ari didn't want to return.

"It is not much of a town," Bella said, bringing him back to the present.

Kell whined. Sam snapped his fingers, bringing him closer. "No, it's not."

"At least if she is here, it will be easy to find her."

If Ari was here, they would have her well hidden. Word had gotten around that Hell's Eight was searching for Ari Blake. It complicated the hunt. "Let's hope."

A man stumbled out of the saloon into the dirt street. Too inebriated to stand up, he fell to his knees and immediately started vomiting. Isabella turned her head away and put her hand to her stomach. Sam couldn't help picturing a man this drunk stumbling to the back room where the whores waited on their customers. Ari was identical to her, Desi had said, yet softer, and Desi was pretty damn fine-boned, all blond hair, big eyes and spirit. It was hard to imagine anyone being softer than Desi, hard to imagine anyone as soft as Desi surviving a line of filthy drunks making use of her body day after day, the poison of their touch eradicating her sense of who she was, the memories of the life she used to have.

I will not live with his touch on my skin.

Bella's statement became a lot more believable.

Another man came out of the saloon. He wasn't drunk. He looked up the street, and straightened. It wasn't hard to figure what had his attention. Bella was more woman than most men saw on their best day. A shiny gold nugget in a pile of dung.

"Bella?"

"What?"

Reaching into his vest pocket, Sam pulled out a couple of gold pieces and handed them to her. She stared at the gold and then at him. He jerked his thumb over his shoulder. "Why don't you go buy yourself a hat that fits."

"But—"

He shook his head, cutting her off. "I'll be back for you in a few minutes." Glancing at the stranger again, he handed her one of his revolvers too. "Wait for me inside."

To Kell he said, "Guard her."

Bella bit her lip, but didn't argue. For that he was grateful. He waited for her to enter the tiny mercantile before directing Breeze down the street toward the stranger. The man didn't move, just watched his approach. Sam assessed him from the tight black brocade pants to the long dark hair blowing about his shoulders. No gun belt, which more than likely made him a gambler rather than a shootist. Sam dismounted and dropped Breeze's reins to the ground, tying him as effectively as if he'd hitched him to the post.

"Howdy."

The man struck a sulphur and nodded. "Gringo."

Sam took his rifle out of the scabbard.

"Nice horse."

"I'm fond of him."

"Not fond enough if you leave him here."

"Horse thieving a problem 'round these parts?"

The man ground the sulphur out under the heel of his fancy black boots. "No more than any other place in Tejala's territory."

Sam touched his finger to his hat. "I thank you for the warning but I think I'll take my chances."

"Your kind always does."

"My kind?"

The man sneered around the thin brown stalk of the cigarillo as the spicy smoke curled around his face. "Gringos who think everyone owes them something."

"Careful your back doesn't break under the weight of that chip on your shoulder."

"I am not the one that needs to be careful."

"As I said, thank you for the warning."

Sam stepped around the drunk leaning against the hitching post. The scent of vomit and urine followed him into the dark interior, intensifying in the close quarters. Too many bodies left too long in this small room imprinted the scent of desperation into the very walls. He walked up to the makeshift bar which was little more than boards laid across crates. "Tequila."

The bartender put a none-too-clean glass on the board and filled it with liquor. It probably was a good thing it was dark inside. Sometimes didn't pay a man to look too closely at what he was ingesting.

From outside came Breeze's scream of outrage followed quickly by the sound of a man swearing, ending with the distinct tattoo of hooves finding their target and then a more distant thump. Sam smiled and tossed back the liquor. Breeze wasn't fond of strangers either. The liquor hit his stomach. His lips peeled back at the raw burn. Quality was not in that bottle. He tossed the bartender a gold piece. It clinked against a nail embedded in the board. "Any chance a man could find some female company around here?"

The bartender exchanged a look with the man sitting at the end of the boards.

A strange smile curved his lips. "*Sí.* There is a chance."

Sam pushed his hat back. "And that chance would depend on what?"

"It would depend on how picky you are."

"Well, I am partial to pretty little blondes."

"Tired already of *la mujer* you rode in with?"

Sam pushed his glass forward. "Nothing wrong with a little variety."

The bartender exchanged another look with the man at the end of the bar as he refilled the glass. The hairs on the nape of Sam's neck stood on end. Retrieving his glass, he took a sip with a nonchalance he didn't feel.

The bartender asked too casually, "Would you be interested in a trade?"

"For what?"

"Our blonde for the *puta* you came in with."

"I'm not that interested in variety permanent like. I just thought I'd take a poke with my drink."

He put the glass precisely down on the bar. It settled with a soft click. "Now, are you offering comfort to men here or not?"

"Yes, but she will cost you more than this gold piece." He tossed the coin in the air. "Blondes are rare, as you know."

"Natural ones are." Many a saloonkeeper forced his girls to bleach their hair. And many a man didn't care that it was an illusion any more than they cared that the women weren't looking forward to servicing them.

Another look and then, "She's as natural as you're going to get."

Probably the first honest thing said today. Sam finished off the last of his drink, taking another gold piece out of his vest and tossing it on the counter. "That ought to cover it."

The gold piece disappeared into the man's dirty hand. "Follow me."

There wasn't much need for a guide to follow. The room was ten steps across, the dirt floor partitioned off by a moth-eaten blanket.

"Betty is a hot one," the bartender tossed over his shoulder with a leering grin as he held the curtain back. "So whenever you're ready, don't be afraid to just climb on and get to it."

"I'll keep that in mind." He stepped through the small opening, keeping his eye on the bartender. No window lit the tiny space just big enough for a mattress laid on the floor. The only light was cast by a near sputtered-out candle. On the mattress a woman lay unmoving, covered by a blanket as ratty as the one that served as the door. Definitely white based on her skin color. Strawlike strands of blond hair stuck out from the edges of the black mask that covered her face.

Looking back over his shoulder, he jerked his thumb toward her face. "What's with the mask?"

"Sally is a sweet lady of mystery."

"Why isn't she moving?"

"She is trained to wait on instruction."

Maybe, but Sam wouldn't bet his share of the Hell's Eight on it. He waved to the doorway. "Do you mind? I don't fancy an audience."

"You can earn back some of your fee if you can stomach one."

Taking two steps to the door, Sam muscled the other man backwards. "No thanks."

He yanked the curtain closed, noting as he did several of the eyeholes were at face level. "And in case anyone's interested, if I even think I see peeping I'm going to plug a bullet in the son of a bitch first and ask for explanations later."

"As you wish, *señor.*"

Yes, it would be. "Glad to hear it."

He turned back. "Ma'am?"

There was no response. Bracing his rifle against the wall, he hunkered down by her side. "Ma'am?" He touched her arm. "Ari?"

The woman's torso heaved in a convulsive jerk. He slid his arm behind her back, feeling the cut of bone. There wasn't a spare ounce on the woman. She jerked again, her ribs expanding spasmodically. She was trying to breathe. The blanket, stiff with dirt, slipped down her chest revealing the hollowed-out dent over her breastbone and an open sore.

"Fuck."

The buckles on the mask were stubborn, her body so much dead weight. Sam grunted as he hefted her torso up against his knee.

"Betty giving you a good time, *señor?*"

He didn't answer, just grunted again with a sense of urgency. The bottom buckle gave. He got the next undone with a lot less work. He lifted the edge in time to hear a very distinctive breath rattle in her throat. "Sweet Jesus."

The woman went completely limp, sliding off his leg. He caught her shoulders, easing her to the floor. Steeling himself, he unbuckled the rest of the straps until he could lift the mask from her face, revealing gaunt bones, red open sores and hazel eyes staring past his shoulder to a place the living couldn't see. "Son of a bitch."

It wasn't Ari. That was some consolation, but not much.

He took a breath, rage rising cold and deadly, and placed his fingers on the woman's lids and carefully closed them. Something he'd learned to do when he was thirteen when the soldiers had finished with his mother. Only then he'd been closing her eyes so he wouldn't have to see the lingering horror and his failure reflected back at him.

He sighed and shook his head. "I'm sorry, darling."

Sorry for whatever quirks of fate that landed her here, sorry he hadn't found her earlier, sorry he hadn't gotten the goddamn mask off in time so her last breath hadn't been smothered. Sorry men were such callous asses. Pulling the blanket up over her disease-ravaged body, he made her a promise. "If I can find your kin, I'll let them know."

Not where she'd died or how she'd looked—the woman deserved better than that—but he'd let them know she passed. Opening the small chest against the wall he moved items around, searching for any clue as to who she was, any hint of where he could find her people. There was nothing beyond the items of her trade, highlighting more than anything else how small her world had become, extending no further than this dusty, dingy room.

The curtain slid back with a scrape of metal on metal. "You killed our Betty."

They'd set him up. The knowledge came first and then the rage, coiling and tightening to a point of focus. His shotgun was an arm's reach away. He'd given his revolver to Bella. Sam palmed his knives from his boots.

"She wasn't nearly the hot ride you promised. I think you owe me my money back."

"And you owe us a new whore."

Bella. They wanted Bella. He smiled. "Now, there I disagree."

A gun cocked. "That is of no importance."

"I don't suppose it would be."

He spun, releasing the first knife in the direction of that metallic click. It landed with a satisfying thud in the chest of the man who'd been at the end of the bar. Movement out of the corner of his eye had him diving to the right. A gunshot exploded as he hit the floor. He rolled to a crouch, the bullet crease burning anew. Chunks of adobe fell over him as he spun and released the second knife. Too wide. It lodged in the bartender's shoulder. Not an incapacitating blow. Shit. His rifle was too far away. He'd never make it. Gathering his feet beneath him, Sam dove for the other man's knees, hitting him hard, driving him back through the curtain into the main room. The fabric ripped and came down over their heads, tangling them in its rank folds. As rapidly as the sound came at him, Sam processed it, tables being pushed back, booted feet beating a retreat. And others, coming in.

Shit. It was going to be a free-for-all.

With a snap of his head against the bartender's chin, Sam freed himself. Tossing the blanket to the side, he grabbed for the gun as the bartender stumbled backwards into the makeshift bar and slid to the floor clutching his shoulder and moaning. Sam only had a split second. Shock wouldn't hold the man forever. He was halfway to his feet when the order stopped him.

"Drop it, gringo."

Sam looked up. The man who'd tried to steal Breeze stood in the doorway, blood trickling from his lip. He was favoring his left side. His grip on the gun was all too steady, however, and the barrel centered on his chest guaranteed a lethal shot.

"Shit."

"*Sí*, you are in shit. We do not like rangers down here."

"Funny, we have the same feeling about no-account chicken-shit outlaws back at Hell's Eight."

There was the barest flicker of the man's eyelids. So he hadn't known who he was. "So you just go on ahead and pull that trigger and see how much is left of you and Tejala when the Eight come riding for vengeance."

"They will never know."

"You can't hide from Shadow."

Another flicker of his lids. Reputations really did come in handy. "And for sure you'll never get Tracker off your ass."

"Tejala will take care of the Hell's Eight."

"Tejala's days are numbered."

The bartender's body was two feet ahead and to the right. Sam just needed a distraction and he could make a dive for it and get the knife. The man in the doorway didn't take his eyes off him. No help there.

"Yours are too short even to count."

That was looking to be the truth. Sam balanced his weight on his toes, the bullet wound from the other day burning, and watched the stranger's eyes. He knew the exact moment the man made the decision to shoot. Sam dove for the knife. A gunshot exploded in a flash of fire. A burning pain seared along his thigh. Damn it! Not again. Then there was another shot. And another. The report sounded familiar. The snarl definitely was. Kell.

Yanking the knife free of the bartender's shoulder Sam came up into a crouch and in one smooth motion sent the weapon spinning toward its target. But it wasn't an outlaw in the doorway. Instead, there was Bella with a gun in her hand.

"Shit!" The knife flew from his fingertips. The blade buried in the doorjamb beside Isabella's head.

Jumping to his feet, Sam swore again. "I told you to stay put!"

Kell snarled around the throat of the man he had pinned to the floor just as Sam heard the scuff of a boot. The bartender.

An elbow to the face dropped the man again. Sam finished the job by breaking his neck. A quick look back showed Isabella still standing in the doorway, staring at his knife quivering in the doorjamb as if she couldn't figure how it got there. She had the gun pointing straight at him.

From outside, he could hear the voices of curious townsfolk.

"Time to go."

He got to his feet. Isabella still didn't blink. He took a step to the left, out of the line of fire. Bella turned with him. The gun traveled with her. "Bella?"

She didn't blink, move or give any other indication she heard him. He heard a shout. They didn't have much time.

He crossed the distance between them, snapping his fingers as he got to Kell. "Leave off."

The dog moved back, still snarling. Sam squatted down briefly to check the pulse on the man Bella had shot, though the pool of blood left little doubt he was dead.

"Is he dead?"

"Deader than mutton."

She looked at him then, her eyes wide with shock. "He was going to kill you."

Sam was close enough now to take the gun out of her hand. He did carefully, uncocking it, being careful of the hair trigger. "That he was."

"I couldn't let him kill you."

"For that I'm grateful, duchess."

He pulled her away from the doorway and looked out

onto the street. The good citizens of this hellhole were gathering their courage. "Bella, I need you to get on Breeze, ride over to the mercantile and get your horses."

"I already brought them over."

She was full of hidden surprises, and still feeling the repercussions of killing a man. Not good. He needed her sharp. "I can't afford for you to fall apart on me right now, all right?"

Her brows snapped down in a frown. "I do not fall apart."

From what he could see, she was a hairsbreadth from it. "Good." He checked the revolver, put two more bullets in the chamber and handed it back to her. "What I need you to do right now is to tuck yourself in behind the door and keep that gun trained outside. If anybody approaches, shoot."

She moved to the side of the door and glanced over at him, her eyes wide, her hands shaking. "What if they are friendly?"

"Trust me. Anybody with any sense isn't going to be coming over here on the back end of a gunfight."

Her frown increased. "They could be nice but stupid."

That they could. "We'll just have to take that chance."

She bit her lip, her gaze dropping to his leg. "You are bleeding."

"Just got grazed." Blood soaked the underside of the tear ripped into the thick cotton of his pants. While it burned like fire, it didn't interfere with the use of his leg. "I'm fine."

She didn't look convinced, but she nodded. When he was sure she wasn't going to drop into hysterics, he headed to the back room to retrieve his shotgun. The prostitute lay where he'd left her, a discarded bundle with no more use to anybody. Likely she'd be taken out to the canyon and her body dumped for the coyotes to dispose of. He couldn't see the residents of this town breaking a sweat to bury a worn-out whore. He shook his head. A sad ending to a sad life. He turned his head away.

"Sam?" Bella called.

"Yeah?" he called back, heading to the door.

"You found the woman, yes?"

The lightness of her voice, the melodic flow of her accent were completely out of place in this harsh place of depravity.

"Yes."

"It is your friend's sister?"

He turned to look at the body again. "No."

But if it had been, he would have taken her body with him, danger or not, out of respect for Desi. Taken her home to her family. At the very least buried her properly with the blessing of a padre.

"You will bring her anyway, *si?*"

Another woman would have objected to even being in the saloon, let alone accepted the company of a prostitute, but Isabella had a way of ignoring right and wrong and focusing on what she wanted. And from that sweet-as-pie command, she did not want a woman left behind in this place. She had good instincts.

"Anybody ever tell you you're a bossy little thing?" he called.

"I merely point out what is the right thing."

Yeah, she did. "What's it look like out there?"

"People gather their courage."

In other words, not good. He didn't have time to mess with a dead body. Images from the past flashed through his head. His mother dead and bloody, the Mexican army all around in the countryside, no time to do anything more than whisper he loved her and drag her to where his father lay. He'd gone back years later. The house had been abandoned and falling down, his parents' bodies had been nowhere to be found, probably carried off by wild animals, the remains disposed of with nature's sense of efficiency. Under the floorboard in the bedroom he'd found his mother's bible and the stash of love letters she'd kept. The ones in which his father talked of the future he was going to build for them in the republic. The ones in which his father spun the dreams his mother had grabbed hold of with all her heart, believing in the man she loved, believing they'd have a life together, that moving to the republic was a start of something fine.

Sam hadn't had any bodies to bury, so he'd buried those letters instead, along with his dreams of family and love. A man that chose to live out here had no right spinning dreams for a woman. Dreams like that just got a woman killed.

"Sam?" Isabella called again when he didn't immediately respond. "You will bring her?"

He tucked the blankets around the corpse. Betty might not have had someone to stand up for her in her last years, but he'd be damned if she'd be short a proper burial now that she'd passed on.

"Yeah. I'll bring her."

11

Isabella stood across the fresh grave from Sam and studied his very controlled, very ungiving expression. He was a puzzle. His reputation portrayed him as the scariest member of Hell's Eight, cold-blooded and ruthless, able to kill with a smile. Yet he'd taken the time to carry out of town the body of a woman that others would consider garbage, losing precious time and putting himself at risk to give a stranger a decent burial. And he had done it with all the respect he would have shown a member of his own family. But yet, she shook her head at the illogic, she should see him as unredeemable.

Sam tossed the last shovelful of dirt on the grave and headed back to where Breeze stood. Not one muscle in his face moved to show he was upset, but ever since he'd walked out of the cantina carrying Betty's body, Bella had wanted to wrap her arms around him and hug him tightly. The urge was not going away either. It just kept getting stronger. And she did not know why. She just knew there was an emotion in his eyes she wanted to ease.

The wind blew across the plains, whipping down out of the hills in a mournful wail. Sam lifted his head, following its path with his eyes, giving her a full view of his profile—the sharp blade of his nose, the square, slightly jutting thrust of his jaw. His lips parted as he took a breath.

His gaze swept over to her, to the grave and then back to the shovel he was securing to the back of Breeze's saddle as if nothing had happened, but it was too late. She had seen the hunger in his eyes, and in a flash of insight she knew what the emotion was that she often saw haunting Sam's gaze.

Loneliness. He was lonely, this man who could care about a woman that life had discarded. Maybe too much so. Drumming her fingers on her arms, she considered the matter. Something about this woman's plight had touched him. She wished she knew what it was. She had a feeling it was the key to understanding all the pieces of the puzzle that made up Sam Mac-Gregor.

Sam came back to the grave. She waited for him to speak but he just stood there, his expression like stone, a legacy of pain in his eyes, until she could stand it no more.

"Will you say the prayer?"

Anger compressed the edges of his mouth the way it always did when she mentioned prayer. Or hope.

"I don't pray."

In this case what he wanted did not matter. A woman was dead. She had just been buried. "The proper words must be said."

He took off his hat. "Then maybe you'd better say them."

She shrugged. "I do not know the words in English."

"I don't expect Betty will mind."

No, she did not suppose Sally would. Isabella made the sign of the cross and bowed her head. At first, the words wouldn't come. Instead, there came the memories of how Betty had looked as Sam had laid her out by the grave, her body wasted by disease, her flesh ravaged by sores, as if the abuse she had suffered over the years were injustices that couldn't be kept hidden.

That was her future. When Tejala caught her, that would be her life, one long, endless scream until it ended in some dirty room. Likely the man who found her body would not be decent like Sam. Likely her body would be tossed to the pigs for disposal. Likely no one would whisper the words of passing. She blinked and took a deep breath. She would not let it come to that.

She found her voice, found the prayer and whispered it loud enough so Sam could hear. He said he did not pray, but if it was important to him to give Betty a proper burial, then the ritual would be important and maybe the words would give him comfort. When she was done, she crossed herself again. Sam put his hat on and turned back to Breeze. She stayed by the grave a moment longer, holding her hair back, needing to say more. She said it in English, just in case Betty's spirit lingered.

"I am sorry, Betty, that we did not find you sooner. I am sorry that your life ended as it did, that you passed without knowing that someone had come for you." She glanced to where Sam stood beside the horse, checking the pack, tall and strong as if none of this affected him. As if he was apart from it all. She did not believe it.

She let the wind take her hair, crossing her arms over her chest. "Because, he did, you know. Sam might be looking for this woman named Ari, but he would not have left you behind. He would have taken you with him. He would have kept you safe."

Like he had her.

"He would have done it simply because he is a good man who believes in doing the right thing." Picking up a handful of the freshly turned dirt, she let it rain down from her fist, symbolically sealing the grave in a final gesture before whispering, "There are not so many of them anymore, so please, do not haunt his dreams." She bit her lip, her gaze drawn to him by the pain he would not share. "I think he has enough ghosts."

Two hours later Sam was still stewing in that melancholy way that worked on her nerves. Bella was used to his silence, used to his empty smiles, had grown attached to his real ones, but she did not think she could ever get used to this. He rode only eight feet ahead, but it was as though he was alone in the world, living in a dark place where no one could touch him. She did not like seeing him that way. It was not right, and she was not going to tolerate it.

Slumping in the saddle she called, "Sam?"

He shifted sideways, looking at her over his shoulder, his beautiful mouth set in a straight line. "Yeah?"

Even his "Yeah" was flat. "How much farther?"

"Why?"

She hunched her shoulders a little more. "I was just wondering."

Breeze came to a stop. In some ways Sam was very easy.

"You're tired?"

"I am sorry. I am not used to riding so much."

He eyed her suspiciously. "This wouldn't be an excuse to get your arms around me, would it?"

She pasted a smile on her face and straightened her spine. "You see right through my ways." She waved him on. "We may go."

He didn't move. His hat was set too low to see his eyes but she bet he was frowning. She tugged her own hat over her face. All the advantages should not be his.

"Are you really tired?"

"I will be fine."

Still he didn't move. She urged Sweet Pea forward. Sam leaned over and caught the reins.

"I can't take you up in front of me."

"I understand."

His eyes glittered at her from under the brim of his hat. "It wouldn't be safe."

"I do not argue."

Kneeing his horse over, he sighed and held out his hand. "You can ride behind me and rest against my back." Motioning with his fingers, he ordered, "Hand me the reins."

She placed the strip of leather in his hand. "Thank you."

Kicking his foot free of the near stirrup, he shrugged. "We've been riding hard."

It was a long way to the ground and her muscles let her know they were not happy to be put to work supporting her once she got there. Sam had her arm immediately, steadying her.

"Careful."

She turned, abandoning the horse for his thigh. The horse had more give, his thigh more appeal. She held on tightly.

The saddle creaked. His arm came around her back, catching under her armpit, knocking her hat off her head. "Step into the stirrup."

The order whispered down her spine. How could he make such a simple practical thing sound so exotic? She did as he asked, having to lean back, finding his strength there to support her, help her.

He lifted. "Swing your leg over."

She did, settling behind Sam. Her skirt bunched up, barely covering her knees. Even with the pants Sam had made for her she was embarrassed. Her mother would be horrified. She wrapped her arms around his lean waist and snuggled up against his back. She didn't care. This was Sam, and for now, he was her reality.

"Comfortable?"

She nodded, breathing deeply of his scent. Man tinged with sweaty horse and the lingering fragrance of tobacco. "Yes."

"Good."

With a cluck of his tongue he put the horses in motion. It was a surprisingly sensual experience riding behind him. With every step the horse took, she rocked against his back, her nipples rubbing in an erotic rhythm. Pressure, then release. Pressure, then release. The edge of the saddle bit into the inside of her thighs heightening her awareness, and the ridge of the low back rubbed against her clit, bringing it to hunger. She moaned. Never would she make two hours like this.

"You all right back there?"

"I am fine."

"Sounded like you were having a little bit of a problem."

The irritant! He knew what she was feeling. And maybe he had been keeping his hand on her leg to heighten her awareness? Well, two could play that game. "I am just enjoying being close to you."

He stiffened. She smiled. That was not the least of the honesty she intended to indulge in. His shirt was warm from the sun. Beneath the thin cotton, she could feel the heat of his skin waiting. The tingle in her fingers spread to her palms. He was a fine man and touching him was such a pleasure. "You must have many women wanting to touch you."

"I think you've got things backwards. It's a man that does the touching."

"Not so much today," she whispered against his back, feeling bold and daring, wanton even. "Today it is my wish to pleasure you."

"Shit." His hand came over hers. To stop her or encourage her?

Running her palms down the hard planes of his stomach, she found the buttons on the fly of his pants. "Do you not want me to pleasure you?"

"You're a virgin."

She laughed and kissed his spine. "This does not make me an *idiota*, Sam."

"Never thought it did."

Two buttons gave. She slipped her fingers in the opening, finding hot flesh and an intriguing line of hair that curled around her knuckles. She tugged. He jumped. This was going to be fun. "Then what did you think being a virgin meant?"

"Shy and hesitant."

Another button gave. "And perhaps unschooled?"

His breath hissed through his teeth as she took advantage of the loosening of material to slide her hands downward until she hit the barrier of his cock. "Yes."

"I am not hesitant, Sam."

"So I noticed."

The rough edge of his drawl excited her almost as much as the thought of pleasuring him did. "I am adjusting my shyness, but I will be always be unschooled…"

This time when she put her mouth to his back, she let him feel her teeth. His whole body stiffened. Her hand closed around the thick base of his cock, straining to hold him even as he strained to her touch. "Unless you teach me."

"Hell, woman, you don't play fair."

She nipped his shoulder blade, feeling the shock go through him. "You would be disappointed if I did."

He didn't answer. She did not need him to. What she needed was for him to lift up so she could work his cock free. "Help me, Sam."

With a curse, he yanked her hand away. She leaned back as he worked his cock free. Freedom did not come easily but when it did, she was there to catch its heavy weight. He groaned. She sighed and rested her cheek against his back as she ran her fingers up the solid length.

"I like very much how you feel in my hand, strong and hungry for the pleasure I will give you."

His hand covered hers. Again she felt the battle his conscience waged with his desire. She sabotaged the effort with a light squeeze and a request she knew he could not resist. "Teach me to please you, Sam. Just this once."

"It won't mean anything."

She nodded, knowing he felt the gesture. "I know."

"It won't be good for you."

The extra warning made her smile. He had no idea what was good for her, just misguided images of what he wanted for her. "I would still like for you to show me what gives you pleasure."

In her hand, his cock jerked. Against her cheek his ribs expanded. She drew a breath with him, enjoying the sweet summer air and this break in his defenses. This moment when he would let her in.

His "Like this" was gruff, his instruction matter of fact as he worked her hands up and down his shaft. She didn't take offense. She could not expect a man she was tempting past what his honor dictated to smile. But she could expect his cooperation.

The rhythm he set was hard and fast. She frowned. Not at all what she expected. He always teased her first with light touches and easy strokes to bring her body to a desperate need. This was more like the end when there was nothing left of her control, nothing she could accept but the merciless drive to completion. His hips pushed up into her downward stroke. The muscles in his back tensed. His hands fell away, giving her back control. She took it with a whisper-light touch that had him shuddering. "I think you are rushing me, Sam."

"What makes you say that?"

"This is not how you touch me."

"Men don't need sweet touches like women do. They like it fast and rough."

She frowned, pondering the depth of truth in the statement. Sam never lied but he would shade the truth if it served his purpose. "I think you would like sweet from me."

He needed sweet more than anyone she'd ever met. Deserved it. He was always caring for those around him, always doing the right thing. A man like that should be rewarded. Should be given the softness he wouldn't ask for.

"I'd like to come without getting my ass shot off."

Another word to add to her vocabulary. "There is trouble?"

"We are out in Tejala's territory, out in the open with potentially a posse on our trail. There could be trouble at any time."

The thought did not terrify her like it should. "But there is no sign of trouble now?"

"Not that I can tell but that means nothing. There could be an ambush set just over the next hill."

"Or there could be nothing."

He shook his head. "The ambush is more likely."

She came to a conclusion. "You are trying to scare me."

"I'm trying to get you to see sense."

No, he was trying to distract her, trying to get her to rush this moment because… The why escaped her, but instinct told her despite his words to the contrary, Sam craved the sweetness he always so easily gave her. "I think I will give my gift my way."

"Come hell or high water."

His interference was becoming tedious.

She stroked him in a long leisurely pass, cupping the broad head in her palm, discovering a silky drop of fluid at the tip. She had not known men got wet, too. She slid a bit of the moisture to her fingertips.

This time his grip on her wrist was inescapable. He turned in the saddle, maintaining his grip on her hand, forcing her to lean around. "Do you want to really pleasure me, duchess?"

His eyes burned down at her full of passion and anger. She might have pushed him too far. She refused to be afraid. Whatever revenge he wanted for daring to exploit his vulnerability she was willing to pay. "Yes."

"Then give me your mouth."

She did, holding his gaze with hers as she parted her lips slowly, inviting whatever he needed. He needed so much, so much more than sex, but it was all he would take. She understood that. Accepted it, but while she was with him she would not leave him wanting. He had passion to give her. She had softness to give him.

The blue of his eyes darkened, his expression hardened. He was going to be mean. She braced herself for it.

He brought her wet fingers to her lips, so close she could smell the sweet scent of his musk. Like freshly crushed grass, yet spiced with something deeper, something compelling.

"This is all I have to offer you."

She leaned the quarter inch forward, curling her tongue around his essence, taking it into her mouth, still holding his gaze, letting him see her accept his seed in the manner he demanded. It was salty and earthy and for as long as she lived, she knew she would never forget his taste. She swallowed and licked her lips.

His hand slid across her cheek until his fingers cupped her head. He pulled her down almost helplessly as he growled. "I need my ass kicked."

It took her a second to figure out what he was doing. Memories of his mouth on her pussy flashed through her mind. He wanted her mouth. On his cock. Excitement flared through her in a shock of lust. She licked her lips again. The residue of his need coated her tongue in pure temptation. She would like to know him like that. Would he be as helpless under the whip of her tongue as she had been under his? It was an intriguing thought. She so rarely got the upper hand with him.

"I desire you very much, and I would most like to take you in my mouth right now the way you do me."

His eyes narrowed and his breath caught before releasing in a growl of words. "Think long and hard before you do this, Bella. There'll be no pleasure in this for you and there will come a point after which I won't stop, even when you want me to."

When, not if. "What makes you think I will want you to?"

"You're a virgin. You have no idea what you're asking for."

"Then you will have to teach me."

"Not like this. Not on a horse in the middle of nowhere."

"This is what we have."

"You deserve better."

Always he thought she deserved better, more. She curved her hand around his cock, tilting the thick shaft toward her. "You are what I want."

"You can't always have what you want." But she could, and from now she could extract a memory to hold on to later, whenever the bad times came visiting. And they would come. Tejala was relentless. She brushed her thumb across the head. Broad and velvety soft, a cushiony hardness topping steel. Powerful like Sam himself. And hers. "I can have you, *sí?*"

His hand was heavy on her head, his fingers gentle on her cheek, his drawl weary with acceptance. "*Sí*. For now."

"Then we will make now very good." She worked her way over. The back of the saddle cut into her hip and she was stretched too far.

"Bella…"

She didn't want to hear any more regret. "You sound so sad, when I am very sure this will make you very happy."

"It won't make you happy."

"You are wrong."

She stole his answer by taking him in her mouth. His immediate groan and shudder smoothed like a balm over her unease. He was much bigger than she anticipated, and it was not so easy as she expected to take him. She opened her mouth wider, shifted closer. He slid deeper. Breeze stumbled. His cock speared deep, bumping her cheek before hitting her throat. She scrambled to pull back.

"Shit!"

Instead of pulling her off, Sam held her there, hands and hips straining as her throat worked with the effort not to gag. Two heartbeats and he eased off, cradling her head in his hand again rather than restraining her. "Sorry, duchess. You bring out my wild side."

The head of his cock rode her tongue in shallow strokes.

He always drove her to the edge before delivering her bliss; she would do the same for him. "I like you wild."

He stopped her before she could try. "I prefer this." His fingers threaded through her hair, massaging her scalp in small circles, gentling her as his passion hoarsened his voice. "This is good."

It was too late, he'd shown her what he liked. And that was his cock deep in her mouth. No matter how he tried to hide it, she could feel the urgency within him. The need to thrust controlled by his position. The need to dominate subdued by his promise. Just because he would not unleash it did not mean she did not sense it. Or did not want it.

She pulled back. "Let me go."

"No."

Drawing her lips back, she let him feel the edge of her teeth.

He tipped his head back and smiled, the rough pad of his thumb rubbing over her lips. "Tempting me isn't going to get me to change my mind."

She was not tempting him, she was threatening him. Her thoughts must have shown on her face.

"I like it rough."

Then so did she, because the challenge to take him past his control the way he took her past hers was a shiny lure too bright to resist. She had this one night. This was the start. And she was not setting the tone with caution or any false modesty he insisted she had to have because she was a virgin. She shook her head.

"You are in for a big surprise, Sam, when you see who I really am."

"I'm doing my damnedest not to."

"Not to what? Be surprised?"

"See you for who you really are."

"Why?"

"Because it won't be good for either of us."

She borrowed one of his own expressions. "I would chance it."

"I won't."

"Then we are back to this."

Leaving the responsibility of keeping her on the horse up to Sam, Isabella took him back in her mouth. His shudder was very much to her liking. So was his taste, his scent, his groan. She lowered her head on his cock, setting a fast pace, a hard pace, alternately raking the underside of his cock with her tongue and her teeth, confirming one thing with every scrape of her teeth—he did like it rough.

"Use your hands," he grunted.

It took a minute to get the rhythm he liked, but when she found it, the rewards were high. His pleasure obvious. His cock went rock-hard and swelled even further. She took him deeper, sucking harder, nipping the tip before soothing it with a pass of her tongue, pumping with her hand, coaxing him to climax. She so wanted him to come for her.

She removed her mouth from his hard shaft just long enough to whisper one plea, "Do not hold back."

She could not bear it if he held back. Not this time. Not with her. She needed him to need her. Needed him to let go for her. Her pussy flowered and ached. Her body wept and her nipples burned as if on fire.

"I won't, baby. I'll give you all I've got."

His big palm cupped her cheek and his voice was hoarse and deep. "And you'll take every drop, won't you?" His fingers grazed her throat. "Every drop down this sweet throat."

Scared, excited and eager, she nodded.

"Then take me deep, Bella. Take a breath and take me deep."

She did, taking him past her need to gag, taking him as deep as she could, raking his balls and cock lightly with her nails, sucking hard until he grabbed her head and pulled her to him. His head dropped back, his cock jerked and his hot seed flooded her mouth in a salty tang. She swallowed, milking him with her hands, taking what he had to give, needing him to give to her, even if only this. When the last pulse faded, and his cock rested quietly on her tongue, she eased back.

"You are pleased?"

"Yes."

"Good, because it will make the next easier."

"Easier?"

She pushed back up. She would not have made it without his help.

She snuggled into his back, whimpering when the saddle pressed against her swollen clit. "I have decided what you owe me for saving your life."

"So what do you want?"

"You to take my virginity."

"That's not much of a prize. First times are rarely good."

"But that is the special part. I want you to make me feel as good as I just made you feel when you do it."

"Shit, you don't ask much, do you?"

She kissed his spine, breathing deep of his scent even as she ran her tongue over her lips, gathering in the last of his essence. "I only ask what I know you can give."

12

Bella was offering him his dream. No strings attached. A night of the best sex of his life—it would be the best—and all he had to do was not make it a nightmare for her. Not a bad deal for a man not wanting commitments, so why was it rubbing him raw?

Sam glanced across the campfire in time to catch Isabella running that tongue over her lips again. She always did that when she was nervous. And why wouldn't she be? She'd leveraged the game out of the realm of play to the harsh truth of reality. Any intelligent woman would rethink her plan when it came to the crunch. He sighed and flicked his smoke into the fire and told his aching cock to take a rest. Nothing was going to happen tonight.

"Having second thoughts?"

Isabella looked up from the cup of coffee she'd been toying with for the last fifteen minutes. Firelight played across her face, shadowing her eyes in mystery, augmenting the aura of femininity she wore like other women wore a fancy hat.

Shit. It was going to kill him to walk away from her tonight.

"No. What makes you ask that?"

"The way you're sitting there getting more agitated by the second."

"I am being silly." She put the cup on the ground beside her. Another stroke of her tongue over her lips. Lust poured through him in a hot, liquid heat riding his blood before pooling in his cock. What was it about the woman that she made him one continuous hard-on?

"Silly or not, let's hear it." He might as well deal with her fears as they occurred.

"Ever since this afternoon, you have been putting distance between us."

"Nothing new about that. I've been trying to put distance between us since the day we met."

She shrugged. "This is different. Now that night is here, I do not know how to get from here…" She made a descriptive motion with her hand from her feet to him "—to there." She hitched the blanket up over her shoulder. "So I am now worrying."

He wasn't sure he was hearing her correctly. "About what?"

"I do not know what is proper, what is improper. What will work. What won't."

He blinked. Of all the concerns he figured she had,

he hadn't figured on that. "You don't know how to seduce me?"

Bella glared at him like it was all his fault. "*Sí*, this is what I do not know."

She was always surprising him. Despite the regret he knew he was going to feel once this night was over, Sam still felt like smiling. "Pardon me. This is my first time out as a defiler of innocence."

A little of the lift left her chin. "This is true?"

Of course it was true. What the hell kind of man did she think he was? "Innocence should be protected."

"As you protect me?"

"It's part of my job. I'm a Texas Ranger. We have the Creed. I live by it."

"And making you do this violates this creed?"

He could say yes. She'd promptly feel so guilty about making him violate his creed she'd back off. But it wouldn't be the truth. And, he wasn't the man he should be. He wanted what she offered. A taste of what Caine had. What his parents had had. Hell, who was he kidding? He tossed the rest of his coffee. He wanted Bella.

"No. You just make me wish for what can't be."

"But already we talked. Tomorrow does not exist."

"So we agreed."

It still wasn't sitting well on his conscience.

"You do not look happy. If we do this, you will have regrets perhaps?"

He glanced across the fire at the sweetness of her

face, her curvaceous figure, the dimple creasing her left cheek, the courage in her eyes, the desire she didn't even bother to hide. "There isn't a goddamn thing I'll regret about loving you, but once I take care of Tejala, you're going to realize this is all for nothing."

"I think, Sam, that even if Tejala were not a problem in my life, I would be here tonight with you."

Shit. He was beginning to think honesty should be outlawed.

"That doesn't change the fact I'm not the kind of man a girl should be throwing her first time away on."

She stood, tucking the blanket under her arms. "Ah, this is the problem." She walked around the fire slowly, deliberately, her hips swaying side to side, the smile on her lips a siren's temptation. "You keep thinking of me as a girl."

"You're hardly out of pigtails."

She stopped just out of his reach, dropping the blanket. It slid off her body in a slow glide, falling to the ground without a protest. He couldn't help thinking there should be a protest. From more than just him. Beneath it she was dressed in her shirt and skirt and the smile gracing her face was the one a woman wore when she bared herself before her man. Shy with innocence, sultry with expectation. It was the kind of smile that turned a man inside out.

She stepped over the blanket. "I am a woman, Sam. I know the value of myself." She pulled the thick rope of her braid over her shoulder and made short work of the tie. She tossed it to him. He caught it more out of habit than thought. He couldn't take his eyes off her.

"You can still back out."

She winked and flashed him a dimpled smile and turned around, leaving him looking at the voluptuous outline of her figure. She really was built like a little Venus, all rounded curves and seduction. She glanced at him over her shoulder from under her lashes, that smile on her face evident in her voice.

"I know the value of a man like you." Sliding her hands behind her neck, under her hair, she turned, raising her arms as she did. "I know the value of what we have together." Her dark gaze locked on his as her hair poured around her face in a silken waterfall. "I think the question maybe should be—do you?"

He had to struggle to find his voice. "I thought you didn't know how to get from there to here."

"I did not, but you reminded me." She put her hands on her hips. Her weight naturally fell forward on her right foot, emphasizing the curve of her hip, the small-ness of her waist. His fingers twitched. The waist he could span with his hands. The hips that would fill those same hands to overflowing. Those incredibly soft hips. "You are a very helpful man."

Not helpful enough. "If I showed you, how come you're still over there?"

"Because you have not shown me everything."

The gentle comeback was a warning. A challenge. He sat a little straighter, everything male in him responding to the blatant femininity in her. Her hands went to the buttons at the collar of her shirt.

"What did I miss?"

"You did not show me you want this, too."

His cock was so hard it felt like the skin was going to split. "I would think that's evident."

She dropped her hands from her throat in a languid gesture, moving them down to her groin. "Not here." She moved her hands up to her breasts, covering her heart. "But here."

Her hands were too small to cover the generous curves. He flexed his fingers. She needed bigger hands. His hands.

She tilted her head to the side. Her hair fell over her delicate shoulder, swinging past her hip in a thick curtain. She smiled in a way that had that dimple in her left cheek flashing at him with the life that was so strong in her. "It is not my wish to rape you, Sam."

The last of his resistance faded under the lash of amusement. And tenderness. She was so much more than he could resist. He held out his hand, palm up. An invitation. "You could never rape me, Bella."

She placed her palm in his with that absolute trust that devastated him.

"Because you are stronger than me?"

He shook his head, pulling her down onto his lap. "Because you would never find me unwilling."

She frowned. "But you fight what is between us."

He placed his finger on the faint line between her

brows, smoothing it with a gentle pressure. "Because I know what's coming if you stay with me. And I know you deserve better, and I want it for you." He ran his finger over the fringe of her lashes. He wanted her happy and safe. "You're a duchess, Bella. You deserve a duke."

She snuggled into his shoulder. "Will this duke love me like a woman, Sam, or will he put me on a pedestal and always expect proper duchess behavior?"

"He damn well better treat you well."

"Or what? Or you will come beat him up?"

He'd kill him. "I'll always be there for you."

"What kind of marriage will that be, Sam? With you always standing between me and this duke. A threat to him, a lure to me?"

"You'll forget about me once you get back home and the threat of Tejala is removed."

"Because I am young and do not know my mind?"

Pain flashed through him. He buried it before it could reach his eyes. He couldn't keep it totally out of his voice. It snapped out in a harsh "Yes."

She shook her head and sighed. "I will not argue that lie with you tonight, but soon you will have to face the parts of you you hide and make a choice." She patted his chest. "Patience is not my best virtue, Sam. I cannot promise to wait forever."

"I never asked you to."

"*Sí*, this I know. It is almost as regrettable as the other."

He frowned. "What other?"

She pushed on his shoulder. "Do not pretend to not know."

He couldn't think of a thing he'd missed. It wasn't until he saw the sparkle in her eye and the grin twitching the corner of her mouth that he realized he'd been set up. He played along, knowing how much she needed the illusion of being in control. "You'll have to fill me in."

She gave an exaggerated sigh. "I can see this is another area of your reputation that has been poofed up."

"You mean puffed."

"Poofed, puffed." She waved her hand. "It is a big disappointment."

"What is?"

"I am alone in the dark with the notorious Sam Mac-Gregor, lying in his lap—" she motioned to the three open buttons at her throat "—half dressed, and I am still a virgin."

The smiles were coming easier to him now, slipping past his instinctive need to check them. The woman was incorrigible. And she brought out his sense of play like no one else ever had. "And?"

"I was led to believe that any of those *cosas* would leave me ruined and…"

"And what?"

She waggled her eyebrows. "Panting with satisfaction."

* * *

He took her down to the ground in a slow tumble, sliding his hand under her back, keeping her from hitting the ground too hard. Tonight was going to be less than what she probably expected. He'd heard pleasuring virgins was a tricky business, and he had no experience with the breed for the simple reason he'd never wanted to.

Except with Bella. Bella made him want all sorts of improper things. Which didn't lessen his responsibility to make tonight the best he could for her. And that didn't mean starting it off with bruises.

Isabella leisurely placed her arms around his neck, linked her fingers behind his head and waited. If he wanted to prove to her he was a son of a bitch, this was a time to do it. He brought his weight down over her.

She licked her lips. For all her bold talk she was nervous.

"You can change your mind anytime, Bella. Nothing has to go further than you want."

She sighed and frowned up at him. "Sam?"

He kissed the end of her nose. Her cheeks, corner of her mouth. "What?"

"If you tell me that again, I will slap you."

He propped himself back up above her. Humoring her was one thing, but he wasn't a tame puppy. "Duchess?"

"*Sí?*"

"If you threaten me again—" he placed his fingertip on the end of her nose "—I'm going to tan your hide."

Her head canted to the side. "Like a child?"

He scooted down a bit. The open neck of her blouse revealed the hollow of her throat and the pulse pounding beneath the soft flesh. "No, like a woman."

His woman. If she were his woman, he'd likely be tanning her hide at least once a week for the sheer pleasure of watching the blush of her orgasm match the blush of her spanking. The fire was dying down but it still cast enough light for him to see instead of being intimidated, she was intrigued.

He could picture it all too easily. The skin of her rear flushed from her spanking, as pretty a pink as her pussy and just as enticing. The creamy flesh would be hot against his thighs as he parted her lips, centered his cock, pressed into her snug little channel. And she would be snug. He'd have to work the head in, a little at a time, torturing them both with the slow culmination. His balls burned and pulled up tight to his body. Shit. He could come from the fantasies she inspired alone.

He unfastened the next two buttons of her shirt, making more room for his kiss. He nuzzled the collar aside. The subtle womanly fragrance of her skin smoothed over his senses as he traced the line of her collarbone. Addictive, sweet, an echo of the deeper spice he would find between her thighs. "Tonight we're going to take this nice and slow."

This was their night. He wasn't going to rush it.

He touched his tongue to the underside of her chin,

teasing, tasting the salt of her desire, feeling her tremble.

Opening another button, he nibbled his way down over her collar to the scented valley between her breasts.

"I want to hurry," she panted.

To the good part. She had no idea what she was asking for. No idea what she was cheating herself out of. "You might as well resign yourself, I'm opting for slow."

Her head dropped back on the bedroll. "Why did I know you would say that?"

"Because we have all night, and I'm a thorough man."

"Do not forget that I wish to be a thorough woman, too."

"I won't forget. By morning, you'll be a thoroughly satisfied woman."

She cuffed his shoulder. "And panting."

He pushed the shirt off her right shoulder, tugging the material out from the waistband of her skirt, exposing her breast and its makeshift support. "Pretty."

"Always they embarrass me."

"Funny, they pretty much delight me." He cuddled her breast in his hand, slipping the support off so there was nothing between his hand and her skin, except heat and anticipation. Her skin was incredibly soft there, smooth and inviting, the color a shade lighter than her face as though an extra dollop of cream had been added to the lushness of her complexion. He plumped her breast up, watching the blush rise over her torso, adding a bewitching pink to the café au lait tint. He could barely make out the faint lingering mark of a bruise. "That was cruel how you bound them. You won't do it again."

"They are *my* breasts."

He glanced up at her from between the high mounds. "Tonight they're mine."

He kissed the underside of the sweet mound, lingered a minute before kissing his way up the convex arch, letting her feel the edge of his teeth as he skimmed the aureole.

Her nipple prodded his cheek. Turgid, hungry, it all but begged the caress of his tongue. He raked it once, twice, three times in a small tribute, before taking her into his mouth, relishing her soft moan, before closing his lips over the plump nub. He started out lightly, gentling her into the moment, sucking at a steady pressure, giving her an easy rhythm until she caught fire, arching beneath him. At the same time, her fingers sank into his hair and tugged. Hard.

He let her nipple slide out of his mouth in a slow gliding, lashing the tip one last time before it popped free.

When he glanced up, she was staring at him. Big brown eyes dark with more than a hint of worry. "You wouldn't by any chance have something on your mind?"

Her lip came between her teeth. "I do not want you to think I am not eager."

He slipped the support off her other breast. The mound flattened and spread in a wanton cry for attention, the nipple already peaked. The perfect topping to a sweet dessert. "I know."

He reached for the waistband of her skirt.

"I need to know what will happen, what is allowed for me to do. I do not want to just lie here."

He would love it if she just lay there, but that wasn't Bella. Bella was joy in motion, always seeking control, always exploring. If he wanted her relaxed he had to give her something to do. And he had to make it seem like it was her idea, otherwise she'd worry on the other side of the equation, which would be—was she forcing him into something he didn't want to do? "You serious?"

"*Sí.*"

He skimmed his lips up her neck, brushing his mouth over hers. Her lips parted immediately. He didn't take advantage, just let the anticipation build. "You didn't finish undressing."

She blinked before looking down. "I am not undressed enough?"

"Not hardly."

She reached for the waistband of her skirt. He shook his head. "Not here."

"Where?"

"Over there by the fire."

Understanding came in a bad-angel smile. "You wish for me to finish what I started?"

"Oh yeah."

"And afterward you will make me pant?"

He guided her upright. "I'll make you scream."

Like a shot she was out of his lap and standing in front of the dwindling fire, clutching the front of her shirt closed, gaze speculative, her sense of challenge obviously coming to the fore. "But I am thinking maybe, my Sam, I will make *you* pant first."

She walked around the fire, the sexy sway of her hips baiting him to follow. She reached the other side and spun around, coming to a stop with her hands on her hips and a challenging toss of her head that sent all that glorious hair flying around her shoulders and her blouse dropping open.

Firelight danced in an alternating pattern of light and shadow over that narrow strip of flesh, deepening her already impressive cleavage, hollowing out the center of his control.

She slipped her fingers beneath the shirt collar and eased the fabric off her shoulder, the sleeve sliding down her arm, while the front caught on her heavy breast, one breath away from full disclosure.

He tipped his hat back off his forehead, his mouth going dry, his libido prodding him to get up, cross over, and give that thin piece of material the push it needed.

Her whole face lit up with confident sensuality. "Ah, you like my breasts."

"No," he corrected, "I love your breasts."

She reached for the other side, giving it a nudge. It

followed the same path, getting caught on the same point.

One, two, three seconds and the damn thing didn't fall. "Duchess, do you think you could bring yourself to take a deep breath?"

She shook her head. "If you want to see my breasts, you must show me your chest."

"I could just walk over there and take what I want." The hitch in her breathing showed how much she liked the thought of that. He leaned forward.

She shook her head. "But you will not."

"I won't?"

"No."

She was a little too fond of giving him orders. "Why not?"

"Because you like teasing me as much as I like teasing you."

So he did. "But you should know there's a price for teasing me."

"I will pay it."

"You don't even know what it is."

"I do not need to. I trust you."

His control was a frayed thread, ready to snap at the least increase in tension. He yanked his shirt free of his pants and stood. "You shouldn't."

She let her blouse drop the ground. "But I do."

13

It took him two seconds to get to her side, to capture her against him. Her body flowed into his without a ripple of protest. She had no instinct for survival.

The depth of her cleavage drew his eye. The weight of her breasts dragged them down just a bit. Just enough to fit perfectly into the palm of his hand. His fingers curled in anticipation. Sam brought his hand up, offering the support he'd promised. She turned into his embrace. Her fingers went to the buttons on his shirt. A flush tinted the ledge of her cheekbones. "So it is fine for me to want to see you naked?"

"Better than fine."

She glanced up at him through her lashes. "And if my nerves are overcome by so much masculinity?"

He chuckled and brushed his thumb over that intriguing blush. "I promise to wake you up pronto."

Her laugh floated between them, bonding them in the

moment, wrapping around them tighter than passion. "Thank you."

He'd loved to laugh as a kid, and for sure he'd created plenty of opportunities to laugh as an adult, but those had often been black moments of dark humor and usually ended up with someone dead. But with Bella it was always laughter as it should be, for the sheer enjoyment of the moment.

He slid his hand across her waist, pulling her back into his body. Lowering his mouth to the delicate curve of her ear, he rubbed his tongue over the tip, a smile tugging at his desire as she immediately shivered in response. "I want you."

She turned in his arms, folding hers across her chest, one eyebrow raised in question as she danced backward toward the bedroll. "Do I look like I resist?"

The woman probably didn't have a clue how crossing her arms like that pushed those gorgeous breasts up and out, putting serious strain on the fabric of her shirt. He, however, couldn't take his eyes off the miracle. He followed.

"Was that a challenge?"

Her gaze dipped to his mouth. She blinked, then dropped her gaze to his groin, where he knew damned well his hard-on was visible. Her eyes widened. Her breasts swelled with her indrawn breath, and she took a step to the side. That slight sting of amazement soothed the wild side of him. Anticipation hovered in his chest, blending with the heavy flow of desire.

"Because I assure you, Bella," he drawled as he followed her, "I can ride you for as hard and as long as you want."

She took another step back. She was almost at the bedroll. "Talk is inexpensive."

She was still staring at his cock. "Cheap. The phrase is talk is cheap."

"Does it not mean the same thing?"

Another step and Sam was close enough to count the heartbeats in Bella's throat. "It loses some of its punch."

Her gaze met his.

Holding it, he took that last critical step, the one that brought him within reach of all the wonder that made her the woman she was. He rested his index finger on that frantically pounding pulse. "You're not scared of me, are you?"

Her tongue lashed her lips, leaving them moist and trembling. "No."

"Then why the backing up?"

She jumped, glanced behind her then back at him.

"You know I wouldn't hurt you, Bella."

Her palm on his chest was warm and soft, very feminine in the delicacy with which she claimed him. "I know this."

He lifted her into his arms and knelt, taking them both to the softness of the bedroll, coming down over her, catching his weight on his forearms, smiling into her eyes. "So why the nerves?"

Her hands opened against his chest, not caressing, not pressing, just resting there as if she were measuring his response. "I want so much for tonight to be what you want."

"This is just me, Bella, loving on you. Nothing big."

She rolled her eyes. "You are the biggest thing I know, Sam."

He moved a strand of hair off the corner of her mouth, tenderness welling. She wasn't afraid of anything. "You can handle me."

His reward was a return of the bad-angel smile. Her palms stroked his muscles and that smile he loved dimpled her cheeks as she arched in invitation. "Yes. I think I can."

Gathering up her skirt, he tucked his hand beneath, finding shockingly bare skin, riding the discovery upward to the soft hair covering her mound. The springing curls immediately wrapped around his fingers. He gave a little tug. The pupils of her eyes dilated and her breath hitched in a sexy moan. He leaned in, catching the end of the soft sigh in his mouth.

"Sweet."

Her lids drifted shut as her mouth flowered beneath his, opening slightly, teasing him with her flavor, daring him to take more. He did, bringing his hand up to her jaw, squeezing until she obeyed the command, holding her in that position, open and helpless until she moaned again, straining in his hands. Only then did he kiss her, tangling his tongue with hers, stroking the sides, teasing the sensitive inner lining of her lips before sucking her tongue into his mouth, drawing on her flesh, her spirit. Willing her to give in. She did with an inarticulate cry and a twisting of her torso.

"See, that's all you need to do, Bella, to make this perfect. Just let me see who you are, how I'm making you feel."

"You make me feel so much."

The sweet scent of her arousal drew his touch. She was wet and swollen. Eager. "Ah, duchess, this is one hungry little pussy."

"What do you expect when you flaunt yourself before me for days?"

Another chuckle. "Not much else, I guess."

He squeezed and she jumped. When her hips came back down he pressed up with the heel of his hand against the point of her pouting clit, rubbing gently as he tested the tightness of her sheath with one finger.

"Sam!"

"Right here."

He pressed again and her head thrashed from side to side as her hips shoved up into the newness of the sensation. He kissed her cheek, the corner of her eye….

"Do that again."

If he did it again she'd come and he wasn't ready for her to come. "Not yet."

Her fist collided with his back, dislodging a smile. "I cannot wait."

"You will."

Her hands waved in the air for a second, finally settling on his shoulder. The heat of her touch burned through his shirt. He wanted all that silken heat against him. He tugged on the waistband of her skirt. "Lift up."

She did. He worked the skirt off her hips. Her thighs fell open. Pearls of moisture caught on her dark curls, reflecting the glow of the fire. Beyond, the swollen folds of her pussy beckoned with a different kind of fire. Holding her gaze, he parted her folds, settling two fingers into the well of her vagina. She shivered, her lips catching between her teeth.

"You're beautiful, Bella."

"So are you."

"Men aren't beautiful."

Passion deepened the husk in her voice. "You are."

Shifting his weight onto his forearm, Sam eased his fingers in, watching her soft pink flesh take him to the first knuckle, stopping when she gasped and clenched. "Easy."

"I am too small." It was almost a wail.

"No, you're just new to this." Her clit, sitting high and swollen, stretched toward him, begging for attention. Her scent surrounded him, clean and fresh like spring, full of potential just waiting to be unleashed.

Sam couldn't wait to set her free. To feel all that passion raining down on him, breaking over his cock. He wanted her with nothing between them. Not the past. Not the future. Not her fears or anyone's expectations. He wanted the way she always was, full of hope and positive thought. He wanted her to remember tonight with a smile.

He touched her clit with his tongue, just a bare whisper of sensation across the turgid tip. Just enough to taunt the fire that burned so brightly in her. Her high-pitched cry echoed around him. Pinning her hips with his forearm, he settled deeper between her thighs. "I'm going to taste you now, Bella...."

"I will come if you do."

"No—" he lifted her right ankle over his shoulder "—you won't." Skimming his hand down the outside of her left leg, he lifted that ankle, too. "You're going to enjoy what I do to you, but you won't come. Not until I give you permission."

"Who are you to tell me this?"

"Your lover."

The declaration hung between them, ripe with implication. Testing her readiness with another pulse of his fingers, keeping her gaze locked to his, he suckled her clit lightly, a mere breeze of the caress he wanted to paint on her swollen flesh before kissing the tip, stroking her thighs when she jerked. She shoved her hand between her vulva and his mouth. Circling her wrists with his fingers, he slid his thumb between her mound and his palm. "Trust me, Bella."

Tenderness suffused lust as she hesitated, a stutter in the trust she was giving him, but then she let him enfold her much smaller hand in his, her fingers weaving through his the same way her faith wove through the relentless tide of lust surging through him, gentling it to a manageable level that stayed just short of mindless.

He smiled and nipped her clit, holding her as the shock went through her in a wave of sensation mirrored in the undulating tensing and relaxing of her inner muscles. A fine sheen of sweat burnished her skin.

"Tell me what you want."

The flush on her cheek intensified. He might be pushing her too hard, but then she shook her hair out of her eyes and rose to his challenge, meeting his gaze, his desire with her own. "I need your…cock in me. Please, Sam."

He could give her that. With a last swirl of his tongue over her pert little clit, he eased his fingers from her tight channel and positioned himself between her thighs. His shadow covered her, blocking the light from her eyes. "Put your arms around my neck and hold on."

She did what he ordered without hesitating. Trusting him. Sam gritted his teeth against the need to take her hard to drive deep as she kicked off the remains of her skirt, almost unmanning him in the process, but then he was holding her, skin to skin, heartbeat to heartbeat. Emotion rolled over him in a stampede. All his life he'd denied himself this, and now it was here, and he'd allowed himself only this one night. This one night before Bella moved on to the life she should have. Heaven and hell wrapped up under one sky.

"Please, Sam."

It was that second *please* that did him in. Isabella so rarely said please, it sounded almost like begging, re-minding him that for all her talk and honesty, this was new to her and she was uncertain. He didn't want her begging in his bed. He wanted her wild and hungry, but not begging.

"You can have whatever you want from me, Bella. No pleases. Just tell me what it is."

I want you to love me.

Isabella froze.

Por Dios, had she said that out loud? She hadn't meant to. Hadn't even known the stupid hope had lingered through all her efforts to bury it. Sam was still staring at her, his blue eyes deep with the passion so elemental to his personality. Still waiting for an answer.

She closed her eyes on a sigh of relief. She had only thought the revelation. Isabella twisted her grip tighter in Sam's hair. "Make me feel good. Better than I've ever felt before."

She didn't expect him to be thrown off by the challenge, and he wasn't. He laughed, kissed her and slid down, nibbling on her neck, her collarbone, the upper swell of her breast as he went, leaving a trail of flames in his wake, so many it felt as if her skin was on fire. She gasped as his lips skimmed the valley of her breast, the softness of her stomach, the point of her pubic bone, the top of her mound.

His eyes met hers, sharp, hot and intense as his tongue nestled under the lip of her vulva and curled around her clit. Heat, fire, shock flared through her system in a breath-stealing combination. Her channel clenched. She pushed her hips up into the press of his mouth, gasping breathlessly when he lashed her with his tongue, the totality of his possession pulling an invisible thread in her spine, arching her into an offering for more. More of his touch, his play. More of whatever he wanted.

She'd been primed for too long. Needed him too much. He might think she would find joy in a safe life, because he refused to see her, but she knew differently. He was what she'd always searched for, why she would never settle for the men and the life her parents pushed toward her. He was her nemesis. Her salvation. Her hope.

The delight of his tongue on her heated flesh was unparalleled, driving through the fear of surrendering, burning so deep it branded her anew. Sam's. She was Sam's. Her womb clenched on the bliss of his fingers parting the tight muscles of her sheath, clamped down on this moment, wanting to preserve it, not wanting it to end.

His purr of satisfaction ratcheted the knot tighter, the need higher.

"Sam?"

She needed release, needed to come, but just when she reached the edge, just when she was about to shatter in climax, he backed off, sprinkling tender sweet kisses across her pussy, surrounding her clit with warmth, tenderness and care, everything but what she needed—the hard touch that would send her hurtling over the edge.

"What?"

"I am going to kill you."

His husky laugh was just one more incentive to carry through the threat.

"No, you're not." One long, lingering swipe of his tongue and he was kissing his way back up her body the same way he'd gone down. As if they had all the time in the world. "You're going to come for me. Long and hard, all around my cock."

He pressed his mouth so hard against her throat she could feel his teeth. Another shudder went through her. One more shift of those gorgeous muscles and he was covering her, his big body sheltering her from reality.

"Like I've dreamed of," he finished on a growl of anticipation.

The blankets by her head rustled as he adjusted his weight on his forearm. Shadows swirled over the passion in his eyes as he kicked off his boots and his pants. Shadows she recognized because she lived with them herself. It was comforting to know he was also plagued with what-ifs.

"Tonight, if you dream with me…" She reached up, curled her palm over the hard muscle of his shoulder, her thumb settling into the indent of an old scar. So many wounds, so many scars, the new ones earned defending her. "You will be happy."

His eyes glittered down at her. "You're the one who's going to be happy."

She grinned at him, letting him take them back to comfortable ground. "Then you must make me pant."

"Oh, you'll definitely pant, but..." The kiss he pressed on her lips was hard, more of a statement than a caress. "Not until I tell you to."

Her soul picked up the shiver that had started in her body and ran with it. As much as she tried to suppress her nature, she couldn't change it, and when Sam took charge, there was only joy inside.

His cock nudged her pussy, nestling into the well created for him. "That little shiver mean you approve?"

She gasped as he pressed in, bold and intimidating. She braced her other palm on his chest. "Yes."

"I'll do my best not to hurt you, Bella." His palm turned her face to his. "You know that."

She blinked, then realized even as her sex flowered to his thrust, that she was pushing him away. Hard. She took a breath. The cool silk of his hair brushed her cheek. His lips followed quickly. "Do you want to stop?"

She heard in his voice how much it cost him to offer that. She also knew why he did. Sam was not a man who easily hurt those he cared about. And he cared about her, even though he fought her. She shook her head. "No. I want to know what it is like to hold your body within mine. Very much."

His hips flexed spasmodically, and his breath raced over her skin. "Damn, Bella, you can't say things like that when I'm trying to be easy."

She arched a little, taking a little more, feeling the wonder as her body strained to accept his possession.

"Maybe easy is not right between us."

The muscles in his throat worked as he swallowed against the need she could feel pulsing within him. He was such a good man who saw himself very wrong. So much so he could not see the truth.

She opened her mouth to argue more, but his covered it, cutting off what she wanted to say with a stroke of his tongue and an invite to kiss him back—which she did until she was clinging to him and he was supporting her, with his hands, his body, the softness of his words.

"I know you have worries. Big worries in your mind that hold you back, so why don't you give them to me and let me take care of them tonight?"

"What worries?" she asked suspiciously.

He smiled the softest smile she'd ever seen on his face and traced her mouth with his thumb. "Your breasts aren't too big, your spirit isn't too wild, your sense of humor isn't inappropriate." The way he cradled her cheek was at once protective and possessive, the light in his eyes so much more. "You're perfect, Bella. You're sweet, giving and courageous, and any man lucky enough to be the center of your attention should drop to his knees and thank his lucky stars."

She sighed and snuggled into his strength, bringing her legs up around his hips, a little of her nervousness slipping away. He did sweet very well.

He kissed her again, softly, coaxingly. Ah, she loved his kisses. The downward press of his hips stole some of her bliss. He was very wide, the moment very intimate, made more so by the intimacy of having him see her take him this time, this way. As her muscles parted for the intimate burn of acceptance, she gasped.

He stopped, not in her but not totally apart. His fingers threaded through hers, pinning them back down beside her head.

"Just a little trust, Bella. That's all you need."

The fact that she had a death grip on his hands did not keep him from working his palms under her head. He just took her hands with him. The brush of his lips across her eyelashes tickled. One of his hands freed itself from hers. It skimmed her cheek, her breast, her side before settling on her hip. His thumb eased between her curls, finding the nub of her clitoris as his lips settled over hers. The pressure of his cock increased. So did the burn. "So sweet, I need more."

"I think I have changed my mind."

Tucking his cock tighter against her, he stroked his tongue over her lips, tickling the corners so she gasped, spiking her passion with slow circles of his thumb, then sliding past the barrier, filling her mouth with his heat. His taste. Not demanding as she'd expected, but more coaxing. His tongue leisurely tangled with hers, again as if there was nothing more urgent going on than a kiss. But there was and the proof of it prodded her in time with his pulse.

She pulled her mouth free. "Sam…"

His "Shh" faded to the quiet of breath against her

cheek. Sensation between pleasure and pain had her scrunch up her neck. His laugh chased the shiver down her spine. The touch of his tongue inspired another shiver that ended in a clench of her pussy against his cock.

"Sweet." A pause for another kiss and then, "Just relax and let me in, duchess."

The familiar endearment buffeted her fears, shaking a few clear of their moorings. His mouth worked over her neck, nibbling, kissing, lapping, finding the most sensitive spot at the curve of her shoulder and neck and then lingering. His cock worked deeper. Pleasure rose on a wave of rapture, overriding the pain, lifting her hips into his thrust.

"No. Stay still. Just let me do this, nice and easy."

Another thrust. Inside, something gave with a breath-stealing flare of agony. She cried out and shoved at his shoulders. He didn't back off, just held her through the erotic first, holding her while she struggled with the reality of penetration. She had taken Sam into her body. She was no longer a virgin. There was no going back. Digging her nails into his shoulders, she arched her hips up, taking more, needing the reaffirmation that it was really happening.

"Thank you."

The softest of kisses touched her mouth. "I believe that's my line, and you're about ten minutes early with the delivery."

"I don't care."

"I do."

Within her his cock flexed. She braced herself for the pain. "No, don't tense up."

His drawl was deep and slow, adding another layer to the seductive spell he wove so effortlessly.

"You are part of me."

"Hell, yes."

His hips pulsed. His cock pressed impossibly deeper, felt impossibly bigger. "Relax. You can take all of me."

There was no way she could take more. He was too big. She was built too small, but still she could not deny him. Not with her body, her heart, her soul, which hungered to be everything he needed.

The slow pass of his fingers over her clit sent a shiver down her spine. The next pass reflected it back, and the third amplified it until the burn of desire flared higher than the burn of possession.

"That's it." His thighs spread hers wider, his cock nudged deeper. "Feel how good it's going to be."

Desire returned, softly at first, riding her wonder, her need to please, skating the edges of his touch until it found a foothold in the wonder. Returning with a vengeance as his cock rubbed against a certain spot inside. Stronger than before, as if it really had not gone away, but rather just lain in wait for the pain to fade.

As if he knew what was happening inside her, Sam growled, "Put your hands behind your head."

She did.

"Lace your fingers together."

She had to untangle them from her hair to do that.

A hard kiss on her mouth indicated the approval she could see in his expression.

"Present your breasts."

The order fell into the accelerated cadence of her breathing, driving it higher. She followed his command, inching her shoulders back as she arched her spine, presenting her breasts for his pleasure.

"Hold it right there."

There was an almost painful arch that shifted her hips down onto his cock the slightest bit. As he slid forward, along with the burn came an incredible bolt of sensation she wasn't braced for. It shot up into her center, twisted as he worked his cock back, straightening out as he worked his big cock back in, splitting her desire into separate camps, one begging for slow, the other cheering for hard.

"Stay arched."

This time his voice was deeper, hoarser. A quick glance at his face revealed why. His gaze was focused on her breasts. She stiffened her spine, the move bringing her clit in contact with the short strokes of his cock, her breasts closer to his mouth.

"Oh!"

She didn't know what was hotter, the exquisite sensation of his cock, slick with her juices, sliding along her sensitive flesh as he filled her hungry sheath, or the passion-tight expression on his face as he watched her breasts shimmy while he worked deeper and deeper within her. Her moan was involuntary. Her lips parted for his kiss, her vagina for his possession.

"Yes."

Hoarse and dark, his approval fanned the flames of her surrender. The impulse to squirm was almost as irresistible as the one to bear down. The first she resisted, but the second she indulged. Squeezing with her inner muscles, holding Sam to her with everything she had. His cock jumped in her tight grip. "Do that again and this won't last as long as I'd planned."

Oh, she liked the sound of that, liked knowing she could do this for him. For herself.

Those sharp eyes raked her face as she smiled, then they narrowed and he swore before closing them completely and arching his back, spearing his cock deep to her center. "Fuck."

It was too much. He was too much. She shuddered as he pressed against her, the wiry hair on his groin rasping over her already sensitized clit, adding fire to the burn before pulling out and working back in, every wiggle, every inch a hard-won victory of persistence over resistance. Friction over glide. The tension built. Her world dissolved to the focal point of his cock in her pussy and the burning pleasure of his possession. This was good. So good.

Her breath broke on sobs she couldn't control. Her reserve broke on control she couldn't maintain. She was so close. So close. As if sensing her need, Sam palmed her hips in his big hands, the bite of his fingers in her

buttocks just one more sensual assault on her frag-
mented nerves.

"Let it happen, duchess. Let yourself come for me."

For me. Over and over the words played in her brain,
mutating out of perspective, taking on a higher note.
Yes, she wanted to come. For her. For him. Especially for
him. Fixing her gaze on Sam's face, she let herself see
only him, feel only the way he made her feel. No fear.
No worries. She arched her back farther, defiantly, challenging him to take her higher, silently encouraging
Sam to hurry. Adding a verbal plea to the one howling
inside when he slowed his pace to a tease. "Hurry."

"We've got plenty of time."

She shook her head so hard, his face blurred to a
streak of colors. "I need you to come now." Before she
could think of all the ways this could end, all the ways
it could go wrong.

She squeezed hard with her inner muscles as he
pulled out, gasped with relief when he swore and jack-
hammered back in. He was losing control. That was
good. She wanted him as wild as she was.

"Bella…"

Ignoring the growl of warning, she did it again and
again until the sheen of sweat glistened on Sam's skin
and his lips pulled back from his teeth in a feral growl.
With a growl of her own, she dragged herself up and
bit him—hard—on his left pectoral, the salty tang of his
skin spreading over her tongue in an exhilarating spice
as he surged against her.

"Damn you!" His grip was as furious as his expression as he rode her hard, as if he wanted to leave a mark, prove his ownership. *O Dios*, she wanted him to mark her. Isabella clung to that fantasy, imagining the possibilities as she drove her hips up into his, chasing completion. With a thrust that had her breasts bouncing, he ground against her. "Come for me."

She wanted to. She strained to. His hand came between them. His thumb covered her clit, centered her with an easy rub, commanded her with a firm pinch, and then there was no holding back. There was just a terrifying feeling of shattering as the violent pleasure sent her hurtling over an unseen edge. She screamed for Sam, heard his echoing shout and then his arms were tight around her, anchoring her as the pleasure continued as he thrust once, twice and then with a hoarse shout of her name, he shuddered, his cock jerking within her, finding the twinges of her climax and bringing them back to life.

And then just as suddenly he jerked out, leaving her bereft, as the heavy weight of his cock landed on her stomach and warm liquid bathed her skin. His seed. She arched into the next splash, gasping at the third as he nipped at her neck, husked his pleasure in her ear.

She held him, stretching out the pleasure, her pussy clenching in sympathetic ecstasy with each jerk of his cock until the spasms lessened, until his chest relaxed against hers, unable to let go, unable to let it end.

Sam rained butterfly kisses over her face. The heat

of his hand enfolded her breast, soothing the remnants of hunger rippling through her.

"Sweet… You are so sweet."

Another shudder of his big body drew her hands to the sculpted perfection of his back. She traced the rise and hollow of his muscles as he took his ease with her body, sweat making his flesh glisten. Her forearms appeared very white against the dark of his tanned skin, highlighting more than ever the differences between them. Differences she loved.

His hand dropped to her stomach, covering the warm weight of his seed. He shifted to his side, watching as he massaged it into her skin, smoothing his hand up to her breast, scooping a bit more to coat her nipples. Marking her. She turned so his palm covered her nipple, his seed and their sweat sealing them together, flesh to flesh.

He glanced up, that strange intensity still in his eyes. "Are you all right?"

"I am very fine."

"Good." The brush of his thumb over her nipple jerked her high against him, her breath stealing from her in quick bursts as he did it again. There was no mistaking the mischief in his eyes as he murmured her name.

"What?"

"You're panting."

So she was. And he was gloating. She hummed, kissed his chest and smiled.

"I bet you cannot make me do it again."

14

The attack came before dawn. Kell's warning growl jerked Sam from a sound sleep. He shoved Isabella out of his arms and off the bedroll, taking the knife thrust to his shoulder instead of his chest. Agony screamed through his arm. He clamped it off with a ruthless surge of cold anger.

Whipping around, Sam blocked the next blow, grasping his assailant's arm and jerking down, using the man's momentum to knock him off his feet. Kell came flying in, teeth gnashing, instinctively going for the man's throat. While he was finishing the job, Sam leapt to a crouch, scooping up his gun belt and slinging it over his good shoulder. His revolver slid easily from the holster and into his hand.

"Playtime."

He cocked the hammer and took a shot at movement in the shadows ten feet away. There was the sound of a bullet hitting flesh and the shadow dropped. Sam sprang to his feet, casting a glance to the side. Isabella lay where he'd shoved her, eyes big, clutching the blanket to her breasts. She was still in shock. "Kell, guard."

The big dog took a position just to the right of Bella. Sam nodded. Across the fire, another shadow flitted from right to left. *Shit.*

Grabbing Bella by the arm, he drew her up and shoved her over the fallen tree that had served as his seat last night. "Lie flat and don't move."

He needed to know where she was. In the predawn, everything was a shadow. Shooting at the wrong one could cost them all. Twigs snapped and boots scraped across rock as their attackers found new positions. Dropping into the shadow of the rock wall he circled 'round, drawing the gunfire away from Bella's hiding place.

Kell whined. Sam motioned him back with a sharp gesture. As best he could tell, there were still three men out there. They had the trees for cover, but they'd have to stay at the edge to get in a shot. One of the reasons he'd selected this site was the rock wall behind and the drop in front. It gave him the advantage. Something he always appreciated.

A bullet winged over his head, pinging off the rock. Sharp splinters stung his cheek just below his eye. He fired back in the direction of the flash, knowing he wouldn't hit. Running along the wall, he tracked the positions of the men by the noise they made. The fact that only an occasional bullet came his way was telling. They were after Bella. He smiled, grim confidence blending in with his rage. He could work with that.

The end of the rock wall was a little more than a slit between the gray of the rock and darkness of the forest. He eased in cautiously, the hairs on the back of his neck standing in warning. Someone was close. Pressing his shoulders to the rough bark of a tree, he wrapped his gun belt around his waist. Leather glided through the buckle with only the slightest of sounds. He popped the bullets out of their pockets and, making no noise, reloaded the well-oiled gun. The same couldn't be said about the man who stalked him.

A twig snapped a couple feet away. Sam eased the chamber closed. Brush rustled in a hushed betrayal. Whoever it was was just on the other side of the tree. Sam reached for his knife. It wasn't in the sheath. Shit. Only one person could have taken it. Bella.

I won't live with his touch on my skin.

Fuck!

The rank stench of stale sweat reached him first followed quickly by the unmistakable sound of a shoulder brushing bark. Sam smiled. Nice of the outlaw to make it easy for him. In a near silent move, he stepped around the tree trunk.

A man dressed in black jumped back. *"Hijo de la—!"*

He never got to finish the curse. Yanking him forward into the force of his blow, Sam hit him in the windpipe before shoving him back. The man stumbled, arms flailing. The hilt of a knife protruded from the waist-band of his pants. Perfect. Diving in, Sam landed on the man's torso, pinning his arms with his knees. The outlaw's gun discharged harmlessly to the right. The man was strong and resourceful. Sam only had a few seconds. Covering his mouth with his hand, he reached back and grabbed the knife.

"Did you get him, Ricco?" The call came from the other side of the clearing.

Sam met the other man's gaze squarely, rage burning hot inside, and placed the blade across his throat. "Tell your companions 'Yes.' Nothing more."

The man swallowed. Sam pressed the blade in. A line of red immediately spread along the sharp edge. With a glare, the outlaw shouted, *"Sí!"*

"Good. Then you can come help us with this one."

"She's naked and ready," another called.

Sam slapped his hand over the son of a bitch's mouth, grinding the heel into the man's chin as he informed him, "Bella is Hell's Eight."

Understanding widened the man's eyes in fear and understanding that came too late.

"More than that," Sam snarled, letting the rage loose, "she's mine."

Blood sprayed in a hot red splash against his cheek as he drew the knife across the man's throat, ending his life in one quick slash. Too quick. This man had come for Bella. Not to kill her, but the life he'd planned on delivering her to? That would have murdered the joy that shone so brightly within her. For that he deserved a long torturous death. Sam wiped the blade clean on the man's shirt. It galled him to no end he hadn't given it.

Pushing to his feet, Sam put the knife in the sheath on his belt before blending back into the shadows. Moving quickly and carefully through the woods, he circled around to Bella's position, determination rising with every step. None of them would touch her. Ever. When he got done cleaning this mess up, he was going to get her settled back in her home, and then he was going after Tejala and when he was done with him, there wouldn't be enough left of the son of a bitch to even be a shadow on her memory.

Kell's low snarl pulled him to the edge of the tiny clearing. Dawn shed its weak light over everything, lending substance to what had been shaded. The two other men had Bella's position flanked. She stood naked behind the felled tree, her hair hanging in an obscuring shield about her torso, back braced against the wall, head up, the knife in her hand. Kell was in front of her, head down, lips pulled back in a menacing growl. The only thing keeping the men from shooting the dog was the fact that any bullet aimed at him might hit Bella. Which meant Sam had about two seconds before they changed positions and that obstacle was removed. No time for finesse.

He cleared the trees with a roar, filling the morning calm with the Hell's Eight battle cry, running across the clearing with guns drawn. The men whirled. His first shot hit square. The man on the left spun around on impact and went down. The man on the right brought his gun up. Not at Sam but at Bella.

Son of a bitch. "Take 'im, Kell!"

The wolf sprang into action, all flashing teeth and raking claws. His jaws clamped down on the bandit's arm. The man screamed again and fired. Isabella screamed and dropped.

"Bella!"

No answer. Kell yelped and held on. The outlaw whirled, struggling to get the gun to his good hand. Kell spun with him. Sam jerked the barrel up in the nick of time to avoid shooting Kell. The outlaw put the gun against Kell's side.

The dog was a sitting duck. Knowing it was too late even as he gave the order, Sam hollered, "Down, Kell."

The dog didn't listen. He snarled and leapt in again, biting and slashing, going for the arm that stuck out in a deliberate lure, not understanding the trick.

Shit.

Sam worked to the side. He couldn't get a clear shot at the outlaw and he couldn't bring himself to risk shooting the damn dog. He'd be lucky at this rate if he didn't get them all killed.

For one instant, Sam had a clear shot. He squeezed the trigger. There was a wild scream from Isabella and she threw herself onto the outlaw and directly in the path of his shot.

Sam yanked his arm up, and the bullet went high. The cold wave of nausea at almost shooting her didn't pass as easily.

He ran in. "Damn it, Bella! Get out of there."

She didn't answer. The outlaw stumbled backward under the force of her weight and Kell's attack. Further away from him.

Isabella's hand came up. Steel flashed in the dim light. The outlaw's gun went off. Kell crumpled to the ground, his snarls abruptly silenced. The outlaw fell too, taking Isabella with him, trapping her beneath him. Blood spread outward from where they landed.

"Bella!"

Goddamn, if she'd gotten herself shot he was going to kill her. Sam didn't breathe, wasn't even sure his heart beat for the five seconds it took to get to her. He dragged the bandit off, heaving him to the side. When he looked back, Isabella was staring at him, eyes big in her blood-smeared face. She was alive. He released the breath he wasn't aware he'd been holding.

"Son of a bitch! I told you to stay put."

She didn't even blink. Her mouth worked. Her eyes grew moist.

"Don't you dare cry, woman, I'm mad as hell at you."

And he wanted to stay that way.

Anger replaced shock. "Do not tell me what to do!"

"Then don't damn well cry."

She glared back at him, tears hovering but not falling, her beautiful skin covered obscenely in blood. First chance he got he was giving her a bath. He held out his hand. "Are you hurt?"

"No." She rolled over, flinching away from the man's corpse, arching to see Kell. Sam followed her gaze. The dog was lying where he'd fallen, not moving.

"Kell. *Dios mio!* Kell!"

Sam reached for her shoulder. "Let me go first."

He didn't know what he could do, the aggravating mutt was probably dying if not already dead, but if there was a way to protect Bella from it, any of it, he wanted to. She shrugged out from under his arm. There was no stopping her. She scrambled over to the dog, sinking her hands into his bloody fur, murmuring to him soft words in Spanish as she searched and found the first wound, crying out as if she'd taken the bullet herself, searching some more until she found the next, crying out again...

Sam came up beside the dog. He was still alive. In his eyes, Sam could see his pain and his devotion. His plea for help. It was a punch in the gut. He didn't have what it took to save the dog. He wasn't a doctor, wasn't much of anything. Grief washed over him. He pushed it back as he did with all emotion, focusing on what the dog needed to hear rather than on what he wanted. "You did good, Kell."

Kell wagged his tail, the thumps slow and uneven. In the dog's eyes, Sam saw the understanding. He was reading the goodbye in his voice. So was Isabella.

Her gaze narrowed. "You will not talk in goodbyes."

"He's hurt too badly, Bella."

"You will help him."

He'd give anything right then to have the power to grant life and death. To give Bella what she wanted. To reward the dog that was his friend with a merciful death, but he couldn't. It always came down to that with the ones he loved. Choices he couldn't live with but he had to make anyway. "I'm not a doctor, Bella. Killing's what I'm good at."

Turning on his heel he went back to his bedroll and picked up his rifle. He could feel Bella's stare like an ever growing weight. When he turned around, she was still kneeling beside the dog, glaring at him. She was so young. He picked up the blanket and brought it to her. She didn't say a word, just stared at him, her expression a mix of disbelief and anger. He wrapped the blanket around her shoulders.

"Where do you go?"

"I need to go make sure this was all of them."

She nodded. "Go. We will be fine without you."

His temper caught up with his emotions. Did she think this was easy for him?

"One of these days, little girl, I'm going to stop humoring you and you're going to find out who wears the pants in this relationship."

Maybe she did have a sense of caution after all, or maybe he just looked in that moment like the mean son of a bitch he was, because instead of arguing, Isabella merely lifted her chin and glared. He turned and left.

Before he did something they'd both eventually regret. Like pull her into his arms and show her what it really meant to be his woman.

Isabella hugged the blanket to her and watched him go, confident always, the broad set of his shoulders projecting his strength, hiding his pain.

Little girl.

He had been right to call her *la niña.* She had behaved like a child, focusing on her emotions, her wants, ignoring his. Sam loved Kell as much as she did. Probably more. Because he didn't show it didn't mean he didn't feel it.

She needed to remember that in times when she was emotional as well as times when she was happy. Sam had too many scars when it came to where he loved to be obvious about how he felt, covering with laughter or silence, but he felt. Deeply. The image of him coming out of the woods on a run, deadly powerful, wild, his muscles glistening with sweat as he attacked the men who threatened her. She stroked her hands over Kell's head. Sam was a very brave man when it came to sacrificing his life for others. Very brave.

Killing's what I'm good at.

She glanced around at the corpses and agreed. He was very good at killing. What he didn't seem so sure about was his skill at loving. Kell whined and licked her hand. "Do not worry, *mi amigo.* We will fix you, and then maybe—" She shrugged and smiled. "Maybe you and I will teach Sam how to live."

Kell whined again. "*Sí,* it will not be easy, but he is very worth it."

From the lick he gave her hand, she assumed he agreed. She patted his head again. "To fix you we need to leave here, which means I must prepare. I cannot sit here like a bulge on a log and leave all the work and worry to Sam. This would not make me much of a partner."

Kell wagged his tail. She smiled at him, suppressing the tears that burned her eyes as she saw once again all the blood. "Do not worry. I will not let you die. It is not how one thanks another for saving their life."

She would not let Kell die for that reason...and for one other. She'd seen the way Sam looked at Kell in that split second before she'd demanded he fix things. Like his heart was being ripped away from his soul. Like he couldn't take another loss. She'd also seen the guilt that came after. He blamed himself. She shook her head and walked over to the man she'd killed. Sometimes Sam was not sensible.

She stared at the man. He did not look so scary now. She should feel guilty. Her mortal soul was in jeopardy. But she did not. This man was evil. He had tried to kill the ones she loved. She would forgive him eventually for the attempt—her God demanded that—but she would never regret putting an end to his attempt.

Forgiveness, however, wasn't going to help her with what she needed to do. She needed the knife. It stuck up from where she'd buried it in the curve where the outlaw's shoulder met his neck. She reached for it. Her stomach rose. Kell moaned. She bit her lip and forced the nausea back. Sam would not hesitate. He would just do what needed to be done. So would she.

The blade grated against bone as she pulled it out. She felt the vibration all the way up her arm. It was more than her stomach could take. The second the knife came free, she turned and vomited. There was nothing in her stomach to lose but the nausea didn't care.

"I do not think I will make a good bandit," she told Kell breathlessly as she grabbed a stick from the small pile by the remains of the fire.

Stirring the ashes, she found a few viable coals. She nurtured them to flame with slow breaths and tiny pieces of grass. To that she added twigs and then bigger sticks. Inside, impatience whispered, "Hurry, hurry." The flame took its own sweet time catching. Inside her the urgency grew at a much faster pace.

Kell was bleeding to death. She did not have time for dawdling fires. Finally, the flame bloomed high enough to take the few logs left over from last night. She tossed them on. She didn't have time to watch to see if they caught. Glancing at the sky, she grabbed up her petticoat from the pile of clothes. "This I leave to you. Make it burn."

"I don't think you're supposed to give God orders."

Sam. He was back and he had that easy smile that meant nothing on his face. The one that hid what he really felt. She sighed. Her task might be harder than she thought.

She stood, gathering up her knife and petticoat. "I would not presume to tell God what to do."

He glanced at the knife in her hand and frowned. "Where'd you get that?"

She motioned to the dead outlaw. "From him."

"Jesus, Bella."

If she hadn't been watching carefully, she would have missed the guilt that flashed in his eyes, it came and went that quickly. He was very good at hiding his emotions.

"It was necessary. I can do what is necessary."

"That's not the kind of thing a woman should have experience with."

"It is the kind your woman would need."

"You're not my woman."

She rolled her eyes. "You begin to bore me with these words all the time." She held his gaze as she walked up to him until her breasts pressed against his bare chest through the blanket. Switching the knife and petticoat to one hand, she slid the other over his uninjured shoulder, curving it around the back of his neck, pulling him down. He bent, not touching her, giving her what she wanted up to a point like he always did. His eyes searched hers, his gaze empty. When his mouth was a scant breath from hers, she whispered, "I am sorry, my Sam, for my words. I do not always think before I speak, and sometimes the words I say paint a picture other than the truth."

He breathed in, hopefully taking her words deep to

the part of him that hurt so maybe the wound she'd caused could heal.

His "You were right" held no emotion.

She shook her head, holding tightly to him, not letting him pull back. Kissing the corner of his mouth, she whispered, "I felt very helpless, and I thought giving orders could fix things. But I did not say the things I wanted to say. They were stuck inside."

"Like what?"

Like I love you.

She couldn't say that right now. She was beginning to understand him. Sam could deal with emotion as long as he could create safe spaces for it. Such a blunt declaration would not fit neatly in a safe place.

She kissed him lightly. He didn't respond. He was being very stubborn. "It scared me when you disappeared into the dark. I could not see if you needed me."

His fingers sank into her hair, ruthlessly holding her gaze to his. "The one place I will never need you is in the middle of battle."

She could have taken that as an insult. She didn't. "Because you want me safe."

The tension in him increased. A tremble started in his hand. "Yes."

The hardness of his erection pressed against her as she leaned against it. She cuddled it into the softness of her stomach. "I must have scared you very much when I protected Kell."

She couldn't bring herself to say "stabbed that man."

"Hell, yes." He shook her. "I almost shot you."

The tension in him was near the breaking point. He would need to release it soon or it would become another scar inside he didn't need.

She looked at him innocently. "This means I was very bad?"

He frowned and growled. "Very."

She dropped her head as if ashamed. "I am sorry."

Immediately his hand came to her shoulder. A concession because for all his growling he was very soft when it came to those he cared for. Not comfortable when they were upset.

"Then maybe, after we get Kell comfortable—" she touched just below the nasty cut on his upper arm "—and your wound is tended, you had better spank me." She looked at him from under her lashes, the way that always made the desire burn in his eyes. At the last second she decided to add a little wiggle. "So I remember not to make the mistake again, *si?*"

Shock, desire and something she couldn't identify flashed across his expression.

"Fuck."

And then she couldn't see anything except the deep tan of his skin as he drew her so hard to him she thought her bones would snap. Above her head he snarled, "Count on it."

His cheek pressed to her head, Sam held her as if he was never letting her go, his breath coming first in ragged jerks and then in carefully measured draws as he slowly regained the control he held so dear. And she said nothing. Letting him take what he needed, understanding for him this was a big thing. He did not do so well with needing. When the calm returned to him she whispered, "Sam?"

His lips brushed over her hair in the gentleness he always gave her when he was in control. "Yeah?"

"We have things to do."

His chin slid along her hair as he glanced over at Kell. "I know."

He sounded so sad as he let her go. "I'll take care of it."

She pulled the blanket around her as he walked over to the dog and squatted down beside him. She couldn't hear the words he said, but she recognized the gentle murmur for what it was. An expression of love. She took the knife over to the fire. It was burning brightly. A positive sign. She glanced up as she knelt. "Thank you."

She placed the knife blade in the fire before looking over at Sam. He was still talking to Kell, his arms resting across his knees. The only sign of how upset he was lay in the curl of his fingers. He was just short of making a fist. She reached for the petticoats, judging how big a bandage to tear.

As she watched, Sam reached out and stroked the dog's shoulder before moving up to his ruff. His fingers clenched in the thick fur and there was a flinch around his eyes before he shifted his hand up to the dog's head.

Kell turned on a pained whine and licked his wrist. Sam swore. Kell dropped his head back. Before it could hit the ground, Sam caught it and eased him down the last inch, keeping the dog from hurting himself in his weakness. Isabella smiled. He was a good man. He would make a good father—playful, watchful, loving.

With a grimace Sam sat back. He petted the panting dog, regret and apology in every stroke of his hand. With a sigh, he put his hand over the dog's eyes. With another he reached back to his holster. Isabella watched in complete disbelief as he placed the muzzle against the dog's big head. His "I'm sorry, boy" came clearly to her.

She leapt to her feet. "Stop!"

Sam looked over at her, his expression one of grim resolution. "Look away, Bella."

"I will not."

"He's in pain."

She threw the petticoats at him. "So are you."

A rock would have been better. The petticoat merely flew two feet before drifting to the ground. She stepped over them. "Yet you do not see me with a gun to your head."

He looked at the petticoats, at her and then back at the dog. "If I ever get this bad, you have my permission."

"Never." She dropped to her knees by his side, snatching the gun from his hand. "Never will I give up on you."

Kell whined and struggled. The anger in her voice was distressing him. She took a breath and struggled for calm, not understanding why Sam was doing this. Yes, it was what anyone else would do, but not Sam. "This is not how we are, Sam."

"It's not?"

How could he not see it? She placed the gun far on the other side of her and stroked her hand soothingly over the wolf, calming him. "No. Kell needs our help. We will give it."

Sam put his hand over hers, halting her stroking.

"He's just a dog."

She turned her hand and threaded her fingers through his, squeezing tightly as she met his gaze squarely. "Who we love."

Sam shook his head, looking at her but not seeming to see her. "It'll be hard, duchess, and in the end he might die anyway, after a hell of a lot of unnecessary suffering."

And there was her explanation for his strange decision. He was protecting her from the pain of trying and failing.

"He also might live. That is the hope I will fight for."

Sam's mouth tightened to a grim line and he no longer saw her, his gaze in the past. "If he doesn't you're going to feel guilty. Trust me, there's no end to the hell someone can put a person through in a selfish need to keep them alive."

Another clue to the way he was. She squeezed his fingers. "Who did you fight for, Sam?"

Who did you fight for and lose?

"It was a long time ago."

"You will tell me anyway."

His gaze hardened. "You don't give me orders."

She suppressed the urge to roll her eyes. Of course she did. The same way he gave them to her. "That was not an order. I merely say the facts.

"Do not look angry at me," she interjected before he could say something mean. "This is a good thing."

"Tell me that later after you've held Kell down while he screams in agony."

She swallowed hard. He painted a very vivid picture. "Why would he scream?"

It was a stupid question which he answered evenly. "I have to dig those bullets out."

And the doubt in his eyes said he didn't think she'd be able to endure it. She squared her shoulders.

"You have much to learn about me, Sam MacGregor."

15

Sam eyed Isabella as they rode out, Kell trailing on a makeshift litter behind the most docile of the bandits' horses. Which wasn't saying much. The animals were mistreated and green broke to the point he wouldn't have bothered at all if the other horses weren't played out. They spooked at every sharp noise and movement. He shook his head. It was a damn shame. A good horse meant a man's life out here. Either the bandits had no reason to fear nature and the elements or they were just plain stupid with the overconfidence that came from belonging to Tejala's gang and striking fear into all they met. His money was on the latter.

What was said about a good horse also applied to a good woman. He eyed Isabella as she rode on his other side. She was a good woman, and she was right. He did have a hard time seeing her the way he should. Not because he didn't appreciate her. He reached for his smokes. But because he appreciated what her looks, youth, and position could attain for her if she wasn't caught up in the false intimacy of their situation. She could marry any man she wanted, virgin or not. Men with wealth, not aspirations for it. Men who could keep her protected and sheltered. Men who could guarantee she'd never be in the position of having to drag a knife out of a dead man's neck in order to cut bullets out of a dog.

Her horse stumbled, causing her breasts to sway beneath her shirt. He tucked his makings back in his pocket. But that man hadn't made his appearance yet. And right now Bella was with him. And he sure as hell wasn't a saint.

"Bella?"

She didn't turn around.

"How long are you planning on giving me the cold shoulder?"

"Until my anger at you dies."

They'd been riding two hours. He'd never known her to be silent more than two minutes.

"How long will that be?"

"I will let you know."

He gave an exaggerated sigh, watching her closely. "You're a hard woman, Bella Montoya."

Her head turned just a little. Sunlight glinted off the blue-black of her hair. "No longer the *little girl*?"

He smiled. "No little girl could hold silent this long."

"I thought you wanted me silent."

"So did I."

"You have missed my talk?"

"There's no need to go hog wild with supposition."

That might have been a snort. Hard to tell as she wasn't looking at him. He squeezed with his knees, urging Breeze faster. The horse was eager to comply. He wasn't one for following either. Unfortunately, the bandit's horse wasn't so inclined. He balked, jostling Kell, who whined.

"Easy, boy."

Bella turned. "Do you talk to the horse or the dog?"

"Whichever one will listen." He countered the pack horse's yank back with a slight redirect to the side. Kell struggled in the travois. The packhorse panicked. Sam had the devil's own time, keeping the other horse from bolting as Kell flopped on the makeshift sled behind. He heard Isabella cluck with her tongue, had a brief glimpse of her calves as she rode by and then she was at the other horse's head, singing a soft song. The horse rolled his eyes but quit yanking back.

"Whatever you're doing, keep it up."

Her brows arched as she looked down her nose at him, appearing every inch the aristocrat he suspected her to be.

"Is that an order?"

She was throwing his own words back at him. The perverse side of him liked it. The lustful side reveled in it, anticipating the moment he'd reinstate the balance to their relationship. Desire surged at the challenge. "Defiance comes with a price, duchess."

"I merely ask."

The woman never *merely* did anything, let alone ask. Taking advantage of the packhorse's distraction, he lined the horse straight in the makeshift traces.

A cluck of his tongue put Breeze in motion. Bella wasn't far behind. "You might want to stay back with Kell. His horse seems to like yours."

"*Bueno.*" She held out her hands for the third horse's reins.

Sam held them back for the sheer pleasure of seeing her get her dander up. She was something when riled. "I don't know. He spooks easily. You might not be able to hold him."

"He likes my horse. They will be fine."

"You sure?"

"You will doubt me on this, too?"

"You're not much of a rider."

She rolled her eyes. "It does not take much to lead a horse at a slow walk."

He pretended to debate it before he handed over the reins. "Move slow."

With a snort, she took the reins. "I am not stupid."

No, she was clever, sexy and despite her comparative youth, more than enough woman for him. She tied the reins around the horn, before moving her horse so close to his their knees touched. "You want something?"

"I would like a kiss."

He blinked. She was always surprising him.

"There isn't another woman in the world like you, Bella."

She held up her arms. "So you must appreciate me."

"I suppose I must." He hopped back onto the horse's flank. Before she could realize what he was up to, he hooked his arm around her waist and pulled her sideways onto the saddle. "How's this?"

"Your arm!"

"Is the better for being around you," he finished for her as he looped her horse's reins around his saddle horn. Bella twisted in his lap lifting the edge of the bandage. Her hands were very tender on his shoulder as she checked the wound. He didn't stop her. It'd been a long time since a woman had fussed with him. "You should have let me sew you up."

"There wasn't enough catgut for Kell and me."

"I could have made do."

"We agreed. Kell was worse off."

She waved her hand. "Pfft! You just do not like to be sewn."

She had him there.

He pulled her against his chest.

She all but melted in his arms, snuggling into his shoulder with a hunger that struck him hard.

He tilted her head back. Her lips parted as easily as her smile welcomed him. She took his kiss the way she'd taken him last night, with a soft gasp and a trust that humbled him. The wildness he'd been trying to contain ever since they were attacked, sprang free in a lust he couldn't contain.

Pulling back, he smoothed the remnant of their kiss into her lower lip. "This wasn't such a good idea."

"I am liking it very much."

He dropped his forehead to hers. "Not for much longer you wouldn't. I'm never stable after a fight."

"I do not understand."

"I'm on edge."

She frowned. He sighed.

"I want you, Bella."

"Right now?"

"Yeah."

She looked intrigued. "How is this done?"

He shook his head. She had no idea what she was offering. "I wouldn't be gentle like last night."

She unbuttoned the top button of his pants. "Maybe I will like rough."

Two more buttons gave, his cock pressed against the material, searching for freedom, searching for her. Her hand, softer than satin, brushed his stomach. Her fingers twined in the hair leading down, tugging, teasing. Her gaze didn't leave his, free of shyness, full of confidence. He didn't hide the effect she had on him, didn't smother his groan when her hand closed around the head of his shaft, his shudder when she swiped her thumb across the tip.

He undid the rest of the buttons himself. He lifted her up. She panicked and grabbed for his shoulders.

Her magnificent breasts were even with his mouth. The nipples made small points under the pale blue fabric. Her short nails dug into his shoulder. Her lip slipped between her teeth, the peachy pink flesh plumping around her bite.

He eased her a little more to the right. "Swing your leg over."

Startled, she glanced at him. "This is possible?"

He could tell she liked the idea from the way her lids lowered and her breath caught. When her thigh slid over his, he leaned in and caught her right nipple between his lips, nibbling gently on the taut nub, waiting for her to make that little sound in her throat that told him he'd found the pressure she liked. "Pull your skirt out of the way."

Her hands cupped his head, fluttered down to his shoulders, and then came back to his head. "Now."

The shiver that went through her confirmed his impression. As much as Bella loved to take control with words, when it came to her pleasure, she wanted to surrender. He could work with that. "Nice and easy, sweet," he warned as she jerked about. "We don't want to spook the horses."

She tugged again. "My foot is stuck in my skirt!"

It was almost a wail. He'd never seen Bella flustered, but she was now. Because he'd given her an order and she couldn't fulfill it. Holding her with one arm around her waist he reached down and covered her hand with his. "I've got it."

He centered her hips against his torso and slowly

eased her down. About three inches into the descent, she jumped and gasped. "What?"

"The buttons."

He glanced down. Her pussy was aligned with the placket of his shirt. "Does it hurt?"

She blushed and didn't answer. "Well?"

"No."

"Then enjoy the ride." He lowered her down.

If her subsequent gasps as he lowered her were anything to go by, she enjoyed every little flick to her pussy. His cock notched into the well of her vagina through the slit in her long johns. She was hot, wet and slick. She flinched.

And sore from last night. "Easy."

"You said you did not want easy."

He didn't. He'd planned on fucking her fast and furious, to release the tension in a violent emotionless pounding, the way he always did. "I forgot how good you feel." Lowering her slowly, gently, to let the weight of her body take them past that first resistance, controlling it. Her head fell back. Her lip went back between her teeth. "Sam!"

He didn't have to ask, he knew. Too much too soon.

"Brace your knees on my thighs."

"Why?"

"So you can be in control."

"And what will you do?"

"This." He placed his thumb on the damp point of her clit and made a little circle.

"Ah!"

"Any complaints?"

Her braid whipped back and forth as she shook her head. "No."

"Then why don't you take us both for a ride."

"O Dios!"

Bella opened her eyes in time to see the stern line of Sam's mouth soften. His head tilted infinitesimally to the side. His fingers brushed her cheek and tiny smile lines fanned out from the corner of his eyes. No words, just the utter comfort of knowing he liked what he saw. What he felt. She had to bite her lip to keep the tears at bay.

His cock throbbed between her thighs, nudging her intimately, melting her with his heat and strength.

The weight of his hand on her shoulder urged her down as if he'd pushed. "Lower yourself onto me."

She bit her lip and tried. His cock felt so much bigger like this. Too big. Too demanding. As if he understood, Sam's lips whispered across her forehead, traced her right eyebrow and then her left, patient, coaxing.

She closed her eyes and relaxed into him, not smothering her cry of distress, of joy, as that broad tip wedged the first inch into her pussy, the intimate burn spreading outward, fanning the pleasure simmering deep inside. Her fingertips curled into the solid muscle of his shoulders. Oh God, she loved this. Loved him. She took more, a little awkward as the pommel caught her hip.

It was nothing compared to the sharp ache as her inner muscles were forcefully parted.

Immediately, Sam's palms cupped her bottom, holding her still, supporting her through the discomfort, preventing her from taking more of that pleasure pain she craved. "Gently, Bella. Gently."

Sam didn't like gentle. He'd already told her that and if she was going to walk away from this affair with one thing, it was going to be the knowledge that she'd pleased him. No wondering. No what-ifs. She was going to know. Maybe in her dreams their next time would be with candles, champagne and sweet murmuring, but dreams weren't reality. Right now, Sam was very real. Very potent. And just out of reach.

Isabella forced a smile and an "I'm fine" as she steadied herself. She rose up with the horse's gait until the wide head of his cock just pulsed against her, teasing herself and him with the promise of her descent, feeling the cream spill from her body and her muscles, still stinging from her last attempt, flex in anticipation. His cock answered with a pulse of its own. A more genuine smile welled from deep inside.

This was Sam. She knew what he liked and she knew making it good for him would eventually make it good for her. She just needed to get this first time behind them. When her body re-accustomed to his, it would be her turn to fly.

Instead of smiling back, Sam's gaze wandered her face, lingering on her cheek, her chest, places where she could feel the heat of her blush. A frown settled over the passion in his expression. Oh, damn, she'd waited too long, let him see too much…

"You're sore."

"I am fine." She wiggled in his grip, sinking the tiniest fraction onto his heat, shuddering as it seeped into her channel, gasping as her very womb clenched in anticipation. "More than fine."

She'd bear any amount of pain if she could just feel him like that again, deep and hard, possessing her fully inside and out. The truth came spilling out as his cock jerked against her. "I need you, Sam."

His expression sharpened with the force of his emotion in direct contrast to the softness of his voice, his gaze. His fingers grazed her left nipple, catching it between the knuckles, squeezing.

She arched her back until her shoulder blades hit Breeze's neck, offering her nipples to his mouth, his teeth. The bite of his fingers into her hips was as erotic as the flare of his nostrils.

Levering herself up and down she asked, "What is the word for what I do now?"

"Making love."

She shook her head, going a little faster. "What is the dirty word?"

He hesitated. Leaning forward, she nibbled on his neck, letting the rocking gait of the horse impale her in tiny increments on his cock. "If you teach me the dirty word, Sam, I will use it in a sentence for you."

He swallowed hard. "Shit."

She sucked the flesh on the side of his neck into her mouth. With a pulse of her hips she tempted him more. "Tell me."

His hand anchored in her hair, pulling her head back. His mouth bit at hers before he growled. "Fuck. The word is fuck."

"Ah. No wonder men use this word so much."

His eyes burned with dark heat. She made him wait. Running her tongue along her lips, letting him see her teeth, the moisture within, waiting for his breath to catch, his gaze to become razor-sharp. Waited until his grip tightened, drawing her in. Inching her way up, she found the lobe of his ear, bit it once, nibbled twice before whispering, "Fuck me, Sam. Let me feel your power surging in me. Show me how much you want me."

"Goddamn!"

He said he wouldn't be easy and he wasn't. It was as if the use of the words broke something inside him. Something he'd been holding back. He pushed her down, powering hard inside her, spearing though resistance too fast for her to absorb, pulling back as she caught the fragment of sensation, yanking her back onto it. She held on as he did it again and again, his thick cock parting her muscles over and over again, scraping along her inner walls in the most perfect tension. It was like riding a beautiful violent storm, scary, exciting, overwhelming. And there was nothing she could do but hold on. His thrusts grew harder, deeper.

"Come with me, Bella."

Impossibly deep. She bit her lip as an inner wildness rose in answer to his, growing with every thrust.

"Sam."

Breeze pranced to the side. She gasped as Sam's cock stretched her a different way, touched a different spot, ripping a high-pitched scream from her throat.

"That's the spot?" he grunted, his voice a harsh rasp. "Right there?"

She didn't know. She knew nothing beyond the hard throb of desire that demanded satisfaction. He rubbed his cock over that bundle of nerves in short hard jabs, tilting her hips so every thrust rasped her clit along the thick cotton of his pants. Her pussy got tighter, his cock bigger, and the swelling in her womb knotted to the point of agony.

"Sam!"

"Damn, you're going to burn us both up."

"I cannot…stand it," she gasped. "You must come."

"Shit."

His body jerked. She tightened her legs around his hips, holding tight, finding a fragment of her voice as he started to pull out. "In me. Come in me."

She wanted to feel his seed, rich and hot, inside her.

For one moment she'd thought she'd won, but then he yanked her up. His muscles were stronger than hers, giving him his way and his cock pulled free and her pussy was empty, clenching on air.

"No. I want—"

"This is what you want."

His hands curved around her buttocks. His fingers dipped into the deep crease between, pulling the firm globes apart, stretching her anus in an erotic prelude. His shaft slid in the thick cream pouring from her pussy, snagging on the tight rosette of her anus, startling a dark forbidden hunger to life. Pressing, parting the tiniest bit, letting the clench of muscle seal them together. "This is what you want, Bella." His head fell back. "What we both want."

The first spurt of seed hit like an erotic punch, burning hot over ultrasensitive nerve endings, jetting deep in an unfamiliar sensation.

She twisted away. His cheek dropped to hers as the second spurt built on the first.

"No. Bear down. Let me fill you this way at least."

She did as he asked, trusting him as she buried her face in his neck. Another jerk of his cock, another spurt of warmth. Another rub against her clit.

"Bear down and take me, Bella."

She could feel herself opening against this pressure. "This does not seem right."

"It's right, Bella. Let me just give you a little more, and you'll see."

This was suddenly too much. She tried to pull off. He wouldn't let her.

"It hurts," she moaned as the intimate ache spread.

He shuddered as his cock jerked, another warm bath.

"Shh, just let it happen. Just rub your clit against me and let it happen."

It was happening whether she wanted it to or not. His cock, greased with her cream, slick from his seed slowly won the battle over muscles uncertain whether to invite him in or push him out.

Sam brushed his lips over her ear. "It's going to hurt for a minute. A virgin's pain again as your body accepts mine this little bit. Just take it slow and breathe."

She couldn't breathe, couldn't stop, part of her welcoming this dark possession, part of her afraid of it. Panic started as the pressure built. "I can't."

"You already are."

The burn intensified, stretching outward, finding her nipples, her clit, swelling them to hard eager points.

"See. Just a little more."

They were almost at the point of no return.

"Sam?"

"What?"

"Kiss me. Hard and wild. As wild as you feel inside."

He didn't hesitate, mating his mouth to hers, kissing her deeply, thoroughly stealing her breath, her will, her fear, leaving her only with the anticipation of the pleasure he promised.

His lips parted from hers, just a hairsbreadth. "Give me your ass, Bella. Now."

Holding her breath, she pushed down. His cock surged. There was a popping give and then an impossible fullness.

Her torso whiplashed into his. His hand left her hip, riding her spine pressing between her shoulder blades, bringing her against him.

"Shh, just relax."

"It is too much."

"No." His expression was tight. "It's just right."

His other hand slid around until his thumb pressed on her clit. The feeling was incredible. Pleasure and pain spiraling outward in an indescribable joy.

"Rock on my cock now. Just a little."

She did tentatively at first, experimenting until she found a rhythm she could handle. The spiral tightened. His cock swelled. She needed more. Her head fell back as she closed her eyes.

"That's it. Go with it."

She didn't have a choice. This was wilder than anything she'd ever imagined. Decadent. But right. So right that she give herself to Sam this way. So right he know her like this.

The wildness in her rose, took over. She turned her face, inhaled his scent and bit his chest, bearing down harder as his hips jerked, taking more of his cock, gasping as it again became too much.

His fingers jerked on her clit, pinching sharply, sending another spike of pleasure pain through her. "Again," she gasped, wiggling her hips in a vain attempt to work him deeper. She just needed him to do it again.

He pinched her clit, sending that shivery spike deep.

It wasn't enough. "Your cock," she moaned. "I need your cock, too."

"Jesus."

"Please."

Another pinch of her clit that wasn't enough and then, "When I get you to a bed, I'll fuck your ass raw, but you're too dry now. You'll tear."

"I do not care." She worked her hips again. "Please."

"Are you almost there?"

"Yes."

He massaged her clit in rough strokes, giving her what she needed there, what he denied her elsewhere. "Do you want to come now, Bella? Do you want to come like this with my cock tucked up this sweet ass?"

"Yes. *Por Dios*, yes."

He clamped down hard, pulling her clit away from her pussy as he rocked his hips. "Then come."

She did, shattering under the sharp spike, smothering her scream against his chest, her ass clamping down on the tip of his shaft, clenching in a hard milking that had him groaning and then his cock was jerking again, filling her with his rich seed, coating her sensitive flesh with thick warmth, easing the way for a deeper penetration.

Against her ear, he growled, "Mine."

She didn't argue with him, just collapsed against his chest as the burning ache of his complete possession rode the last shudder of her climax to sear its way to her soul.

"Always."

16

Isabella felt conspicuous the minute they entered the town limits. This wasn't a town on the edge of nowhere, clinging to existence. This town had a livery, a boardinghouse and a saloon. This was a town with expectations of growing. This town had women—not all of whom worked at the saloon. And it was the way the good women were looking at her that made her acutely aware of Sam's seed coating the still-sensitive flesh between her legs and tender tips of her breasts. Did the sin she'd committed with Sam brand her for all to see?

She lifted her chin and met the gaze of a very properly dressed blond woman leaving the mercantile. The woman looked away. For the first time since she met Sam, for the first time since she decided what was right, Isabella felt shame.

"You keep that head up, Bella. Speculation is normal when anybody new walks into town."

She glanced over at Sam. He had that mean expression on his face. As if he was ready to go for the throat of anyone who looked at her wrong.

"I am not ashamed."

"Then why are you blushing?"

"Because now I know what they speculate when they look at me!"

"And that bothers you?"

She shrugged. "I do not like the thought of others picturing me naked with you."

The brim of his hat pulled down low hid his eyes, but his lips twitched. "You had to go put that thought in my head, didn't you?"

He could not be serious. "You do not think women think this way?"

"Can't say I ever did before this moment."

She nodded toward the woman in the simple gray dress. "That one for sure wondered."

"You think? She doesn't look the type."

"What is the type?"

Sam motioned toward the saloon where three women lounged against the building, enjoying the warm sun. They were dressed in bright dresses that barely covered their knees and exposed the tops of their breasts. Isabella blushed for a whole new reason. Even in her small town with Tejala's influence everywhere, women did not display themselves so. It just was not done. Maybe this town was not as civilized as it would like.

"I think that one would be judging how much money you carry, rather than seeing your body with mine."

He nodded. "You're probably right. But that doesn't make it any easier to imagine a proper woman speculating about me with someone."

She rolled her eyes. "Women are no different than men. They wonder. They imagine."

"Well, hell." He glanced at her from the corner of his eye. "I'm not going to be able to go to a social anymore without blushing."

It was such an outrageous thing to say, and so impossible to believe, there could only be one reason he was saying it. He was distracting her. "I think that I would like to see that."

"Me blushing?"

"No, you at a social. I think you would be interesting to see around others."

"Decided you want to know all my secrets, eh?"

"*Sí.*" She looked around. People were beginning to notice them, stopping on the street to stare. Curtains in windows fluttered. Anytime a stranger entered town, it tended to be time for gossip, but the fact they had a dog strapped to a travois behind them was bound to raise more talk than usual. That and the fact that she was *castellaña* and this town appeared to be mostly Tejanos. Memories of the war were still strong and tempers were still very high between the two races.

The two men talking to the saloon girl moved away

from her and stepped into the street. She recognized them. They were close to Tejala.

"Put that hat on your head, Bella, and switch on over to my other side."

She didn't hesitate. She would feel much more comfortable with Sam between her and the men who watched her with such hunger. "This does not seem such a friendly town."

The men did not move back into the overhang of the building. And with the heat the way it was, that alone was cause for suspicion. Sam held out the packhorse reins. "Mind taking over for a spell?"

"No." The leather reins were warm and damp from his skin. She put her fingers in the indents left by his, wanting the connection. "Where do we go?"

"You are going to someplace safe, and then I'm going to look for Tucker."

She didn't know if there would be someplace safe in this town for someone like her. "Tucker is your friend?"

"Yes."

Her mouth went dry. "You are close to him."

He was still scanning the street. "Yup. He's family. You'll like him."

Her liking him was not a question. Tucker liking her was a big question. Family could be very picky about the women their members associated with. "What is the name of this town?"

"Lindos."

Her day was getting worse and worse. "We are not far from my home."

"I figured that. Montoya is two towns over. You live there, right?"

"How did you know?"

The half smile that could seduce or annoy her played on his lips. "It wasn't hard to put together, duchess. The way you put on airs, and that last name along with being in Tejala's territory kind of did narrow down the field."

She felt so foolish. She thought her secret was well hidden. "I have no wish to visit home."

"We'll talk about that later."

The two men came into the street, not far enough to block them but enough to make her heart jump in her chest. "Sam?"

"I see them." He flipped his cigarette into the dirt.

"What do you want me to do?"

His hand slid down to his revolver. "Stay where you are and think about what you're going to say to your momma."

The last time she'd seen her mother, they had fought. And if she saw her again they would probably fight again immediately, because her mother wanted the security an alliance with Tejala would bring her. And as much as Bella probably should do for her family, asking her to marry Tejala was too much. Tejala only wanted her to prove a point. When that point was made through her submission, he would kill her, then maybe her family too. He was that kind of man. She had to raise her voice for Sam to hear her. "I will not go."

He raised his hand acknowledging he heard her, but she noticed he didn't nod. He was going to be stubborn about this.

She stood in the stirrups, leaning forward, dread filling her as he kept going forward to those men so clearly ready to start trouble. She wanted to call him back. All that came out of her mouth was, "I can be stubborn, too."

He still didn't look back, but he saluted her with two fingers. "Never doubted that, duchess."

He kept Breeze walking slowly and steadily toward the men. Why did he always have to look for the fight? The closer he got to the men the more nervous she became. Not only because there might be trouble but because there were things she had not told Sam. Things he might hold against her if he found out. She gripped the pommel in her hands. It was too late now. She just had to hope the men did not disclose everything.

Finally Sam pulled his horse up. He touched his finger to the brim of his hat. "Can I help you gentlemen?"

The one on the right with the meticulously groomed handlebar moustache stepped forward. She struggled to remember his name. He stroked his fingers over his moustache and she remembered. Manuelo. The clean-shaven man in the back positioned himself a little to the left and to the side. His name she could not remember. "The woman you are with. She looks familiar."

She borrowed one of Sam's favorite curses. *Shit.*

"The woman is mine."

Even hearing him say it with a threat in his voice gave her a thrill. The man widened his stance.

"I think you are wrong."

"Wouldn't be the first time."

It was nice to know she was not the only one with whom Sam could be perverse.

"The woman is Tejala's."

"By right or claim?"

"By contract. She is his intended."

Hope died. Sam knew all now. She was engaged to another man and she'd slept with him. A betrothal contract was as good as marriage. He would hate her.

"You don't say." He shifted his weight in the saddle. It looked like a casual gesture but Breeze shifted, too, and when he settled Sam was at a better angle and she was no longer in the line of fire. Would this come to bullets?

"You mean paperwork was drawn up and everything?"

That didn't sound like hate in his voice. It sounded like goading.

"By her father."

Sam tipped back his hat. "I thought her father was dead."

"He signed before he died."

He had. Right before she blacked out from lack of air. She touched her throat, feeling again the agony of straining for breath that couldn't come, hearing again her father's pleas for her life. Hearing the gurgle as he choked on his own blood after he'd signed and Tejala had slit his throat.

"Well, where I come from we don't sell women like we sell cattle, and since he's not here to discuss it, I'd call that deal empty."

"Tejala will not be happy." Manuelo tipped his hat back. "You do not want to see Tejala unhappy."

"He's welcome to pull up a chair any time he gets a notion to discuss it."

There was a tension developing between the men. Worse, more men, obviously friends of the first two, were wandering out of the saloon. She didn't like it. Men, liquor and provocation were never a good combination. She liked even less that she did not have a weapon.

"You can have the discussion with us."

"You don't look the type capable of intelligent discourse."

"¿Qué?"

"My point exactly. I'll talk to Tejala if he ever gets his chicken ass out of hiding."

Manuelo bristled. The crowd pressed in, scenting the spill of blood. "Tejala is not a coward."

"Seeing as I've never seen him do anything but bully women and children, you'll have to pardon me for holding my own opinion."

Why was he goading them?

"You are a very foolish man, *señor.*"

Bella agreed and intended to lecture him about that as soon as she got him out of here.

"So I've been told, but I've got a message for you to take to Tejala."

"And what would that be?"

"Bella is Hell's Eight now."

Manuelo's beady eyes narrowed to slits. "Who are you, gringo?"

"The name would be Sam MacGregor."

From the crowd came the whisper of "Wild Card."

The clean-shaven man stepped back. Manuelo's fingers twitched. "What do Texas Rangers do this far in Tejala's territory?"

"Hunting."

"For who?"

"I could say antelope, or mountain lion or—"

Manuelo pulled his revolver. Sam was faster. Two shots sounded in rapid succession. Manuelo fell to the ground, blood spreading in a bright red blossom over his chest. His accomplice stumbled back against the wall clutching his chest, eyes wide. His gun fell from his fingers to the ground. He followed it down in a slow slump.

Sam shook his head. "Looks like I'll have to find me a new messenger." He reached in his vest pocket and pulled out some coins and tossed them to the feet of one of the bystanders. "See that they don't stink up the street."

The man nodded, but he didn't move. No one moved. The gunplay had happened so fast, Isabella hadn't had a chance to feel terror, but it was on her now, icy cold, leaving her light-headed. With relief or anger she couldn't decide, but she was leaning toward the latter. Sam could have been killed, might still be killed, and all she could do was watch. She tugged the packhorse, who didn't seem at all distressed by gunfire, forward.

The blond woman Isabella had noticed earlier came pushing through the crowd, ignoring the guns and the danger. She knelt beside the clean-shaven man. As if the moment could not explode into violence at any second, she opened the man's shirt and checked his wound. Her mouth set in a straight line, she shook her head before looking up at Sam. "If thee paid for two burials, thee are owed money back."

"I can remedy that."

She shook her head. "Not today thee won't."

Sam's head came up. "I beg your pardon."

"It's not my pardon you should be begging but God's."

"God and I aren't on speaking terms."

"God talks to everyone. Even fools." She snapped her fingers at two men inside the saloon. "Enrique, Paolo, bring this man to my house."

"That's not necessary, ma'am."

The woman stood, brushing the dust off her skirts. Her white lace cap ruffled in the breeze. She was tall, with a pretty square face, pale blond hair and a very competent manner. "It wouldn't have been if thee had tried talking instead of shooting."

"He's an outlaw."

"He's an injured man and in need of care."

"He's just as likely to stab you in your sleep."

"Dying isn't to be feared, Sam."

Sam opened his mouth and then closed it. Isabella knew exactly how he felt. Never had she seen a woman handle men so.

"Might as well give it up, Sam. There's no getting a word in edgewise when Sally Mae gets her dander up."

"I'm getting that impression."

Isabelle blinked at the man who stepped out of the saloon. She'd thought Sam was big but this man was a giant. As he came up beside Sally Mae it was a study of opposites. While Sally Mae was fair and willowy, the man was dark, with big bones and layers of muscles piled on top. He wore a leather vest over a blue shirt with the sleeves ripped off. His muscled arms were as massive as the rest of him. The darkness of his skin merely emphasized the deep cuts of his biceps. The only similarity was their eyes. They both had gray eyes. Hers were dark calming gray while his were so pale beneath the brim of his hat, they seemed to almost glow.

Sally Mae did not look pleased to see him. Her eyes narrowed. "I have not given thee permission to use my given name, Mr. McCade. You will kindly refrain from such an overly familiar manner."

There was another similarity. Both were very confident.

Tucker didn't look any worse for the reprimand. If anything, he looked amused. "That last name of yours is a mouthful."

Her chin came up. "Thee are not an ignorant man. Endeavor to learn it before we meet again." She turned on her heel and marched away, skirts swaying at her brisk pace.

"Now there's a bit of ass I wouldn't mind taming," a trail hand with lank brown hair hanging from under his hat declared.

With seeming nonchalance, McCade reached out and grabbed him by the throat. With a move equally as casual, he tossed him through the glass front of the saloon. Glass shattered in a cacophony of discordance.

The packhorse jerked at the reins and whinnied. Isabella held on to the ends of the reins, making shushing sounds the horses ignored. Kell whined. The third time she was almost jerked from the saddle, Sam rode up, sliding his hands around the reins until he got close to the horse's head. She let go in response to his tug. She didn't know where to focus. On Sam or Tucker.

A shout came from inside the saloon.

"Damn it, Tucker!"

Isabella blinked again. This was the "nice" friend Sam expected her to like? This giant who tossed men through glass windows?

"Put it on my tab, Brian," Tucker called over his shoulder before his gaze met hers.

"That doesn't cover the inconvenience," Brian grumbled from the dark interior. Tucker didn't take his eyes from her, approaching with a fluid grace leaving her with an impression of being stalked.

"Uh-huh."

He was a handsome man in a brutally harsh sort of way. There was no warmth in his gaze, just a cold assessment as he glanced at her then at Sam.

"Thought we agreed we'd only bring back blondes?"

What did that mean? She turned in the saddle to look at Sam. He was checking on Kell. "Bella here proved just too tempting to pass up."

Tucker reached up and took her hat off, studying her as if she were a horse. His gaze dropped to her mouth. "She does have potential."

She snatched her hat back. With a snap of her hand, she used it to knock his off his head. He caught it without any sign of awkwardness. To her surprise, all her violence had done was make him smile.

"Push her much more, Tucker, and we're going to have words."

For all the languor in the statement, Isabella heard the threat.

"Like that, is it?" Tucker asked.

Sam stood. "Pretty much."

"Desi sent us out after blondes."

"No shit."

"She's not blond."

He made her dark hair and caramel-colored skin sound like a deficit. Him with his black-as-sin hair, scary eyes and much darker skin.

"Sally Mae is right," Bella snapped. "You are overly familiar."

His gaze cut back to hers. "It's my nature."

She wasn't so sure about that, but he was something. Either very bad or very good. She couldn't tell which.

Sam came up beside her. His fingers curled around hers. It was a subtle gesture, but as they were in public, a declaration of intent. He'd been sending her these signals for days, but saying nothing. Was he trying to tell her something?

"I need a place for Bella to stay."

Tucker sighed and looked down the street where Sally Mae stopped in front of a fenced yard. "The only place for a decent woman to stay just got complicated."

"Don't tell me."

"Sally Mae runs the local boardinghouse."

"Is that where she took Tejala's man?"

"Yup."

"Well, sh—shoot."

Bella glanced at Sam askance. He'd never watched his language around her before. First the hand-holding and then this. What was he doing?

"Mrs. Schermerhorn has deep beliefs."

"I thought you did not know how to say her name?" Bella queried with an arch of her brow.

The faintest of smiles touched his lips. "The ability comes and goes."

More than likely with his need to irritate. She looked over to Sam. "I'm beginning to see the family resemblance."

Sam took her hat and popped it back on her head, tapping it down until it covered her eyes. "Everyone does eventually."

She pushed the hat back. The man Sam had tossed money to grabbed the hands of the dead man and hauled him away, dragging him across the street. Sam was still on the subject of the woman's behavior.

"Is she stupid? That man will rape her first chance he gets and probably slit her throat before he's finished."

"To her that's unimportant."

"How can this be unimportant?" Bella asked.

"She's a Quaker. She believes she is to do no harm, that all life is sacred and the rest is up to God."

Sam reached for his makings and took out a paper. "So, she's stupid."

Tucker went still. "No, she's not."

Sprinkling tobacco on the paper, Sam brought the paper to his tongue. Isabella couldn't look away. A shiver ran down her spine as Sam ran his tongue along the edge. Between her legs her pussy flexed and fresh cream gathered. He had a very skilled tongue.

With one last flick that had her shifting in the saddle, Sam twisted the ends. "What is she then?"

"A woman of principle."

"Who's going to get herself killed."

"I keep an eye on her."

"From the saloon?"

"From the barn behind the boardinghouse."

Sam's lips tightened. "You set yourself as guardian for a woman that doesn't even see fit to let you rent a room under her roof?"

"It was my choice."

"I bet."

Something lashed in Tucker's eyes. Isabella couldn't identify it.

"Shut the hell up, Sam."

"The hell I—"

The emotion flashed again. This time she did recognize it. The big dangerous man cared for the woman. Isabella put her hand on Sam's thigh. "It is not your concern, Sam."

"The hell it's not."

Tucker looked at her hand. His brow arched. She tipped up her chin and matched him stare for stare. She didn't care what he thought. But inside, the part of her raised to always submit to propriety cringed. Just a little.

"Maybe the saloon has rooms."

To her surprise, Tucker's "no" beat out Sam's.

"It's not a place for a proper lady, miss."

She might as well take the bull by the horns.

"Maybe I'm not so proper."

"For Sam's sake, I hope not."

She blushed. Tucker laughed. Sam wrapped his arm around her shoulder and pulled her close. She tipped her head for his kiss. She felt much better once his lips met hers. This was familiar. This made her comfortable. This was the Sam she knew.

"I'll sit on Tejala's sidekick," Tucker offered.

"You're just looking for an excuse to irritate Sally Mae."

"True enough." He walked around the back of the packhorse to the travois. "Who is this?"

Weakened and ill, Kell still managed to raise his head and display his fangs.

"Kell. I picked him up on the other side of the mountains."

"He looks pure wolf."

"He's got to be part dog seeing as he's domesticated." Kell snarled.

Tucker smiled. He had a nice smile, Isabella decided.

"No need to go insulting him."

He reached out.

"Kell doesn't like to be touched," Isabella called, worried despite herself.

"I'll keep that in mind."

Tucker took off his hat and set it on the ground beside the travois. His shoulder-length hair fell forward, hiding his face. As he spoke to the dog in a low singsong language she didn't understand, Kell continued to snarl. But when Tucker lifted his bandages and looked beneath, he didn't bite even though it had to hurt and there was plenty of Tucker within striking distance.

"How did he do that?" she asked Sam.

He shrugged. "Tucker has a way with wild things."

Tucker stood. "His wounds are infected."

"Oh no." Isabella did not want to hear he was going to die.

"Know someone that can take care of it?" Sam asked.

"Yeah, but you're not going to like it."

"Sally Mae?"

"She won't turn him away and she has a real talent for healing."

"Seems all roads lead to Sally Mae."

"So it would seem."

"She any good?"

"Her husband was a doctor."

"Was?"

"He was killed last year by a dissatisfied patient."

"Sam needs care, too," Isabella interjected. For her interference she got a glare from Sam.

"I'm fine."

Tucker grinned and took the packhorse's reins. "Let me guess, he needs stitches?"

"How did you know?"

Tucker clucked to the horse and started down the street. "He's always been squeamish when facing a needle."

Isabella smiled very sweetly at Sam. His blue eyes glittered a warning from beneath the brim of his hat. She ignored it.

"He will not be squeamish today."

"What makes you say that?" Tucker asked, glancing over his shoulder.

"Because he promised me."

* * *

"You're leaving me?"

Isabella sat on the rail-back chair in her bedroom in the boardinghouse and stared at Sam, the towel with which she'd been drying her hair pausing halfway to her lap.

"There aren't any more rooms. I'm going to be staying with Tucker in the barn and keep an eye on things."

She reached over and smoothed her hand over the mattress of the double bed. "The bed is big enough for the both of us."

Sam didn't even seem to notice the way her borrowed dressing gown gaped.

"We're in town now, Bella. We can't be carrying on like we did before."

The sick feeling in the pit of her stomach grew. "You do not want to be seen with me."

He slapped his hat against his thigh. "You have a reputation to protect."

"I do not think riding around with you in the wilderness has left me with any."

"No one here knows that."

"They do not need to know to speculate."

"You hear anyone saying anything untoward, you send them my way."

"Sam, I knew what I faced when I had relations with you. I have no regrets."

"What we do is between us and not up for speculation."

The part of her that hoped to hear him say he had no regrets withered.

She twisted her hands in the towel. "Why is this so important?"

"Tomorrow I'm going to take you home to your mother. I don't need to give her any more reason to meet me at the door with a shotgun."

He would not budge on taking her home.

"She will be too happy that you bring me home to care in what condition."

He took a step into the room. Though he came closer, she felt like the distance between them widened.

"I find that hard to believe."

"Because of what you know of your mother, but *my* mother married as her parents ordered. She was not happy leaving Spain. She is not happy here. She has waited a long time for an opportunity to improve her position."

"No woman who raised a daughter as independent as you would be worried about position."

She smiled, happy memories pouring over her. "My mother did not raise me. She had…other pursuits."

"Who did?"

"My father until my mother noticed, as you said, how independent I became."

"And then?"

Her mother had been very shocked, when in a moment of coherence she'd seen her racing up the stairs in a pair of pants. "Life was not so exciting."

Sam sat on the bed beside her chair. He turned her

face to his. "You mentioned she had other pursuits. What were they?"

She didn't want to say.

His thumb rubbed her bottom lip. "Did she enjoy other men?"

"*Dios mío,* no!" Her mother was very reserved. Not given to touch. Very proper. "She took medicine for her pain."

"She'd been injured?"

"I think in her heart for a very long time."

"Ah. She took laudanum."

His arms came around her. Strong, warm. She turned, wrapping her arms around his neck. He pulled her as close as she could dream, so close she could hear his heart beat. Steady. Like him. She closed her eyes. "I know I promised not to cling, but I need you to hold me. Just for this little bit."

His hand smoothed over her hair. "Duchess, I'm just going to be out back."

"I know." She also knew it was the first step to putting distance between them. Taking her home to her mother would be the second. Sam never promised her forever, but he wouldn't be cruel with the goodbye. He would ease her into it. Like this.

"Then why do I feel you shaking?"

Her control wasn't what she wanted it to be. "I am afraid to go home."

She didn't want to lose the magic she had with him, didn't want to go back to her stifling existence. She didn't want to live with the gaping hole in her soul—all that would remain of her love when he left.

"Tucker and I will take care of Tejala."

She shook her head. "I do not want this. He is too dangerous."

His chuckle stirred her hair. "I'm not exactly a tabby cat, duchess."

"It is an unnecessary risk."

She covered his newly stitched arm with her palm. The arm that would bear an ugly scar because he'd refused to take the catgut that Kell needed. He was always making sacrifices. She tilted her head back so she could see his expression and more importantly, so he could see hers. "I do not want to be one of your sacrifices, Sam."

"Who said anything about sacrificing you?"

"I just think it is important that you know how unhappy I will be as your sacrifice. I will pine, mope." She frowned at him. "Most likely *cry*."

He shifted her up onto his lap, and the towel fell to the floor. There was no laughter in his voice, no amusement curved his lips, but she felt his smile in the glide of his palm over her cheek, the thread of his fingers through her damp hair. "Are you blackmailing me?"

She stroked her finger down the stubble of his cheek. He had not had time yet to bathe. "Will this work?"

"Try it and see."

She was tempted. Very tempted. But if Sam was going to stay with her it could not be because she forced him. "No. That would not be right."

His eyebrow quirked up. His smile deepened. His lips brushed over hers. "How about persuading me? Would that be right?"

She wished it would. Digging her fingernails into her palms, she kissed him back. "No."

"So it's all on me?"

He did not sound upset. His palm slid inside her robe, curled around her breast. Her *"Sí"* was more gasp than word as his thumb stroked over her nipple. "Well, that makes things easy."

With a chaste kiss to the end of her nose, he set her back on the chair.

"Makes what easy?"

He didn't answer, just scooped up his hat and sauntered out the door. Whistling. Whistling! She grabbed the pillow off the bed and threw it at his back. It missed. His chuckle floated down the hall.

She wanted to scream. She wanted to hope. She could not do either.

Movement in the doorway snapped her gaze up. Sally Mae stood there. Despite treating the outlaw, Kell and Sam, her hair was still in place in a neat bun at the base of her skull. She bent and picked up the pillow.

"Men can be infuriating, can't they?"

Isabella sighed. "Sam more than most."

Sally hesitated in the doorway. "May I come in?"

Isabella stood and tightened her sash, pulling the top closed. "Of course."

Sally put the pillow on the bed and sighed. She ran her hand over her immaculate hair. "This is awkward."

"Then you must just say it."

"I know who thee are. Thee are the woman Tejala has been searching for and—"

Isabella sighed. "You want me to leave."

"Dear heavens, no!" The woman's shock was genuine. "I wanted to offer thee refuge."

The small house was hardly the fortress that would be required to repel Tejala. "Why?"

"Edmund Burke once said, 'All that is necessary for the triumph of evil is that good men do nothing.'"

"You are not a man."

"That doesn't mean I will stand by and let a man drive a woman out of her home and do nothing."

"Even though you are a woman?"

"Rather than a man?"

"Yes."

"My religion does not hold men above women."

An interesting concept. "What else does your religion teach?"

"That all people carry the seeds of God in them and have the power of choice, that it is our duty to help where we can, and that it is wrong to do harm to others."

"And this is why you helped the outlaw?"

Sally sighed. "Yes, though sometimes doing what's right is harder than it should be."

She just bet. "Tucker said you were a woman of principle. He admires you."

A blush tinged the pale cream of the other woman's cheeks. "I bet he said a lot of other things along with it."

Isabella didn't lie. "He does have a sense of humor."

Sally frowned as if she were annoyed, but Isabella didn't miss how her gaze went out the window to the backyard where Sam and Tucker were talking. Nor did she miss the wistful hunger disguised by the brusque tone as she grumped, "It needs adjusting."

"Maybe he just needs the touch of a good woman."

"Maybe." Sally shook her head. "But it would take a very brave woman."

Said the woman who'd offered her shelter from the most feared *bandido* in the territory. "I think you are a very brave woman."

Sally blinked and then smiled sadly. "But not the woman for him."

Isabella wasn't so sure.

17

"That girl has a passel of trouble riding on her heels," Tucker said, resting his shoulder against the trunk of the big elm in the back of the boardinghouse and looking up at Isabella's bedroom window.

Sam finished rolling his smoke before tucking his makings back in his pocket. "Not as much as Desi had."

"Trouble enough." He took a draw on his cigarette. "Did you have any luck with those leads on Ari?"

"None panned out. How about you?"

"Nope." He shook his head. "I never knew there were so many blond whores until I started looking for one."

Sam knew exactly what he meant. "I'm going to hate to bring the news back to Desi."

"For sure that will break her heart."

"Yeah."

"So what are you going to do about Isabella?"

Sam struck a sulphur on the heel of his boot. "As

soon as I get her settled back at her mother's, I'm going after Tejala."

"Taking on Tejala will be a big job for one man. The man's crazy. Word is the pox is eating his brain."

Sam lit his cigarette, took a drag, and shook out the sulphur. "It's got to be done."

Tucker leaned back against the tree. "That doesn't mean you have to be the one to do it."

"I've kind of warmed up to the idea."

Tucker smiled and blew out a stream of smoke. "I get that impression."

"Bella won't be safe as long as he's alive."

"She'd be safe enough back at Hell's Eight."

Tapping the ash off his cigarette, Sam glanced through the window across to Bella's room. Through the sheer curtains, he could see her and Sally Mae talking. It was a very homey scene, one that made him hunger for the permanence it implied. "That's assuming I can get her back to Hell's Eight alive."

"If you're planning on eventually taking her back to Hell's Eight, aren't you taking a chance taking her home to her momma? I heard her mother favors the alliance with Tejala."

"Her mother can favor all she wants. Isabella will never marry that piece of shit."

Tucker shrugged. "Of course, there's always the possibility after Tejala's gone that a pretty little thing like Bella isn't going to want to marry up with a geezer like you, either."

Sam closed his teeth on the stub of his smoke. That was more likely than not. "I know."

"I was joking."

"I wasn't."

Tucker snorted. "You're shitting me, right?" He waved his hand toward the house. "That woman wants to marry you more than anything in this world."

"I know she thinks that now, but once the danger's gone and she makes up with her mother, she might reconsider."

Tucker swore and flicked his cigarette through the air. The glowing end carved a thin red path through the descending dark before it hit the ground and smoldered. "You want her, right?"

"Yes."

"Then why the hell are you setting her up to have a choice?"

"Because it's only fair."

"Fuck fair. She wants you. You want her. Take that as a sign and grab some happiness for yourself."

Sam cut Tucker a glare. "The way you grabbed up Sally Mae?"

Tucker's expression closed up tight as a drum. "That's different."

He just bet. "How so?"

Striding over to the cigarette butt he'd discarded, Tucker ground it into the dirt with the heel of his boot. Dust puffed up in a small violent cloud. "She's white. I'm Indian. She's Quaker. I'm not. She's a pacifist. I'm a gunslinger." Tucker's expression remained impassive as he turned back. "Go ahead, pick one and work with it."

"That's a heck of a lot of differences."

Tucker motioned to the upstairs window. "And yet the only thing standing between you and Isabella is your own stubbornness."

"And about ten years."

Tucker shook his head. "You're your own worst enemy sometimes, Sam."

"Maybe." He dropped his cigarette by his feet and snuffed out the butt with the toe of his boot, grinding it down into the dirt. "Or maybe I just don't want to wake up a year from now to an empty bed and a whole bunch of regrets."

"That's why you slept with her?"

Sam sighed. There wasn't much he could keep from Tucker. "No, that was weakness, pure and simple."

"It's not weak to love someone."

"I keep telling myself that."

"But…?"

One thing about being to hell and back with someone, they tended to understand. Without a lot of preface he cut to the truth. "I've been having dreams."

"About Texana?" he asked, naming the town they'd grown up in, the town that no longer existed.

He nodded. "It always starts three days after the army left."

"The day your mother died."

"Yeah. In the dream I walk up to her, but when I pull the hair back, it's Isabella's face I see."

"Damn it, Sam. How many times do I have to tell you. What happened to your mother wasn't your fault. Nothing could stop that infection."

But maybe he could have stopped the rapes that caused the infection. If he hadn't gone back in to get the deck of cards his father had bought him, she wouldn't have come back for him. She wouldn't have been trapped in the house. She might have gotten away. "I know."

Tucker sighed. "Now why don't I believe you?"

Probably because he was lying through his teeth. "I have no idea."

Blowing out a breath, Tucker clapped his hand on his shoulder. An unusual gesture for Tucker. He wasn't a demonstrative man. "I can't do your thinking for you, Sam, but I can tell you this. If Sally Mae were Isabella, and I were you, I'd grab her up and every bit of happiness I could and to hell with the consequences." His hand dropped to his thigh.

Sam glanced over. "You would, huh?"

"Shit, yes." His fingers curled into a fist. "We just don't get so many chances for happiness that I think it's worth throwing one away." His silver eyes met Sam's. "Whether it's for the best of reasons or for the worst."

It was damned uncomfortable having a man look into your soul, having that man be your best friend, knowing he not only understood your pain but shared it, and then realize that while he knew it could work out for you, it would never work out for him. Not only did it make him ache like a son of a bitch, it was humbling.

"You've got a real way with words, do you know that?"

Tucker's lips twitched at the corners in a parody of a smile. "I save them up for special occasions."

"What makes this a special occasion?"

"Shoot." The arch of his brow was eloquent. "There isn't a lady in or out of the territory that hasn't set her cap for you. It's gotten to the point where the ladies won't even give a man the time of day until they know you're not available."

"And that's cause for celebration?"

Wry humor painted Tucker's grin with the edge of sadness. "Sure is. When word gets out that you're taken all those mourning ladies will need consolation. And there will be plenty of men ready to give it."

Sam laughed despite himself. "And you're planning on being one of them?"

He shrugged. "I imagine I'll work my way up to it."

And pigs would fly tomorrow. Tucker wouldn't be consoling anyone. Not until he got over whatever it was he felt toward the widow Schermerhorn. Tucker didn't play around. When he came in from his solitary excursions, he did seek company, but it was never with a whore or a young innocent. And it was never a case of a different woman in every town. For him there always had to be at least an illusion of more than bodies satisfying a need. "You could always just steal Sally Mae away."

"The thought did cross my mind."

"But?"

"She'd consider it an act of violence and never forgive me for it. Sally Mae is real big on choice."

"Damn."

"Yeah."

Sam leaned back against the tree and watched the night fall in a curtain of black velvet. Crickets picked up their chorus. Cicadas joined in in a deafening symphony. Tucker settled in beside him and watched the half-moon struggle to clear the hills.

"Are you really going after Tejala?"

"He killed Isabella's father, choked her almost to death, chased her from her home, put a price on her head, what the hell do you think?"

"I think that would be a yes."

"That's how I saw it."

"You want some company?"

"I wouldn't mind."

"When are you heading out?"

"Tomorrow afternoon I'll take Isabella to her mother's down by Montoya. I see leaving from there by early afternoon."

"You'll have to double back this way to get to Tejala's stronghold."

"I heard he was holed up in Catch Canyon."

"That was the word."

"I've got some stuff to get together here, but—" he pointed to the southwest where Sam could make out the jutting outline in the faint light of the half-moon "—how about I meet you out by the fork in the river at the base of that ridge by nightfall?"

"That'll work." He tipped his hat back. "Do you by any chance have a bottle tucked out in the barn?"

Tucker always had a bottle stashed away. Not because he was much of a drinker, but being part Indian and looking his heritage, frequenting saloons could be more trouble than it was worth. "Of course."

Sam glanced up at the window. The light went off. He pushed off the tree. "Well in that case, how about we check on it just to make sure it's not getting lonely?"

"Can't hurt."

But it probably wasn't going to help. Sam sighed and fell into step beside Tucker. It was going to be a long night, but at least tomorrow he'd start to put things right. And from there, he'd just have to see.

Isabella had been gone for six months and topping the rise above her home she could see that nothing had changed. She pulled Sweet Pea up. The Montoya ranch spread across the valley in a neat organized sprawl with the fortress that was the hacienda in the middle like the crown jewel of her father's dream.

Breeze did a little sidestep as Sam pulled up beside her. "Very nice."

"My father had big dreams."

"Looks like he realized them."

"In part. Unfortunately, he never had a son to pass them on to."

"There was just you?"

"*Sí.*"

"So your mother favoring Tejala has more to it than just wanting to be safe?"

Isabella nodded. She loved her mother very much, but that didn't make her blind to her faults. "My father was a third son. He came here to build a future."

"And got a damned good start on it."

There was a strange note in his voice. She looked around the ranch with pride. "Yes, he did. However for my mother coming here meant giving up all position, all society. That was hard for her. She loved the parties and her social life."

"It's a hard life for a woman out here."

"Things grow better. More families come. More community builds."

"And as the woman with the biggest spread, she gets to be queen bee?"

She nodded. "This is very important to her. She cannot return to Spain except to live as the reclusive widow on the charity of her family. Her life is here now. What she wants is here now."

"But she needs to hold the ranch to hold her position."

"Yes."

"She's a wealthy widow, she shouldn't have any trouble finding a husband."

Isabella couldn't look at him.

Breeze shifted his feet in response to the tension creeping into Sam's body.

"Bella?"

There was no hope for it. She was going to have to tell him. It was unfair. He already held so many marks against her.

"The ranch does not go to my mother."

His sigh as he kneed Breeze closer cut to her heart.

"Let me guess, you inherit the whole kit 'n kaboodle?"

She ran her finger along the seam of the leather gloves Sally had loaned her. *"Sí."*

"I always figured there had to be more to the story of why Tejala wanted you." His finger curled under her chin, lifting it. "So why didn't he just marry you when he had the chance?"

"Marrying me does not get him the property."

"How does that work?"

She tried to jerk her chin free. The movement was checked before it really got going by the shake of Sam's head. It was her turn to sigh. She narrowed her gaze and set her shoulders. "If I tell you, you are not allowed to hold this as an excuse to decline my suit."

"You don't tell me what to do."

She folded her arms across her chest. "If you do not agree, I will not say."

"Duchess, men do the courting and men set the limits."

She pushed his hand out from under her chin. "Ha! I've been courting you since first we met."

That half smile she hated played about his lips. "Is that how you see it?"

"Yes, and you have not been running very hard."

To her surprise he smiled. "You might want to ask yourself why that is."

"I have often."

"And?"

"I do not have an answer."

"I do. Do you want to hear it?"

Her stomach dropped to her toes. She didn't trust what he would say when he smiled like that.

"No."

His eyebrow quirked. To her surprise, he let the subject drop. "Then maybe you'd better answer my original question."

She copied her mother's most haughty look. "An honorable man does not resort to blackmail."

He hooked his hand behind her head and kissed her hard, puffs of his laughter striking her lips as he pulled back, letting her see the humor in his eyes. "I never said I was an honorable man."

No, he hadn't. He hadn't needed to. He wore his honor easily, displayed it in everything he did. And as much as she feared how he would respond to the fact that she was a wealthy woman, she owed him the truth. "The ranch does not transfer unless I approve the man I marry."

He blinked and slowly drew back. "Son of a bitch, your father hog-tied your mother, didn't he?"

She nodded. "He worried for me."

"So he gave you all the power he could."

She nodded, tears burning as she thought of the way he died. "He did not think it would go the way it did. He died protecting me."

"I'm sure he did not regret it. Tejala must be spitting bullets."

"He is not happy with my 'stubborn nature.'"

"But I bet your father is sitting proud in heaven watching you."

The reference to heaven surprised her. "Why?"

He touched her cheek with the tips of his fingers in a gesture reminiscent of a kiss. "Because you're an amazing woman."

She frowned. "You said I was young."

He smiled. "Young and amazing."

More conflicting signals, pulling her close where before he would have pushed her away, taking control where before he would have given it to her. She didn't like it. "I do not understand you anymore."

"Figuring out why that is will give you something to do until I get back."

She grabbed his hand, squeezing hard, searching his expression for the truth. "You are coming back?"

This time when he kissed her it was with all the softness he hid so deeply inside him. "Never doubt it."

"Why?"

He looked around at the ranch below. "I'm beginning to wonder."

She dug her nails into his hand. "Look at me, Sam, not at what I own. I am more than that."

His brows snapped down in a frown. "You don't have to tell me that."

But she did, because unlike others who might want her because of her wealth, Sam was more likely to not want her because of it, to keep her safely ensconced in it. Away from the harm he thought he brought her. "I was born to this, but I do not need it."

"It's a hell of a lot to give up."

She should not push him now. It was wrong, but he was leaving to fight a battle she worried he could not win. For her. "Ask me for what we both want, Sam."

His mouth set in that stubborn way he had. "No. I'm not leaving you with regrets if something goes wrong."

"So instead you would leave me with the emptiness of the unfulfilled wish?"

Yes, Sam thought, he was, because wishes brought into the day hurt more than those that were conceived but never born. His mother's words, spoken through fever-cracked lips in a bruised and broken face whipped out of the past, flaying him anew with regret. After all this time.

It'll be all right, Sam. I'll be better in a bit and then we'll go back East to your father's brothers. They'll take care of us. You'll play with your cousins, have all the candy you want, get a good education. Just wait a few days.

Except she'd never gotten better. There hadn't been any candy. He and the others had all but starved to death waiting for his father's brothers to come. He'd hated his mother for years for giving him that hope. Hated himself for being stupid enough to believe in it to the point he'd almost killed the other members of Hell's Eight by insisting everything she'd said would come to pass. That they just had to wait.

It wasn't until he was a man full grown that he found out the telegram his mother had had him send had never arrived. By then it'd no longer mattered. He'd learned to survive on his own, without wishing. Without holding on to false hope. And without giving out false hope to anyone else.

He smoothed his thumb over her mouth. "Yes."

Her lips parted, wrapped around his work-roughened flesh in a soft nibble before sucking lightly. His cock hardened, his body hungered. His heart hungered harder.

She was everything he'd ever wanted. Everything he shouldn't take but he was going to. If he came back, and if she still wanted him after she had time to reacquaint herself with everything she would be giving up, because as beautiful as the Montoya ranch was, he wouldn't be staying. He was Hell's Eight and always would be. He slid his thumb free. "Hold that thought until I get back."

"It is not I who should hold that thought."

The smile she could always conjure from him slid across his lips. She never gave up. That was for sure. "All the way to the grave." With a press of his knees he urged Breeze away. "Now, why don't we give those guards with the bead on us a break and head on down so you can introduce me to your mother?"

The introduction didn't go as expected. Sam expected anger, coolness, and maybe a bit of leftover hostility from Bella's mother. After all, he was Texan, of no particular family connections, and a Protestant. Not to mention he looked every bit as disreputable at the moment as the outlaws he hunted. Instead, Mrs. Montoya took one look at him standing behind Isabella as she hugged her daughter and burst into tears. Not the violent emotional kind he'd seen Tia and Desi indulge in a time or two, but big silent ones that poured down her still smooth cheeks in a wrenching display of grief that went no further than him. She blinked rapidly as Bella tried to step back, hugging her again, clearly not wanting her daughter to see her distress. If he'd had a handkerchief, Sam would have handed it to her. He didn't have a handkerchief.

"Bella, your manners are slipping."

Predictably, Bella spun around and frowned at him. "This is not the time for your provoking, Sam."

He grabbed her hand and tugged her to his side, giving her mother a bit more time to compose herself. "When would be better?"

"When it is not the time for you to be making a good impression!"

"Bella!" Mrs. Montoya snapped. "This is not the way a proper young woman addresses a man."

Bella flushed and glared at him as if the reprimand was his fault.

"I am sorry, *Mamá*."

"It is not me you should be apologizing to."

It was very clear from where Bella got her tendency to give orders.

"No apologies are necessary, Señora Montoya. Bella and I have an understanding. I provoke her, and she gets to call me on it."

The woman did not look appeased. "She was raised better."

"I'll make a note of it."

Bella shot him a look so perking with frustration, he got the impression if her mother hadn't been there, she would have kicked him in the shins. "Sam MacGregor, this is *mí madre*. Bettina Montoya de Aguero."

He nodded. "A pleasure to meet you, ma'am."

She inclined her head, the break in her composure as if it had never been. "It is a pleasure to meet you also." She motioned to Bella. "Especially as you bring back to me my daughter safely."

"That also was a pleasure."

Bella flushed a brilliant red. Mrs. Montoya's brows snapped down in a frown as Bella gasped, "Sam!"

"She's got a great sense of humor," he clarified, albeit a little late. "Can make a man laugh at the darkest times."

The woman's gaze sharpened in a look he'd seen many a time before. One that usually sent him running.

"She has always had this gift."

"*She,*" Bella said, "is right here."

Mrs. Montoya never took her eyes off him. "Bella, please go to the kitchen and prepare some café for our guest."

Bella hesitated, clearly not trusting him alone with her mother. No doubt afraid of what he was going to say if she wasn't there to limit him. "Can not Leila handle this?"

"Leila is no longer with us."

"What happened?"

"I sent her away." With a wave of her hand she dismissed Bella. "Now, please hurry before your ranger thinks we do not know how to treat a guest."

She didn't go without a fight. "Sam?"

"Yes."

She touched her finger to the back of his hands. "Please remember this is *mí madre.*"

"There's no doubt about that, duchess. You look very much alike."

Bella's mother had the same fine skin, same thick dark hair, same aristocratic cheekbones, same autocratic manner, and same, he suspected, inner vulnerability.

"Sam."

He caught her hand in his. It was a blatant breach of etiquette, but what did he care about rules when there was that fear in Bella's eyes? Rubbing his thumb across the fine bones of her hand, he held her gaze and whispered, "Relax, Bella. I do know how to behave when the occasion calls for it."

"I am sorry." Her lower lip slipped between her teeth. "It is just…"

"Your mother," he finished for her.

"*Sí.*"

"Go get the coffee, Bella," Mrs. Montoya ordered.

The tone of the order brooked no denial. With one last anxious glance, Bella turned and headed to the archway, leaving him alone with her mother.

With another elegant wave of her hand, Mrs. Montoya motioned him to the comfortable parlor. The wine-colored curtains were drawn against the noon sun. He caught the woman's anxious glance toward the covered windows. Or maybe, he considered, drawn against something else.

"You indulge her," she said, turning back to him.

He took a seat where she indicated in the wing-back chair across from the horsehair sofa. "She's easy to indulge."

The response prompted another frown. "She is headstrong and without a firm hand will get herself in trouble."

He smiled. "Like running away rather than marrying up to a ba—monster like Tejala?"

"You also defend her."

"Again, she's easy to defend."

"Are you involved inappropriately with my daughter, Mr. MacGregor?"

"I'd say we've done everything right."

"I have heard of your reputation."

He didn't think she was talking about his reputation with guns.

"You are said to have many women in many towns."

"A lot of things are said."

"That is not an answer."

He sat back. The chair was comfortable. Built for a man of about his size. It was a pleasant change. "Probably because you haven't asked me any questions."

Her eyes narrowed and then she smiled. Just a little, and it was tight around the edges, but it was a smile. "Like my husband, you are very direct."

"I find it saves time."

"So did he."

She looked around the room, memories in her sigh. "He loved it here. Loved what he'd created."

"Bella says you weren't so enthusiastic."

"I was not the best mother then."

"There's still a whole lot of future ahead of you."

"Why are you being so kind?"

He shrugged. "Bella loves you. Since I can't see Bella being happy if I stand between you and her, I'm inclined to be generous."

"But?"

He met her gaze squarely. "You betray her to Tejala, and I'll kill you myself."

She sat back, eyes widening. "Not so kind, after all."

"No," he agreed, placing his hat on his knee. "Not so kind."

"But you love my daughter."

It was a statement of fact.

"That I won't discuss with you."

"Because you don't feel it?"

"Because Bella deserves to have it discussed with her first."

"Ah." She smoothed a wrinkle from the sofa, attacking it again when it popped back up. "My daughter is in a lot of trouble."

"I'm going to fix that."

"By killing Tejala?"

"Yes."

Footsteps sounded on the tile. Bella returning. Mrs. Montoya cast another anxious glance at the doorway. "The trouble will not go away with Tejala's death," she said in a low urgent voice. "There will be other men wanting what she owns."

"I know."

"It will take a strong man to hold this ranch for her children, but she would make it worth his while."

Bella was almost upon them. "Are you offering me Bella in exchange for her safety?"

"Yes."

"Son of a bitch!"

Mrs. Montoya sat back, her face bleaching white.

Bella came in the room, took one look at the scene and swore with a word she must have picked up from him. The coffee cups rattled on the tray.

Sam got up and took it from her before she dropped

it. She glared around him at her mother. "You offered me to him, didn't you? Like I was some cow in the pasture to be bargained away for a profit."

"Bella…" Sam cautioned.

She shoved past him, advancing on her mother who didn't say a word, didn't stand up.

"No. She offers you the ranch, like I matter for nothing." Her voice rose with the pain of every syllable, imitating her mother's more precise pronunciation. "You can have this wonderful ranch if you will but take my worthless daughter off my hands."

"Bella!" her mother gasped.

"That's enough." Sam put the tray on the table.

She spun around, her hands slamming down on her hips. "No, it is not. First cousin Aguerro, then Tejala, now you and tomorrow maybe someone else." She threw up her hands. "When does what I want matter?"

She meant more than with just her mother. Sam grabbed her arm and tugged her around. He held her gaze. "I said, enough."

She was furious but beyond that, hurt. Ignoring her mother and all the rules of propriety, he pulled her to him.

She struggled, taking a halfhearted swing at him. "Let me go."

The blow landed lightly against his ribs. Holding her close he smoothed his hand over her hair, feeling her tremble, feeling her pain, hating that anything but a smile touched her. "Enough, Bella."

Her hands fisted against his chest. She thumped him on the shoulder, rocking her forehead on the plateau of his breastbone. "I am more than this, Sam."

"I know."

She waved her hand indicating the room and all its elegant furnishings without lifting her head. "I wanted *you* to see me as more than this."

"Bella, I fell in love with you when I thought you didn't have a pot to pee in."

She went still against him, still not looking. "Say it again." Before he could open his mouth she added, "Just the first part."

He smiled. It hadn't been the most romantic declaration. "Look at me first."

"No."

"Why not?"

"Because if I do I'll wake up and it will be a dream and I could not bear it."

"Your dreams are so poor this is the scenario in which you imagine a man will propose?"

Her head popped up then. "Propose? I did not hear a proposal."

"And you're not going to either until I get back."

She propped her chin on his chest, as always a combination of flirtation, humor and that incredible feminine strength. "But words of love, you will tell me those."

It wasn't a question, which just made him smile. He traced the outline of her mouth with his index finger. "Yeah. I'll tell you those."

In front of her mother, before he went off and maybe got himself killed, he would give her words of love. Give her hope. Oh yeah, he was a prize.

Something of his thoughts must have shown in his expression because she frowned. "And no regrets, Sam. I do not want them with regrets."

She wanted them any way she could get them, the same way he wanted them from her. He tipped Bella's head back, and parted her lips with his thumb. Her mother cleared her throat. Sam tempered his intent. Placing his mouth against hers, he gave her a chaste kiss rife with tenderness instead of passion. "I love you, Bella Montoya."

Her hands crept up to his neck, nails stinging in erotic little enticements, holding his mouth to hers when he would have pulled back.

"This is not a dream?"

"No, duchess. No dream."

Relaxing against him, she came up on her toes, fitting her body more intimately to his. Her "Good" sighed into his mouth.

He waited. She didn't return the sentiment. As the seconds passed, he became more and more aware of her mother watching. More and more aware of her silence. He pulled back. She smiled contentedly up at him. And still she said nothing.

"Is there something you want to say to me?"

"When you come back, when you give me the rest of what I want to hear, then I will give you the words you want to hear."

"Are you blackmailing me, Bella?"

"*Sí.*"

And she did it without a lick of shame, too.

18

"You have chosen a very hard man."

Bella glanced away from the window to look at her mother. "I have chosen a good man."

"He will not let you always have your way."

"He always lets me have my way."

"Because he humors you."

Yes he did, and it pleased Bella even as it irritated her for a reason she didn't understand.

"If you choose him, he will control you," her mother continued.

It wasn't the annoying thought it should have been. She turned her attention to the scenery beyond the window. Specifically to the rise Sam had ridden over. "He will try."

"Men do not like women who see themselves as their equal."

In a flash of insight, Isabella understood the problem in her mother's marriage. Her mother was strong and intelligent, and could be seen as a threat by a man who already struggled as a third son. "He is not Papá."

Her mother sighed and came up beside her. They were the same height. She'd never realized that before.

"In some ways all men are the same. They want to be the only one and they want to be in charge."

Sam did like to be in charge. And he was possessive, but that did not mean that he would want her to be less than herself. He had not grown up in the old world, had not grown up expecting her obedience as his due. "Not Sam."

She pushed the other panel of the curtain aside and stared out. Silence stretched uncomfortably, until finally her mother spoke in a sad whisper. "I wasn't trying to sell you to him."

Bella couldn't look over. It hurt too much. "Then what were you doing?"

Out of the corner of her eye she saw her mother lick her lips. A rare nervous gesture. "Getting for you what you wanted."

She'd never even thought to look at it that way. "What?"

"You clearly wanted him. And he was resistant. This is a big ranch. A prize. A man would have to be a fool to not want it."

"Or Hell's Eight."

"What does this mean?"

"It means he is a man that cannot be bought."

Bettina glanced over. "He will walk away from your heritage?"

"He does not want it."

"Every man wants it."

Bella didn't know how to explain to her mother the loyalty that burned so brightly in Sam. He did not come from a society where children were traded in marriage as pawns for power, where always it was a battle for position and what went on behind the scenes was often more important than what was displayed to the public.

"He is a very straightforward man." Her fingers tightened on the curtains. Bella bit her lip. "If he chooses me, I will be a very lucky woman."

"Why would he not choose you?" Her mother frowned, her lips tightening as she pulled herself up straight. "What is wrong with him? You are young, beautiful, smart." With a jerk of her chin her mother punctuated the last claim with the arrogance she wore so effortlessly. "A Montoya. He should be grateful that you even smile at him."

That was the mother she remembered.

"I will be sure to tell him that." Imagining Sam's smile if she did inspired one of her own.

There was another long pause, and when her mother broke it, it was with a voice as tight as her expression. "If you go with him, you will be alone."

There was no if. "*When* I go with him, I will have Sam."

"And when he tires of you or becomes embarrassed because you are not white like the women around you? What will you do then? You will have no family to protect you. No one to run to."

They were genuine concerns. They just weren't hers. "I think I should warn you, Mamá. Sam is not at all proper."

Her mother's brows snapped down again. "And this means what?"

"He has not much interest in society's dictates."

The expression in her mother's eyes was old. "He will when the children come. The words spoken against his choice then will matter."

Sam would be a fiercely protective father. "Then society had best watch out. He is not tolerant of those that hurt the ones he loves."

Turning, her mother put her shoulder to the window and studied Bella with an assessing look in her eyes. When she was younger and had made foolish decisions, the look alone had been enough to make Bella squirm and confess. "There is no doubt in your voice and I must wonder as you have not known him long. Do you know him so well or does love blind you?"

She didn't even have to think. "I know him so well."

There was another long look from her mother.

"He is worthy of being a Montoya?"

An easy question. "Yes."

"And you will have no other? You have not met Xavier Alvarez's nephew. A fine-looking man just a year older—"

"I will have no other," she snapped, only to see the teasing smile softening the edges of her mother's mouth too late.

It had been a long time since she'd laughed with her mother. Impulsively, she leaned over and hugged her. "I love you, Mamá."

Her mother stood frozen for a second and then she hugged her back. Hard and quick. "I thought you had forgotten."

"The last years have been so confusing. Especially when you gave me to a monster."

"I did not give you to Tejala. The plan was never to deliver you to him but only to buy time, but you did not believe and you ran and it all went bad."

Bella stepped back. "Did Papá know?"

"He did not approve." Her mother didn't release her, maintaining contact through the tips of her fingers on her arms. "So why does your man not snatch you up?"

"He thinks I am too young and that if he gives in to his feelings, he will be taking advantage of me and steal the future I should have."

Bettina shook her head and sighed, letting go of her hands. "This is what happens when men think. They get everything wrong. You have never been young."

Her mother did know her. "Papá might have understood."

"Not in time." A wistful tone entered her voice. "Your father could be stubborn."

"Very stubborn," Bella agreed, sharing the memories caught in her mother's smile. Her eyes stung with tears as she remembered the time he'd bought a burro to power the gristmill. "Do you remember when he bought Felix?"

"*Sí*. Felix. Your father wanted him to walk in circles."

"Felix only wanted a straight line. So Papá decided to train him."

"And spent hours walking in circles beside it only to find that was how it always must be."

Felix still lived on the ranch but they did not have a gristmill.

"I told him another burro might be different—"

"But—" her mother laughed with her, wiping at her eyes "—he said he did not have the time to train another one."

The tears in her mother's eyes gave her pause. They were not all from humor. "You cared for him?"

Bettina looked surprised by the question. "He was a good man. We lived together for twenty years. Why would I not?"

Isabella felt like a fool. Indeed, why would she not? "Maybe Sam was right." She sighed. "Maybe I am too young."

Bettina shook her head. "Now is not the time to doubt yourself."

"Why?"

"Because your Sam could go either way when he comes back if he has such guilt."

"He had a lot of guilt."

"Why?"

"It involves his mother."

"She was an evil woman?"

"No, he loved her very much but she died in a way that has left scars." Sam had not told her, but Tucker had. Someday Sam would, but until then at least she had the knowledge.

And the life he lived after left many more scars. So many she ached thinking about them. So many he felt unworthy of her. Which was the most ridiculous exasperating thing.

Her mother went back to staring out the window. Isabella searched for Sam, even though he'd only left a few hours ago. She didn't know what her mother searched for.

"If he wants you, you really will go?"

"I will go whether he wants me or not."

That sent her mother's eyebrows up. "You will not abide by his decision?"

"If he decides I should live without him, no."

The corner of her mother's mouth twitched. "Does he know this?"

Isabella's own lips twitched in wry amusement. "He should. I have not exactly been complacent to this day."

"A man like this will be angry."

"His anger will not be as big as mine should he throw our love away."

Her mother let the curtain drop and turned. "What is your plan?"

Innocence was getting harder to feign. "What makes you think I have a plan?"

Bettina snorted. "You have always had a plan since you were old enough to think."

Her mother did know her. "If he leaves me, I will follow."

"And then?"

She blushed. That part of the plan she didn't think she could share.

Her mother did not need a picture drawn. "You plan on seducing him."

The words were shocking coming from her mother's mouth. Even more shocking was the lack of blush as she did so. "Yes."

Her mother raised her brows. "Haven't you already done that?"

"Yes, but I have not conceived."

"You would trap him with a child he does not want. Why?"

"Because he does want it." She was sure of this. "Sam takes care of everything he meets. He...substitutes strangers for the family he is afraid to have." She remembered how his hand cradled her stomach low down where his seed had spilled. The hungry expression on his face as he'd rubbed it into her skin. The intensity of the emotion pouring off him as he'd kissed her breasts, her stomach, her mound afterwards. "He can face death without fear, but he cannot face bringing harm to one he loves."

"And he fears harming you? Why?"

The snap in Bettina's voice yanked her head up.

"Not because of any lack in himself. He would die for me. It is the life he leads he fears." She shaped her hands into a closed ball. "He wants me in a safe cocoon like a butterfly."

"You would go crazy living like that."

She smiled, rubbing her arms as a cloud chased across the sky, briefly casting the room in shadow. "I am waiting for him to realize this."

"That could be a long wait, and you have little patience."

"I have patience enough for this."

Despite her words to the contrary, she could wait forever for Sam.

"You want him this badly?"

"He is the only man I will love."

Her mother scoffed. "Spoken like a child."

Isabella looked out the window, up the path Sam had taken when he'd ridden from her life, ready to sacrifice himself so she wouldn't face danger. "No. Spoken like a woman who knows her heart."

She frowned as a rider appeared on the hill. First one then another. Not comprehending what she was seeing until three gunshots went off in rapid succession. Warning shots.

Her mother grabbed her arm and dragged her back so fast she stumbled. "Get away from the window."

Isabella spun around, looking over her shoulder. Riders spilled over the hill in a cloud as dark and as threatening as the one that had just passed. Someone rang the bell in front of the main bunkhouse. It chimed loud and urgent. There were shouts in the yard. Doors crashed against walls. Booted feet raced over wooden porches.

"¿*Qué pasa?*"

Her mother shot a glare out the window as she crossed to the gun cabinet.

"Tejala comes for you."

"Something's wrong."

Tucker's declaration merely confirmed the sick feeling in Sam's gut for the last fifteen minutes they'd been climbing toward the stronghold. There should have been guards. Someone should have challenged their approach, taken a shot at them. It should not be this quiet.

He swung down off Breeze's back and crouched down by the tracks. Pushing his hat off his forehead he glanced down the trail perpendicular to the one on which they'd come in. "Everyone's heading out. No one's going in."

"Maybe Tejala's moving again. Enough people knew about this hideout to make him nervous. "

One of the reasons Tejala avoided capture was that he rotated between hideouts, always keeping them secret, never staying long enough in one to be caught.

"Maybe." He scooped up a handful of dirt and poured it into a hoofprint. But he didn't think so.

"You think they went after Isabella?"

Sam stood. "I don't think Tejala would leave the area without securing her."

Tucker spit out the piece of grass he was chewing on. "Seems a damned high risk to take just for a woman."

"Bella isn't just a woman."

"Uh-huh. I'd expect you to say that."

Sam shook his head. "I'm not that lovesick."

"But you are lovesick."

"Don't rub it in," he growled.

"So what's the big draw for Tejala with Bella?"

"The Montoya ranch is inherited through Bella."

"Well shit, no wonder Tejala wants her so badly."

"There's more."

Tucker pushed his hat back off his face and sighed. "There always is."

He turned Breeze back down the path and stopped. There was something wrong with the tracks. "Along with her mother, Bella has to approve the match or the ranch doesn't transfer."

Tucker pulled up beside him and studied the ground. "Who the hell thought of that?"

"Her father."

"He wasn't thinking much, was he? A will like that opens a woman up for every schemer that steps off the stagecoach."

"I know." Sam motioned to the ground. "That strike you as odd?"

"Yeah."

Dismounting, they followed a too-clean path to a

tumble of rocks. Dirt and debris splattered the sides of the biggest and sprinkled the tops of the small ones. Debris just didn't fall that way naturally, but it did fall that way when swept about in an effort to cover tracks. And the only reason someone covered tracks was that they'd left something valuable behind.

"Interesting." He studied the rocks. The slide was taller than his head. Stepping back, he couldn't see any clear opening. Tucker walked around the left side. "See any signs of a cave?"

"Not so you'd notice."

Sam took another step back, squinting against the bright sun. The need to get to Bella gnawed at him. At the same time, his gut said he was missing something important. Tucker moved around the right side, when it struck him. The debris sprinkled upward in a straight line.

"Tucker."

"Yeah." He leaned back around the rock.

"I'm thinking up's the way we need to go."

"It figures." Tucker took out his bowie knife.

Sam snorted and pulled his normal-sized knife. "Why don't you just go holler to the snakes that they terrify you?"

"Just because I don't like them, doesn't mean I'm terrified." Tucker flipped the wicked knife with its wide blade that curved to a lethal tip.

"Then what's a knife like that supposed to say?"

"Get the hell out of my way."

Despite the tension, Sam grinned and waved him forward. "In that case, you go first."

Tucker cut him a glare. "Just remember this when it's time to escort a lady across a river."

Sam grimaced. Desi, Caine's wife, had gotten him good that time, tricking him with an appearance of complacency, almost drowning them both in her escape attempt. It had been a damn cold ride home and he'd yet to hear the end of it that a little slip of a thing got the better of him. He still didn't know how anyone that delicate looking could get up to so much mischief. "Just climb."

Tucker smiled, his teeth clenching down on the heavy blade before he started up. Sam followed, his own knife between his teeth. He wasn't any more fond of snakes than Tucker was, but he had a lot less reason for his fear. Being thrown into a snake pit and left to die put a mark on a man.

Tucker reached the top and whistled.

"Find something?"

"A nice little hidey-hole."

He heaved himself up over the last boulder. The back of the rocks spilled down to a cave. The opening was about five feet high and wide enough for a man to get through. "Think there's anything inside?"

Sam took his sulphur out of his makings and started down the other side. "Only one way to find out."

Tucker sighed. "Figured you were going to say that."

The reason for his reluctance was easy to figure.

There was a higher likelihood of snakes in the cave. He glanced over. Tucker was breathing evenly. Too evenly.

Sam cut him a glance. "I'll go in. You keep an eye out here."

"Like hell."

"It's not necessary to push like this."

"That's not your call."

"You don't have anything to prove to me."

Tucker moved toward the entrance. "Wasn't aware that I was trying."

"You are one stubborn son of a bitch, Tucker McCade."

"Yeah," he mocked back. "And you're the obliging sort."

"Sweet as pie. Just ask the ladies."

Tucker ducked into the interior. "I think I'll just ask Isabella."

Sam followed. "That's underhanded."

"Funny. I just see it as an easy way to get to an honest answer."

Sam struck a sulphur, moving with Tucker into the cavern a few feet at a time until the weak light illuminated the far wall.

"Son of a bitch!"

Cases of dynamite lined the wall. An open crate lay on the floor, packing hay strewn about.

Tucker waved his hand and stepped back. "Put out the goddamn sulphur."

Sam shook it out. He took a step back himself. Dynamite could be damn unstable. As the cave plunged to darkness, a dry rasping rattle filled the cave, echoing off the walls, making it impossible to locate the source. He heard Tucker's indrawn breath. He struck another sulphur. Snake trumped dynamite as far as immediate threats went. In the wavering light, he saw Tucker staring at a spot directly behind him. Shit.

"Don't move."

The rattle came louder. "Wasn't planning on it."

Sam could see the sweat on Tucker's forehead, knew the sound alone had to be eating at his mind, but when he sheathed the bowie knife and pulled the throwing knife, his hands were steady. With slow easy movements, he walked to the side, easing the knife into throwing position as he did.

The snake wasn't impressed. Its rattling took up a frantic rhythm. "Hold up that light," Tucker ordered. "When I say, 'jump,' hightail it to the left."

"Don't worry, I'll have wings on my feet."

Tucker's eyes narrowed. "Ready."

The sulphur burned almost to his fingertips. "Can't be soon enough for me."

"Jump."

He jumped. The knife whizzed past his head. The flame blew out. There was a thunk and the rattling hit a discordant rhythm. Sam rolled to his feet, ripped a sulphur out of his kit, and struck it. In the wavering light he saw the snake was dead, its body severed in half. Not a surprise. Tucker never missed.

Sam retrieved the knife before Tucker could force

himself to and stuck it in his belt. He prodded the dead snake with his foot. "At least we've got dinner."

"Not hardly."

In the flimsy light Sam saw a torch propped against the wall. It flared to life at the touch of the flame. The stench of kerosene followed the burst of light. Holding the torch up, Sam counted the boxes of dynamite. Ten in all. Enough to blow up half a mountain. Enough to cause problems for a bunch of soldiers. He smiled. Enough to cause problems for Tejala.

He patted one of the cases, holding the torch well away, and looked at Tucker. "Are you thinking what I'm thinking?"

"Probably." Tucker came over and motioned Sam back. "Which, you realize, only makes us both crazy," he grunted as he hefted the box up and headed back toward the entrance.

"And what's wrong with that?"

"We don't have enough time to discuss it," Tucker called back.

Sam stayed behind, holding the torch high, studying the stash. Nine boxes could do a lot of damage. Kill a lot of men. Hurt a lot of innocent people.

"Tucker?"

"Yeah?"

From the sound of things he'd cleared the top of the slide and was working his way down the other side. Sam dropped the torch in the loose hay on the floor by the boxes.

"Run!"

* * *

They made the ride back to the Montoya ranch in record time despite the dynamite tied to the back of Sam's horse. Cresting the rise, he realized it wasn't fast enough. The neat orderly ranch was in chaos. Ranch hands milled in the courtyard, saddling horses, some cursing while others shouted orders. Wagons were turned over as makeshift barriers. Curtains fluttered out of broken windows. The front door hung off its hinges.

"Son of a bitch," Tucker breathed.

The sick feeling in Sam's stomach grew. "Yeah."

He kicked Breeze into a gallop, uncaring of the risk, needing to get down there, needing to see Bella, needing to know she was all right.

A clanging rang in his ears as Breeze ate up the distance with long hungry strides. A man to his right shouted and pulled out his gun, getting in his way. Sam drew his Colt and fired. At the last second his arm was knocked up and Tucker was between him and his target. He heard Tucker shout something. He didn't know what. He just knew that men melted out of his way and there was nothing between him and that ominously listing front door. Breeze slid to a stop. Sam didn't. Using the momentum to propel him forward and onto the porch in a flying dismount, he burst into the house.

"Bella!"

No one answered. Crossing to the parlor he looked

inside. Shards of glass sparkled on the polished wood floor. The door to a half-empty gun cabinet swung open. A dark stain marred the cushion on the maroon settee. The stain drew him forward against his will. He reached out. Touched it, confirming what he'd already known. Blood.

He spun around. "Bella!"

This time there was a response. The scrape of a shoe on wood. The squeak of a door hinge from somewhere in the interior. Pulling his Colt, he ran in the direction. Rounding a corner he nearly ran into a short plump woman. She screamed and dropped back against the doorjamb.

He grabbed her arm and snarled, "Where's Bella?"

She clutched her chest. Her mouth worked. He shook her. "Where's Bella?"

"Sam?"

He dropped the woman's arm with disgust and pushed into the room. Bettina lay on the bed, a bloody bandage wrapped around her chest, her expression as stark as her long black hair against the white sheets. She looked so much like his Bella it hurt him seeing her there because she was alive and safe while Bella...Bella might be—he cut off the thought. Leaning over he wrapped his fingers in Bettina's hair, holding her gaze to his. "Where is she?"

She licked her dry lips, but didn't look away. Her voice was a hoarse rasp. "He took her."

"Who?" He already knew, but he needed to hear it.

Needed to hear how he had failed Isabella. Hear how empty his promises to keep her safe had been.

"Tejala."

He only needed to know one more thing. "Did you betray her?"

"No."

Her gaze didn't flinch. In it he saw pain, anger, but no fear. He straightened and let go of her hair. "I believe you."

He turned on his heel. She caught his sleeve. He turned.

She struggled up on her elbows. "You go for her."

"Yes."

"He will rape her."

The words hit him like bullets. "I know."

"Do not tell her until you get back."

"Tell her what?'

"That you no longer consider her for your wife. It will break her."

He didn't remember moving, but he had Bettina's shoulders in his hands and he had her raised off the bed, rage pouring from him. "Did you tell her that filth?" He shook her. Her head rocked back and forth. "Did you tell her I wouldn't want her if he touched her?"

A woman was screaming. Boots thudded down the hallway. Hands grabbed his shoulders. All he could see was Bettina's face and the truth. All he could hear was Bella's certainty.

I will not live with the touch of him on my skin.

"Jesus. Sam. Back off."

More hands grabbed his wrist, jerking it free. He clung with the left as if keeping the contact could block the truth. As the third man joined the fray, he was pulled off.

He closed his eyes. Bella was strong. Strong enough to kill herself rather than be dishonored. Strong enough to defeat Tejala the way she felt she had to. He didn't fight the men dragging him back, his attention focused inward, reaching for Bella with a desperate prayer.

Don't do it, duchess. Don't do it.

There wasn't any answer. Just the never-ending echo of his own plea.

When he opened his eyes, two hard-eyed Montoya men along with Tucker stood between him and the bed, ready to leap if he went crazy again.

"We'll get her back," Tucker said.

Sam shot Bella's mother a look of disgust. "When we do, she's not coming back here."

Dead or alive, he was not bringing her back here.

"This is her home," Bettina gasped, holding her shoulder. "Her birthright."

"Her home is with me."

"You do not understand—"

The rage swelled almost beyond his ability to contain it. He cut her off with a slash of his hand. "No. You don't. You don't understand her, and you don't understand me, but try to understand this. There's nothing in this world that could make Bella anything less than perfect to me, and if anything happens to her because you convinced her otherwise…" He looked out the window at the men readying to ride and then at the men between him and Bettina. "Well, lady, you'd better hire on a bigger army because I'll be coming for you."

Bettina opened her mouth, closed it, struggled to sit up. Fresh blood stained her bandage. The plump woman came to her side. She waved her away. Her expression tight with pain and anger, Bettina propped herself on her elbow. Sam didn't want to hear what she had to say. He headed for the door. Behind him he heard Tucker follow. Bettina's threat stopped him as he reached the threshold, paralyzing him with a need to respond.

"Know this, Ranger. If you do not bring my daughter home, I will be coming for *you*."

Tucker's palm in the middle of Sam's back shoved him on through the door before the rage could cut loose.

"Lady, shut the hell up."

Outside, men waited in the twilight. They were armed to the teeth, standing by fresh mounts and they were looking at him expectantly. The dynamite lay beside the porch. One of the men walked a saddleless Breeze, cooling him down gradually from the hard ride in. Tucker's horse was being cared for the same way. Their gear had been packed on two fresh mounts.

"What is this?"

One of the men following came around to stand in front of him. There was a tear in his shirt at the shoulder. Blood on his sleeve. "We ride with you."

"No." He would not risk Isabella to men he didn't know.

The man's eyes narrowed. "She is our *patrona*. Stolen on our watch. It is our right to return her to her home."

"She's not coming back here." His hand dropped to his gun. "Now, get out of my way."

The man didn't budge, merely pointed to a man in his forties with gray at his temples. "That is Miguel. He has been with the Montoyas for twenty years. He picked out *la Montoya*'s first pony and cart. He taught her to drive." He pointed to a young man still in his teens. "That is Guillermo. He and *la Montoya* were playmates, always in trouble together. When Isabella fell into the river, he jumped in and pulled her out. He was six at the time." He pointed to three men roughly about his age. Tall, lean with a fighter's tension. They had his hard eyes and their array of weapons was both impressive and practical. "These are my brothers. Our job has always been to protect Isabella."

"And you are?"

"Zacharias Lopez."

"Well, Zacharias, it's one hell of a job you're doing."

"That was unfair, Sam," Tucker interjected. "Tejala is crazy with the pox. No one could expect this."

"Fuck fair." He didn't care about fair. Tejala had Bella. He'd worry about fair when he had her back. Sam grabbed up the case of dynamite and swung it up onto the horse's withers, keeping the rough wood on the extra blanket. The chestnut snorted and pranced at the awkward weight.

"Easy boy."

When he turned, Miguel was there with a length of rope. Calm. Capable. Determined. He didn't let go when Sam grabbed hold. The tension stretched along the length, joining them. Miguel's gaze caught and held his.

"Men died to protect *la Montoya* here today. More will die before we get her back. The deaths do not matter. We gladly make the sacrifice for Isabella. She is Montoya. She is family. Not you. Not Tejala. Nothing will keep us from getting her back."

There wasn't a quiver of uncertainty in the older man's voice. He meant what he said.

"And when you do?" Sam asked.

"Then *la Montoya* will make the decision of where she will go."

Even if she didn't want to go with him. Sam understood that. Even respected it. Isabella's father had hired good men.

"Fair enough."

Miguel let go of the rope. *"Bueno."*

A ripple of satisfaction went through the men. As quietly as he'd approached, Miguel resumed his place.

"Anybody have any idea of what direction Tejala took her?" Sam asked, tying off knots.

There was a disturbance behind the line of horses. A

boy who looked about eight was furiously kicking the sides of a barrel-bellied burro. The burro trotted along at the same pace, its short legs setting a bruising rhythm the boy went with.

As soon as the boy saw Zacharias, he started yelling in Spanish too fast for Sam to translate.

He looked over at Zacharias. "What's he going on about?"

Zach shrugged. "I have no idea."

The boy kept coming like the demons of hell were on his heels, showing no indication of slowing when he neared the horses.

As he got closer, Sam could make out part of what he was saying.

"La Montoya! La Montoya!" He could also make out blood on the boy's shirt. A lot of it.

"Give him room."

The men already were. The Lopez brothers converged on the boy and burro, snatching him off before laying him on the porch amidst a string of harsh curses.

"Who is he?" Sam asked, as Zach stripped the shirt from his chest, revealing a bullet hole high on the left side.

Zach rolled the boy onto his side, ignoring his frantic gasps of *"Escucha me."* The bullet had gone clear through. That was at least a blessing. He said something to his brother before answering Sam. "My little brother, Jorge. The foolish one."

"Why foolish?"

Zach smoothed the hair from his forehead. "He followed Tejala when he left."

"On that burro?"

"*Sí.*"

He arched his brow at him. "You didn't stop him?"

Zach's eyes narrowed at his brother. "We did not know."

"Are all of you that determined?"

Zach glanced up. The fires of hell had nothing on the fires burning in Zach's eyes. "Yes. And Tejala will pay for this, too."

At the mention of Tejala's name, the boy grabbed Sam's arm, the small blood-covered fingers with their ragged nails surprisingly strong. He again spoke too fast for Sam to understand. All he got was *la Montoya*. The kid knew something about Bella.

"What did he say?'

Zach took a breath. "He says you must hurry before Tejala hurts her."

The sick feeling in his stomach grew. "Where are they?"

"Not far."

That at least was good news. "Where?"

The boy pointed to the canyon.

"In the caves," Zach said. "They must have holed up for the night."

He asked the question of the boy. "What about *la Montoya*?"

Zach listened and then translated. "He said *la*

Montoya was disrespectful." Sam closed his eyes, knowing what was coming. *Ah Bella.*

"Tejala struck her and then took her off alone to one of the caves."

There was more Spanish. A hesitation before Zach translated. Sam opened his eyes, waiting.

"He says the men all laughed when *la Montoya* screamed and fought. It made her mad. She grabbed a knife."

Sam's heart froze in his chest. The child was too young to know why Bella panicked. Why she grabbed that knife. *No.*

"He says many screams came from inside the cave. Much noise." Zach's gaze dropped from his.

"What?"

Tucker came up beside him and put his hand on his shoulder. "Let it go, Sam."

"What did the kid say?"

Zach shook his head. Tucker answered in the flat direct way he had when delivering bad news. "He said she screamed your name and then all went quiet."

"Son of a fucking bitch."

Dear God, don't let her be dead.

The small fingers on his arm squeezed once. Twice. He looked down. The boy stared back at him with too-old eyes in a too-white face and whispered in broken English on broken breaths, "She…waits…for you."

Shit, he hoped so.

19

The caves were dark. Sam slipped along the ledge that rimmed the openings, conscious of the dynamite tucked into his belt, hoping like hell it was as stable as it seemed to be, but not taking chances by scraping it against the wall. According to Jorge, Tejala had Bella in the third cave from the right. If Jorge hadn't been so foolhardy as to risk his life by following Tejala's gang, he never would have known they were here. No fires burned by the entrances. No smell of smoke tinted the air. According to Zacharias, the caves went deep into the mountain with many connecting tunnels which probably meant they vented elsewhere, too. Put a fire deep enough in them and no one would know.

Sam looked out into the desert. He owed Jorge. Without his tenaciousness, Sam would have ridden right past, wasting precious time. Maybe costing Bella her life. If the day ever came when Jorge called in the debt, it would be gladly met. By Sam or any member of Hell's Eight.

Sam glanced along the ledge behind him. Other shadows followed in his tracks, not by a scrape of a boot betraying their presence. Isabella's father might have made some mistakes in his life, but the men he hired was not one of them. The Montoya ranch hands were a force to be reckoned with under normal circumstances, but with vengeance on their mind, there were like death blowing in on a cold wind. He held up his hand to indicate for the men behind him to stop. Across the way he could see the other group led by Tucker clearing the edge of the ledge and getting into position. The sharpshooters were there, though they were not visible. A cloud drifted across the moon, throwing them in darkness.

Shit. The ledge was too narrow to traverse without some light. The left side of the ledge was a sheer drop into the plain below. It'd taken them two hours to climb the side of the mountain but they could probably get back down to the bottom in a couple of minutes if they were willing to give flying a try. Sam didn't feel like flying, but he did feel like killing. Every one of the sons of bitches who'd taken Bella, but especially Tejala. That bastard he was going to take great pleasure in killing. Slowly.

Don't give up, Bella.

He refused to think she already might have. Refused to think on how badly she would be hurting if she hadn't. With every second that ticked by during which he was forced to wait, the wildness inside surged and the recklessness grew, one thought overriding all others with the urgency. He had to get to Bella. She was close. She needed him. He had to get to her.

His breath came hard and a cold sweat broke out on his body as the past bled over the present. He saw his mother held down by soldiers. Felt the raw burn from his bindings as he struggled, saw the hopeless plea in her eyes. A plea he wanted to answer but couldn't. He was just ten feet, just five steps away if he could only move, but he couldn't. Couldn't move, couldn't help her even as he heard that last horrible scream as something ruptured inside her under their torture. Saw her lips move in prayer one last time, saw the acceptance in her eyes as her God and her son failed her. Saw her give up in that moment and as he called to her, begged her mentally to stay, her face became Bella's. Her eyes, Bella's. Her pleas, Bella's. Her prayers, Bella's. He closed his eyes. For sure, Bella would be praying.

Sam glanced at the heavens, toward the God Bella so believed in.

Don't you fucking fail her.

A hand touched his shoulder, snapping him out of the nightmare. In a whisper so soft so as not to carry past his ear, Zacharias whispered, "Shoot for more respectful. The odds aren't that much in our favor."

Sam blinked. He'd said the last aloud. Shit. He was losing control. He nodded. Light began to leach back into the landscape. He took one breath and then another, forcing Bella from his mind, gathering the cold anticipation of battle around him as a shield. Bella didn't need him crazy. She needed him doing what he did best. He pulled his knife from his boot while motioning to the others he was going forward. From across the length of the ledge, Tucker raised his hand in acknowledgement.

This was the most dangerous part. Sam had to get past the first two caves without being detected. He crept forward, watching for dark spots on the ground that would be pebbles. He couldn't afford any noise. Not now. He got to the edge of the first cave. No noise came from within, nothing to indicate if someone was sitting on the other side, ready to shoot. Glancing up at the sky he only had a few seconds to wait. With the moon obstructed, he'd be able to cross in front with no one the wiser. He knew Tucker was making the same approach from the other side. And behind him, a line of men were ready to take his place. The only one getting out of these caves alive tonight would be Bella.

Memorizing the narrow path, Sam waited for the cloud to make its push. Light faded with a slide of black over gray. He moved quickly, chasing it across the entrance, glancing inside as he did. Two men sat in the entrance, their attention on the cards between them. He faded into the shadows on the other side as the men looked up. The cloud moved on. Tucking into a crevice in the wall, he signaled back to the others. Two men inside.

He had to wait longer to clear the second cave. Impatience clawed at his skin, as a wisp of a cloud approached the moon. It was doubtful it would even cast a shadow. He didn't have all night. Every second was precious. He could see the third cave just ahead. Twenty feet. If he ran straight through he could be there in under a minute. Dead, but he'd be there. Sam tightened his grip on the knife and took several steadying breaths. His corpse would be worthless to Bella. She needed him alive. She needed him to keep his promise.

The next cloud that approached the moon was an insubstantial one at best with nothing bigger close behind. Their advantage was shrinking fast. Sam needed to make a decision. Either he waited for however long it took for a new cloud to make an appearance, or he made do with what he had. A tall man came out of the third cave where Bella was imprisoned, hitching up his pants and fastening his fly.

The man laughed and said something over his shoulder. The world slowed as Sam's vision distorted at the edge, all the details blurring away like so much unnecessary clutter, leaving only the man's profile in vivid detail, the jugular clearly delineated. The knife burned Sam's palm. His fingers twitched, he imagined the bastard raping Bella. Imagined how good it would feel to bury the blade deep in the bastard's throat, to watch him struggle. The man turned his head and grinned. Sam's restraint snapped and he leapt to his feet, his gaze never leaving its target.

There was a shout behind him as he started running. Sam ignored it, his focus on vengeance. The man turned as the cloud cover flitted away, and suddenly Sam could see the slight droop of his right eyelid, the shock in his expression as his greasy hair dropped into his eye as his hand went to his gun. Sam's heart thundered in his ears, blood rushed through his veins. The man's revolver cleared the holster. With dreamlike slowness, the muzzle pointed up and outward. Sam pushed himself harder, not caring about the bullet in the chamber, seeing only the smile on the bastard's face, hearing only the laughter. With a roar, he leapt in, catching the man behind his neck, pulling him into the thrust of his knife. The blade cut through muscle and tissue as if it were butter.

An explosion rocked them both. Sam hung on, pulling the knife out before driving it back inward on an upward thrust. Blood spewed from the outlaw's mouth, spraying Sam's face. The man crumpled to the ground. Sam let him fall, breathing hard, blinking as the world came back into focus.

"Goddamn it, Sam." Something hit him hard in the midsection and took him down. Bullets whined above his head. Tucker slammed him back down into the ground when he would have gotten up. "This was not the time to lose your goddamn head."

Sam spat the dirt out of his mouth. "Get the hell off me."

"Not until you're clear on what we're doing," Tucker growled as the volley of shots from the interior of the cave subsided.

With a backward jab of his elbow, Sam knocked Tucker off and sprang to a crouch, grabbing his Colt off the ground where Tucker had knocked it. "I know exactly what I'm doing."

There were two men inside the entrance of the cave hunkered down behind rocks. Sam waited. They would do something stupid. Men always did when they had the numbers to make them confident and all they'd seen were two men. What were two against twenty?

They didn't make him wait long.

On a "Now" they sprang to their feet. Palming the hammer, he put a bullet between each of their eyes. Their guns discharged in a flash of sound. Their bodies didn't hit the ground before he was heading into the cave.

"Hell!" Tucker said, catching up to him. "Are you trying to get yourself killed?"

"No." He just wanted to get to Bella.

Tucker grunted, pressing his back against the wall. "Well, try not to be reckless when you've got dynamite sticking out of your belt."

He'd forgotten about that. Sam looked down. The sticks were still there. The cave veered to the right. The wavering glow of torchlight extended past the corner. Beyond he could hear the sound of someone breathing hard combined with the sounds of a struggle.

He lunged forward. Tucker grabbed his arm and hauled him back. "Think."

Sam leaned against the stone wall. *Shit*. He needed to think. If that was Bella, barging in there could get her killed.

"Damn it, *puta,* you bite me again, and I'm going to break those teeth out of your head." A man's voice.

"Touch me again and I will kill you."

It was Bella, though the words were distorted. Sam closed his eyes in relief. And she was still fighting.

"Big talk for the camp whore."

"Big talk for the camp coward."

There was the sound of a fist hitting flesh and a small cry. "Your mother gave you to me."

Sam inched along the wall behind Tucker.

Bella's voice was shaky but full of fight. "She did not. She tricked you."

"Those ropes say otherwise."

"My Sam will kill you."

Her Sam was going to castrate the bastard first.

"Your Sam isn't going to want my leavings."

Bella didn't have an answer for that. Sam adjusted his grip on the gun. She was really angling for that spanking he'd promised her. She knew better than that.

Tucker crouched down, gun drawn, and nodded he was ready. Sam glanced quickly around the corner. What he saw made him sick. Bella was tied spread-eagle on the ground. Rough ropes wrapped around her ankles and wrists. An obese man with his pants hanging off his hips straddled her chest. In one hand he had a gun, the other was in front of his body out of sight. It wasn't hard to figure what he was doing. It wasn't hard to figure out why Bella's voice was strained. The bastard was crushing her under his weight.

Beyond the cavern the battle raged. The even repercussions of well-placed shots indicating the Montoya sharpshooters were doing their job, keeping the outlaws pinned down until such time as Bella was free and all hell could be set loose. He took a step. The room tilted off-kilter. Sam blinked and leaned back against the wall, putting his hand to his side. It came away soaked in blood.

Tucker glanced up, saw his hand and mouthed, "Fuck."

Sam shook his head, wiping his hand on his pants. The wound was nothing. He wouldn't allow it to be more.

From the other room came the click of a gun being cocked. The bottom dropped out of his stomach. Tejala was forcing the issue with the threat of death. It wouldn't work. Dying wasn't what Bella feared.

"Open wide, *puta*, and we will see how laughable you find my cock."

Tucker cocked his eyebrow at him. Sam took a breath and held it. The walls still bulged and swayed. No. He hadn't warned Isabella against ridiculing a man's pride and joy. And even if he had, it wouldn't have made a difference. Caution wasn't part of Bella's nature. She came out swinging with whatever she had. Even if it got her hurt. Damn, she must so hurt…. He blinked again and took a breath.

The room righted. Pausing to make sure it was going to stay that way, he gave Tucker the thumbs-up and stepped around him into the room. The rage took over immediately. Bella thrashed beneath the body of the huge man, fighting her bonds and his efforts. Tejala fell forward, bracing his weight on his arm, his other hand fumbling between them.

"Hear those gunshots?" he grunted as he struggled to obtain his goal. "That's your Sam dying as he falls into my trap." He bounced on Bella's chest. Air exploded from her in a pained gasp. "This is all there is for you now. My cock and my pleasure. You suck me good and I might consider holding off giving you to my men."

Three more steps. Sam just needed three steps to reach Tejala. He concentrated hard on making those steps without roaring like an animal, without pulling his gun. A bullet would be too easy for the bastard. Too quick. One step.

Bella screamed, "Sam!"

He thought she saw him until her cry split into a high note of loss. And then it ended altogether as Tejala bounced on her chest again, his stomach obviously getting in the way of his goal.

Two steps.

"He will not come for you, *puta*. And even if he does, he will die in the trap."

Sam wrapped his forearm around the son of a bitch's throat. "Her Sam will always come for her," he snarled in the outlaw's ear. "Always." His muscles screamed as he dragged Tejala back. Fire shot out from his abdominal wound. Blood dripped down over his hip. Tejala stumbled, almost toppling them both with his weight. As he righted him, Sam had his first glimpse of Bella. He'd thought he'd prepared himself for the fact that she'd likely be beaten, but the blood caked on her swollen split lip, her beautiful eyes bruised and swollen, the handprints around her throat…shit, nothing could have prepared him for that punch in the gut.

He wrenched his arms tighter. Tejala gagged and failed.

From Bella came a pathetic whisper as she leaned up. "Sam?"

Shit, she couldn't see. "Right here, duchess."

She jerked back. "*O Dios,* no." She yanked at her arms, twisted to the side, fought her bonds. "*Por favor,* do not look at me."

"Of course I'm looking at you." Tejala jabbed back with his elbow. Sam clamped down with his forearm, kicking Tejala's leg out from under him. The man's gasps turned to gurgles.

Sam didn't care. The only thing that mattered was Bella. "You're the most beautiful thing I've ever seen."

"Here, ma'am." Tucker came forward, shrugging out of his shirt and draping it around her. Bella continued to struggle. Blood showed at the edges of her bonds. Tucker pressed her shoulders to the floor, *"Cálmate, pequeña."*

She bucked once, twice and then shuddered into a collapse. "Tucker?"

"Yes."

Even from where he stood, Sam could see the devastation in her expression. "Do not let him see me like this."

Tucker glanced at him. Sam nodded. Tucker could do whatever it took to get her to settle.

"He can't see you now." Tucker cut through her bonds, wincing when Bella cried out.

"But he saw, didn't he?" she asked as she curled onto her side in a ball. She was tearing his heart out. "He saw me dirty with that man—"

With a shake of his head, Tucker cut her off as he guided Bella's limp arm into the sleeve. "Do not worry about Sam," he crooned in that calming way of his while shooting a look at the outlaw Sam held. "He is too busy killing Tejala to notice much."

Sam blinked. He *was* killing Tejala and not even getting to enjoy it. Loosening his hold slightly, Sam drew in raw, ragged breaths, rage and sorrow threatening his stability. It came to him as she got a lungful of air that he didn't want to kill Tejala as much as he needed to hold Bella. "Tucker!" Sam shoved Tejala toward Tucker who caught him easily, his big bowie knife pressed to the outlaw's throat. Tejala stood very still, his chest laboring, his now flaccid cock hanging out of his pants.

Tucker smiled his easy death-is-coming smile down at Tejala. "Give me a reason to twitch, you bastard."

Sam knelt beside Bella, reeling slightly as agony shot up from his abdomen. Reaching out carefully, he placed his hand against the side of her head, catching her hair with his thumb and pulling it aside so he could see her profile. "Duchess?"

"Do not look at me!"

He'd do more than look at her. He bent, nearly passing out from the pain, and gently kissed the one un-bruised spot along her jaw. "My Bella, are you thinking a few bruises could make you ugly to me?"

Her breath shuddered in, stuttered out. Her fist pressed into her mouth, reopening the cut on her lip. "I am not yours anymore."

"Ah, duchess, you'll always be mine."

"Not like before. He tore my clothes off, tore—"

He slid his arm under her shoulders, not letting her finish. "Just like before."

"You saw—"

"I saw my Bella getting the best of the bastard that tried to break her."

He angled her up. Torch light illuminated her face. Her poor little face.

"You have to say that."

Feathering a kiss across her hairline, he glared at Tejala. "I don't have to do anything."

The sounds of fighting outside picked up. Tejala's men were getting desperate. Probably running out of ammunition. The Montoyas didn't have an unlimited supply either. They didn't have time to discuss this now. "Can you stand up?"

"Of course."

"Of course, like our first night riding together or, of course, for sure?"

"I do not know." Tucking her feet under her, she struggled to stand up. Tucker's shirt flapped around her knees as she wobbled. Sam caught her arm, supporting her as she found her center. She stumbled as her ankles took her weight. He didn't let go of her arm when she steadied. She looked incredibly fragile. "Maybe not so 'of course.'"

He held her a few heartbeats longer before, asking. "Are you okay, now?"

"*Sí.* "

It was a bald-faced lie, but he didn't call her on it.

Across the room Tucker swore. "She's bleeding, Sam."

Bella clutched the shirt closer and sobbed. Sam followed the trajectory of Tucker's gaze. Blood dripped in small rivulets over the inside of her knee to her calf.

He let go of Bella and advanced on Tejala. "You tore her?"

Tejala spat at him. "She was a good fuck. Tight. She screamed as she came around me."

"I did not. He did not—"

"Stay out of it, Bella."

"You tell me how to do this!"

"Soon she will be big with my baby."

"He lies!" She lurched toward him, her eyes watering a stream of tears. Sam spun around, catching her before she fell. She clutched at his chest. "He lies."

"I know."

"Tell him how you begged for it, Isabella. Tell him how you—"

Sam motioned to Tucker. "Give him something else to think about."

His eyes eerily cold, Tucker asked, "You want him for barter later?"

"No."

The bowie knife whipped down. Tejala screamed an unholy sound and clutched at his privates.

"Sam?" Bella cried, looking right and left. "What happened?"

Tucker shoved the outlaw forward. "Nothing unexpected."

Tejala fell to his knees, still screaming.

Looking at Bella's poor battered body, the blood on her legs, Sam wished the hell he had been the one wielding the knife. He scooped her up in his arms. The pain in his gut was getting too strong to ignore. "Let's go home, duchess."

"I cannot go home."

Because of how she now saw herself. Dirty. Damn, she was ripping him apart one syllable at a time. Blood dripped into his boot. Arguing was pointless. "Then how about just get out of here, all right? Just out of this dark cave?"

Her arms came around his neck with a tentativeness that made him want to rage anew.

"*Sí.* Leaving this place would be good."

"Then that's what we will do."

"What do you want to do with him?" Tucker asked from behind Tejala.

Gut him. Cut off his eyelids so he couldn't look away. Stake him in the sun and let the buzzards feast on his intestines while he watched. "Leave him to bleed to death."

Tucker grunted and sheathed his knife. "You're too damn soft."

"I'll work on it."

Tucker came up beside him. "While you're working on it, I'll carry her."

Bella stirred against him in the same instinctive protest that shot through him. No one but he should touch her now.

"No." It came out sharper than he intended. Forcing the tightness from his throat, he clarified. "She's comfortable."

Tucker looked at the blood soaking his shirt and pant leg. "You going to make it?"

He had Bella in his arms and she was alive. He'd make it. "Yes."

He no sooner cleared the corner when there was a commotion behind them. Men's voices. Running feet. A lot of running feet. Tejala screamed, "My men come,

Ranger! You are trapped! Do you hear me, Ranger?
She'll never be yours. As long as I'm alive, she'll be
mine!"

"He is right, you must leave me and go."

"Bella?"

"What?"

"That's not going to happen."

"He's got to be crazy," Tucker sighed.

"Yeah." But he was also right. In Bella's mind, he
would always own a part of her.

Bella wiggled against him. He stumbled as she
bumped his wound.

"Can you not shoot him?"

Leaning back against the wall, he took three steadying breaths as the room spun. He could, but the risk
would be that the whole cave would come down, taking
all of them with it. "It's good to see your bloodthirsty
side perking up."

"That would be no, yes?"

He nodded, forgetting. "There's too many for bullets,
but I was thinking dynamite would do the trick."

"We have dynamite?"

"In my belt."

She reached between them again, pulling out a stick
with a small screech. "This is dynamite!"

"It's not dangerous unless it's lit." Normally.

Tucker took the dynamite from her hand before she
could throw it. "Blowing the place up is dangerous."

"That's why I'm going to do it."

"Like hell."

"Someone has to get Bella out."

Tucker glanced down at his side. "You'd better run fast."

"Or what?"

His gaze met Sam's. "Or I'll come in after you."

"No."

Bella's nails sank into the back of his neck. "I do not want you to do this, Sam."

"You don't even know what this is."

"I can tell from Tucker's tone, it is not good."

"Tucker's a worrier."

"You take too many chances."

"Duchess?"

"Do not tell me not to worry, Sam. I may not see well, but I hear trouble in your voice."

"You always hear trouble in my voice."

"Not like this."

From the sound of things, the men were almost upon them.

"Look at me, duchess."

She tipped her face back, wincing as she frowned. The touch of her fingertips on his whiskered cheek was a rasp of regret. "You are all fuzzy."

"I can work with this." He kissed her with infinite care, a bare brushing of lips. "I love you, Bella. Don't ever forget that."

Her gasp buffeted his guilt. "You will not tell me this this way!"

It was the only way he had. This might be the last chance he had. Sam shoved Bella into Tucker's arms. "Get her out of here."

The other man took her, frowning. "What the hell are you doing?"

Grabbing the dynamite out of his hand, Sam smiled, blinking against the dizziness. "Getting rid of vermin."

"Sam!"

He ignored Bella's call. "Don't let her do anything stupid, Tucker. Now or later."

"Hell, that's your job."

Probably not for much longer. "You've got to the count of twenty to get clear. Give the signal to the others when you do."

Bella struck at Tucker's chest, fighting to get down, to get to him. "I do not want this sacrifice, Sam!"

But he wanted it. He wanted her to live. He wanted to imagine her happy, growing old with a family. For that the men had to be stopped and Tejala had to die.

Tucker pinned her to his chest with a flex of muscle, his expression as solemn as his gaze. "Remember to run."

He nodded and pulled out a sulphur. "Remember to take care of Bella."

Tejala was standing when Sam reentered the cavern, fastening his pants with an eerie calm as if his genitals weren't on the ground, as if there wasn't blood soaking the front. Through the back tunnel, the first of the reinforcements arrived. Sam struck the sulphur and touched it to the fuse.

"Welcome to the party, boys."

The boys stopped dead so abruptly the ones behind knocked them into the room. He tossed the first stick. Men swore and scrambled back toward the tunnel. The dynamite rolled across the floor toward the back, driving men back with its hiss of death.

"What are you doing?" Tejala screamed as if they all weren't going up in a big bang in a few seconds. "Shoot him."

The son of a bitch really was crazy. A couple men reached for their guns. Sam lit the second stick. "This one's got a short fuse, folks."

He tossed it, too dizzy to worry about accuracy. Besides, with dynamite accuracy wasn't a must. The fuse sputtered a warning. He had one stick left. He looked at the front of Tejala's pants. That would be a good place to drop it.

I do not want this sacrifice, Sam.

Hell. He swayed. Neither did he, now that he thought about it. He met Tejala's gaze and tossed the stick, letting Fate decide the outcome. "I've got better things waiting for me."

Turning on his heel, he ran for the far side of the cave knowing there was no hope, but trying for it anyway. Fresh air blew across his face. His muscles ached with the effort. The cave exploded. Reaching deep for one last burst of speed, he dove for the safety of the night.

The percussion slammed into his back, sending him flying through the air. He hit the ground, momentum keeping him rolling. The ledge came up fast. He dug in his nails. They scraped across the ground, tore. On the next roll, his hand found only air.

He heard a scream. A man's shout. "Isabella!"

And then small, strong hands latched onto his arm, jerking the momentum out of his spin, slowing it to an inevitable slide toward the bottom.

"Santa María, Madre de Dios—"

"Bella!" Dear God, it was Bella that held him, head arched down, neck muscles straining.

"Let go."

"Do not interrupt!" she snapped out in a hoarse growl, before continuing in staccato gasps. *"Ruega por…nosotros…pecadores, ahora—"*

His weight drew her further forward. Her chest appeared over the edge. Soon it would be too late. He wedged his boot in a crevice, taking some pressure off her arms. Where the hell was Tucker? "Let me go, Bella."

"No!" She continued to pray even as her fingers began to slip. *"Y en la hora…de nuestra muerte."*

He twisted his arm, breaking the grip of her right hand. She lunged forward and dug her nails back in. Jesus, a half an inch more and she'd be overbalanced. He softened his voice, trying reason. "You can't save me, Bella."

She lifted her head. Her eyes glittered behind the

slits of her swollen lids in her battered face. "It is my choice to fight."

Her body jerked. An arm extended past hers. A dark hand snapped around his forearm below her hand. He recognized the scars across the knuckles. "Zacharias, get her out of here."

"In a minute."

"Now." If the ledge crumbled, nothing could save her.

Bella turned her head and snarled at the ranch hand. "If you touch me, I will geld you."

Zacharias didn't even blink. "I am sorry, *patron*. I have a fondness for my man parts. Up you will come." He barked an order to those above. *"Ahora, tírenos hacia arriba!"*

And suddenly there were a lot more hands pulling and hauling them up. Amid the shouts of determination, there came the periodic shots from the sharpshooters, keeping the area clear. And then he was on solid ground, propped against the wall, Bella in his arms, clinging to him. He didn't mind. She could cling all she wanted. Zacharias collapsed beside him. It took everything he had to turn his head. "Thank you."

"Do not thank me." Zacharias rested his head back against the wall, a faint smile on his lips. "*La Montoya* is the one who wanted you."

"And it's your job—"

"To see that *la Montoya* gets what she wants," Zacharias finished for him.

Sam put his hand to his aching stomach, pressing his lips to Bella's hair. "That's going to change."

Bella perked up. "This way is working for me."

"As you see, *patron, la Montoya* has her wishes."

What he saw was too many men indulged Bella's impulsiveness. "The next man who lets her endanger herself will deal with me."

Zach shrugged. "She is a wild one."

"I'm wilder."

Zach smiled. "So I've heard. A wild card."

Tucker came up beside them and hunkered down. "You all right?"

"Been better." But not more at peace. Damn, he wanted to pull Bella into his body and shelter her from everything, just absorb her into him until there was nothing between them. He wanted it so badly his hands were shaking. "I thought I told you to keep her from doing something stupid."

"She's one crazy woman. Wouldn't leave. By the time I realized she wasn't behind me, you came flying out and she went flying after you."

Tucker unbuttoned Sam's shirt, their gazes meeting as he looked at the wound. "Something I'm thinking might not have been that stupid."

"Are you hinting you'd miss me if I wandered off to meet my maker?"

"I'm hinting it might be time for you to start working harder at sticking around." He gave a pointed glance to Bella. "The rewards can be worth it."

"That has been mentioned."

"It has?"

"Yeah." He pulled Bella close and held her tightly as the black at the edges of his vision surged inward. From afar he heard himself say, "Bella tells me I'm an answer to a prayer."

20

Some answer to her prayer Sam was turning out to be. Isabella glanced over to where Sam sat, back braced against the trunk of the tree, munching on a drumstick as if everything he wanted was in that picnic lunch her mother had made. It had been two weeks since he'd brought her home. His wounds were almost healed, her bruises barely showed, and still he had not let her know what he wanted of her. He seemed content to hold her at night when the nightmares came, happy to help around the ranch, and generally keep her in a safe place where nothing, not even he, touched her with emotion. He probably thought this is what she needed to heal. Stupid man.

She needed him, his passion, his bossiness. She needed him to touch as though what had happened with Tejala did not matter. She needed him to take over and not leave everything to her. She needed her Sam back.

"Your mother might be a bit testy to live with, but she sure can cook a chicken, can't she?"

He had her alone on a beautiful day by the river and he wanted to discuss her mother's cooking skills? "She is a very good cook," she agreed.

That was it. Again, the short answer that went nowhere. Bella shifted on the blanket. The stick poking her in the hip through the blanket was just one more irritation in a day that wasn't going at all like she had planned. She considered grabbing another piece of chicken just for something to do, but she was so nervous, if she ate it she'd vomit, and that was one humiliation she could spare herself. "It was a surprise to see Señor Alvarez come calling today."

"Gossip among the men is that he's been sweet on your mother for years." He set the stripped bone on the plate with the others. Nudging the pile straight when it would have tipped to the right.

"I used to fear him. But he is always sweet around Mamá."

His gaze cut to hers. "Was he sweet to you?"

His long fingers were dark against the white china, reminding her of how they looked against her skin. She loved watching him touch her, having him touch her. She shifted again. Stupid stick.

"Always he was nice. Often, I thought he should remarry. He would be a good father."

Sam looked up, catching her watching him. "For

some men, there's only one shot at happy and there's no settling for second best."

What was he saying? The three feet between them took on monumental significance. For a few seconds she couldn't breathe let alone speak. The river rippled over stones and birds sang, but inside her, time stopped. Finally, she got a grip on her dread. She took a breath, licked her lower lip. "And he wanted my mother."

Sam drew up his knee and rested his forearm against it. The tight cotton of his pants cupped his privates with loving detail. The muscles of his upper arm strained his shirtsleeves. "Maybe."

Desire simmered in her stomach. She wanted those arms around her. He was still looking at her. His eyes measuring every twitch of muscle. Her skin, flushed and sensitized, experienced that look as a touch. The irritation of the stick became unbearable. She rose on her knees, fumbled beneath the blanket and yanked it out.

Then she was faced with a decision. She could resume her former position perched on the edge of the blanket, or join Sam in his patch of shadow-dappled blanket. It wasn't a hard choice. The stick went flying and the distance between them decreased from three feet to about six inches. The tension between them rose until it crackled like lightning in a summer storm. She placed her hand on the blue plaid next to his. So close, all he had to do was stretch out his pinkie and they'd be touching. Her nipples peaked with her

daring. She looked up. Nothing in Sam's expression
changed. She shifted her weight onto the arm closest
to him. His lids flickered. In interest or affront? It was
so hard to know what he wanted, would find acceptable
in the wake of Tejala's touch. She'd explained to him
that Tejala hadn't raped her, that the blood had been
her woman's time and that had saved her, but did that
really make a difference? A man with Sam's pride had
to care what others said about his woman.

"I think Señor Alvarez is more than sweet on my
mother. I think he is in love with her."

As she was in love with Sam.

"Then he should do something about it."

Impatience at his composure. So should Sam.

"I think he was waiting for her to give him a sign."

"Giving the lead to a woman like her is a disaster
waiting to happen."

"A woman like her?" She may have fights with her
mother, but that did not mean anyone called her
names.

"Duchess, your mother is looking for a man, not a
puppet."

The notions caught at her longing and tugged it as
tight as her nipples. "That is a strange idea."

The faintest of smiles hovered in the lines fanning
out from the corners of his intense eyes. He wiped his
hands and mouth on the wet cloth packed for that
purpose. "Not that strange. Some women very much
enjoy a man taking their choices away in bed."

Could he tell how that thought affected her? A crow squawked. A bee buzzed by, and she still couldn't come up with an argument.

"Some women, duchess, don't want to make decisions when it come to their relationships." He put the cloth away. "They like their men to take over, define their limits, test them."

Images of his cock testing the limits of her pussy flared through her. Her eyes closed on the memory of the intimate burn. It was always such a tight fit. She swallowed hard.

"Some women, perfectly capable women even, prefer a man to take charge in the bedroom."

Were they still talking about her mother? The flesh of her pinkie burned in anticipation.

Touch me. With your hands as well as your words.

"Some women glory in the surrender to their man."

She took a breath. They were no longer talking about her mother. "And the men, how do they feel when their woman surrenders?"

"Like they just received an answer to a prayer."

She could not stand the not knowing any longer. She opened her eyes. Sam's expression was still carefully controlled, but his eyes, his eyes burned with flames she wanted to step into. "Are you one of these men, Sam? One that needs his woman to submit?"

"Yes."

Just like that, he answered. No blinking, no hiding. She wished she had the same confidence. She licked her lips, and stared at their hands, so close yet so far apart. Indecision battled with hope. Fear with excitement. "And if I were one of these women, yet not saying so for many fears, how would I let you know that I am trapped by those fears? That I need help?"

He reached out, very slowly, as if he feared she would run. His fingers slid along the side of her throat, curled with blessed familiarity around the back of her neck. His thumb under her chin tipped her face up.

"You would say, 'I love you, Sam.'"

Tears burned her eyes. "So easy?"

"So easy."

"Even when the world thinks she was touched by another man, played his whore?"

"The world doesn't matter."

A tear overflowed. "Other men will laugh at him. Pity him for his choice of woman. Say things."

He caught the tear on the edge of his thumb, made it disappear with a swipe. "No one will say anything about my wife."

Her heart skipped a beat. *Wife?* "No one expects you to marry me now."

His head bent, the edges of his lips fitting to hers. "Bella?"

"What?"

Very softly, very tenderly, the order breathed into her mouth, "Say the words."

She clenched her hands into fists, closed her eyes and

took a breath. "I love you, Sam. So much I do not know what to do with it. If you—"

His kiss, very soft, very sweet, cut off the rest. "Loving me is enough."

"What if it is—"

"It's enough." He kissed her again, harder, his lips parting hers with the demand she remembered, commanding her response, accepting it as she gave it, giving her in return the confidence to put her arms around his shoulders and pull him to her. This was Sam. This was good. This was what she needed. When she was breathless and pliant, her fears buried under a wave of sensuality, he pulled back, feathering a kiss across her eyelids.

"Was that so hard?" he asked, his deep drawl a warm cocoon she wanted to crawl into.

She settled for resting her cheek against his chest. "Yes."

"Why?"

She uncurled her fingers, letting them rest against his pulse, and gave him the unvarnished truth. "I do not want to disappoint you. "

The tug on her hair was expected. She tilted her head back, knowing she couldn't avoid this. The set to his mouth was hard, lending more of that aura of cruelty to his face, but there was nothing cruel about his eyes, or his voice. "That works both ways."

Impossible. Sam was not afraid of anything. "It is easier for you."

"How?"

"You give the orders and I follow."

"But if I give the wrong orders and you get hurt, I have to live with it. And, baby, the thought of you hurting about kills me."

"I have a choice."

This time his sigh pressed her cheek first up and then down on a slow expulsion of breath. "Duchess, when I have you bound and naked on my bed, there won't be much choice."

The bolt of lust was stronger than the bolt of fear, but not by much. "This is done?"

"Yes."

"And you do not mind if it excites me?"

His laugh was easy, natural, the way it should be between them. "I thank my lucky stars that it excites you."

Goose bumps sprang up in the wake of the glide of his palm down her back. She shivered as he lifted her across his lap, dropping back into the support of his upper arm as he nudged her thighs apart with a press of his lean fingers. "You, Bella, are sweet, soft, and everything I've ever wanted."

That was hard to believe. Sam was a very experienced man. The first button on her skirt gave and then the next. His fingers found the ties of her bloomers, and tugged.

His lips brushed against hers as his fingers worked beneath the loose cotton and found her wet core.

She felt his smile as well as his approval as he dragged the callused pad of his index finger up her slit, slowing as it approached her eager clitoris. "Very nice."

The most eloquent response she could work up to was a whimper that mingled with his breath.

"Put your arms around me, and hold on tight."

She did, digging her nails into his back, opening her mouth at the touch of his tongue, her hips straining up, needing him to move that finger. Needing him. Just needing him so much.

And then he moved that critical fraction of an inch.

Her head dropped back as every sense focused on that throbbing point of connection. "Oh yes."

"Sweetheart, open your eyes."

She didn't, wanting to hold on to the dream he was weaving.

"Bella."

It was a warning. She cuffed the back of his head. "Do not distract me."

His finger on her clit swirled once, twice. Fire arced hot and bright within. She couldn't breathe, couldn't do anything but ride the brilliant wave as it tore through her.

"Open your eyes."

The brush of his teeth over the arch of her throat pulled the added spice of danger to the conflagration.

She cracked her right lid. Sam was looking down at her, his gaze narrow and intent, his face tight with the desire riding him. It was harder to crack the left eye, but she managed it.

His fingers shifted. Warm pressure enfolded her clit. Ah, she loved it when he got serious.

"Keep looking at me."

And bossy. She loved that side of him too. His fingers shifted in a delicate glide, changing the grip, the caress, switching to a milking motion that incited a cacophony of pleasure that ripped along her nerve endings, building with each draw, swelling with each glide, pushing and pushing her toward the point of no return. She held her breath as passion rose, closing her eyes to focus on it, holding it desperately. "Watch me."

The order snapped her eyes open again. Her reward was a firm stroke of his finger. She arched and gasped. Her hips bucked the half inch his grip allowed. She needed more. So much more.

"Good." It was almost a purr, or maybe a growl. "I want you to come, Bella."

Isabella dug her nails into the back of Sam's neck, clinging to sanity. "I do not think I can help it."

This time the sensation that shot up from her clit was lush and full. Languorous and intense. She shuddered as urgency crested in a high wave, gathering strength, hovering over the agony of anticipation, ready to crash down.

"You're very pretty when you come," he whispered into her mouth. "You're very pretty everywhere."

His forearm rested against her stomach as he worked at the buttons on her blouse, slipping them free one by one, kissing each new inch of skin as it appeared, swirling his tongue across in a leisurely tasting that echoed in her imagination, transferred to her clit. The buttons gave with amazing ease.

"You are too good at this."

"That's not something to be complaining about."

Her shirt fell open. His harshly indrawn breath pushed his chest against her side. His forefinger traced the scalloped edge of her corset until it rested in the valley between her breasts, not moving, not giving any indication where it would go next. Her nipples throbbed.

"Now this I like."

She'd worn a sheer pink camisole today. One that tantalized more than it concealed. It was totally impractical for most things. "I chose it for you."

"Why?"

She blushed and arched her back, presenting him with the gift of her breasts. "Because I knew you would like the way it pushes my breasts up, and the way you can see my nipples through it."

"Then thank you." The front ties offered up no more resistance than her shirt. Her left breast tumbled against him, the right clung to the cup, falling to the side, separating from its mate the few inches…

"Oh God."

His chuckle encouraged her next gasp as he brushed the cup off her breast, exposing her nipple to first the glide of his tongue and then the rasp of his five-o'clock shadow. Bliss ripped from her in a high-pitched cry that echoed in the canopy of sun-dappled leaves shielding them from the brightness of the sun.

"Let me hear that again, duchess."

She shook her head, not sure she could survive.

His "Yes" brooked no resistance. Neither did the brush of his chin, across the tip, nor the heat of his mouth, the swirl of his tongue, the glide of his teeth up the taut stretch of her nipple. He got his cry and more as she arched into his caress, pleasure ripping through her as he spread his palm underneath her shoulder blades, supporting her, taking more and more of her weight as he sucked and nipped at her nipple. His hand worked between her legs and then he stopped, the only stimulation on her ultrasensitive flesh his low, "Look at me."

She did, because he ordered it. Did because the way his finger tapped her clit promised a reward she desperately wanted. His gaze was hot on hers, very involved with her pleasure. Very involved with her. "Whose mouth is on your breasts?"

A soft nip, a delicate sting, and her voice lost its power. "Yours."

"Whose hand is cupping this sweet pussy?" A stroke of his thumb emphasized his point.

"Yours."

Blunt-tipped fingers curled into the well of her pussy, pressing but not entering. The rough pad of his thumb hovered on her clit, promising but not delivering and his breath blew across the aching point of her nipple, teasing but not easing, while his eyes burned with an intensity that seared deeper than lust.

His thumb circled her clit, sending the pleasure burning through her body in a shocking arc that jerked her spine taut. His chin grazed her nipple, the pinpricks from his beard ricocheting the sensation back down to her pussy where the slow steady intrusion of his fingers parted her muscles with relentless demand.

"And who do you come for, duchess?"

"You. Only you."

"Then come for me, Bella," he ordered in a voice aching with tenderness. "Just me."

She expected violence, force, the rough edge of his passion, but instead he gave her easy thrusts, soft swirls and delicate suction. And love. So much love, the kind that understood and healed. The only kind that mattered. "Now."

And she came for him with the same devastating tenderness with which he milked the response from her body, sobbing his name, holding on to him as her body drifted over the precipice, trusting him to catch her, to hold her. Because this was Sam. The only man who could ever touch her. The only man's touch she would hold to her heart. The only man who mattered.

When the last pulse faded from her womb, he was still holding her. His touch was soothing in direct contrast to the urgency she could feel humming under his skin. His fingers grazed the side of her neck with infinite tenderness. "Now, that was nice."

"Yes, it was." The river still rippled in the background. Birds still chirped in the trees and clouds still drifted across the sky. There was no going back. Not anymore. She was Sam's woman. She opened her palm across his chest, disliking the cotton of his shirt which kept her from his skin. It was a good thing to be, even if it complicated things. "Can we stay here forever?"

"If forever is the next four hours, yes."

She smiled. "Always you joke."

The blanket tugged as he rolled on his side. "And always you laugh, so I think that works out fine."

Lines of strain hovered around his eyes and mouth. He still had not recovered from his injury. "You have been doing too much around the ranch."

"There's a lot to do in a place this size."

"Zacharias speaks very highly of you and Tucker."

"Your father hired good men."

"They are not hired like you think."

"I know. Zach explained his family has been in service to yours for a century."

"It is our way to bind our futures."

"I'm not saying it's bad, just different."

She bit her lip. "It will be hard on them when I leave."

They had been dancing around this subject for a week, ever since her mother made it clear that she expected Sam to take over as *El Montoya*.

"I told your mother and I told Zach, I'm Hell's Eight. My loyalty is there."

"Could you not be Hell's Eight here?"

"It's not the same, Bella."

The depth of his frown spoke of his conflict. Sam could be happy here, she knew this, but in his mind he did not have a reason to stay. He did not have something that made it all right for him to make his own place away from the men with whom he had always ridden. In his mind the ranch was hers and for him to stay as *el patron* was assuming a role that wasn't his.

"I do not understand if what is yours is mine why what is mine does not become yours."

"Because a man supports his wife, not the other way around."

Ah, pride. This she understood. She let her hand drop to the hot bulge of his cock trapped within his pants. "You are man enough to support me wherever we are and still be Hell's Eight, my Sam."

She rubbed her fingers over his shaft in the short teasing caress that drove him wild, the roughness of the material caught on her skin in a provocative invitation to take it away. It would be so easy to slip the buttons from their holes, free his flesh, maybe make him as vulnerable as she felt.

The muscles in his thighs flexed, pushing against her forearm. Well, maybe not that vulnerable. Vulnerable was not a word that went with Sam, but maybe just a little less alone. She drew a figure eight on his flesh, smiled when his powerful body jerked and his nostrils flared. His hand caught hers and he knelt beside her, his hands on her lapels spreading her shirt. "We can argue about this later."

"Can we not just agree you are *El Montoya* now?"

His smile made every nerve ending leap to life with the promise it contained. "No, we cannot. Sit up."

She scooted onto her knees as he slid her shirt down her arms. The sleeves caught on her wrists, locking her arms behind her. He didn't immediately remove them, his gaze locked on her bound state, the thrust of her breasts. "Now, that's a pretty sight."

Alarm and passion flared with equal strength. Embarrassment was forced to take third place.

His hand under her elbow steadied her as he ordered, "Stand up."

She did, blushing more as the sun's warmth struck her breasts, very conscious how her corset pushed them up. "Anyone can see."

"All you need to focus on is that I want to see."

It was amazingly easy to do that.

He pulled her two steps forward until she was fully in the sun, supporting her weight when she stumbled, letting her go when she regained her balance. His hand left her arm and two seconds later was tugging her skirts off her hips. The chill that raced over her skin had noting to do with temperature and everything to do with the conflicting emotions raging within. Fear, embarrassment, anticipation, desire.

The last time she had been naked before a man had been Tejala.

She leaned against him as he pulled her right shoe off. "What are you doing?"

"Undressing you."

She rolled her eyes. "If you untied my hands I could help."

"I've got it under control."

So he did. The left shoe came off. Three tugs and two "lift ups" and all she was clothed in was warm air and sunlight.

Sam sat back on his heels, his eyes burning hotter than a touch as they roamed first up and then down, and then up again before stopping at her core.

His tongue passed over his lips. The implication was as good as a touch. Her hips jerked as her clit throbbed and her womb clamped. Sam's low laugh wove through the moment, adding to the illusion of touch. He reached out. It seemed to take forever for his finger to reach her, and when it did the touch was too light. A mere teasing trace of her labia.

His brow arched in inquiry. "Hungry, duchess?"

She swallowed and nodded.

"And you want to please me?"

Pressure from the back of his fingers separated her thighs. She nodded again. The breeze whispered over her flesh. She shivered. His gaze sharpened. His eyes narrowed. His finger dipped lower. "I like you like this, bound and poised, ready for whatever I decide."

His finger slipped between the inner lips of her pussy, pushing inward and upward, circling the well of her vagina still too light. Still too knowing.

She swallowed back her whimper and squared her shoulders. She could take this.

"Oh yeah, thrust those pretty breasts out."

His finger entered, hooked on her pubic bone, pressing against a spot that seared with sensation. This time she couldn't help her cry.

"Come here." She went, three steps stretching into eternity as the movement rubbed his finger against that bundle of nerves that hurtled her toward another climax. When she straddled his knees, her pussy level with his mouth, Sam slipped his fingers free. Her pussy clenched around the devastating loss. Cream wept from her body as her knees buckled. He caught her hips in his big hands, holding her in position.

"Not yet."

"Yes."

His grip on her rear tightened. His "No" blew across her clit and it dawned on her that this position also had possibilities. She held still, not daring to breathe as he leaned in, the red of his tongue a fleeting glimpse before he got too close to see anything. But she could feel. The heat of his mouth, the moisture of his breath. The slightly rough, featherlight rasp of his tongue over her clit.

"Stand up straight."

The order didn't process at first. Neither did the

sharp sting on her ass but then the heat of the spank burned through her haze, gaining her attention. The sting of the next sent strength through her knees. "Come closer."

She looked down. How much closer could she get? She shuffled forward a few steps. Sam leaned in and she discovered how snugly his tongue fit the crease in her mound. The slightly rough surface flowed over the smooth tip of her clit in a heartbreaking prelude before withdrawing. The brush of his lips on her inner lips was exquisite. The kiss he placed there tender.

"I'm feeling lazy, duchess. So I'm just going to sit here and enjoy your sighs and taste while you find your pleasure."

"Sam, I can't hold back."

His laugh teased. "I'm not asking you to hold back, I want you screaming but I also want you to do the work."

"I do not understand."

The tip of his tongue flicked her. "Work yourself on my tongue, baby, until you come. And don't hold back. Let me hear every whimper." He flicked her again with a stinging whip of sensation. "Every sigh. Every gasp. They're mine and I want them."

This time when his tongue came out, it stayed, firm and soft against her clit. She didn't have to move much to find the pleasure. Just a pulse of her hips, a bend of her knees as she was riding her way to bliss. More. She needed more something. She pulled him harder against her as the agony spiked to an unrelenting demand. To move. To cry out. To give him what he wanted.

His fingers dug into her buttocks, drawing her harder against him when the ability to hold herself upright collapsed beneath need. And still she couldn't come, couldn't climb over the ledge to the place he wanted. She needed and she needed but she couldn't achieve. She yanked on his hair. "Sam. Please. Please."

At first, she did not think he was going to answer her plea, but then his grip tightened and she was yanked forward. He nuzzled his face between her legs and caught her clit between his teeth as he sucked and lashed, giving her the edge she needed to cling to, giving her a wave to ride until she was no longer climbing but hurtling over into the sun, searing her inside and out as she bucked and fought, unable to get away, forced to take her pleasure as he willed it. And he willed her so much. Too much for one woman to withstand. She exploded with a scream, collapsing into Sam's hold, giving him the responsibility for anchoring her as her climax ripped reality away.

Damn, she was something, Sam thought, laving her clit gently as her pussy spasmed, prolonging the moment for her as long as he could. When the last quiver rippled through her damp folds, he stood, her taste on his tongue, her scent in his nostrils, his cock pounding to the rhythm of Bella's rapid breaths.

She collapsed against his chest, murmuring a

protest as he lifted her up, twisting in his arms as the wind blew over her swollen flesh. He carried her over to the sunlit boulder, stripping the rest of her clothes from her while she quivered in the aftermath of her pleasure. A simple push of his hand had her rolling over on the rock, her hands still bound behind her. He brushed the hair back from her cheek. Her face was flushed, her eyes drowsy, her legs splayed and limp, a wanton invitation to his desire.

He covered her body with his, bringing his chest down over her slender back. "Duchess?"

"*¿Qué?*"

The airy little question was barely audible.

"I'm going to make you mine now."

"I have always been yours."

Yes, she had. "But since you seemed to forget that, we'll just call this a refresher."

He brought his cock in alignment with the soft, wet heat of her pussy, letting it drop into the well. The red swollen flesh welcomed his eagerly, conforming to the broad helmet of his cock with a lover's thoroughness, wrapping around and holding him as he settled into the shallow well. His cock looked huge against her delicate flesh, appearing almost brutally big against the lush folds. She whimpered. Her pussy twitched. Tension entered her muscles. He stroked his fingertips down her spine.

"Trust me, duchess."

She took a shuddering breath. And then muscle by

muscle relaxed. He pressed in. She took him as she always did with a feminine surrender that went deeper than the physical. Deeper than she wanted to accept, but she took him. He kept going, not pulling out, filling her with a steady pressure. "That's it, Bella. Just relax and let me in."

"You're so—" her breath caught "—so big."

"And you like that."

Her lips slid between her teeth. The flush on her cheek deepened as muscle gave and she took another inch. Her "yes" came out on a groan.

"You almost have all of me."

Her hands clenched to fists.

"Almost?"

He couldn't blame her for the high squeak. He was bound to feel bigger to her this way. "Just a little more."

He put more of his weight into the slow thrust, inexorably filling her past the point of denial for either of them. Her right buttock shone, a creamy taupe bright sun. His shadow covered the left. He put his hand over the right, pressing in with his fingers, marking her flesh as he marked her pussy. When he removed his hand, the imprint lingered a moment and then disappeared even as his groin pressed into the pad of her pussy. She groaned and shuddered.

Her breath came in short pants as she held him, her inner muscles flexing and releasing in little flutters that had his balls pulling up tight.

"Are you all right?"

She was so tight sometimes he wondered how she took him at all.

"Oh yes!"

"Good." He worked his cock out, groaning himself. The friction burned with erotic perfection. No one ever made him feel like Bella, no one ever fit him like she did. In bed and out. He leaned over, rubbing his chest along her back, delighting in the feel of her vertebrae against his abdomen and chest, maneuvering so the ridge of her spine nestled into the deep groove in the muscle of his torso linking them from torso to navel, absorbing her shudder as he whispered in her ear, "I'm going to make love to you now, Bella. The way I've wanted to since the day I met you."

A long pause, another shudder and then a subtle tension entered her spine as her hands opened and then her fingers curled as if grabbing hold. Her feet shifted on the ground. Her toes found purchase. He kissed the nape of her neck for the moment of anxiousness. She still had a lot to learn about him.

He eased himself back in, slowly, lazily, ignoring the inner urging that said to ride her hard. His Bella knew too much about his hard side and not enough about the part of him that found everything about her a wonder, something to be treasured, respected, loved. The echo of her moan filled the clearing as he filled her. He kissed that corner of her lush mouth. "I'm going to love you like this, Bella. Slow and sweet, so sweet when you come, you're going to lose yourself, and when you find your way back, I'm going to be there holding you, keeping you safe, the way it's supposed to be."

A tear glistened in her eye. He smoothed his lips over the corner. "No tears, no sadness. Just you and me, baby."

He slid his hand under her cheek cushioning her face from the hard stone. The heat of the rock seeped into his hand, the heat of her skin warmed his palm. "Push up with your toes."

As always she followed his order, the trust she gave him a gift he valued. Bracing his weight on his elbow, he slid his other hand under her belly. "Settle down now."

She did, with exquisite slowness and a little gasp that breezed over his fingers as the calluses on his palms scraped her engorged clit. "Keep going."

She hesitated. "I'm sensitive."

"Hmm." He kissed the curve of her ear as he feathered his index finger over the swollen nub. She flinched. Very sensitive. "I can work with that."

"What are you going to do?"

"I told you. Love you. Now." He snuggled against her. "Rest yourself on my hand and let me get to it."

Her shivery sigh of his name accompanied the lowering of her hips. Sam accepted her weight the same way he accepted her trust. Completely. "That's my girl."

The echo of his own words resounded through his head as he pumped slowly in and out of the tight confines of her pussy, glorying in her response. She was his. Had always been his and while he might have been fool enough for a spell to think he could let her go, he was never letting her go again. A woman like Bella was special, deserved a man strong enough to keep her. For Bella, he was going to be that man.

In and out, in and out, he slowly, surely joined them together. Over and over, canting his hips to the angle that had his cock striking that spot halfway up her channel, so her moans punctuated the rhythm he set, adding a rhythm of their own. She alternated between grinding her mound down on his hands and pushing her hips back into his descent, every muscle in her body trying to hurry him on, but he didn't want to hurry. He wanted to stay inside her forever.

Her mouth turned into his palm, her teeth biting the pad of his fingers as he leisurely stroked her clit with a touch too light to give her what she needed to come, but everything he needed to feel. Her want. Her desire rising beyond her control, beyond safe. "That's it, Bella. Go with it. "

She shook her head. He lowered lips to her ear, nuzzling his way through her hair, creating a provocative haven where only he and she existed. "Yes. Come for me, sweetheart. Let me feel that sweet pussy clamp down on my cock, let me feel your orgasm, milk me to my own." He increased the speed and pressure of his touch on her clit, pinning her to the rock as she jerked, holding her steady as he rubbed faster, harder, as he pumped deeper, longer. "C'mon, duchess. Give me what I need and I'll give you my seed. All of it."

"Sam!" Her muscles snapped tight. Her teeth bit down on his hand, and then his little duchess growled, a feral needy sound that shot straight to his groin.

"Come for me, baby."

And she did, hard and violent, screaming his name, holding tight with her teeth, and her inner muscles.

And when she came back to herself, he made sure he was there, holding her, kissing her, smoothing the tears from her lashes with his lips. And when she opened her eyes, and looked at him, he came for her, giving her everything he had, every drop of his seed, every drop of emotion, wanting to fill her as much as he could, so full that emptiness that had been in her eyes after Tejala would never return.

As the last pulse faded, a robin sang in the tree above them. The sun warmed his back. He eased the shirt from her arms and draped himself back over her, sheltering her from the breeze and any insecurities that might come calling.

Beneath him, Bella sighed and wrapped her arm around him. "I love you, my Sam."

He caught the lobe of her ear between his teeth, and flexed his cock inside her, enjoying the intimate kiss of her muscles clenching back. "I love you, too."

"Enough to stay with me here and make a home for our children?"

He smiled. She was determined. And it was a

tempting offer. The Montoya spread was a good one, but showing the lack of management in recent months. It needed care to not go under. But these were Bella's people, not his, and he didn't think he could live comfortably as a charity his wife saw to. But he didn't want to argue about it now. Not when she was soft and welcoming in the aftermath. "How about I promise to think about it?"

"I can work with that."

21

They were waylaid before they made it through the gates. Jorge, dressed in his Sunday best black shirt and black pants with his hair slicked back and still dripping water, stopped them before they could enter the compound. Kell, who'd taken a liking to the boy from the day Tucker had brought him to the ranch, stood at his side. Jorge's face was pale, and his eyes anxious. He was thinner than he should be but well on the way to health under the eagle eyes of his brothers. Sam pulled Breeze up short. "What can I do for you, Jorge?"

The boy bowed his head. *"Patron, Patrona."*

"Jorge."

He shuffled his feet in the dirt, uncomfortable beneath Bella's greeting. After one last kick of his feet, he squared his shoulders.

"I have come on a man's business."

Sam smothered a grin, both at the boy's demeanor and Bella's indignant gasp. "Well, now, that sounds serious. Do you want to talk here or at the house?"

The boy glanced anxiously over his shoulder. "Here would be good."

Sam lifted his leg over Breeze's neck and hopped down. "Then why don't we take a walk?"

The boy nodded with another anxious glance. "That would be good."

It probably would be if one was worried about one's brother catching up to him. "Bella, can you get Breeze settled?"

She hopped forward into the saddle. "I will try not to do him damage."

He gave Kell a pat on the head. "I'll give you my thanks later."

She blushed and clucked Breeze forward.

Left alone with the boy, Sam turned on his heel and started walking. The boy showed no inclination to talk. Sam was tired and hungry. He gave him a verbal nudge. "So, what's on your mind?"

"I wish to discuss your debt to me."

That was pretty formal language indicating the boy had probably rehearsed his speech. Probably had his eye on the jar of penny candy in town and knew his mother wouldn't approve. "Discuss away."

"*La Montoya* loves you very much."

"Yes."

"We love the Montoya very much."

Sam's "Yes" wasn't that easy this time. He had a feeling where this was going and it wasn't to a jar of hard candy and peppermint sticks.

Jorge drew himself to his full four feet of height. "You said I could ask anything I wanted of the Hell's Eight and it would be paid."

"So I did."

"I want the Hell's Eight to let you go."

That was a hell of a request. "Why?"

"So you can have a home."

Christ, did even little kids think he was pathetic? "Here?"

The boy's chin came up. "Here is good. There is good food and fun." His eyes narrowed as he pulled out what was obviously his trump card. "Here is *la patrona*."

It was a good card. "I could take Bella with me."

Jorge shook his head. "Here *la patrona* is respected. No one spits on her."

Sam looked at him sharply. "Someone spit on you?"

The boy nodded. "Zach was not happy."

Sam just bet. And he bet Zach made whomever had spit on the boy pay.

Jorge continued. "*La patrona* does not know what it is to be hated. Everyone loves her."

"True."

He kicked a stone with the toe of his shoe. "You love her."

Sam smiled. "That's not the best guarded secret."

"I heard my brothers talking." Jorge looked up. "They do not hate you."

The kid was taking his time getting to his point. "That's good to know."

"It is. If you were not a good man, they would kill you."

Sam didn't doubt it. "Because it's their job to protect *la Montoya*."

"*Sí*. Also because they love her." He shrugged. "*La patrona* is very easy to love."

It'd better be a platonic love. The Lopez brothers were a damn good-looking family. "Do you have a point to all this?"

The boy nodded. "If you love *la patrona*, you will not take her away from her home to a place where people will spit on her." His eyes glittered. He looked very much like his brother right then. "I would not like for her to be spit on."

Laughter floated through the air from the direction of the barn. Bella came out of the barn, walking backwards talking to someone still inside. She looked at home, at peace. He could feel the walls closing in. "Neither would I."

"So, you will stay?"

He hated to disappoint the kid. "This isn't my home." But it was a damn fine home for someone.

"You do not have a home."

He thought of the Hell's Eight. Of all the work he'd put into it, the dreams wrapped up in it. "I'm building one."

"We have already built one for you."

"It's not mine."

The boy frowned in confusion, his fingers wrapping in Kell's ruff. "But you are *la patrona*'s chosen. Always we hold the ranch for you. That is why *la patrona*'s *papá* always told her to choose a strong man, because together she and her *marido* must build the future."

Sam hadn't thought of that. Bella's father had had a dream, had planned for that dream to grow through generations. He had known Bella would have to marry to hold the ranch, had even prepared the way with his people for a stranger to find his place within their tight ranks. Had prepared Bella. Sam pushed his hat back off his brow. He wished to hell he'd gotten to meet the man so he could have prepared him.

The Montoya ranch was a huge spread set up in dangerous territory. It'd be a challenge every day just to hold on to it against those that would take it. Growing it would take even more effort. A little spark of excitement lit his blood. "I always did like a challenge."

"It's not enough to like the thought, you must make it happen."

A surprising bit of wisdom for a child to spout. "That has the sound of something you hear often."

Jorge screwed up his face with disgust. "*Mi madre* likes those words."

Bella stood on the porch, a hand to her eyes, looking at him, a shaky smile on her face. The truth struck him hard. It wasn't enough for him to love Bella and want her to be happy. He had to make that happen. Even if he had to sacrifice a bit of pride. "They're good words."

He turned around, retracing their steps. Jorge immediately went back to looking nervous. It wasn't hard to see why. Zach was standing by the porch, a frown on his face.

Sam cut the kid a glance. "You weren't, by any chance, warned against having this conversation with me, were you?"

Jorge went from scared to righteously stubborn in the blink of an eye. "You made me the promise. You said I could ask for anything."

"Yes, I did."

Jorge stopped. "Are you going to keep your word?"

"Well, I'm not going to leave Hell's Eight. I made promises there first, but—" He didn't get the *but* out fast enough to prevent the boy's face crumpling. "But I don't see why I can't add the Montoyas to my family."

The kid could change expressions faster than lightning could strike. "This means you will stay?"

"Yeah. It means I'll stay." He grabbed the boy's arm before he could take off. "I'll make you a deal. You let

me break the news and I'll square things with Zacharias."

He nodded. "It is done."

Sam extended his hand. Jorge grabbed it, pumped
it once and then took off on a run and a whoop, Kell
loping by his side. He made it halfway to the front
before he started yelling.

Sam shook his head as everyone looked his way.
Bella's smile faltered and then was reborn as she came
running toward him, skirt flapping. She was a good
five feet away when she launched herself into his
arms.

He caught her, pretending to stagger back a step.
She cuffed his shoulder before wrapping her arms
and legs around him. She buried her face in his
throat, pressing her lips to his pulse almost desperately. "Is it true, my Sam? Will you stay and build a
dream with me?"

He kissed the top of her head, pretending a grump
he didn't feel. "Damn kid stole my thunder."

Tipping her head back she offered him her mouth.
"Do you really mind so much?"

She wasn't asking about Jorge's revealing his decision.

"I don't mind at all," he admitted, accepting the invitation, tasting her sweetness, her passion. "It's a good
place, Bella. A good dream."

Her head cocked to the side. "A good gift for our
children?"

Damn, they would probably have children. As often as he was at her, probably a whole brood. And with Bella as their mother, each and every one would likely be a handful. His smile grew, spreading inward. "Yes."

"I think you will have to toughen up before we have children, though."

There was no missing the mischief in her voice. His cock went hard, snuggling up to her heat through layers of clothing. Tugging her head back, he checked her expression.

"Why?"

Her pout was as fake as her happiness was real. "You have disappointed me."

"How?"

"Zacharias thought for sure you would...paddle Jorge's rear for such impudence."

As if Zach would allow anyone to touch his brother and live. "And?"

Her legs slid down the outside of his thighs, her breasts pressed into his abdomen scant inches above his straining cock. Her smile turned sultry. "I was going to offer to take his place."

She skipped back a step. "But now that cannot happen."

"Like hell."

He grabbed for her. She squealed and darted away, predictably to the right. He caught her hand, and tugged her toward him, ducking his shoulder into her stomach and hefting her up before striding to the house, quelling her struggles with a firm swat to her rump. "I deserve some compensation for putting up with your mother."

Her hands caressed his ass, cupping the cheeks, slipping between his legs to graze his balls. "Would you like me to paddle your butt?"

He almost dropped her on her ass.

"Bella?" he managed through his laughter.

"What?"

"Hush."

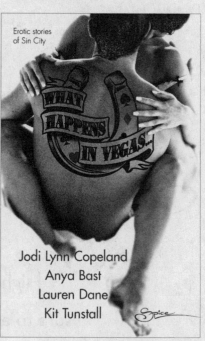

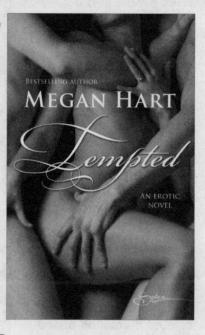